FICTION   Herman, Richard.
HER
           The Trojan Sea.

DATE			

The
TROJAN SEA

The
TROJAN SEA

RICHARD HERMAN

WILLIAM MORROW
75 YEARS OF PUBLISHING
An Imprint of HarperCollins*Publishers*

HarperCollins books may be purchased for educational, business, or sales promotional use. For information please write: Special Markets Department, HarperCollins Publishers Inc., 10 East 53rd Street, New York, NY 10022.

FIRST EDITION

Designed by Nicola Ferguson

Printed on acid-free paper

Library of Congress Cataloging-in-Publication Data
has been applied for.

ISBN 0-380-97700-1

01 02 03 04 05 RRD 10 9 8 7 6 5 4 3 2 1

For Sheila,
who made all this possible

To be vanquished and yet not surrender, that is victory.
JOSEF PILSUDSKI, POLISH GENERAL AND STATESMAN

The world continues to offer glittering prizes to those
who have stout hearts and sharp swords.
F. E. SMITH, FIRST EARL OF BIRKENHEAD

If he can't fly a good jet—and he hasn't the
heart of a hunter—he'll
never be a fighter pilot.
PAUL WOODFORD, FIGHTER PILOT

The
TROJAN SEA

Prologue

The Caribbean

Jane Ryan huddled under the dodger as the sailboat met the eight-foot swell head-on. It was almost 6:00 A.M., and she was cold and sleepy as she neared the end of her four-hour watch. *Temptress* took the swell easily. Jane loved the forty-two-foot boat with its cutter rig, classic lines, and strong hull. In many ways it was her alter ego, a seagoing version of what she was: sturdy, totally reliable, a little too broad of beam, and handsome in an old-fashioned way. No one would ever call Jane Ryan slim or beautiful. But perceptive people did look at her twice. Just like *Temptress*.

But she had a problem. Mike Stuart, the boat's owner, had worked hard, taken all the required classes, and been certified by the U.S. Sailing Association for offshore passage-making. As a final touch he had hired her to be his instructor for a test in the real thing on a six-week cruise in the Caribbean. But something was not quite right. She moved the problem to a back burner. They could talk about it in Miami, another three or four days away. Automatically, she checked the barometer at the navigation station just inside the cabin. It was falling rapidly. *Strange*, she thought. The forecast twenty-four hours ago had called for good weather with the possibility of a tropical storm well to the south of them. She shook away the cobwebs of sleep as the eastern horizon glowed with the first golden red of sunrise. Mike Stuart climbed out of the companionway to take the next watch. She squeezed past him and stood on the ladder. "Coffee?" she called.

"Super," Stuart said, his voice raised against the wind.

She disappeared into the cabin as *Temptress* slammed into a wave and shuddered. "Update weather," she mumbled to herself. She braced herself against the roll of the boat, lit the stove, and within a few minutes handed Stuart a mug of steaming coffee. "Breakfast?"

"How do you do it?" Stuart asked, taking a welcome sip. "I could never cook in all this motion."

"Practice," Jane answered. She was given to one-or two-word communications, and she considered anything more than four blabbering. She studied Stuart for a moment. Forty-one years old and five feet eleven inches tall, he was remarkable mainly for his red hair and bright green eyes. *Too bad about the glasses*, she thought. *His eyes are his best feature.* She ducked back into the galley, still thinking about him. After cruising on *Temptress* for over a month in tropical climates, she had come to enjoy his dry humor and gentle manner. An image of them in bed with her responding to his tender touch played in her mind. *Where did that come from?* She was being a blabbermouth and hit her mental delete key to obliterate the image. But it wouldn't go away.

Stuart stuck his head inside the companionway. "Jane, the wind's starting to kick up. Should we furl the jib and take a reef in the mainsail? Maybe fly the staysail?"

"I'll help," she replied. If it were her watch, she'd have done it by herself, without asking. Why was she coddling him? Deep down she knew the answer. Mike Stuart was truly one of the good guys, and there was something about him she wanted to mother and protect. Or was it caress and cuddle? She couldn't make up her mind. She slipped into her life vest and harness.

Stuart had already furled the jib on its roller reefing and turned *Temptress* into the wind, all simple tasks. He was clipped onto a tether and ready to go forward to reef the main while she stayed in the cockpit. They were a well-practiced team, and within minutes they'd shortened the big sail down to its first reef. Stuart worked his way aft, tidying up the lines and the reefing tie-downs.

Now there was enough light for her to study the sky. She didn't like what she saw. "Mike, head north."

"North is Cuba. That's never-never land." He grinned at her, and she felt her heart do a little flip-flop. "I can never, never go there. Never." Stuart was a lieutenant colonel in the U.S. Air Force with a security clearance that forbade his even thinking about going to certain places. Cuba was high on that list.

"Big storm to the south. North is away."

"Right. Any port." Another thought came to him. "Isn't this too early in the season for a hurricane?"

"Tell the hurricane that." She climbed down the companionway and sat at the navigation station. Her hands darted over the single-sideband radio as she hunted for an open frequency. Twelve minutes later she had a current picture of the weather and for the first time in her sailing career she was deeply worried. She laid in a course to Cienfuegos in Cuba and its sheltered harbor before joining Stuart in the cockpit. She gave him the new compass heading, and he dialed it into the autopilot. "That tropical storm southeast of us," she told him, "has turned into the granddaddy of hurricanes. Caught everyone by surprise."

"The weather gurus blow it big time," he quipped dryly. "That's what comes from never looking out the window before they make up a forecast. How bad is it?"

She shook her head. "It's gone all the way—a category five. That means winds greater than a hundred and fifty-five miles per hour."

"Ouch. How big will the waves get?"

"Don't even think about it."

"I'll try not to." He gave her his lopsided grin. "Are we in deep doo-doo?"

"Not yet. By going north, we should outrun the worst part."

"Can the boat take it?"

"Oh, yeah," she replied.

Again the wry grin. "But can we?" He started the diesel engine to charge the batteries and make sure it was running properly.

Four hours later they took the second reef in the mainsail and reduced the staysail to half. By noon, they had taken the third and final reef in the main. Just before she finished her noon-to-four watch, Jane furled the main and flew a fourth of the staysail, relying on the diesel for power. Stuart took over then, and she went down below to secure the cabin, stow all loose objects, and rig lee straps on the settee for sleeping. Then she fixed their last hot meal and forced Stuart to eat it. Finally, she prepared a large thermos of hot soup and tied the thermos in the sink.

With the galley cleaned up and all the drawers pinned closed, she lay down on the settee to rest.

She was sound asleep when a rogue wave knocked *Temptress* down, laying the boat flat on its port side. The lee straps saved her from tumbling about and injuring herself. "Come on," she coaxed. Slowly *Temptress* righted herself, and Jane felt the boat stabilize as Stuart restarted the engine. But it wouldn't catch. Rather than drain the batteries, he gave up. "Good boy," she said. She donned her life vest and harness and went topside. It was dark, and Stuart was at the helm, guiding *Temptress* down the backside of a huge wave.

"No damage up here," he called. "How's down below?"

"No problem," she shouted, clipping a tether to her harness. "The bilge is dry." Even if there had been damage or spillage below, she would have ignored it as long as they weren't taking on water. She worked to control her voice. "Mike, we're going too fast. We need to slow down coming down these waves. Otherwise we're going to bury the bow and pitchpole."

Stuart gulped visibly at the thought of the bow's digging into a wave and *Temptress* somersaulting onto her back. Again, the grin. "And here I was having fun."

She shook her head and smiled in spite of herself. That was the Mike Stuart she loved. "You lying scumbag." Back to business. "We need to rig a drogue."

"*No problemo, señorita.*" She shook her head at his fractured Spanish and took the helm. "Hey, I'm just practicing the lingo if we're going to Cuba." He opened the cockpit locker and pulled out the stern anchor rode, dumping all 250 feet of thick line on the deck. Then he pulled out a small tire off an old trailer that Jane had insisted they bring for just such an occasion. He tied the tire to the end of the line.

"Hurry!" Jane shouted as they crested a huge wave and rocketed down the backside. Stuart threw the drogue over the stern and watched in horror as all 250 feet of line paid out and then disappeared. He had forgotten to cleat off the end of the line.

"I can't believe I did that," he moaned.

"Get the small anchor and tie it to a docking line," Jane said, ever practical. Stuart clipped his tether to the jackline that ran along the deck to the bow, where their smallest anchor was stowed. A wave rocked the boat so hard that he fell to his knees. "Shorten your tether!" she shouted. But he didn't hear this last command as he crawled forward. *Temptress* bottomed out in the trough and dug her nose in as water crashed over the deck. Slowly the boat rose to meet the next wave, shaking itself free of the tons of water on the deck and in the cockpit.

Stuart had reached the last handhold on the cabin trunk. He had lost his glasses and could barely see. "Go!" Jane shouted. "You've got time!" Stuart darted forward, pulled the anchor out of the forward storage locker, and started back. He reached the mast before another wave hit and had to hold on. But before he could move, *Temptress* crashed over the crest and steamed down the backside of the wave. He dropped the anchor and held on to a halyard with both hands.

"Oh, shitsky!" he shouted as *Temptress* dug her bow into the wall of water at the bottom of the trough. The stern started to lift, threatening to pitchpole them forward. But at that exact instant a cross-wave broadsided them, knocking the boat over on her side. The force of the water tore Jane's grasp off the wheel, and only her short tether kept her from being swept overboard. Her harness twisted around her arm as she fell. She almost passed out from pain as her left shoulder dislocated.

Eventually, *Temptress* righted herself. Jane pulled herself to her feet and grabbed the wheel as the cockpit rapidly drained. She looked forward. "Mike!" But he was gone. Then she saw his tether trailing around a shroud and over the side of the boat. The tether was stretched taut from his weight. She looked over the side of the boat. He was being dragged alongside and banging off the hull.

Rapidly running out of time and ideas, she spun the wheel and laid the boat abeam, or across the waves. Their forward motion stopped, with Stuart sheltered on the lee, or downwind side of the boat. But Jane wasn't sure if *Temptress* could lie abeam of the waves. There was a very real danger of the boat's tripping on the face of a wave and rolling over. But she didn't have any other options. She crawled forward and grabbed Stuart's tether, bracing her feet against the low bulwark. If a wave washed him overboard, one could wash him back on board. She timed her move and waited for the boat to rock as the next wave hit. She felt the tether go limp and then pulled for all she was worth. Stuart came crashing out of the sea and onto the lifelines, the plastic-coated cables that acted as a railing. He was sputtering with life but on the wrong side of the lifelines.

Jane felt *Temptress* start to go over.

She grabbed the back of his harness with her good hand and pulled, dragging him over the lifelines. He fell on her, and she passed out from the pain.

Temptress struggled upright.

A blast of water jolted Jane back to consciousness. Somehow they were still on board, and Stuart was pulling her into the cockpit. But they were still abeam the waves. Another wave crashed into them. Luckily it wasn't a big one, or they would have capsized.

"A fine mess you got us into, Stanley," Stuart muttered. No answer from Jane. He looked up as they rose to the top of the next wave, still on the verge of a capsize. A prolonged burst of lightning illuminated the night, and even without his glasses all he could see was wave after wave marching down on them.

"Turn," Jane groaned. "Run before it." Stuart grabbed the wheel and gave it a spin, trying to bring *Temptress*'s stern into the next wave that was bearing down on them. Nothing happened. Then, with maddening slowness, *Temptress* responded. The wave crashed over them, and Stuart felt the boat shudder. Jane washed up against him, banging them into the steering pedestal. For a moment he was certain they weren't going to make it. But *Temptress* shook off the wave, and the bow came up. They accelerated down the front of the wave and surged up the next one, again going far too fast. At the top the boat leaped out of the water and slammed down.

Again the lightning flashed, and Stuart saw a dark gray mass on the far horizon. "Oh, my God," he whispered. The fear of all sailors held him tight. They were running out of sea room and being driven by the storm onto a lee shore. Once more they crashed off the top of a wave, rocking violently. *Temptress* tried to respond, but she was taking on water in the cockpit and was too sluggish.

Stuart set the autopilot. He timed the next wave and slid open the cabin's hatch. He lowered Jane down the companionway as the next wave crashed over them, and washed him down the open hatch. The cabin was awash in a foot of water as he placed her on the settee and jammed a sodden pillow between her and the lee straps, immobilizing her shoulder. The storm had beaten him to a pulp, and he was out of ideas.

Jane looked at him, paralyzed by the pain. A voice from Mike's distant past echoed through him. It was his father, urging him on, telling him to do something, even if it was wrong. He grabbed a handhold as the autopilot let go and *Temptress* broached. "Help her!" Jane shouted. The boat rocked violently, and he held on, unable to move. He was certain they were going to capsize. Again *Temptress* fought off the raging sea.

Something inside him snapped. "I'll be back," he promised. He worked himself over to the companionway. He paused at the navigation station and found another pair of glasses. Then he hit the bilge-pump switch. Over the noise he heard a soft whirring sound. Or was it his imagination? Then he knew. The bilge pump was working. *Temptress* was not ready to give up, not yet.

And neither was he.

He hauled himself up the companionway and slammed the hatch shut in time to save the cabin from another inundation. Looking around, he saw the anchor he had dropped. It was hooked on a lifeline near the mast, and only a near miracle had kept it from being washed overboard. He snapped Jane's tether to his harness and scooted forward on his hands and knees to retrieve it. Within moments he was back in the cockpit and had secured the anchor to a dock line. This time he tied the bitter end of the line to a cleat and dropped the anchor off the stern.

Almost immediately *Temptress*'s stern slewed into the waves. He grabbed the helm and felt the rudder respond. With the anchor and sixty feet of line acting as a drogue, *Temptress* slowed, and the waves went rushing past. The violent rocking motion eased, and they were coasting down the waves, not accelerating out of control. "I'll be damned," Stuart said to himself. "That worked." A wave passed under them, and they rose up.

Then he saw the dark mass of a ship. For a moment he stared, not believing the sight. It disappeared as they went down a wave, still very much in control and stable. They rose up on the next wave, and again he saw the ship. Were they on a collision course? He forced himself to calm down. "I should see the navigation lights, red light on the left, green light on the right, with two white masthead lights. But I'm only seeing one white light. It's gotta be the stern light. We're behind you."

He checked his watch. "How long have we been at this?" he asked himself. Suddenly the answer didn't matter—he was going to gut it out no matter how long it took. He tried to start the diesel while he waited for the next wave to lift them up. The engine refused to start, and he gave up, saving the batteries. Then he saw the ship again. Were they overtaking it because the ship had slowed for the storm? He wasn't sure.

He reached for the handheld VHF radio that was stowed in the steering pedestal and hailed the ship on Channel 16. There was no answer. Twice more he tried to raise the ship with the same lack of success. "Screw you," he muttered.

His instincts told him to fly a little staysail to control their pitching. He pulled on the staysail sheet, unrolling about a fourth of the small jib. The boat stabilized and was more controllable, but again they were going too fast. "More drag," he told himself. He reached into the locker under the cockpit seat and pulled out another dock line and a canvas bucket. He punched four large holes in the bottom of the bucket and tied it to the dock line. Then he cleated off the bitter end of the line and threw the bucket overboard. *Temptress* slowed.

"How 'bout that," he announced to no one. He engaged the autopilot and allowed himself a grunt of satisfaction when it held. The combination of drag and slower speed was working. Satisfied that *Temptress* could take care of herself, he considered his next move. He went below to check on Jane. The bilge pump had drained the cabin, and he shut it off. He reached into the refrigerator and pulled out a water bottle, surprised at his thirst and hunger. He took a long swig and then worked his way forward to check on Jane. She was awake but still in pain.

He held the water bottle to her lips, and she drank greedily. Carefully he felt her shoulder, not sure what was wrong. She gasped. "It's dislocated, happened before. Reset it."

"I don't know how," he said.

"Feel it."

His fingers moved over her shoulder, feeling the dislocation. "That's it," she said. "Pull out and push." He did. At first nothing happened. "Pull harder." Stuart pulled as hard as he could and felt something give. Then he pushed her shoulder back into place. She screamed in pain and then relaxed, tears in her eyes.

"I'm gonna get you to a doctor," he said. It was a promise he meant to keep. He told her how he had set the drogues and staysail. He ended with "There's a ship out there in front of us, and we're getting pretty close to Cuba."

"How close?"

"I saw land."

"And the ship is headed for it?" Stuart nodded. "Check the GPS."

He went to the nav station to check the Global Positioning System and verify their position. "It's not working," he told her.

"The antenna's probably washed away," she said. "I'm guessing that the ship is making for port. Follow it."

Stuart went topside and checked on the ship. Much to his surprise, they were still behind it, going at the same speed. But it had turned to a new course, more to the northwest and parallel to the coast. He released the autopilot and turned to the new heading, surprised that *Temptress* was responding so well. He thought about the landmass he knew was out there in the dark. "You better know where you're going," he muttered. He tried to reset the autopilot, but it was dead. "Steer the boat," he told himself as they dipped between waves, losing sight of the ship, before rising up so he could see it again.

The hours dragged, and fatigue slowly drove Stuart down, demanding its price. Despair was on the verge of claiming him when the glow of dawn on the eastern horizon sent a jolt of hope through his body. Then, as they rode to the top of a wave, a flashing light winked at him. He counted the interval. "Six seconds," he mumbled to himself. He watched as the ship headed straight for the light. "It's got to be a harbor entrance." The waves were closer together now and steeper as the bottom shallowed out. Without the diesel it was all Stuart could do to keep *Temptress* headed in the right direction.

The waves grew bigger, and he could hear the crashing of waves as the flashing beacon grew brighter. Ahead the ship rose up on the back of the wave, its bow high in the air. He shook his head in disbelief. The ship was much shorter than he had guessed and very wide, like a wedge or arrowhead. He watched in horror as a huge wave engulfed the ship and it disappeared from sight. Automatically he turned around to see what was overtaking them. Fear claimed him as the enormous wave rose up in the fading darkness, its mass rising well over sixty feet.

At that instant the hatch to the cabin slid open and Jane's head appeared. She was looking directly at the wave. She pulled herself up and looked forward. Ahead she saw the flashing beacon and the ship's navigation lights, now motionless in the calm waters of a harbor. "Cut the drogues!" she yelled. "We're crossing a bar." But he froze, worn down by fatigue and fear. "Do it!"

Stuart snapped out of it and quickly cut the two drogue lines. *Temptress* surged ahead as the gigantic wave started to break over them. Now they were accelerating and surfing down the face of the wave. He spun the wheel, shouting like a madman. *"Come on, Mama!"* They shot past the beacon, and the wave crashed behind them. Stuart was vaguely aware of a mass of black rocks on his port side as the wave pushed them into the harbor. He clutched the wheel as he wobbled, his inner gyros confused by the sudden calm.

For a brief moment a feeling of total elation swept over him. Then it was gone.

"Drop anchor over there," Jane said, pointing to an open area well away from the ship. Stuart turned in the direction she had indicated, as *Temptress* coasted to a stop. He went forward to drop the anchor, still wobbling. They set the anchor on the first try, and he staggered back to the cockpit and clambered down the open companionway. Jane was in the galley, heating water.

He collapsed on the settee, instantly asleep.

✳

The aroma of Malt-o-Meal filled the cabin, and for a moment Stuart was back in kindergarten on a cold winter morning. "Here," Jane said, handing him a steaming bowl laced heavily with granola. He wolfed it down.

"How's the shoulder?"

"Hurts like hell," she said. "But I'll survive." Her left arm was in a makeshift sling.

Stuart looked around. The cabin was clean and shipshape, a far cry from the chaos he remembered. "How long have I been asleep?"

"Nine hours."

He finished the bowl and stuck his head out the companionway. They were anchored in a secure harbor. He gulped when he saw the narrow harbor entrance. How had he managed that? The wind was dying down, but waves were still crashing into the harbor entrance. "Being the skipper and all, I should know this. But where the hell are we?"

"Cienfuegos in Cuba."

He smiled ruefully. "That's gonna piss off a few people when I tell them. What about customs and immigration?"

"The port captain's been and gone. No problems. Didn't even stamp our passports. Gave us a temporary insert. Real friendly."

"What happened to the other ship?"

"Left about noon."

Stuart climbed into the cockpit and studied *Temptress*. The boat was none the worse for the storm. "She's a good boat," he allowed. No answer from Jane. Suddenly it was all back, the wind, the waves, the fear—all that he had fought against. He gave her a sad look. "I screwed up out there, didn't I?"

"A little," she allowed. "But you got your act together."

"Sure. But I froze at the very last, coming over the bar."

"Mike, you were tired. You did good. Real good."

But he couldn't accept the truth of it. "If you weren't here . . ." His voice trailed off as he contemplated a watery grave.

"That was your first storm, the worst one I've ever seen. What did you expect?"

He didn't have an answer. But he did know what his father would have expected. And he didn't meet the standard. "You know, all I ever wanted to do was get through the next eighteen months, retire from the Air Force, and go cruising. Now I'm not so sure."

"Two days ago I would've agreed with you. But not now. Mike, you can do it."

"Yeah, sure." He stared out to sea.

1

Dallas, Texas

Ann Silton and Clarissa Jones sat in a corner of the large two-room suite in the Regency Hotel as the convention's executive committee gathered for a late-afternoon meeting. Neither woman wanted to be at this particular meeting, and both had their arms and legs tightly crossed, sending an unmistakable signal. But they had no choice. Front Uni, the latest and largest coalition of environmentalist groups, was on a roll, growing daily in power and influence. The unbelievable success of the convention was a tribute to John Frobisher, the brains and organizing force behind Front Uni.

"I told John," Ann said, "that we have no business talking to *her* just because *she* happens to be available." Ann shot a hard look across the room and speared John Frobisher, hoping he would get the message. Clarissa, the younger of the two, followed Ann's lead and tried to emulate her stare. But Clarissa only managed to look doe-eyed, sweet, and naïve, a reflection of her true nature.

"Why did we even hold the convention here?" Clarissa asked.

"Because John got an excellent deal and the hotel offered us the conference rooms free of charge. It was too good to turn down."

Clarissa gave a pretty shake of her long blond hair. "Well," she conceded, "the rooms are very nice. And I love the big bathroom with all the towels and free toiletries."

"It's too nice for what we're paying," Ann muttered, going even deeper into her mental defensive crouch. Another thought came to her.

"I wonder if *she* had anything to do with all this?" They fell silent when the subject of their conversation walked in.

Although Ann and Clarissa had seen Lee Justine Ellis on TV, they were not prepared for the sheer physical presence of the woman. L.J., as she liked to be called, simply devoured a room by the force of pure charisma. For Ann it hurt even more. She and L.J. were both thirty-eight years old, but L.J. looked ten years younger. L.J. was tall, with a mass of naturally curly, dark-blond hair pulled into a loose bundle at the base of her neck. She was wearing a man's white shirt with rolled-up sleeves, loose-fitting jeans that hinted at her trim figure, and cowboy boots that made her long legs seem even longer.

At first glance her shirt and jeans looked as if they came off the rack at some bargain-basement sale. In reality the custom-tailored shirt cost three hundred dollars and the jeans over six hundred dollars. A connoisseur of Western wear would have recognized her cowboy boots immediately and guessed their value at over fifteen hundred dollars. He would have been half right. Lee Justine Ellis was a masterpiece of the kind of casual, down-home understatement that only the very wealthy can afford and the very beautiful carry off. And with her blue eyes, high cheekbones, and perfect mouth, she was drop-dead gorgeous.

"She's not wearing a bra," Clarissa whispered. "Look at John. He's all but stepping on his tongue."

"It's not his tongue he's stepping on," Ann said, feeling squat and dowdy.

John Frobisher introduced L.J. to the five other members of Front Uni's executive committee. "I think you all know who Miss Ellis is." The environmentalists nodded in unison. L.J. was the president and chairman of the board of RayTex Oil, a small but feisty oil company she had inherited upon the death of her father. Many environmentalists shared the belief—it was part of Ann and Clarissa's private mantra—that any oil company was inherently evil and had to be destroyed to save the world. For the two women, Lee Justine Ellis was a beautiful incarnation of Lucifer himself.

L.J. gave Frobisher a warm look, studying his features. His shaggy, prematurely gray hair and pudgy body reminded her of the teddy bear she'd loved as a child. Like most women, she had an irresistible urge to cuddle him. But there was more to it. Like a good general, L.J. had scrutinized the opposition and dissected the environmentalist movement. John Frobisher was a political operative and on the upper end of the environmentalist food chain. He was a savvy lobbyist and wore a suit and tie. He also understood the process of change and believed in engaging the enemy in a constructive dialogue, which was why he had invited L.J. in the first place. Of the four groups that made up Front Uni, he represented the one faction L.J. feared. But at the same time she respected him for what he was. And there was that teddy bear image that touched a childhood memory.

Ann and Clarissa were from Greenpeace, the revenue-generating machine and propagandists of the movement. But Greenpeace was running out of steam and hadn't had a win since the "Save the Whales" campaign. They desperately needed an issue that looked good on a bumper sticker and would rally the faithful—and shake loose their checkbooks.

Of the three other men, two were scientists. They did the real work of the movement and dealt in the truth, which would never translate to a bumper sticker. Because they were complex, rational, and legitimate thinkers, they were never mentioned by the media. The last man was from Earth First. He was a true believer and an ecoterrorist not above spiking trees in old-growth forests or sabotaging oil refineries.

"I hope you're enjoying Dallas," L.J. said. She pulled up a chair and sat down next to the two women. The four men hurried to join her, forming a tight but casual circle in one corner of the room. L.J. crossed her legs and leaned forward. She clasped her hands and gave a little smile that was both timorous and half apologetic. "It is nice of you to take the time to see me." Her voice had a soft, barely discernible Texas accent. "I was hoping we could talk."

"Miss Ellis," Ann said. She paused to take a deep breath.

"Please, I do prefer L.J."

Ann frowned. "Drop the phony act and cut to the chase."

L.J. gave Ann a knowing look, taking her measure. Like John Frobisher, Ann Silton was a person L.J. could respect, and under the right circumstances might even like. But they were adversaries about to engage in mortal combat. L.J. gave a little nod, accepting the challenge. Ann had no idea what she had started. "I'm not the enemy," L.J. said. "In fact, we share many points of common interest."

"Why do I doubt that?" Ann shot back.

"Please," Frobisher said. "At least we can listen to what L.J. has to say." Ann gave a tiny snort and fell silent.

Again the little nod from L.J. "I feel like Marc Antony at Caesar's funeral." She paused for effect. The allusion to the famous speech from Shakespeare's play was not lost on the environmentalists. Like Antony, L.J. was facing a very hostile audience, many of whom would be glad to see her quick demise, preferably in a public and humiliating manner. She started to speak, her words matter-of-fact, her tone friendly. "Oil is the world's biggest business because it's the linchpin of our civilization. Petroleum pervades our life, and we are, whether we like it or not, a hydrocarbon society. Oil is so critical that in the twentieth century it meant money, power, and mastery."

"Honey," Ann said, her voice dripping with sweetness, "this is the twenty-first century. Things change."

L.J. gave her a smile and the little nod. "Have they? Petroleum has changed every aspect of our civilization, and I don't see us getting along without it."

"And I don't see how we can live with it," Ann said, her voice calm and reasoned. "Oil is the great polluter. It's killing the environment."

"I agree," L.J. said. The silence in the room was absolute, surprise on every face. "Unfortunately I don't see Hydrocarbon Man giving up his cars and suburban way of life."

L.J.'s ready agreement startled Ann. "You got the 'man' part right."

"There's no need for us to fight," L.J. said.

Frobisher sensed that it was time to intervene. "There are two issues on which there is no compromise."

L.J. turned to look at him, her blue eyes full of understanding. "Oil spills and air pollution."

"Correct," he said. "And I repeat, there is no compromise."

"In both of these areas we have many points of common agreement where we can work together to make things better."

"Why?" Ann asked, genuinely interested but still doubtful.

"It's complicated," L.J. replied, "and I can't explain it in ten seconds. But in a nutshell, it's in my economic self-interest to do so."

"You'll have to do better than that." This from the ecoterrorist. "A lot better." His face was granite hard, a perfect reflection of his voice.

L.J. pulled off the gloves. "The environmentalist movement is laboring under the illusion that environmental improvement is basically 'free,' a matter of regulation, and there is no price tag, no bill to be paid. That's totally wrong." The two scientists nodded in agreement. "Oil is so integral to our economy," L.J. continued, "that any change will involve money, massive amounts of it. Also, I know change is coming, and I want to be part of it."

The ecoterrorist was the type of alpha male Ann Silton detested, and she liked the way L.J. stood up to him. Ann repeated her question, the hostility in her voice gone. "You still haven't answered why."

"Because," L.J. answered, "I'm going to make money when the bill is paid. Lots of it. But there's another reason, and whether you believe it or not, I am an environmentalist and I care."

Ann wanted to believe her, but there was still so much between them. "You are one conflicted woman if you believe all that."

L.J.'s laugh filled the room with music. "My father claimed I'm part Southern belle and part feminist. How much more conflicted can you get than that?"

"Maybe," Frobisher allowed, "there are areas where we *can* work together."

L.J. gave him a look that made his knees go weak. "Oh, I hope so. Now, where do we begin?"

❋

At exactly nine o'clock the next morning, Lloyd Marsten, the CEO of RayTex Oil, entered the company's executive offices on the top floor of the Fountain Plaza Building. As always, he moved with a measured, purposeful dignity, and nothing betrayed his impatience. His secretary, Mrs. Shugy Jenkins, sprang from her seat and held open the door to the CEO's corner office. "Good morning, Mr. Marsten. Tea?" She was a prim, childless, birdlike woman in her mid-forties, a Southern Baptist whose faith was the only thing that flourished on her parent's hardscrabble farm in west Texas.

"That would be nice, thank you." Marsten's British accent matched his outward appearance. He was tall, gray-headed, slightly stooped, and impeccably attired in a Savile Row suit, not the regulation Brooks Brothers ensemble worn by his fellow CEOs. The suit helped highlight the differences between him and his American contemporaries. He was the epitome of the European oil man—suave, cultured, intelligent, technically competent, and aristocratic. But underneath the smooth and urbane exterior lurked a shark, a very hungry predator. "Is Miss Ellis in yet?"

Shugy worked hard not to frown at the mention of L.J. "Not yet." She couldn't help herself. "Her chauffeur dropped her off at the Dallas Regency yesterday afternoon for the meeting with the environmentalists. He never picked her up."

"Ah," Marsten said, not missing a beat. "Perhaps she was offered another way home."

If she went home, Shugy thought, hurrying to get Marsten's tea. She worshipped the very ground Marsten walked on and considered L. J. Ellis a Jezebel.

Marsten settled into his chair and gazed out the window. It was an unbelievably clear day for September, and Fort Worth's skyline etched the far horizon. But he didn't really see it as his stomach churned with anxiety. The door opened, and Shugy wheeled in a tea cart. L.J. was right behind her, still wearing the same clothes as the day before. The secretary poured two cups of tea and stirred in the right amount of milk and sugar for Marsten. "Thank you, Shugy," Marsten said, sending her on her way.

L.J. sipped her tea and waited for the door to close. "Is Shugy her real name?"

"I believe it is," Marsten replied. "A diminutive derived from the word 'sugar.' "

"She reminds me of my old spinster aunt. The poor thing believed if you enjoyed something, it was sinful. But she did like her soap operas."

He arched an eyebrow. "I've often wondered what you Texas ladies enjoyed."

"I enjoyed last night," she replied.

"Were there, ah, developments?"

"No, I did not sleep with John Frobisher. But he thinks we might." She considered the possibility, recalling the teddy-bear image and the urge to cuddle him.

" 'A promise made is a debt unpaid,' " Marsten quoted.

" 'And the trail has its own stern code,' " L.J. added. She laughed, and as always, he was enchanted. It helped calm his growing apprehension. " 'The Cremation of Sam McGee.' When did you start reading Robert Service?"

"I am trying to understand you colonials." Again he arched an eyebrow, still waiting for a full report on the night's activities. If it were germane to RayTex Oil, she would tell him.

"I had to tame the two women on the executive committee. The older one, Ann Silton, has a brain and isn't afraid to use it."

"Which you like in a woman," Marsten added.

"We do have a lot in common," L.J. said. "She's aggressive and wants to make a difference. The younger one, Clarissa Jones, is in need of an ego. We sat up most of the night talking about women's issues. It turned into a girl's slumber party." She thought for a moment, a sadness in her eyes. "Have ARA check them out." ARA, or Action Research Associates, was the firm of private investigators RayTex Oil used. Like the CIA, ARA had global reach; however, there was one big difference. ARA was very good at what they did.

Again the expressive eyebrow from Marsten.

"No, I did not sleep with either of them."

"A promise made . . ."

"I'm not that kind of girl," L.J. said.

"Do they know we're picking up the tab at the Regency?"

"No. But it would have been cheap at ten times the price."

"Your search for allies is admirable," Marsten said. "I just hope it isn't misguided."

"Change is coming, Lloyd. We can't stop it. But we can delay. For that we need friends at court."

"Ah," he replied. "The slow roll."

"The slow roll," she acknowledged.

Marsten paused, judging his timing. "By the way, Steiner arrived last night."

An eager look flashed across L.J.'s face. Just as quickly it was gone. "Did he bring it?"

"It's in my safe."

"And Steiner?"

Marsten walked over to the safe hidden in the wall. He held his right hand against the palm-print scanner. "Safely ensconced in the Parke Royale with two ladies of his choice." The safe door clicked and swung open. Marsten extracted two CD-ROM disks. His hands shook slightly as he inserted the disks into the small but powerful computer tucked away in the credenza behind his chair. The keyboard rolled out from a slot in his desk, and he typed a command. He turned ninety degrees to face what looked like a painting by Constable hanging on the wall. The picture on the high-definition plasma display smoothly transformed from a bucolic landscape into an image familiar to anyone in the oil industry: the seismic reflection cross-section of the geological structure of Saudi Arabia's Safaniyah field, the world's largest offshore oil field.

In theory, seismic mapping was easy to understand. Prospectors fired a small pyrotechnic charge to send an acoustic signal into sedimentary rock sections beneath the earth's surface. Using a string of geophones, a special type of seismograph, they measured the time taken by the waves to travel from the explosion into the earth and then bounce back to the geophones, anywhere from one-thousandth of a second to six seconds later. The data were recorded on a magnetic tape and later processed through a computer to determine the subsurface geological formations. Long experience had taught what formations might hold oil and, equally important, those that didn't. While it wasn't insurance, it was the next best thing.

"All very familiar, yes?" Marsten said.

"I wish we had the concession," L.J. allowed.

A sad look crossed Marsten's face. "Not very likely in this day and age." He tapped a command on the keyboard. The image on the screen split, and a second seismic reflection cross-section appeared. "Here is an area where Steiner recently shot seismic using the traditional methods. Nothing here to interest us, yes?"

She nodded. "A total waste of time and money to drill."

Again his fingers danced on the keyboard. "Here he surveyed the same area using his new Seismic Double Reflection technique that allowed him to probe deeper than ever before—and voilà! we have . . ." The second image on the screen metamorphosed into a seismic map very similar to that of the Safaniyah field.

L.J. gasped. "Does this mean what I think it means?"

"It does." Nothing betrayed the emotion Marsten felt. "You are looking at what may be the largest elephant of all time." In oil-industry lingo an "elephant" is a giant oil field. "But it's deep. Very deep."

Raw emotion coursed through Lee Justine Ellis like a huge earthquake leaving severe aftershocks in its wake. For a moment she was so overwhelmed that words escaped her. Then the one demon deep inside that she had never been able to control came out of its hidden lair. She wanted the elephant. It had to be hers, no matter what the cost or what she had to do. It was a need so overpowering, so central to what she was, that it could not be denied without destroying her. "How big?" she finally managed to ask.

"Bigger than Saudi Arabia."

She looked at Marsten in shock as her demon raged in demand. Saudi Arabia possessed one-third of the world's known oil reserves. "Where?"

Marsten shook his head. "Steiner won't say."

Nothing betrayed the emotions tearing at her. "Really? As I recall, we're paying the bills."

"He seems oblivious to that minor detail."

L.J. considered her next move. "Who knows about this?"

"As of now, three of us. You, me, and Steiner."

She fixed Marsten with a hard look. "Keep it that way."

Lloyd Marsten understood perfectly.

The Pentagon

The summons came after lunch, much earlier than Stuart had expected. He stood up in his cramped cubicle and carefully adjusted his tie and uniform coat. His boss, Colonel Roger Priestly, was an obsessive compulsive and a stickler on dress and appearance. Lately there had been an epidemic of pant cuffs being altered a fraction of an inch to conform to regulation length. *It gives him something to do*, Stuart thought. He heaved an inner sigh of resignation and walked resolutely to the colonel's office. *My first day back from leave, and it's already hit the fan*, he told himself silently. For a moment he wished he were back on *Temptress* in Miami. But just as quickly the image vanished. That was all behind him.

Peggy Redman, Priestly's secretary, was sitting at her desk. She was a heavyset African-American in her mid-fifties with short-cropped hair and a flair for finding stylish clothes at sales and outlets. She smiled at him, glad that he was back. The atmosphere in the office was always much more pleasant when he was around. "How was the Caribbean?"

Stuart returned her smile. "You might say we got rained on."

Peggy looked concerned. "It wasn't what you expected?"

"We were caught by Hurricane Andrea."

"That must have been terrible. But welcome back. We missed you." She waved him into the colonel's office.

"Lieutenant Colonel Michael Stuart reporting as ordered," Stuart said, snapping a sharp salute.

Priestly waved his fighter-pilot salute back. It was a cocky blend of informality and arrogance, allowed to the Priestlys of the world but not the likes of Stuart. On the surface Roger "Ramjet" Priestly was a fighter pilot's pilot—tall, ruggedly good-looking, athletic, articulate, and well sponsored, thanks to a good marriage. The fact that he had never flown combat and avoided cockpit assignments whenever he could hadn't hurt as he clawed his way up the rank structure. His current assignment to ILSX, Pentagonspeak for Installation Logistics Supply Plans, was a slight detour in his quest for his first star and flag rank.

Priestly had fought for a slot in Contingency Plans, the hotbed of new ideas. But some quirk in the colonels-assignment system, probably because both had "plans" in the title or someone had a sense of humor, had landed him in ILSX. His sponsor had urged him to take the assignment with the promise that once in the Pentagon, he could transfer to Contingency Plans or to the Joint Chiefs. But so far he was stuck in ILSX. Normally ILSX was headed by a veteran supply officer, and thanks to his predecessor, Priestly had inherited a superefficient and well-run organization that needed little tending and less expertise on his part.

Stuart, on the other hand, was nonrated, a ground-pounder without wings on his chest. He was one of the faceless officers, a combination of technician and bureaucrat, who made up the infrastructure of the Air Force and kept it working on a day-to-day basis. Because of officers, NCOs, and airmen like Stuart, planes were fixed, supplies delivered, control towers manned, accounts balanced, buildings painted, computers programmed, telephones repaired, laws enforced, dining halls opened, and the sick cared for.

In Stuart's particular case, he managed the complex and baffling world of petroleum, oil, and lubricants—or POL for short. His job, in the simplest of terms, was to ensure that JP-A, kerosene-based jet fuel, would always be available, especially in time of war. Michael Eric Stuart would never be in harm's way or see the inside of an airplane except as a passenger, but what he did was essential to the Air Force mission. His only claim to fame was Air Force Manual 23-110, the sixty-page regulation he authored that detailed how fuels were managed.

Priestly left Stuart standing to keep him off balance and send the message that he was less than happy. He tossed a report onto the desk between them. "What's this piece of shit?" he asked almost good-naturedly.

Stuart cocked his head and eyed the title through his glasses. "Our input into the Quadrennial Defense Review."

"And you expect me to sign off on it?"

I'll be glad to witness your X, Stuart thought. Wisely, he stifled that thought and said, "I just crunch the numbers."

"Crunch them again."

"Will do, sir. But the results will be the same."

Priestly leaned forward. "The mission of the Air Force is to be able to fight two major theater wars simultaneously." He tapped the offending report with a forefinger. "Now you're telling me we can't do that."

"I didn't say that."

"What exactly did you say? Educate me."

Not possible, Stuart decided. "I said that we do not have the necessary access to tankerage to guarantee the flow of POL to two major theater wars being fought simultaneously."

"There's no way I'm going to tell the committee working on the Quadrennial Defense Review that the Air Force cannot meet its mission."

Stuart tried to be reasonable. "The operative words, sir, are 'cannot guarantee the flow.' There are work-arounds described in Appendix C."

Priestly kicked back in his chair and steepled his fingers, studying the man in front of him. He sighed. "Stuart, you're just another thumb-sucking milicrat"—Priestly's term for a military bureaucrat—"who wants to get down to the third floor." The third floor of the Pentagon was the "money floor," where the defense budget was assembled. For the professional bureaucrat it was considered a plum assignment with real power. Stuart wanted to say that he only wanted out the front door—in eighteen months. "It's too bad," Priestly continued, "that you can't see the big picture for the trees. It would help if you had ever strapped on a jet and been on the cutting edge of what the Air Force is all about." He paused, gathering steam for his favorite lecture about being a can-do Air Force. Stuart braced himself for the tirade. He had heard it before and accepted it as the penultimate act before Priestly sent him back to his cubicle in disgrace.

Unfortunately, the telephone rang before Stuart could escape. The colonel answered it with a curt "Priestly." He listened for a few moments and stared at Stuart. "This is the first I've heard about it, sir. I assure you—" His faced flushed as the caller cut him off. The colonel was not used to being on the receiving end of a harangue. Then, "Yes, sir. I'll check into it." He carefully dropped the phone into its cradle. An image of a monk handling a holy relic that delivered ecclesiastical messages directly from God flashed in Stuart's mind.

Priestly took a deep breath. "That was my boss, Brigadier General Castleman. What exactly in God's name were you doing in Cuba?" Before Stuart could answer, Priestly shifted into overdrive. "Your security clearance prohibits you going there, and you should've reported you were in contact with a hostile foreign power. By not reporting that contact, you took all my options off the table. I have no recourse but to ask for an Article 32 investigation leading to court-martial."

"Sir, I tried to tell you, but—"

Priestly held up a hand and interrupted him. "Air off, Stuart. I don't want to hear any lame-ass excuses." He glared at the lieutenant colonel. "But how in the hell did Castleman learn about it?"

"Because I reported it, as required, when I signed in from leave this morning. It was early, you weren't here yet, so I left a memo for the record on your e-mail."

Priestly shook his head. "That's a load of bullshit, and you know it."

"It's a matter of record, sir. And there are mitigating circumstances, which are outlined in the memo. It's all in your computer."

Priestly shook his head in wonder, as if he couldn't believe what he was hearing. He tapped the offending document lying on his desk. "First this report and now Cuba. What's got into you?"

Good question, Stuart thought. He was standing up to Priestly, when not too long ago he would have been running for cover.

Priestly made his decision. "I'm sidelining you until I can get to the bottom of this. Report to the Administration Section and make yourself available for whatever shit detail they have. They're always hollering for help."

"Is that all, sir?"

"Dismissed," Priestly muttered. Stuart snapped a salute and, without waiting for it to be returned, spun around to leave. "You're on the edge," Priestly said, stopping him. "One more screw-up and I'll push you over. You can kiss your retirement good-bye. Think about it."

I am thinking about it, Stuart thought.

※

The Pentagon is aptly named for its five sides, five concentric rings of offices, five floors, and the five-acre center courtyard that has been called Ground Zero. The inhabitants of the Puzzle Palace, or Fort Fumble, as it is sometimes known, don't think it's funny, because it was a commonly accepted fact that in the heyday of the Cold War, the Soviets had fed the center coordinates of the courtyard into at least five ICBMs. This was not attributed to a Russian sense of humor but to the reliability, or lack of it, of their missiles and warheads.

"Big" is the adjective that best describes the Pentagon, and with over 6.5 million square feet, it's easy to get lost. If the casual visitor should see a man in uniform talking to a pretty civilian employee, it's not because he's trying to score but because he's lost. Yet everyone will think he's hitting on her, which even in this day of political correctness is much better than appearing to be asking for directions, a major violation of the male ethic. When the $1.2 billion renovation that was started in 1993 is completed in 2006, the added 200,000 square feet of office space will only make the situation worse.

But in spite of its size and idiosyncrasies, the occasional scandal about contracting and budgeting, the personal ambitions stalking its offices, and the egos that define the command corridors, the Pentagon is an efficient place, and the taxpayers get good value for their money. For the next two days Stuart worked in an administrative limbo, making it even more efficient, shuffling the never-ending flow of paperwork that flooded the Air Force. "Paperwork" was really a misnomer, since most of the Air Force's business was conducted on computers. But the devilish machines had not streamlined the military's penchant for documentation. In fact, they'd only made it worse. Consequently the first file Stuart opened contained over thirty unanswered queries, letters, and one inventory form to be filled out and dutifully forwarded. He went to work on the inventory, the most time-consuming project.

Late on Wednesday afternoon Peggy Redman, Priestly's secretary, telephoned. "You can come back. Everything's fine."

"What happened?"

"Cooler heads prevailed and decided you did the right thing by riding out the hurricane in Cuba. And, can you believe it, your report was forwarded, unchanged, to the committee working on the Quadrennial Defense Review?" She gave a low, very wicked laugh. "No one knows how that happened or how to answer the committee's questions, least of all Colonel Priestly. It seems you're suddenly the indispensable man around here. The good colonel has dropped the investigation."

Stuart shook his head in amusement. Peggy Redman had saved him because she had what management experts call "institutional loyalty." An untold number of trees had died providing the paper describing this phenomenon but, in short, it was nothing more than a blend of dedication and common sense. Peggy believed in what her office did and knew what it took to get the job done. It also helped that she liked Mike Stuart and hated Colonel Roger "Ramjet" Priestly with a pure and refined passion.

"Thanks, Peggy," he said, vowing to send her a large bouquet of flowers. He was certain she had forwarded the report to the committee by simply misrouting it. He returned to the inventory he was working on because it grated on his nature to leave projects incomplete, no matter how trivial. He worked hard, but it was after 8:00 P.M. by the time he finished. He turned out the light in the admin office and hurried to catch the next Metro. For Stuart, as for so many who worked at the Pentagon, it was easier to take the subway than fight the traffic and parking. But at that late hour there were only three other passengers on the train.

As the crow flies, it was less than four miles from the Pentagon to Stuart's basement flat in Capitol Hill, the multiracial residential area immediately east of the Capitol. The journey normally took about thirty minutes, depending on how quickly he transferred lines at the midway point, and it was a short walk from Eastern Market, the station where he got off, to his apartment just past Archibald Walk. During daylight it was a safe enough walk, but after dark he preferred to catch a cab, if one was available.

Stuart came out of the station and decided to wait a few minutes to see if a cab might drive by. He checked his watch. *Come on*, he thought.

Three African-American teenagers, all wearing the latest gear, ambled by and stopped at the entrance to the Metro station. They were full of life and trading good-natured insults as they discussed the merits of certain young females. It was all part of the life in his neighborhood and one of the reasons he liked living there. A fourth teenager joined them, and the insults grew loud as the words flew back and forth. Stuart got a good look at the newcomer when he stepped under a streetlight. He was much older than the three boys and definitely not a teenager.

Alarm bells went off in Stuart's head, and he moved away. Again he checked his watch. *No taxi tonight*, he thought. He decided to walk just as a street-sweeper truck lumbered around the corner. Suddenly the words changed tone, now ugly and menacing. Stuart hurried past, moving toward the approaching sweeper as the four young men started to push and challenge.

Stuart saw a knife flash, and the latecomer broke away, running directly at him. Stuart froze. The man barreled into Stuart and knocked him into the path of the oncoming sweeper. The screech of brakes deafened Stuart as headlights blinded him. He knew he was dead.

Something snapped inside, filling him with rage.

He threw himself to the ground, centering up on the sweeper's bumper, anything to get away from the big wheels. He flattened his right cheek and stomach against the asphalt as the truck rolled over him. He felt the back of his coat rip as it slammed to a stop.

Stuart lay under the sweeper, afraid to move. He could feel the weight of the truck on his back and his glasses smashed under his cheek. He saw feet run past and heard shouting. Then the cab door swung open, and he felt the driver getting off. The belly of an incredibly overweight man appeared as the driver knelt down beside the truck. Then his face emerged. "Am I hurt?" Stuart asked.

"You're talking," the driver said. "I'll get a flashlight and call for help. Don't move."

"Don't get back into the truck!" Stuart shouted. But his warning was too late, and the truck rocked on him. Stuart moaned. "He got back in."

The next few minutes turned into an eternity as the police and then a fire truck arrived. Everyone kept telling Stuart not to move, and finally a paramedic, a slender woman, crawled under the truck. "Well," she said, "good evening, sir."

"Does your husband know we're meeting like this?" he muttered between clenched teeth.

"He's not the jealous kind." She examined him and took his pulse. "I think you're okay. We're going to jack up the truck in a few minutes."

He closed his eyes as the emergency crew shoved a hydraulic jack under the chassis and started to pump. Someone grabbed his ankles and gently pulled him free. He looked up into the smiling face of the paramedic. "You are one lucky man," she announced.

✳

It was after midnight when Stuart got home. He dropped his ruined uniform coat in a chair and headed for the shower. He stripped off his clothes and examined himself in the mirror. Other than a few minor scrapes and bruises, he was fine. He could feel the onset of stiffness the examining doctor had warned him about. The hot water felt good as it coursed over his body. He got out, toweled himself dry, and padded into the kitchen, ravenously hungry. The flashing light on his answering machine announced that he had two messages.

The first one was from his ex-wife. "Hi, honey. This is Jenny. Give me a call whenever." He gave a little snort. The unspoken protocols of their divorce were well established, and she wanted money. If the call was about Eric, their twelve-year-old son, she would have said, "Mike, we have a problem." But Eric was with Stuart's parents, touring England. He decided to put Jenny's call on a back burner until "whenever" felt right.

The second message was short and to the point. "This is Jane. Call me anytime."

For reasons he didn't understand, he wanted to talk to her. He dialed her number, and she answered on the third ring. "I know it's late, but you said to call anytime."

"It's okay," she said. "You're hard to contact."

"A lot of pressing matters around here," he replied. "How's the shoulder doing?"

"Better. Question: What about *Temptress*?"

The empty feeling in his stomach was back, and it had nothing to do with the lack of food. The last time he had seen his boat was in a slip in Miami. It was gleaming in the early-morning sun, none the worse for wear after the hurricane and the sojourn to Cuba. "Sell her, I guess."

"Good time to sell. Beginning of the season here. How much?"

"Whatever's fair."

A long pause. Then, softly, "I'd like to buy her. Can you carry the loan?"

The gentleness in Jane's voice touched him. "Okay by me," Stuart replied. "But I need some cash up front."

"I'll talk to a bank," she said, breaking the connection.

Stuart smiled to himself as he hung up. *That's Jane*, he told himself. *A woman of few words.*

2

RAF Cranthorpe, England

The boy kept bouncing against his seat belt, not wanting to miss any part of the old English air base. "This is neat, Gramps," he kept repeating.

Colonel William "Shanker" Stuart, United States Air Force (retired), smiled at his grandson's unfeigned enthusiasm. He was glad he had brought Eric to RAF Cranthorpe for the air show and the dedication ceremonies. The old Royal Air Force Base had been restored to its glory days during the Battle of Britain and was being dedicated to those "so few" men who had accomplished so much. "Yeah, it is neat," Shanker admitted. He inched their rental car into a parking space and got out.

A large group of men and women carrying signs and placards were gathering in the parking lane in front of them. Shanker estimated their number at over two hundred, and the signs they carried worried him. He watched in silence as they unfurled a large banner. The last thing Shanker wanted to see was a demonstration ruining the ceremonies. Too many volunteers had worked too hard to keep RAF Cranthorpe alive.

Eric read another one of the signs. "What's 'Ban the Bomb' mean?"

"It's a throwback to another time, son, when people were worried about nuclear war."

The two Americans watched as three well-dressed men approached the group of protesters. "I'm afraid I must ask you to leave," one of the men told the demonstrators.

"Who are you, mate?" a scruffily dressed woman shouted.

"I'm from the CAA, and—"

The crowd started shouting, "Hell no, we won't go," and drowned out the CAA man. The three men gave up and retreated to the safety of their car as the crowd grew larger and the chanting louder.

"What's the CAA?" Eric asked.

"That's the British government's Civil Aviation Agency," Shanker answered. "It's the same as our FAA, the Federal Aviation Agency."

"I thought you didn't like the FAA."

"I don't dislike them, son. I just think they're a pain in the ass. Like all bureaucrats."

"Dad says he's just a bureaucrat in the Air Force."

"That's different," Shanker replied. *But not much*, he groused to himself. All he ever wanted was for Michael to be like his older brother and fly jet fighters. But Mike's poor eyesight had precluded that, and as a result he was a nonrated officer with a desk job. His younger son was one of his life's major disappointments. He put his arm around his grandson's shoulders. "Come on. They got an F-4 here like the ones I used to fly."

"That's neat, Gramps. Can I sit in it?"

"We'll see, son," Shanker said, feeling much better. There was hope for the family yet. They followed the crowd out to the old parking lots, where three generations of warbirds were on display. Shanker paused when he saw the old F-4 Phantom II, and for a moment the memories came rushing back. It was 1972, and he was a young captain walking out to a bomb-laden Phantom for a mission over North Vietnam. "We were young then," he said in a low voice.

"I'm afraid you were born old," a voice with a clipped English accent said from behind him, bringing Shanker back to the moment.

Shanker turned around. The speaker was a tall, lanky man his age. A mass of unruly gray hair framed a ruddy face, and close-set, bright blue eyes twinkled above an outrageous RAF-style handlebar mustache. He was wearing an olive-green flight suit with leather gloves protruding from a leg pocket. "Chalky!" Shanker shouted. "You old reprobate! The last I heard, you were flying for the Saudis."

"I was until they phased out the Lightning and bought F-15s from you Yanks."

"Can't say I blame them," Shanker allowed.

The Englishman shook his head. The old, long-forgotten, good-natured rivalry was back. "Who's the young gentleman?"

"Wing Commander Seagrave, may I present my grandson, Eric Stuart. Eric, Wing Commander Robin Seagrave, better known as 'Chalky' because of his hair, which turned white the first time he flew in a real jet."

Eric extended his hand. "Pleased to meet you, sir." The two shook hands, the Englishman impressed with the boy's good manners.

"Eric," Shanker said, "don't pay any attention to what Chalky says about the Lightning."

"What's the Lightning?" Eric asked.

Seagrave laughed. "Obviously your grandfather has neglected your education. Come, I'll show you." He led the two to another parking lot, where a jet fighter was parked. "Well, lad, what do you see?"

Eric studied the airplane for a moment and concentrated hard. He glanced at his grandfather, and Shanker nodded his encouragement. "Well," Eric began, "I see a single-place jet fighter with a big intake in the nose." He walked around the old jet and screwed up his face. "It's got funny-looking clipped wings, almost delta-shaped but not quite." He smiled. "It's got a big vertical stabilizer sticking up like a B-52." His eyes opened wide in amazement when he walked around the back. "It's got two engines! One on top of the other!"

"Very good," Seagrave said. "Right on all counts, except it's a *two*-place. The pilot and passenger sit side by side. A bit cramped. Specifically it's a BAC Lightning, model T.55. Lightnings were in service with the RAF from 1960 to 1988." He explained how Saudi Arabia had also flown the jet until 1986 and then given this particular one to a group of English aviation enthusiasts for preservation. "Unfortunately," Seagrave explained, "the CAA won't allow me to fly it. Never said why. Some bureaucratic nonsense. Probably afraid to make a decision."

"Then why the flight suit?" Shanker asked.

"They will allow a high-speed taxi demonstration down the active. I'll light the reheat but shut it down at a hundred fifty knots and deploy the brake chute. That should delight the crowd."

Shanker was jealous. "You lucky dog."

Seagrave wouldn't let it go and had to rub it in. "Wait until you see my passenger." He pointed to a young woman waiting near the boarding ladder to the cockpit. "On local control with the CAA. Going along to make sure all is correct. Liz," Seagrave called. "Someone I'd like you to meet."

The woman walked over to them. Her flight suit was molded to her figure, and she moved to an inner music that created an image of beauty and grace. Seagrave made the introductions and escorted her back to the boarding ladder. "Lucky dog," Shanker muttered under his breath.

"She's really pretty, Gramps," Eric said.

"I'm glad you noticed, son." They watched in silence as the two climbed into the Lightning, donned their helmets, and started engines.

Eric studied the jet as it taxied out to the main runway. "Was the Lightning a good fighter, Gramps?"

Shanker was absolutely honest. "It was a real hot rod in its day and still nothing to sneeze at. I flew against it in an exercise once and got my eyes watered. But it didn't carry enough fuel and had a limited range. It never saw combat, which is the real test."

"Wing Commander Seagrave is really cool. Is he a good fighter pilot?"

"He's one mellow dude in the hot tub and a damn good pilot, but since he never flew combat, we'll never know for sure about the fighter thing. Just like the Lightning."

❉

Seagrave glanced at his passenger. "You okay?"

Liz took a deep breath. "Fine, thanks. This is most exciting."

"Much more thrilling if we could fly." He pointed at the handle for the brake chute in the upper right-hand corner of the instrument panel. "When I ask for the chute, just a smooth straight pull. But not until I tell you." She nodded, her eyes bright. She tentatively touched the handle.

Seagrave keyed the radio. "Cranthorpe Tower. Lightning One is holding at 'C' ready for taxi run."

"Cleared to enter and hold," the tower answered. Seagrave acknowledged and taxied into position on the runway. "Lightning One, you are cleared for your high-speed taxi run, surface wind is two-fifty at twelve knots, temperature plus eighteen."

Seagrave answered, "Winding up and rolling in twenty seconds."

"Roger, Lightning One," the tower replied. "Runway is clear."

Seagrave fed the power into the two Rolls-Royce Avon Mark 302C engines. When the RPMs touched 92 percent, he called "Brakes off"

over the intercom and shoved the throttles full forward. "Reheat now."
He lit the afterburners and called their speed, his voice calm and matter-
of-fact as their speed quickly built. "Very good. One-twenty, one-thirty—
Christ!" A swarm of people surged onto the runway, directly in their
path. They were holding a huge banner across the runway proclaiming
SAVE OUR CHILDREN—NOT CRANTHORPE! Their intent was obvious:
They wanted the Lightning to split the banner while video cameras
recorded the image for the evening news. But they'd misjudged the space
the Lightning needed to clear on each side and hadn't given Seagrave
enough distance to drag the accelerating fighter to a stop. There was only
one option left.

Rather than plow into the demonstrators, Seagrave pulled back on the
stick, and the Lightning lifted into the air, shaking off its earthly shackles,
and returned to where it belonged. Seagrave allowed a tight smile when
he saw the protesters fall away as the jet barely cleared their heads, accelerating through 190 knots. He snapped the gear handle up. Again his
voice was amazingly calm as he keyed the radio. "Tower, Lightning One
is lifting off. No choice in the matter. We're overweight and need to burn
off fuel before landing. Please clear the runway."

The tower controller was frantic. "Remain within ten miles of the
field. You are cleared to maneuver at your discretion. I, ah, we have no
idea what's going on. I'm ringing security to clear the runway."

"Capital idea." He turned to Liz. "Well, this is a bit more than I bargained for. I do hope we didn't singe too many hairs."

"Not me," Liz answered.

The old habits were back, and Seagrave scanned the instruments as he
leveled off at four thousand feet on the downwind side of the landing pattern. The left main landing-gear light flickered from green to red for a
few seconds. Out of habit he tapped the light, not that it would have done
any good. The light flickered again. "Probably a microswitch," he told
Liz. "But it could mean the gear is not up and locked properly." The light
flickered again, and he considered recycling the gear. Then the light
went out, indicating all was well.

He keyed the radio. "Tower, I had an 'unsafe gear' light, but all
appears well now. Would appreciate a visual."

"You're cleared for a low approach and overshoot," the tower answered.
"The circuit is reserved for you to maneuver at your discretion."

"Cleared for the approach," Seagrave replied. He turned final and lined up on the runway as they descended. He slowed to 240 knots and kept the gear and flaps retracted. Ahead of them he could see the runway, still packed with protesters at the halfway point. "What are those fools doing?" he muttered. He flew past the tower at fifty feet and pulled up, again accelerating.

"I have no idea," Liz said. "But you did get their attention, and a few are leaving."

"Your gear doors appear to be fully closed," the tower radioed. "Your underside scans clean."

"Very good," Seagrave replied. "What are those bloody fools doing down there?"

"Security reports demonstrators are sitting down on the runway and refuse to move. We've called for help."

Seagrave hid his irritation as they did two turns in the circuit, holding at four thousand feet. Liz studied the crowd on the runway each time they flew past, her exasperation growing at the lack of progress. She reached over and touched his arm, her eyes sparkling. "Maybe we could do a high-speed pass to encourage a few others to leave, yes?" She tried to look innocent and helpful.

He caught the look in her eyes. She may have been with the CAA, but her head was screwed on straight. "A very good idea," he said. "And we are cleared to maneuver at our discretion." He keyed the radio. "Tower, this time around will be a high-speed pass."

"Roger," the tower answered. "Stay above two hundred feet and no faster than six hundred knots."

Seagrave flew a curvilinear approach to final and leveled off at four-hundred feet. "I don't believe they've seen us yet. But they soon will." He inched the Lightning down to two hundred feet and stroked the after-burners, the airspeed bouncing off six hundred knots. He passed over the demonstrators and rotated. "Full reheat now," he said, shoving the throttles into max afterburner.

Liz twisted her head, looking back and fighting the G's as she gave the demonstrators the finger. "Bastards!" she shouted. "That singed the odd hair or two."

Seagrave allowed a tight smile. His passenger was a fighter pilot at heart. He leveled off at eight thousand feet and flew a wide downwind, rapidly descending back to four thousand feet. He automatically scanned the instrument panel once again. "Not good," he muttered. "We're losing hydraulic pressure." He pointed to the Services Pressure Gauge. "It should be steady at three thousand PSI." The needle was slowly dropping, falling toward the red sector.

"Is that bad?" Liz asked.

"It will be if we don't get down." He keyed the radio. "Cranthorpe, we have a problem. I'm losing hydraulic pressure and need to land immediately."

"Stand by," the tower answered.

"I can't stand by too long," Seagrave replied. "Request vectors to the nearest suitable field for landing."

A much-relieved tower controller answered, "The runway is open. You're cleared all the way. Check three greens."

Seagrave lowered the undercarriage. Two lights blinked green at him. But the left main gear stayed red. "Tower, I have an unsafe condition on my left main. Request a flyby to check undercarriage down." He selected flaps, hoping there was enough pressure in the system to lower them. There was.

"Cleared for a low approach," the tower answered. This time Seagrave flew by at 175 knots, as slow as possible. He gently yawed the aircraft to help gravity pull the gear down. "Your left main is still up," the tower radioed.

"Selecting emergency undercarriage now," Seagrave answered, his voice still calm. His left hand dropped down beside his seat and he pulled the U/C selector button on the floor. "Just another day on the job," he muttered to himself. But Liz caught it and understood. Like most fighter pilots, Seagrave would rather die than sound bad. Now it was a question of maneuvering as smoothly as possible while getting back around for landing. They entered downwind. He kept talking on the intercom to reassure his passenger. "Flying is a bit more demanding since the artificial feel and autostabs have quit. But it's no big deal."

"I have you in the binocs," the tower radioed. "Your undercarriage appears down and locked."

"How encouraging," Seagrave answered. "But I still have a red." He turned final and again gently yawed the aircraft, hoping gravity might perform some magic. It did, and the offending light turned to green.

Then it blinked red to green and back. "Do make up your mind," Seagrave groused. "No need to amuse the spectators with a gear-up landing." As if on cue, the light turned steady green. The runway, finally clear of the demonstrators, loomed up in front of them. "Crossing in now, one seventy-five, ease back gently, gently, one fifty-five, one fifty, ah, there we are." It was a picture-perfect landing. He eased the nosewheel onto the runway. "Brake chute now, Liz."

Her hand flashed out and pulled the handle, straight and smooth as he had told her. The chute popped out from the base of the vertical stabilizer and snapped open. He tapped the brakes, depleting the last of the pressure accumulator. They stopped on the runway, still going straight ahead. Seagrave's right hand danced on the console. "HP fuel cocks off." The engines died of fuel starvation and spun down. Seagrave keyed the radio. "Cranthorpe tower, Lightning One is down. We'll need a tow back to dispersal. Thanks for the help. Good show all round." He peeled off his oxygen mask and smiled to Liz. "Ground crew will have to use a hand pump to open the canopy. I hope you don't mind waiting."

Liz reached out and touched his cheek. Her hand was warm. "That was the most exciting thing that's ever happened to me."

"You were brilliant. And that entitles you to say the three magic words: 'Cheated death again.'"

"Cheated death again," she repeated.

The car carrying the three CAA officials reached the Lightning at the same time as the ground crew. The crew piled out of the van and quickly installed ground locks on the landing gear. Once the gear was secure, two men fitted a hand pump to the socket on the left side of the fuselage, just aft of the wing's trailing edge. One man pumped furiously, and the canopy slowly opened while Shanker and Eric climbed out of the service van. Shanker gave Seagrave a thumbs-up. "You did good," he shouted.

The CAA headman jumped out of his car, his face bright red, and started shouting the moment Seagrave climbed down the boarding ladder. "This aircraft does not carry a certificate to fly, nor were you authorized to fly!"

Seagrave ignored him and helped Liz climb down, her legs still a little weak. "Are you okay?" Seagrave asked.

"Perfect," she answered.

Seagrave walked around the jet with Shanker and Eric, examining it for damage. One of the ground crew was looking in the left main gear well. "Here's the problem. A gland let go when you retracted the gear. Never happen if the system were exercised regularly."

"It's the same with us," Shanker said. "You got to keep 'em flying once or twice a week or they turn into hangar queens."

The CAA headman was livid with rage as he trailed after Seagrave. "What's your name? What are your qualifications? Who gave you permission to operate this aircraft? Why did you take off? What speed were you going when you flew down the runway? What was your height? What do you have to say?"

Seagrave gave him a sad look. "Which question to answer first? Ah, height. Six feet three inches in my socks. Question one: Robin Seagrave. Question two: eight thousand hours on fighters. Question three: your chaps. Question four: It was either take off or kill half the crowd on the runway. Not a long time to make that decision, and I don't recall hearing any input from the CAA at that particular moment, which would have been most helpful. Question five: six hundred knots. That's six hundred ninety miles per hour for you nonflying types."

The CAA man sputtered. "That's supersonic!"

Seagrave shook his head in resignation, his suspicions about the CAA fully confirmed. "Don't you consider it strange that no one heard a sonic boom?" He didn't wait for an answer. "Try seven hundred sixty miles per hour at sea level for Mach One. What was I saying? Oh, yes, question six: I've already answered that, but if you mean altitude, two hundred feet."

Seagrave leaned into the CAA official, his eyes cold blue steel. "As to what I have to say? Are you naturally thick, or did you take a course? Talk about failed common sense. If you, as the CAA official in charge, had done your work properly, you would have known a protest was planned and exercised proper crowd control or canceled the taxi demonstration."

Shanker had to add his two cents' worth. "I saw the CAA talking to the demonstrators about two hours earlier in the parking lot."

The CAA official whirled on Shanker. "Your contribution was not called for."

Shanker gave him an expressive shrug that was clearly a "fuck you" message.

"Offhand," Seagrave said, rolling in for a second strafing pass on the

CAA, "it appears that your lack of appreciation of the situation allowed those bloody stupid demonstrators to place a large number of people in danger, the least of whom were my passenger and myself. In fact, I plan to raise the issue with my MP."

The CAA official blanched at the thought of Seagrave's MP, or member of Parliament, questioning the CAA in the House of Commons. Now it was his turn to attack. "I want this aircraft towed to the nearest hangar and salvaged immediately. It will never fly again." He stormed away without waiting for a reply.

"Have a nice day," Seagrave called. He took a deep breath and turned to the ground crew. "I'm afraid I cocked it up. Looks like the end for the old girl."

"Maybe," Shanker said, "I can help."

3

Miami, Florida

Eduardo Pinar was the first to arrive at Café Martí, a sidewalk café in the heart of Little Havana. He found a table at the back and collapsed into the chair, his slender body spent from the exertion of walking two blocks in the early-September afternoon sun. As always, he was oblivious to the noise and hustle around him. Just another dreamy young man with a droopy mustache and limpid, brown eyes going nowhere and without ambition.

A waiter approached and made small talk as he waited for Eduardo to order. "The heat has finally broken," the waiter said in Spanish. "Soon we'll see the tourists again."

"Will we?" Eduardo replied in English. "Espresso and a newspaper, *por favor.*"

"*Cuba Libre?*" the waiter asked, not that it made any difference. *Cuba Libre* was the only paper allowed in the café, which was frequented by equal parts anti-Castro exiles, Cuban spies watching the exiles, and FBI agents watching both groups and trolling for recruits among either. For the waiter the only question was which group Eduardo currently belonged to. Allegiances changed almost daily, but he'd sort it out.

A skinny little woman Eduardo knew only as Carita arrived at the same time as the espresso and newspaper. Like Eduardo, she ordered a small cup of the potent brew that could etch a sidewalk. "Where's Luis and Francisco?" she demanded in English.

"Coming," Eduardo replied. He didn't like Carita, but Luis had insisted she join the group.

"Have you heard about the others?" she asked.

"I heard they were arrested and are in jail."

"They'll die there," she said, unconsciously lapsing into Spanish. "The bastards will execute them in their cells."

"Were we betrayed?" Eduardo asked.

"Of course we were," she snapped. "How else—" She fell silent as the waiter returned with her espresso. When he left, she continued. "Our country will never be free." She fought back her tears. "Not in our lifetime."

Eduardo was moved by her tears and reached across the table, covering her hand with his. His eyes flashed with passion, and he spoke in Spanish. "Do not lose faith. For every one of us they cut down, four more will arise in his place. We will free our country of this evil, this abomination to God and humanity. Our children will return to their homeland and not have to live under the cruel tyranny that has driven us into exile." He stopped talking when Luis Barrios and Francisco Martínez arrived. Like Eduardo, they were in their mid-twenties.

Luis Barrios, the group's leader, slumped in a chair and mumbled a few words of deep despair for their jailed comrades. Then he talked about their struggle to win the freedom of their country. Slowly his own words renewed his spirit and filled him with purpose. The movement was not dead, and as the Semtex explosive had been delivered, they had work to do.

Eduardo called for their bill.

❄

The waiter scoffed at the small tip Eduardo left behind and scooped it off the table in disgust. A tall, very pretty woman with dark hair sitting at the next table caught his attention. She often came to the café, always alone, and most of the waiters thought she was either an FBI or a CIA agent. But as he always pointed out, beauty attracted attention, and that was bad for an agent. Personally, he thought she was attracted to Latin men or just practicing her Spanish. Perhaps both. "I couldn't help but overhear," Sophia James said in passable Spanish. "Are they really freedom fighters?"

"Them?" the waiter said in disgust. "They're from Puerto Rico, not Cuba." *She couldn't hear the accents. At least she'll leave a large tip.*

She did.

4

RAF Cranthorpe

Inside the hangar, Shanker and Seagrave sat in deck chairs nursing monumental hangovers while Eric played in the Lightning's cockpit. The boy's dark blond hair kept bobbing out of sight as he fought his version of the Battle of Britain. Outside, a cleanup crew of volunteers swept up the trash from Saturday's air show. "The bastards," Seagrave kept grumbling over and over. "She's too good a bird to turn into scrap." He fell into a pit of deep remorse. "I should have mowed the bastards down."

"A kill is a kill," Shanker muttered, each word a pile driver of agony spiking his headache.

A silver Bentley drove up and stopped in front of the hangar. The chauffeur popped out and held the rear door open. Prince Reza Ibn Abdul Turika climbed out, stretching his tall frame. Seagrave stood and walked, a bit unsteadily, over to meet the Saudi prince. They knew each other from the time Seagrave had trained Saudi pilots in the Lightning. "So, my friend," Turika said, "you have problems."

Seagrave told the prince about the unauthorized flight and how, in retaliation, the CAA had ordered the Lightning to be salvaged for scrap. "All my fault," he admitted. "I should have killed the fools on the runway."

Turika walked around the jet. "Very good," he admitted, admiring the immaculate restoration work. "You did this all with private contributions?" Seagrave quoted the figures in pounds sterling and the estimated number of man-hours that had been volunteered. "It sounds like a labor of love," Turika said. Eric stuck his head out of the cockpit and quickly climbed out. Seagrave introduced Eric and then Shanker, telling the prince how Shanker had flown F-4 Phantoms. Turika was immediately interested. "Did you know a Colonel Anthony Waters?" Turika asked.

A rueful look crossed Shanker's face. "Yeah. I knew Muddy. They don't get any better. I was with him at Ras Assanya. I was evacuated out just before the base was overrun."

"Muddy was a good friend," Turika said. "And Jack Locke."

"I knew Jack," Shanker said. The two men shook hands, bound by a common tie to two legends of the U.S. Air Force.

"Well," Turika said, "Chalky here tells me you can help with our dilemma."

"I belong to a group in the states called the Gray Eagles. We restore warbirds and keep 'em flying for air shows and demonstrations. We're long on volunteers and short on money, but we can take care of the Lightning, providing it was a donation and transported to the States."

"And provided," Turika said, "the CAA doesn't turn it into scrap." He studied the Lightning for a moment. "This was the first Lightning I ever flew. Chalky was my instructor. Do you remember that?"

Seagrave nodded. "Like yesterday. Technically it still belongs to your government and is on loan to us."

Turika exhaled loudly. "The ownership is a confused issue. My government wants nothing to do with it."

"But the CAA doesn't know that," Seagrave said. Turika fell silent, considering his options.

"Gramps," Eric said, "if the Gray Eagles get it, I can wash it and keep it clean. I got lots of friends who'll help me." A thought came to him. "You know what would be real neat?" He was so excited he couldn't contain his twelve-year-old enthusiasm. "We can paint it with Saudi markings, just like when Prince Turika and Commander Seagrave flew it."

"I doubt if the Saudis would allow that," Seagrave said. He looked at Turika. "But there would be a certain poetic justice, since your country has kept it alive."

Turika smiled at the boy, recalling when his sons had been the same age. But they had all grown up, and not one had followed in his footsteps. "Do you want to be a fighter pilot?" Eric nodded vigorously, a big grin on his face. Turika turned to Shanker. "You're a very lucky man to have such a grandson. Let's make something happen, for his sake." He paused, remembering the past. "And for Muddy Waters and Jack Locke." He looked at Seagrave. "Chalky, do you know anyone in your government who might be sympathetic?"

"Miss Liz will help," Eric blurted out. Just as quickly he added, "Excuse me, I didn't mean to be rude."

"Out of the mouths of babes," Seagrave murmured.

❋

"Sorry, Chalky," Liz said, "but I don't have the authority to do anything." She gazed at the Lightning and recalled her short flight from the day before. "What a shame. It is a magnificent machine."

"What if we submitted a letter returning the Lightning to its rightful owner?" Seagrave asked.

"I thought the RAF Cranthorpe Memorial Display owned it," she replied.

"It is my understanding," Turika said, "that it is on loan from my government, along with all the equipment, tools, spare parts, and extra engines."

Liz understood exactly what the men were suggesting. "Well, if you submitted the letter through my office . . ."

"And if you didn't forward it for a week or so," Seagrave added.

"I had planned on taking leave starting tomorrow," Liz said. "I'd be gone a week. It would be on my desk waiting for my return."

"And if I happened to take possession of the Lightning during that time," Turika said.

"Yes, I see," Liz said. "You could move it at your discretion." She warmed to the idea. "Actually, if it was out of the country, the problem goes away, for which I personally would be most grateful—in my official capacity, of course."

"What about an export license to clear customs?" Seagrave asked.

"No license is required for exporting salvage," Liz replied. "Just a declaration and estimate of value to pay customs."

Shanker shook his head. "It doesn't look like salvage to me."

"What does salvage look like?" Eric asked.

"I imagine that customs doesn't really care what it looks like," Turika said, "as long as it is declared salvage and they have an estimate of value."

"I can provide that," Liz said.

"We can't ask you to do that, Liz," Seagrave said. "You're taking too much of a chance declaring it salvage, giving us an estimate, and then sitting on the letter while we abscond with the goods."

"Not to worry," she replied. "Since when has one bureaucracy talked to another?" She gave them a radiant smile. "Cheated death again, yes?"

The Pentagon

Colonel Roger "Ramjet" Priestly was not a happy man as he reread the lengthy memo from the secretary of defense's office. He was unhappy because his name was not on it and Lieutenant Colonel Michael E. Stuart's name was. He threw down the memo in disgust and buzzed his secretary. "Peggy, I want Stuart in here on the double." He didn't wait for a reply before breaking the connection. He checked his watch. Exactly forty-five seconds later Stuart presented himself in Ramjet's office. Peggy had warned him, and not even his glasses could hide his worry. Ramjet threw the memo at Stuart. "I suppose you've already seen this?"

Stuart scanned the memo. "No, sir. This is all news to me."

Ramjet came out of his chair, his palms flat against his desk, his arms rigid, and leaned forward. "In a pig's ass! This has got your pecker tracks all over it. Tell me a major initiative coming from the National Security Council and forwarded to me from the Sec Def, that directs"—he grabbed the memo and jabbed a forefinger at the opening paragraph to quote—" 'A comprehensive review of the Strategic Petroleum Reserve to include movement and distribution affecting defense commitments' isn't tied to your tail." His face turned beet red.

Stuart tried to be rational. "We do this type of thing all the time, sir. I don't see the problem."

Ramjet fell back in his chair. "The problem is that I'm totally out of the loop. It looks like I was asleep at the switch. From now on you will back-brief me after every meeting you attend. Also you will submit nothing, and I mean nothing, without my signing off on it first."

Stuart tried to explain. "Any top-to-bottom review is going to involve the heavy hitters. I'm just one of the troops buried on some subcommittee doing the legwork."

"Remember who you work for and you won't have a problem. Forget where your first loyalty is and I'll be the one who buries you. Do you understand everything I've said?" Stuart nodded. "Good," Ramjet said. "One more thing: I'll hang you out to dry if you ever make an end run around me like this again. Dismissed."

Stuart decided that protesting his innocence was a waste of time, and he hurried out of the colonel's office. *Maybe Hurricane Andrea wasn't so bad after all*, he thought.

Peggy Redman waved a blue memo slip, stopping him before he could escape. "First meeting this afternoon," she told him.

He skidded to a halt. "I was lucky to get out of there alive. He hates my guts, and I don't know why."

"He hates himself," Peggy replied. "He doesn't need a reason." She sighed. "I've seen it before. It's very sad."

"Not when you're the target," Stuart groused. He read the memo and let out a groan. "The meeting's at the NSC across the river. He's not going to like this." The NSC was the National Security Council, and across the river meant the other side of the Potomac and the Old Executive Office Building across the street from the White House. For Ramjet Priestly that was much too close to the president. Stuart had a distinct image of being sent *up* the river and not *across* it.

"I'll tell him," Peggy said.

He gave her his best grin. "Thanks. I owe you."

Peggy made a note and watched him go. She picked up the phone and dialed a friend in the NSC. "Gloria, it's Peggy. Lieutenant Colonel Mike Stuart will be at the meeting. Put in a good word for him, okay?" She listened for a moment. "You'll like him. He's one of the good guys."

❋

Stuart was the only uniform on the third floor of the Old Executive Office Building, and he felt like a fish out of water. But that was typical of the Turner administration with its deliberate muting of the armed services' presence in the nation's capital. Although the president, Madeline O'Keith Turner, preferred to keep the military in the background, she was not hostile to the Department of Defense and trusted her military advisers. It had been that way since the Okinawa crisis, when her own party had turned against her and only the generals had stood firmly behind their commander in chief.*

Stuart found the conference room and walked in. The table was arranged with name cards and handouts at each seat, and flowers, the trademark of the Turner administration, were in the center. It all made him think of a formal banquet. Stuart glanced at the civilian sitting next to him and then his name card. General something, he couldn't quite read the last name. He was gray-headed, hunch-shouldered, and totally nondescript. "Colonel Stuart," the general said, "we're supposed to wear civvies on this side of the river."

"Sorry, sir. I didn't know. It won't happen again."

"Who do you work for?"

"Colonel Roger Priestly, the chief of ILSX."

"I'll speak to him."

Stuart suppressed a groan. That was all he needed. He automatically stood with everyone else and at first couldn't see who entered the room. He caught his breath when he saw Mazana Kamigami Hazelton, the national security adviser.

"Please be seated," the national security adviser said. She remained standing while the committee shuffled into their seats. It was the first time Stuart had seen her in person. She was petite, very short—less than five feet—and beautiful. Her delicate features reflected the best of her Hawaiian and Japanese heritages. Her exquisitely tailored business suit and diamond engagement ring with its matching wedding band shouted wealth, while her last name, Hazelton, signaled power and influence. Mazie, as she liked to be called by her friends, carefully cultivated her image as the administration's Dragon Lady to tame Washington's willful, and often obstinate, power brokers. In the rarefied air of the nation's capital, she was recognized as Madeline Turner's staunchest advocate and a force to be reckoned with. She could also be a very kind and supporting friend.

"Thank you for coming," Mazie began. "Before we start, why don't we go around the room and everyone introduce themselves?" It was quickly done, and Stuart was shaken. Some of the most influential names

---

*Editor's note: Madeline O'Keith Turner's first crisis after she assumed the presidency upon the death of President Quentin Roberts is detailed in the book *Power Curve* by the same author.

in the capital were seated at the table, and he was a tadpole, a small fry, or something equally insignificant. He tried not to look uncomfortable.

"President Turner," Mazie said, "has asked for a complete review of the Strategic Petroleum Reserve and is very concerned about how it impacts on our war-fighting capability. I think you all know how the president works." She stopped to let her words sink in, a little smile playing at the corners of her mouth.

Stuart panicked. He didn't have the slightest idea how Madeline Turner worked. He was way in over his head. *Time to bail out*, he thought. Cautiously, he raised his hand, half hoping the national security adviser wouldn't see it. She did and gave him a little nod. The butterflies in his stomach turned into a swarm of bats in full flight. Very big bats. "Madam . . ." What was the proper form of address? "Ah . . ."

For a moment Mazie was back in time and sitting in the same spot. A warm smile spread over her face. "In a meeting like this, Mike, I prefer Mazie. Or if that makes you uncomfortable, Mrs. Hazelton."

Stuart was so flustered that he missed her use of his first name. But the general sitting next to him didn't. "Ah," Stuart said, "I think I took a wrong turn somewhere. You really want my boss here, not me." No answer from Mazie, just the same encouraging smile. Stuart shook his head. "I have no idea how the president works."

"Efficiently," Mazie answered, "and she's amazingly straightforward. In this case she wants a hard, honest, and complete evaluation without a political spin. If there's bad news, she wants to hear it now, not later when it's too late to do anything about it. Let me put it this way: She hates surprises. Mike, you're here because I briefed her on the shortfalls in tanker availability you predicted. She was impressed. Now, if you'll all turn to paragraph two of the cover letter in front of you, you'll see she wants a total review of the SPR, to include all upstream, midstream, and downstream factors."

Stuart relaxed. The national security adviser was speaking the language he understood. "We need," Mazie continued, "to cut across all departments and leave no stone unturned. Obviously this is a major initiative and will need an executive head to shepherd your work." She looked at the general sitting next to Stuart. "I asked General Butler to chair this committee and he graciously consented. He'll report directly to me. Bernie, it's all yours."

Lieutenant General Franklin Bernard Butler stood up. "Thank you Mrs. Hazelton." He rapidly outlined how the committee would work and what their first goals were. From the ready acceptance around the table, it was obvious Butler was an accomplished administrator and had worked with them before. "I'll need help and would like an assistant to act as the main point of contact and coordination. We need a technician who can see the big picture, keep it all in perspective, and be responsible for all the paperwork. I believe he or she should be from this group." He looked at Stuart, recalling Mazie's comments. "If it's acceptable, I would like Lieutenant Colonel Stuart to step in."

Stuart felt a compelling need to visit the men's room.

Mazie nodded graciously and looked around the table. "All agreed, then?" There were no objections. The meeting rapidly drew to a close, and Stuart escaped to the men's room.

General Butler was right behind him. He was friendly as they stood at the urinals. "Well, it looks like you've a sponsor," he said.

"Sir, it's news to me if I do. Besides, I'm not qualified to do this and, and—"

The general interrupted him. "You're worried about Ramjet, right?"

Stuart nodded dumbly. How did Butler know about Priestly?

"I'll explain it to him," Butler said, zipping up his pants. "And, Mike, when the national security adviser calls you by your first name, you're qualified."

✳

Stuart had barely returned to his office in the Pentagon when his phone rang. It was Priestly. "Mike, I heard the meeting went very well. Say, if you've got a minute, I would like to see you. No hurry, though. Whenever you're free."

Stuart said that he was free, broke the connection, and made record time down the short corridor to Priestly's office. Peggy grinned at him when he skidded past her desk. "Go right in," she said.

Priestly stood up and smiled when Stuart reported in with a sharp salute. The colonel waved his fighter-pilot salute back. "Please, Mike. That's not necessary." He motioned Stuart to a chair at the conference table in front of his desk while he buzzed Peggy and told her to bring in tea. He came around his desk and joined him. They made small talk until Peggy arrived with the tea tray. She banged it down, not happy to be Priestly's servant, and walked out. Priestly smiled again. "Secretaries. They think they own the place." They discussed the meeting at the National Security Council for a few minutes, and Priestly related a funny incident that took place when he was a White House Fellow.

Stuart decided he liked the old Ramjet better than the smooth-talking sycophant he was seeing now. An image of Jane meeting Priestly at a Washington cocktail party played out in his imagination. "General Butler had some good words about the impression you made on the national security adviser," Priestly said. "When you look good, we all look good."

That's why the change, Stuart decided. An urge to bolt swept over him. He was tired of the games they were playing.

Priestly lowered his voice and spoke in confidence. "You didn't tell me you knew the national security adviser."

Stuart couldn't help himself. "You never asked."

※

It was after 9:00 P.M. when Stuart finally arrived home. His answering machine blinked a couple of messages at him. The first was from Jane. As always, she said little. "This is Jane, call me." He grinned. She had gone over her allotted four words. The second message was from Jenny, his ex-wife. "Mike, you haven't called. I have a personal problem and, and . . . well, please call." The "I need money" voice—again.

Two women in my life, and both their names start with J, he mused to himself. *Why do I always go for the middle of the alphabet?* But they couldn't have been more different. Jenny was tall, willowy, and glamorous. Jane, anything but. He hit the speed dial, eager to hear Jane's voice again.

She came directly to the point. "Sorry, Mike. I can't get a loan for the down payment on *Temptress*. I can list her with a broker or try to sell her privately."

Stuart thought for a moment. Did he still want to sell his boat? He made a decision not to make a decision. "Can you bring her up here? I can get a slip at Annapolis."

"Can do for expenses," she replied. "Figure six hundred seventy-eight." She had obviously thought about it.

"I'll send you a check," he said, breaking the connection.

Almost immediately the phone rang. This time it was Jenny. Her voice carried that same, breathless quality that always made him think of sex. "Mike," she said, "why haven't you called?"

"I just came in. It's been hectic at the office. What's the problem?"

"Oh, Mike. I'm in love."

Again? he moaned to himself.

Dallas

Professor Emil Steiner's reputation preceded him into the corporate offices of RayTex Oil. As editor of the most prestigious scientific journal in Europe, a department chair at a respected French university, and twice a runner-up Nobel laureate, he had scientific credentials that were unimpeachable. He also had a reputation for thoroughness and maintaining the most rigid scientific standards. His private reputation was somewhat different. He was a womanizer with an extravagant lifestyle.

What actually walked into Lloyd Marsten's corner office was a short, sixty-four-year-old man with bright blue eyes, a flushed face, and tufts of closely trimmed white hair stuck on his balding head. His expensive suit draped artfully over his rotund body and hid most of his expanding waistline. He walked with quick, bouncing steps, and his incredibly small feet were never still, not even when he was sitting down.

Marsten made the introductions as L.J. and Steiner shook hands. His left hand snaked out and snared her hand between both of his. "I have been looking forward to meeting you," Steiner said, his voice free of any French accent. He didn't let go of L.J.'s hand, and she had the distinct impression she was shaking hands with a trained seal.

"My pleasure," she said, extracting her hand with a little jerk. "I do hope you're feeling better." Steiner had arrived in Dallas four days earlier and pleaded jet lag, delaying the meeting. At last count, eleven call girls had cycled through his hotel suite at the Parke Royale to help him recover. Of course, all were billed to RayTex Oil. Steiner hated being alone.

"I'm much better," he replied. "Thank you."

Marsten played the affable host, and the three were soon seated in a little circle drinking tea and coffee. L.J. gently tapped Steiner's knee.

"The results you've obtained with Seismic Double Reflection are absolutely amazing. But I must admit I don't understand how you did it." Steiner puffed up at the adulation in her voice and gave her a few bombastic simplifications about wave-propagation characteristics. "Ah, yes," she replied before going into a detailed discussion of how he had used multiple seismic explosions to reflect off the leading signal the moment it hit a reflecting surface. The initial result had been a lot of "noise," or confused signals, and she wanted to know how Steiner had filtered, and then modulated, the "noise" into meaningful signals.

Steiner was no fool. The price of entry into the oil industry was technical expertise and hard field experience. L.J. obviously had the first. "May I ask where you studied?"

"I studied petroleum engineering at the University of Texas." She batted her eyelashes at him.

"Their program is much better than I thought," Steiner said.

L.J. beamed at his praise and gave her hair a little toss. His hand crept out and rested on her right knee. He was not above being sweet-talked by a very pretty woman, but there was a price to be paid. Marsten watched with fascination, wondering how much of his hand Steiner would get back. Perhaps a warning was in order. "L.J.," Marsten said, "also worked for seven years in the field, until her father died and she inherited the company."

Steiner understood and snatched his hand back. Field work was the rough-and-tumble side of the oil industry, and to survive for seven years took a special kind of toughness that few men had. "May I ask where?"

Again the adoring eyes that he should ask such a perceptive question. "Where the action was. Siberia, the Kalahari, the Grand Banks." She saved the worst for last. "Eritrea."

Steiner shot Marsten a quick look. Eritrea was on the Red Sea coast of Africa and had been part of Ethiopia until 1993, when it declared independence. In 1998 a border war with Ethiopia erupted, and an oil-prospecting team had been taken hostage by a local warlord. "L.J.," Marsten said, "was the one who negotiated our release."

"You were one of the hostages?" Steiner asked Marsten.

"We were all hostages," Marsten replied in a low voice. The memories and the tension were back, still unresolved issues. "If L.J. hadn't been there, they would have killed us."

Steiner's breath came fast. "The rumors about torture, were they true?"

Marsten pulled into himself, and a fragile, half-pathetic look spread across his face. L.J. recognized the symptoms and changed the subject, leading them away from that traumatic time. "Emil, you're not going to tell us where the elephant is, are you?"

Steiner didn't answer.

She gazed into his eyes and appealed to his sense of loyalty. "We've had such a productive relationship in the past. All the grants for your research when no one else shared your vision, our support when the university wanted to fire you . . ." She let her voice trail off. RayTex had saved Steiner's job, not to mention his reputation, by buying the silence of four young women students and his university's forgiveness with an endowment. It was a large endowment because there was much to forgive: the misappropriated funds, the sexual harassment, the four girls, the faculty wives.

"And I have delivered as promised," Steiner said.

Appeals to Steiner's loyalty weren't going to work. L.J. gave a little nod, accepting the challenge. Marsten caught it and felt sorry for the scientist.

"We need to find a common ground," L.J. said, starting the hard negotiations.

"I was thinking of a percentage of the profits," Steiner replied.

"Perhaps a percentage of the net."

Steiner shook his head. "That is not possible," he said, slipping into French. He quickly corrected himself. "It must be a percentage of the gross." Marsten went stiff at the man's audacity. Even an extremely small percentage skimmed off the top of all revenues from a large oil field translated into millions of dollars.

"And that is not possible," L.J. said.

"Perhaps someone else is interested," Steiner ventured.

"We do want to be reasonable," L.J. said, keeping negotiations open.

"Then it is gross?" Steiner asked.

"Agreed."

Steiner almost giggled at the stunned look on Marsten's face. "I believe fifteen percent is a reasonable figure," the scientist ventured.

L.J. and Marsten stared at him in disbelief. Fifteen percent of the gross would make Steiner wealthier than half the nations of the world.

"One-tenth of one percent," L.J. countered. "We *are* talking gross here."

"You insult me. Twelve percent."

"One-half of one percent."

Steiner stood up to leave. "My CD disks please."

"Dr. Steiner," L.J. said, "you must be realistic. No company can pay the percentages you're asking for. At best you can expect maybe one percent of the net profit, or its equivalent."

Steiner thought for a moment. "Three and a half percent of the gross. This is my last offer."

L.J. gave him a radiant smile. "I believe we have a deal." They shook hands.

"My lawyers will draw up the agreement," Steiner said.

"Of course," L.J. said. "And the location of the field?"

"After the agreement is signed and sealed with the proper advance, I will be glad to reveal its location."

"How much of an advance were you thinking of?"

"Half a billion dollars on signing."

Nothing betrayed what L.J. was thinking. "Until then," she said. She escorted him to the door. Again they shook hands, and he left, a very satisfied man.

"My God!" Marsten blurted. "Three and a half percent of the gross and half a billion up front? You can't be serious."

"Of course not," L.J. said. "We need to explain the situation to him in a way he'll understand." She paced the floor, her anger showing. "What exactly are we dealing with here?"

Marsten had experienced her anger before and knew what she was capable of doing. It was the dark side of her nature that frightened him. But he was the moth to her flame, and he couldn't turn away from her. "Steiner is a brilliant scientist, but he's a very silly person. He's lived too long in academia and lost touch with reality. And he is a very greedy man."

"I want the location of that elephant and, since we paid for it, the computer program for Seismic Double Reflection. Reopen negotiations. The sooner the better."

"Shall I go in hard?" Marsten asked.

L.J.'s face was an icy mask. "Get his attention." She turned and walked out of Marsten's office. He thought for a moment before reaching for the phone.

❋

The four young women were waiting for Steiner when he returned to his hotel room late that evening. At first he thought there was some mistake, they were so beautiful. His surprise was even more complete when two of them spoke fluent French. After a little conversation one of them went into the bathroom to draw a hot bath while another called room service for champagne. He smiled when they all started to undress. "Four is my favorite number," he told them.

❋

Marsten's voice cut through the fog. "Ah, there you are." Steiner came awake and blinked his eyes. "You do remember who I am?"

Steiner nodded, his mouth unbelievably dry. He wanted a drink but his lips were taped shut. Fear shot through him when he realized he was naked and tied spread-eagle on the bed. His eyes darted around the room. The women were still there, all dressed and wearing the coldest expressions he had ever seen. Surely the games they'd played hadn't been that bad? One of them opened an aluminum briefcase and pulled out two syringes and two small vials. With a cold efficiency that matched the look in her eyes, she filled one syringe. He wet the bed.

"Really, Dr. Steiner," Marsten said. "We expected better of you. Perhaps you're wondering what we're doing here." Steiner bobbed his head vigorously. "Think of this as contract renegotiations." The woman holding the syringe sat on the bed beside Steiner and looked at Marsten. "Of course," Marsten continued, "you're thinking that we can't get away with this sort of thing, what with the police and its being the twenty-first century, yes?" Marsten paused for effect. "Please disabuse yourself of that thinking. This is Texas. Actually, we like to reward our friends because we value them. We want to value you, Dr. Steiner. Please give us a reason to do so."

He nodded at the woman sitting on the bed. She grabbed Steiner's arm and jabbed the needle into his left biceps. She quickly filled another syringe from the second vial. "I assure you, it's very painless," Marsten said, his voice friendly. "You will feel a little warmth before lapsing into unconsciousness. That's all. The medical examiner will report the cause of your death as an overdose of a controlled substance, which, of course, laboratory tests will confirm." He pointed to the woman. "She's holding the antidote. But it must be administered within a few minutes, seconds actually, to be effective. Would you like to know the price of the antidote?" Steiner bobbed his head up and down. "Ah, I thought you would. We want the Seismic Double Reflection process as well as the exact location of the oil field." He reached over and peeled the tape away from Steiner's mouth.

Steiner babbled in French while one of the women translated. "He says it's all in his computer. The computer is in the safe. The safe is in the dressing room." She wrote down the numbers as Steiner rattled off the combination. She handed the note to another woman, who hurried into the dressing room.

"I do hope the computer is there," Marsten said.

"Please," Steiner pleaded, "the antidote. I feel very warm."

"I would imagine you do," Marsten replied. "You've soiled yourself." He gave a slight nod, and the woman sitting on the bed administered the second shot. Steiner relaxed as tears streaked down his face in relief. The woman who had left was back with a laptop computer and a stack of nine disks. She handed it all to Marsten. "The password, please."

"There are six." Steiner answered in English. He babbled a string of French words, which the woman acting as translator wrote down in clear block letters.

Marsten carefully placed the computer and the disks into his briefcase. "I do hope this all works," he said, pocketing the note with the passwords. He walked to the door. "I hope you don't mind waiting while I validate your offer." He spoke to one of the women. "It smells terrible in here. I know it's not part of our agreement, but do clean him up."

The drive back to the Fountain Plaza building took less than twenty minutes, and Marsten rode the express elevator to the top floor. He walked quickly through the deserted offices, ignoring the night cleaning crew. He locked the door to his office and sat at his desk. For a moment he stared at Steiner's computer. An inner voice warned him that he was taking a fateful step and there would be no turning back. He drew in a deep breath and opened the computer. Fortunately, Marsten's French was very good, and Steiner was quite pedantic, and predictable, in creating files. Still, it took Marsten twenty minutes to find the correct opening menu. Then it required all six passwords Steiner had given him to reach the directory he wanted.

He looked at the screen in amazement, not believing what he saw. He picked up the phone and hit the speed dial. Within seconds L.J. was on the line. "I do believe you need to see this," Marsten said, his voice calm and matter-of-fact as he stared at the map on the screen.

5

Dallas

The Parke Royale prided itself on its discretion and service, and the two maids never batted an eyelash as they repaired the chaos in Steiner's suite. L. J. sipped her breakfast tea until they finished and handed each a twenty-dollar tip as they left. Then she sat Steiner's laptop computer and the nine disks on the coffee table in front of her. "They're gone," she called to Steiner, who had taken refuge in a bathroom.

A very subdued scientist poked his head out the door. He glanced around to ensure they were alone. Satisfied, he finally emerged, dressed in a conservative dark suit, his tie carefully knotted. He rubbed his wrists as he sat down opposite her. For once his little feet were still, and his normally flushed face was very pale. "I'm so sorry," L. J. said. "I came over the moment I heard." She handed him a cup of coffee. "One sugar, yes?" He nodded, a little surprised that she remembered. She gave him a repentant look and nudged the computer in his direction. "Please, what can I do to set things right?"

"The man's a barbarian. He must be punished."

L. J. reached for the phone and asked the operator to connect her with the Dallas Police Department. "Considering who you are and the circumstances," she said as they waited, "there will be some bad publicity. Reporters never seem to sleep. But it can't be avoided."

Steiner's face turned a paler shade of white. "Perhaps, perhaps," he stammered, not sure what to do.

"Please," she said, "let me take care of it. In my own way." He nodded, and she broke the connection.

"I want Marsten fired, broken, ruined," Steiner said.

"I can do that," L.J. said in a low voice. "But you must understand, Lloyd only thought he was protecting RayTex and me."

"He would have killed me."

"He was bluffing."

Steiner shook his head. "You weren't here."

"But I do know Lloyd." She searched for the right words to explain. "He has . . . well, an exaggerated sense of loyalty to me. It goes back to Eritrea when that group of rebels took my exploration team hostage. He flew in to negotiate our release, but he ended up a prisoner himself." She shuddered involuntarily. "They did unspeakable things to him."

"What did they do?"

She answered in a low voice filled with pain. "Please, I don't like to talk about it." She pulled into herself, for a moment back in time. Then she looked directly at Steiner. "I did what I could and, fortunately, was able to convince them to release us. We managed to get Lloyd to a hospital in time to save him. It created a special bond between us, and I can't desert him, not after all we've been through together. But Lloyd has always felt"—she searched for the right words—"well, that he failed me, and he's never ceased trying to make up for it." She gave him a pleading look. "I do hope you understand. I value loyalty above all else, and I was hoping"—she paused for effect— "I was hoping that perhaps you and I, after this terrible experience . . ." Her voice trailed off. She studied Steiner, reading his body language, correctly gauging his emotional state. Now it was time for renegotiations.

She gave him a tentative smile, little more than a flicker before it disappeared. "I must tell you, I was impressed by the way you negotiated. Half a billion dollars for nothing." She gave the computer a definite push in his direction. A little sigh. "I do wish you were on our team."

Steiner was a very confused man. "Nothing? How can you say the largest offshore oil deposit in the world is nothing?"

"Oh, Emil," she said, leaning into him, keying on the confused look on his face. She patted the couch beside her. "Please." She pulled the computer to her while he moved over to her side. She turned it on and worked her way to the seismic cross-section in question. "Just like Saudi Arabia's Safaniyah field, correct?" Steiner nodded in answer. "But there is one big difference," she said. "Safaniyah is a proven reserve, but we won't know if there's oil here until we drill."

"There's oil there," Steiner muttered.

She sighed. "Have you ever heard of Mukluk?" He shook his head. "Well," she continued, surprised by his ignorance, "Mukluk is near Alaska's North Slope and has a perfect profile. So perfect that the rock-trappers at Sohio thought they had an elephant to rival the Saudi fields. They calculated the odds of finding oil at one in three, not the normal one in eight, and formed a joint venture. Together the companies spent over two billion dollars drilling, and when Dr. Drill finally spoke, they had the most expensive dry hole in history. Oh, the oil had been there, but it had either migrated or leaked to the surface over thirty million years ago."

She had his undivided attention. "There's another problem. Right now oil is a glut on the market. The world is awash in it, and only artificial supports are keeping the price per barrel at the current level. A find like this will drive prices so low that the oil industry in the United States will not be able to compete and will go bankrupt." Her fingers danced on the keyboard as she called up a map.

"Consider the geopolitics," she urged. "Look where it's located. Do you really think he'll do business with the United States? Or any Western democracy?"

"Oil must have a market," Steiner said.

"Exactly," she said. "If oil is there, and if it is put into production, he'll use it as an economic weapon against us. Prices will be driven to half their current level, and RayTex will be one of the first to go under. Not even the majors can survive for long. Obviously you knew that, and that's why you wanted half a billion dollars up front. Absolutely brilliant. Take the money and run."

Steiner was crestfallen. "Then no other company will be interested?"

"Oh, they'll be interested—in keeping it a secret. I imagine they'll react much like Lloyd. But they won't be bluffing." Now she was feeding his paranoia. "I do wish you were on my team. I could protect you, and we might . . . well, who knows what we might be able to do? All at the right time, of course."

Steiner reached over and punched at the keyboard. "Is it all inside their territorial waters?"

"I believe so," she said. Together they leaned forward and studied the map of Cuba.

❋

Marsten was waiting for L.J. in his limousine when she left the Parke Royale. He arched an eyebrow, asking the unspoken question. "He's in," she answered. "For how long, I can't say. Fortunately for us, he's paranoid and doesn't know who to trust."

"He's very bright," Marsten said. "Don't underestimate him."

"I'll try not to. We do have some leverage. Underneath he's furious that he was twice refused a Nobel Prize, and he needs validation. We can dangle that carrot in front of him."

"Sooner or later," Marsten said, "he's going to want money. Large amounts of it. More than we can provide."

"That'll probably happen about the time he figures it all out," L.J. said. "He's such a sneaky little weasel, so have ARA watch him. We must maintain secrecy—at all costs until we can lock in the concessions." She thought for a few moments. "Where's the weak link? Who besides you, me, and Steiner could possibly know?"

"The seismic crew on the research ship?"

"Doubtful," L.J. replied. "The readouts were downlinked to Steiner by satellite. Even if the crew did see something, they wouldn't know what it meant."

"But they would know where they'd been shooting seismic," Marsten said.

"That's a possible connection. Check it out."

Marsten made a note in his diary before handing her a small package. "The videotape from ARA. Good quality. No doubt who they are. Or what they were doing. It is, shall we say, beneficial, when one is paying the bills."

She agreed with him. "It most certainly is." The limousine pulled into the roundabout of the Regency Hotel, and she dropped the package into her handbag. "Do they know?"

"They were contacted yesterday evening. I believe they spent a very sleepless night."

"I'll catch a taxi back," she told Marsten, getting out of the limo.

Ann Silton answered the door, her face ravaged with worry and tears. At first she refused to let L.J. in. "We have nothing to say to you." Her eyes filled with hate. "I don't know what game you're playing," she said, her voice low and cutting, "but you won't get away with it."

L.J. fumbled in her handbag for the package and tentatively extended it to the woman. "This came in the mail. Do you want to see the letter?" Now it was her turn to cry, and tears ran down her cheeks.

The woman hesitated, not sure what to do. But L.J.'s tears decided her. She took the package and opened the door. "Did you get a letter?" L.J. asked. Ann shook her head. "Mine's with the tape," L.J. said, walking into the hotel suite.

Clarissa looked at L.J., unsure how to react. L.J. rushed over to her while Ann read the letter. "The bastards," L.J. hissed. They held hands for a moment. Softly L.J. said, "When I saw the tape, I saw a beautiful, loving moment. There is absolutely nothing for you to be ashamed of."

"It's just that . . ." Clarissa replied, tears streaking her face, adding years to her look.

"I know," L.J. said. "Our society isn't ready to accept people for who they are." She straightened her shoulders. "This has nothing to do with what we're trying to do. I won't have it. I just won't have it." She stood up and paced the floor, taking charge. "Have you shown this to John?"

"He's a man," Ann said, obviously distrustful of Front Uni's executive director.

"He's a good person," L.J. said. "We need to tell him. Now."

※

John Frobisher fumbled with the second cassette, finally inserting it into the VCR. The screen flashed, and an image of two nude women making love on the same couch he was sitting on appeared on the screen. They watched in silence for a few moments, confirming the two tapes were identical. But L.J. split her attention, closely judging Frobisher's reaction. It was a combination of fascination and lust.

"It's the same tape," Frobisher said. "Unfortunately, there's no doubt who it is. When was this taken?"

Ann's words were barely audible. "Monday night."

"Well," Frobisher muttered, "considering it's Wednesday morning, they didn't waste time." He stared at L.J., thinking the obvious. "What's your game, Ms. Ellis?" He stressed the "Ms."

L.J. shook her head. "I don't play games, John." She stood up, full of resolve, and paced the floor. "So what do they want?"

"As the letter says," Frobisher replied. " 'You don't need friends like these.' "

"I don't desert my friends," L.J. said. "Why do you think I came here?" Frobisher didn't answer. "So who do you think did it?" she demanded.

"Your friends in the oil business," he answered.

She shook her head. "They're too sophisticated to try something this crude. No, it's got to be someone else." She stopped and studied him for a moment. "Are you having internal problems in Front Uni?"

"Only the normal disagreements," Frobisher said. "The environmental movement is a loose confederation of highly principled individuals who—"

L.J. interrupted him. "Do any of you have a personal problem?" They all told her no, and her lips compressed into a narrow line. "Do you want to call the police?"

Frobisher thought for a moment. "If they want to disgrace us, make us lose credibility with the public, wouldn't that be playing right into their hands?"

L.J. nodded, conceding the point. "I'm a woman in one of the most male-dominated businesses in the world," she said, feeding their preconceptions and personal biases. She was also telling them the truth. Her face grew cold. "I have to play hardball to survive." She paused. "Give me a little time to get to the bottom of this. Do you trust me?"

"I trust you," Clarissa said. Ann and Frobisher nodded in unison.

The Pentagon

General Butler was impressed. The big poster boards with the yellow Post-its arranged in a flow pattern, the neatly ordered folders, the quick-reference chart for the computer files, and the blue talking folder for Butler's initial briefing to the National Security Council on the Strategic Petroleum Reserve were ample proof that Mike Stuart was an accomplished staff officer. "You did all this in nine days?" Stuart nodded. "When do you go home?"

"I'm divorced," Stuart replied, as if that explained it all.

"I know promotions are tough these days," Butler said. "But this is much more than I expected."

No emotion crossed Stuart's face. "It's pretty clear that I'm not going to be promoted, so I plan on retiring in eighteen months."

Stuart's reply stunned Butler. It was a constant surprise to him that men like Stuart continued to give their best and sacrifice their personal lives even when their careers were at a dead end. He thumbed through the blue talking folder on the current status of the SPR. "Good work," he muttered. "Even I understand it. Okay, what's next?"

Stuart pointed to a third poster board. "The oil world is divided into three parts: upstream, midstream, and downstream. Upstream is exploration and production, midstream is the transportation net that moves crude oil to refineries, and downstream is marketing and distribution. As a user, the military is all downstream. But what ultimately determines what is available to us is the upstream part of the equation. I think," Stuart ventured, "we need to take a detailed look at what's coming on-line in the future, in terms of exploration and production."

"How do you propose we do that?"

"We ask the oil companies what their plans are for exploration in the next five years." From the incredulous look on the general's face, Stuart knew he was on shaky ground.

Butler humphed. "There's no way they'll tell us that!"

Stuart shrugged. "We won't know until we ask. And we promise to treat their answers as secret, not to go beyond this committee."

"Even if we know how much exploration is planned, that doesn't tell us how much oil will be discovered."

"But it gives us some clues," Stuart replied. "We know what the past success rate has been. We can assume a lower success rate in the future and plot it out against the discovery curve of the last ten years to establish a trend."

Butler was even more impressed. "Which gives us a planning factor for the future."

"Which can be revised at any time," Stuart added. "It also gives another indicator. If the overall planned exploration rate by the companies is on a downward curve, then we can assume the oil companies are not worried about their current reserves."

"Do it," Butler said. He gathered up the blue briefing book and headed for his office. "You need a sponsor," he said, almost to himself.

※

Roger "Ramjet" Priestly scanned the proposed survey and then the mailing list. Every oil company that did business in the United States was on the list, and he was worried that the survey would set off all sorts of alarm bells, not to mention phone calls to congressmen and lobbyists. It was exactly the sort of attention he did not want. He picked up the phone and punched at the number for Stuart's cubicle. There was no answer, and he buzzed for his secretary to come in. "Peggy, where the hell is Stuart? Doesn't he know Friday is a normal workday?"

"He signed out on leave for the day, sir. He's going to pick up his son in Dover, Delaware." She paused to let Ramjet's blood pressure go up ten points. "You did approve it, sir."

"Right," he said, not really remembering. He threw the offending survey across his desk. "Put a hold on this until I can talk to him." He almost told her to throw it in the trash can but thought better of it. "No, wait. Better yet, send it back."

"Send it back," Peggy murmured. "Will that be all?" Ramjet nodded, and she returned to her desk. "Send it back," she told herself. "Now, what does that mean?" She answered her own question. "He must mean to General Butler's office." She glanced at the cover letter, which was duly signed by one Michael E. Stuart. She smiled to herself and dropped the survey in distribution to forward it to General Butler's office. Then she picked up the phone and called Butler's secretary. "Joannie, Ramjet told me to return the survey being sent to the oil companies back to your office for action. So will you send it out?" She listened for a few moments. "You've got that right, girl. Without us, nothing would ever get done."

Dover Air Force Base, Delaware

Stuart drove slowly through base housing trying to find the house he had lived in as a teenager, when his father had been assigned to a staff job at the air base. It was one of William "Shanker" Stuart's few assignments outside the tactical Air Force and away from fighters, and it had been a strange time, as his father had hated his job while his family had been most content and happy. In fact, Stuart remembered his three teenage years at Dover as among the best times in his life. It was even more ironic because Stuart had been born at Dover when his father was assigned there as a lieutenant before going to pilot training. But he didn't remember that.

Three good years, he thought. *That's all I got. Eric deserves more. A lot more.*

The wail of turbofan engines split the air, and Stuart instinctively looked up. A massive white transport aircraft, the sound of its four huge engines pounding his senses, flew over. Stuart stared in wonder and shook his head. It was an Antonov An-124, the Russian counterpart to the USAF's C-5 Galaxy. How many times had he briefed pilots on that aircraft during the early years of his career in the Air Force as a young intelligence officer? But he had never seen one, and the actual sight was overpowering. He watched mesmerized as the giant plane seemed to defy gravity entering the landing pattern.

He drove across the main highway and through the gate, heading for the passenger terminal where he was to meet his son and father. He parked his car and wandered toward the terminal, fascinated by the sight of the An-124's tail moving slowly behind the building. For Stuart's first eight years in the Air Force, the plane had belonged to a potential enemy, the Soviet Union, and one of his jobs in the Defense Intelligence Agency as a captain had been to track the status of AeroFlot and Voyenno-Transportnaya Aviatsiya, the Soviet Air Force's air-transport arm. A stand down by either was considered a "trip wire" indicating that the Soviet Union was moving to an attack footing. If both stood down, the United States military would have started to move up the DEFCON as it also prepared for war.

But things had changed. The Soviet Union no longer existed, and Russian Transport Aviation was reduced to hauling commercial cargo to earn money and landing at the bases of its former enemy. And that's why he was there. His son was on the An-124.

Stuart groaned when he entered the terminal. His ex-mother-in-law was standing inside the door, her arms folded tightly across her breasts, her feet apart in a boxer's stance. A man in a charcoal-gray suit holding a briefcase stood next to her. *Barbara Raye always leads with a lawyer,* he thought. He tried to manage a smile, anything to pull her fangs. "Where's Jenny?" he asked, hoping his ex-wife was around.

Barbara Raye Wilson's look turned even harder. "She couldn't make it. She's off with her current scumbag." As a matter of family policy, Barbara Raye never approved of any man in her only child's life, and Stuart had been another casualty in the long procession of men Jenny presented to her mother for sacrifice. Stuart assumed that it was a combination of money and a lone grandchild that kept the two women together. Barbara Raye had won the Powerball Lottery, and Jenny had Eric.

Stuart couldn't help himself. "She did tell me she was in love." The words were no sooner spoken than he realized he had made a bad mistake. Jenny and her mother were at each other's throats again, locked in a deep love-hate battle for dominance, with money and access to Eric the weapons of choice. It escaped his understanding why they couldn't break the tie that binds and go their separate ways, or at least declare a cease-fire in their on-again, off-again war.

Eric burst through the door leading from customs and ran up to his father. "Dad, you got to come out and see it!" Stuart assumed he was talking about the An-124.

"Mr. Stuart," the lawyer said, "letting your child fly on that aircraft was the height of irresponsibility."

"He and his grandfather were suppose to fly United."

Eric couldn't contain himself. "Gramps's friend had a Lightning we had to get out of England to save it from being cut up and another friend's got lots of money and he rented a plane to fly it here and we came with it." He smiled as if that explained everything. "Come on. We can watch it unload."

"Maybe we should wait here," Stuart said, seeing the look of disapproval on Barbara Raye's face.

Eric felt the tension between his father and grandmother and didn't want any part of it. "Please, Dad. Gramps is at the airplane."

"Well, let's go howdy the folks," Stuart said. Eric led them, half running, out to the parking ramp where a small crowd was watching the big aircraft discharge its cargo.

Eric ran up to the rope holding the crowd back. "Gramps!" he yelled, waving at his grandfather. Shanker waved back and motioned them to the entry-control point. "That's Wing Commander Seagrave and Prince Turika with Gramps," Eric explained. "You'll like them."

Shanker escorted the small group to the back of the aircraft to watch the unloading. He introduced them to Seagrave and Turika while four spare jet engines were offloaded. Three pallets of spare parts were rolled onto loaders, followed by a set of wings mounted on a wooden cradle. The last loader drove up, and two spare wings were rolled off, along with twelve tires. Finally the fuselage of the Lightning was rolled out the front of the aircraft, gleaming in the September sun like a wingless dart. "I sat in the cockpit," Eric said. "It's really neat and Commander Seagrave flew it when he shouldn't have but he didn't have a choice and that's why he got in trouble and we had to save it."

Stuart laughed. He had never seen his son so animated. "It sounds like you had a great time."

"It's time he was back in school," Barbara Raye announced, taking charge. "You're coming with me, young man."

Stuart's stomach took a twist. He could not remember Barbara Raye losing an argument to anyone other than Jenny. Tons of money gave her unlimited power and she wielded it like a deadly weapon. Still, he tried to delay the inevitable. "We need to talk to Jenny," he said.

Barbara Raye gave him a cold look. "No we don't. Eric is staying with me."

"Dad," Eric pleaded. His wonderful day had suddenly turned sour.

"Come," Barbara Raye ordered. She reached for Eric's hand, but Shanker knelt down beside the boy, blocking her.

"Where do you want to go?" Shanker asked.

Eric didn't answer and only looked very unhappy. He fought back the tears and shook his head.

"He's going with Mrs. Wilson," the lawyer said.

Eric looked at his grandfather, who looked at Stuart. "Well?" Shanker asked. "You're his father. Make a decision."

Stuart didn't know what to say.

"I want to stay with you or Dad," Eric whispered to Shanker.

"He's coming with me, and that's final," Barbara Raye said, pushing Shanker out of the way.

It was a mistake. Shanker stepped in front of her. "Ma'am, normally I don't cotton to hittin' women. But in your case I'll make an exception."

The lawyer intervened. "Stop right there, Mr. Stuart."

Shanker whirled on the lawyer, fully engaged. "As I recall, Mike and Jenny have joint legal custody of Eric. Unless you've got a court order—"

The lawyer interrupted him. "In the absence of Jennifer Stuart, Mrs. Wilson is empowered to act in her place."

Shanker leaned into the lawyer, his face inches away from the man's nose, and exhaled. "You got a piece of paper from a judge saying that?"

"Don't threaten me," the lawyer said.

"I'm not threatening you, fuckface."

The lawyer backed away, astounded at the pure aggression in the man. "There's no need to get violent," he said.

"When things go wrong, get aggressive," Shanker said. "And you're all wrong."

"You can't get away with threatening people," the lawyer replied.

"I'm warning," Shanker growled. "You as much as touch that boy without a court order and I'll put you down. And I mean me personally, you personally." He paused for effect as a wicked smile spread across his face. "Ain't it fun being an advocate when people advocate back?"

Barbara Raye wasn't having any of it. She reached down and pulled at Eric's shirt. "We're leaving."

Shanker grabbed her hand that was holding Eric, but she wouldn't let go. They stared at each other. Then, with one hand grasping her wrist, he pressed against the back of her knuckles with his other hand, forcing her clenched hand down and her fingers to open. He did it so easily it looked like a caress. He smiled at her. "I do hope you know how to get out of Dodge, ma'am."

Barbara Raye's eyes squinted at him in pure hate. "You haven't heard the last of this," she said, storming away. The lawyer followed her like a puppy dog.

"Nice seeing you again," Shanker called. "Have a nice day." He turned to Stuart and shook his head. The old hurt was back. *Thank God for Dwight*, Shanker told himself, thinking of his older son.

6

Miami

How many times have we been through this? Luis Barrios moaned to himself. He picked up a brick of the gray explosive, working hard to conceal his exasperation. By now they all should have been able to assemble the bomb in less than five minutes. But it wasn't happening and, if anything, Eduardo and Francisco were slower. At least Carita was nearing the goal. "Semtex is a plastique," he told them. "Without an igniter it's harmless. Don't be afraid of it." From the expression on their faces, they still didn't believe him. "Look," he said, desperate to make his point. He dropped the brick. Eduardo almost fainted.

Luis picked up the explosive and flicked open his knife. The blade was razor sharp, and he deftly peeled off a sliver of the explosive. He hated wasting even a few grams, but he had to make his point. He dropped the sliver into an ashtray and lit it with a cigarette lighter. The explosive was slow to ignite and, finally, it burst into flame before quickly consuming itself and burning out. An acrid stench filled the room.

Carita threw open a window. "It smells terrible," she said. "Maybe something is wrong with it."

Luis was puzzled. Nothing he had heard or read suggested that Semtex had such a pungent smell. But he had made his point. "See, it's harmless. I even keep it under my bed."

"Perhaps," Eduardo ventured, "we need to test it. To see if Carita is right."

Luis nodded. He *was* worried about the smell. What if they had been sold a fake? It was a common practice in their business, and even he had palmed off a few bad guns to raise money. But they had only six blocks of the explosive, and he didn't want to waste any of them. Still, Eduardo's suggestion made sense. He rationalized it would also be good training and give them confidence. He made his decision. "We'll use two hundred grams to make a small bomb. But we'll use it on a real target."

❄

Carita drove the car past the sign that announced RTX Farm Supplies. "You all have the map memorized," Luis said, "and should know exactly where you are." Three heads nodded in agreement. Luis had selected an isolated target on the outskirts of Miami that was easily scouted and not guarded. Then he deliberately put them on a short timetable to give them a sense of urgency. They had practiced until it was second nature, and now it was merely a matter of execution. To make things as easy as possible and build their confidence, he deliberately chose a Saturday night.

The car slowed, and Eduardo bailed out. He rolled behind a low bush and keyed his radio. Inside the car they heard the two clicks that meant he was in position as the lookout and all was clear. Luis answered with one click.

Francisco's jaw worked, and he broke out in a sweat. His face turned pale, and his hands shook. "I can't do it," he moaned. The thought of actually penetrating the compound of the fertilizer-processing plant, planting the explosive, and retreating through the fence was too much for his fragile nerves.

Luis snorted in disgust. "*¡Cabrón!*"

"*Francisco es cagado,*" Carita said, calling him cowardly. Her contempt matched Luis's. "I'll do it. But you better drive. He may shit his pants in fear." It was quickly arranged, and she stopped the car. Luis handed her the black bag that held the bomb and the wire cutters when she got out. He slipped behind the wheel and drove off to circle the compound. If their timing was right, they would both arrive back at the same spot at the same time. Then it would be a simple matter to pick up Eduardo and drive away.

Carita scrambled over the low ridge of earth surrounding the tank farm and quickly cut a hole in the wire fence to slip inside. Even in the darkness she had no trouble finding her way among the white tanks that made up the fertilizer-processing plant. She scrambled over the berm that formed a separate containment basin around the largest tank and slid down the inside. She crawled up against the tank that held a liquid fertilizer and placed the bag, bomb, and wire cutters against the main valve.

Like Francisco, she started to shake. Imagination is the curse of all terrorists, and the idea of half a million gallons of fertilizer exploding was overpowering. A dog barked, and she froze. She listened. The sound was coming closer. She reached inside the bag and hit the activate button. But in her haste to get away she didn't depress it long enough to set fully. Instead of fifteen minutes' delay, she had less than twenty seconds. She climbed the bank of the berm as the guard dog came around the side of the tank. It grabbed her pant leg and dragged her back down. She kicked to get free of the growling animal, and much to her surprise the dog let go and disappeared over the berm, barking loudly. The bomb went off.

Luis returned to the pickup point just as the bomb exploded. A bright flash lit the sky, and for a moment he was certain he was dead. But instead of a powerful explosion vaporizing him, there was only the sound of a crashing wave. He gunned the car and sped off as a wave of dark liquid surged over the secondary levee surrounding the tank farm. It engulfed the car and pushed it sideways. The car tilted up and teetered on the edge of a rollover. Then it dropped back onto its wheels, the force of the wave spent.

To Luis's amazement, the engine started on the first try, and he raced down the road to pick up Eduardo. A dripping form emerged out of the shadows, and Luis slammed the car to a stop. Eduardo piled in, and they drove away. "What happened?" Eduardo asked.

"I don't know," Luis answered. "Maybe the tank only burst from overpressure."

"What happened to Carita?"

"She's got to be dead," Luis said.

"What do we do now?" Francisco asked from the rear seat.

"Make the phone call," Luis snapped. Francisco punched at his cell phone and called the *Miami Herald*. When he got the night editor, he announced that the Revolutionary Jihad had blown up the tank farm as a warning to American imperialists. He broke the connection and threw the cell phone out the window. He glanced at the clock in the car's radio. *¡Mierda!* he raged to himself. They were too late to make the Sunday-morning edition. They should make the Monday-morning edition.

"I'm burning!" Eduardo shouted.

"It's the fertilizer," Luis said. He stopped the car beside a canal, and Eduardo dove in, desperate to wash it off.

7

Stuart ignored the insistent ring and tried to go back to sleep. But he had forgotten to set the answering machine, and the phone kept ringing. Reluctantly he burrowed out from under the covers and glanced at the clock radio beside the bed. It was just after seven o'clock on Sunday morning. He picked up the offending instrument. "Yeah," he mumbled.

"Mike," the familiar voice said, "we've got to talk." It was Jenny. "Where's Eric?"

"With me," Stuart said. "I tried to call you, but there was no answer. I left a message on your answering machine."

"I'm not at home right now," she said, not bothering to explain why she was out of touch. "We need to talk."

Her "need to talk" was Jennyspeak for face-to-face. "We're going down to my folks' today."

"We'll meet you there," she said, breaking the connection.

"Who the hell are 'we'?" he grumbled. Unfortunately, he knew the answer; he just didn't know the name. Jenny was a vivacious woman with long red hair and bright green eyes and, at forty years old, looked like she was in her late twenties. She prided herself on still being able to wear a size-three dress and the briefest of swimsuits, which was, to Stuart's way of thinking, part of the problem. As long as her body and looks held, she had no intention of growing up.

Eric bounded into the bedroom, carrying a model of the Lightning he had finished the night before. He held up the plane for Stuart's inspection, proud of his handiwork. "You really like that airplane, don't you?"

Eric nodded. "It's different and Gramps says it's still a real hot rod and maybe someday I can go up for a ride in it."

Stuart scrubbed his hair. "We're going to have to teach you about run-on sentences first."

Eric was undaunted. "And then I can go for a ride? I'll learn today."

"We'll cross that bridge when we come to it. Okay, what would you like for breakfast?"

✳

The four-hour drive to Newport News passed in a heartbeat as Eric kept up a running chatter, his enthusiasm boundless. *What am I doing?* Stuart asked himself. *I've got a great kid, and I'm missing him growing up.* He made a mental promise to change that. They turned down the tree-shaded lane near Langley Air Force Base and followed it to the end, where a two-story brick home was nestled in a surrounding garden. Stuart's mother was standing in her prize roses pretending to work as she waited for her grandson. *Jenny must be here*, he thought. Just being around Jenny upset his mother, a condition both women accepted. Eric jumped out of the car and ran into her waiting arms, happy to be there. Martha Stuart was everyone's grandmother, graceful in her old age, full of love, and perfectly happy with a name that was constantly linked to the famous homemaker. But as she told everyone, "I had it first."

"Jennifer's here," Martha announced, "with her young man."

"How young?" Stuart asked testily.

"Does it matter?" She stopped him. "When are you going to put a stop to it?"

"To what, Mom?"

"To Jenny and Barbara Raye's battle over Eric. He needs a stable home, and you are his father."

Stuart nodded, accepting the truth when he heard it. He walked inside to meet his ex-wife's latest lover. Shanker met him at the door. "She's got a real winner this time," he said. The "winner" Shanker was referring to was a very likable, handsome, twenty-three-year-old named Grant DeLorenzo. The two men shook hands as Jenny waited impatiently.

"Mike, let's go outside and talk." She led the way to the back garden, her legs snapping at her tight miniskirt. She started talking the moment they were out of earshot. "Grant wants to go to Colorado and start a snowboarding school."

"I imagine that's already been done," Stuart said sarcastically. "And I don't think a resort operator is going to encourage competition."

She ignored the obvious practicalities. "We need money," she said.

"And that's where your mother comes in, right?"

"She wants to keep Eric until we're established and he can join us. She said she'd help us get started." It was the old trade-off, Barbara Raye's money for control of Eric.

"Once she has her hooks into him, she'll never let go."

Jenny chewed her lower lip, not liking the truth. "This is so right this time," she said. "I may never get another chance for happiness."

"I'm thinking of Eric's happiness," Stuart said. "You know how miserable he is around your mother. Go talk to him. He's never been so happy and content. I'm not sure what's happening, but I don't want to risk losing it."

"So what are you suggesting?" From the sound in her voice, he sensed she was weakening.

For the first time in their long relationship, Stuart pressed his advantage. "Look, Washington is no place to raise a kid. So why doesn't he stay here with my folks until I can get out of the Air Force? Mom and Dad are all for it." She stiffened. "Jenny, your mother lives in Connecticut, and I'm not going to let him leave the state." He was surprised by the force of his own words, and thanks to the divorce laws of Virginia, neither he nor Jenny could take Eric out of the state without the other's permission.

"What about me?" she wailed.

Stuart sighed. "The money, right?" A little nod from Jenny. "Why don't I help for a while? Say, a thousand dollars a month until you're settled in."

"That's not very much," she said.

He hated himself for buying his son's happiness, but he didn't want to take on Barbara Raye and her money. "It's all I can afford."

Much to his relief, she nodded, accepting the deal.

The Pentagon

Stuart had barely settled into his desk Tuesday morning when Peggy Redman's voice came over the intercom. "He wants to see you immediately." She didn't have to identify the "he" nor what "immediately" meant.

"What's bugging the good colonel now?" Stuart asked.

"He doesn't need a reason," Peggy replied, breaking the phone connection. Stuart bounced from his chair, grabbed his uniform coat, and hurried out of his cubicle. Halfway there he deliberately changed his mind and paid a visit to the men's room. He finally sauntered into Ramjet's office six minutes later. The colonel waved him to a chair before Stuart could report in, an unspoken acknowledgment of Stuart's changed status. Until Ramjet had the new constellation of who was "in" and who was "out" nailed down, he stayed in a deep defensive crouch. When it was safe, he would set matters right and crunch the appropriate heads. With any luck, Stuart's would be the very first.

"Mike," Ramjet said, all smiles and flashing teeth, "we got a disconnect. No big deal, but I would like to keep it from happening again." He tossed a thin document across his desk for Stuart to read. It was the survey sent out to the oil companies. "Since you are the office of primary responsibility for this, and you work for me, I should have signed off on this before it went out." He leaned across his desk, his hands clasped in front of him. "Mike, we've all got to be playing from the same sheet of music or we all look bad."

Stuart wanted to remind him that General Butler was the daddy rabbit for the survey and he was reporting to Butler, even if temporarily, on this project. "I didn't know there was a problem," Stuart hedged. "I did forward it to you." He almost added "as a courtesy" but thought better of it.

"I sent it back to you," Ramjet said. "Somehow it ended up on General Butler's desk without my concurrence."

Stuart shook his head and tried to sidestep the issue. "Sorry, sir. I was on leave, and it never came back to my office. By the way, any feedback yet?"

Ramjet's face turned red as his blood pressure skyrocketed. Feedback was the last thing he wanted. His jaw worked as he forced into his voice a friendliness he didn't feel. "No, not yet. But I'm worried the oil companies will respond negatively to your survey and complain to their friends in Congress."

"Any response to the survey on their part is voluntary," Stuart reminded him.

"Be that as it may," Ramjet concluded. "I'll be the one taking the heat if anything goes wrong." He kicked back in his chair, his teeth grinding. *No little turd like you is going to make an end run around me and ruin my career!* he raged to himself. Again he tried to sound friendly. "Mike, we've all got to be team players on this. I would appreciate it if it doesn't happen again."

Stuart knew he was dismissed. "Yes, sir," he said. He stood and quickly left the office. He shot a glance at Peggy Redman, an unspoken understanding between them. The flap over the survey was a minor bureaucratic squall, worthless in itself but typical of how careers were made or broken.

Ramjet waited for Stuart to close the door before he picked up the phone to call officer assignments at Randolph Air Force Base outside San Antonio, Texas. It was time to sideline Stuart before he could do more harm.

Dallas

The corporate offices of RayTex oil were not what the two FBI special agents had expected. They'd inadvertently gotten off the elevator on the floor immediately below the top floor and stumbled into the working offices. The staff bustled with friendly activity and flowed between functional but cheerfully decorated offices. Down the hall an open door revealed a spacious day care center for children. "My wife would love to work here," the junior agent said.

"You can always tell a woman's touch," the senior agent allowed, alluding to L.J.'s reputation. A junior engineer escorted them to the top floor, which was in total contrast. Dark-suited men and women moved quietly through exquisitely decorated offices.

Lloyd Marsten came out of his office to meet them, further impressing the two agents. "Sorry to keep you waiting," he said. "But I was on the phone with Miss Ellis. She's in St. Louis; otherwise she would be most interested in talking to you." They shook hands as the agents introduced themselves. He led them into his office and motioned them to sit down. "How can we help you?"

"Obviously," the lead agent said, "we're here about the bombing Saturday night in Miami."

Marsten sat behind his desk and steepled his fingers. "Right. RTX Farm Supplies. One of our subsidiaries."

The two agents flipped open their notebooks and held their matching silver ballpoint pens at the ready. "Then, RTX *is* owned by RayTex Oil," the junior agent said. It wasn't a question.

"Certainly," Marsten replied. "RTX is a contraction of RayTex. Most bizarre. Why would anyone want to blow up a liquid-fertilizer storage tank?" As he had worked with the FBI before, he didn't expect an answer. The FBI gave something up only to get more in return.

"We were hoping you could supply an answer to that question, Mr. Marsten," the senior agent said, starting to play him.

Marsten considered his answer. "Perhaps they thought nitrates were present and hoped to spark a sympathetic explosion on the order of the Oklahoma City bombing." The agents wrote furiously in their notebooks while Marsten plotted the sequence of his next moves. "That suggests, at least to me, that they didn't understand chemical fertilizers."

"So you don't think it was an inside job," the senior agent said.

"It may have been," Marsten replied. "But if an insider was involved, she didn't deal with product."

The two agents exchanged glances. "You said 'she,' " the senior agent ventured.

So a woman was involved, Marsten thought. He loved dealing with the FBI. They were so good up to a point. Then they became quite transparent, if you knew how to play the game. It was time to dangle some bait. "Would it help in your investigation to see the personnel files for RTX?"

"That might be useful," the senior agent replied.

Marsten reached for his computer keyboard. "I'll see what I can do, but we'll have to work around the privacy statutes." He faked a sigh. "So misguided. They only help the criminals." He typed a command into the commuter. "Ah, yes, here we go." Then, almost conversationally, he asked, "Can you tell me anything about the body discovered at the scene?"

The agents leaned forward in anticipation. If it was an inside job, quick and complete access to raw personnel files could be a major breakthrough. "Most unusual," the junior agent said. "It was a woman. The preliminary examination of the body and personal effects indicated she was probably a Latina. But we can't be sure." It was a deliberate ploy to lead Marsten on. The FBI's initial forensic analysis of the body, clothes, shoes, hairstyle, dental work, and contents of the stomach had confirmed that the deceased was a Latin American female in her late twenties, had had two abortions but never given birth, and was not a manual laborer.

Marsten looked at them in amazement. "Really? According to the *Miami Herald*, a Middle Eastern group claimed responsibility. I've never heard of them."

The junior agent nodded in agreement. "Neither have—"

A sharp look from the senior agent cut off his partner. Marsten caught it and hit the print button on his computer. The printer in the credenza behind his desk hummed quietly as he waited for the printout. He handed them a thick stack of papers. "Here's everything we have on the employees at RTX," Marsten told them. "I do hope you'll maintain our confidentiality."

"We do appreciate your help," the senior agent said. Marsten escorted them to the door. "We'll get back to you as soon as we have something definite." They shook hands, and Marsten watched them walk to the elevators.

"Of course you will," Marsten said softly. He returned to his office and sat on the couch, deep in thought. He was a good CEO because he anticipated problems and instinctively understood what L.J. wanted. At the top of her priority list was the safety and well-being of her employees, and she expected him to respond accordingly. He probed his memory, looking for connections. Was the bombing of RTX Farm Supplies related in any way to the series of refinery accidents that had plagued the industry since the late 1990s? While he had no proof, he suspected they were not accidents. Was it the handiwork of the environmental extremists like Earth First? He wasn't certain, but knowing L.J., he knew she would expect him to act on his suspicions. The adage "Better safe than sorry" had real meaning for her.

He sipped his tea as he defined the big picture. Slowly he sketched a complicated flowchart on a yellow legal pad, organizing different elements into a new company-wide security plan. But something was missing. What was it?

He shelved that problem for the moment and turned to the action and project folders that seemed to occupy more and more of his time. He worked quickly through them, making decisions, asking questions, and assigning projects. He stopped on the fifth folder. What to do about the two corporate jet aircraft RayTex owned? Given the economics of flying, he would have preferred to sell at least one. But L.J. loved flying the oldest of the aircraft, an old Sabreliner that had recently been completely renovated with new engines, instruments, leather interior, and paint. *Better to keep L.J. happy*, he decided.

The last folder contained a survey from the government requesting information on RayTex's plans for exploration in the next five years. Marsten's immediate reaction fell someplace between fat chance and never. Then the name on the cover letter caught his attention. His eyes narrowed for a moment as he tapped his personal memory banks. He had a prodigious memory and knew how to use it. He turned to his computer and typed in a series of commands to call up the log of the seismic vessel Steiner had used for testing his Seismic Double Reflection technique. He reread the section recounting when the ship had taken refuge from Hurricane Andrea in Cuba. *Coincidence?* he wondered.

He reached for the phone and called Action Research Associates. Within seconds he was speaking to the lead investigator. "Can you confirm that a Lieutenant Colonel Michael Stuart who works in the Pentagon is the same Michael Stuart who owns a sailboat called *Temptress*?" As RayTex Oil paid ARA a hefty retainer fee for their services, he didn't hang up. He had his answer in less than a minute: They were one and the same.

Marsten leaned back and clapped his hands together lightly. Should he talk to L.J. about this latest development? Was it pure coincidence that this Lieutenant Colonel Stuart's boat had followed Steiner's research vessel into that Cuban harbor? How much coincidence did he believe in? Could Stuart compromise what they were doing? *So many unknowns. We need more answers.* He mentally filed that problem away for later consideration. He buzzed his secretary for tea and relaxed in his chair, letting his subconscious work. Suddenly the basic weakness of his security plan jumped out of his subconscious, where it had been festering. To be proactive about security, he needed better intelligence; otherwise they were sitting targets for whoever was out there ready to visit harm on the company. "Harm the company," he repeated aloud. He let his mind run with that topic. Finally he reached for the phone to set up a meeting with

ARA. What he needed to discuss had to be face-to-face, with no witnesses.

Annapolis, Maryland

Stuart stood on the city dock with the marina's manager waiting for *Temptress* to arrive. "There she is," he said. Stuart moved down the slip to help dock his boat while the manager held back. He could tell a great deal by the way any captain docked, and the combination of tide and wind were working against the woman as she guided the forty-two-foot sailboat down the narrow channel. Unless she was very good, he expected a few bangs and bumps as she entered the narrow slip.

"She single-handed it?" the manager asked.

"All the way from Miami," Stuart answered.

"Motored all the way?"

Stuart shrugged. "You'll have to ask her." He doubted if Jane ran the diesel more than absolutely necessary and suspected she was under sail whenever possible. Like the manager, he watched as she guided the boat in. At exactly five boat lengths short of the dock, she slipped the transmission into neutral and glided into the slip. She hit reverse and blipped the throttle at the last moment to bring the boat to a complete stop without touching the dock. It was a low-key, masterful demonstration, and the manager was impressed.

Stuart wanted to hug her for the smooth performance. Then he was honest with himself and admitted he just wanted to hold her. She threw him a stern line and went forward to hand the manager a bowline. "How was the trip?" Stuart called.

"Uneventful," she answered. "I took my time."

"Come up the Intercoastal Waterway?" the manager asked.

"Why do that?" she replied.

Now the manager was really impressed. Only a very seasoned and confident sailor would sail the Atlantic single-handedly instead of coming up the Intercoastal Waterway. "Son," he muttered to Stuart, "don't let this one get away." He studied the boat's condition and was even more impressed. "You want a job?" he asked Jane. "Fourteen dollars an hour."

From her silence Stuart knew she was seriously considering it. "You can live on *Temptress*, if you want," he said, offering encouragement.

She tilted her head to one side, still thinking. She did need a job, and it was time to think about settling down. How much longer could she be a sea gypsy? Besides, she did want to see more of him.

"Why don't you think about it?" Stuart said. "Say, are you up for a ride to Newport News tomorrow? I'd like you to meet my family."

"I'll let you know about the job Monday," she told the manager.

✳

It was perfect weather for the trip to his parents' home in Newport News, and Stuart wanted to make it last as long as possible. But he also wanted to be in time for lunch. Unfortunately, Sunday traffic down the Delmarva Peninsula didn't cooperate, and it was 2:00 P.M. by the time they arrived. As expected, Martha Stuart was in her garden. They chatted for a few moments and, from the very first, Martha liked Jane. "Your father and Eric are at the airport," she told them, "working on that airplane. Dwight's with them."

"I didn't know Maggot was here," Stuart said.

She shooed them away. "Go on now, I've got work to do." She walked with them to the car and watched as they drove away. "I like her, Michael," she said aloud to herself. "For once, be smart."

"Dwight's my older brother," Stuart explained, answering Jane's unasked question. "He's a fighter pilot, flies A-10s. Everyone calls him Maggot."

Jane heard the hurt in his voice. "Your father was a fighter pilot?"

"Yeah. And I'm the big disappointment in his life." They rode in silence to the airport, both lost in their own thoughts.

Eric saw Stuart's Ford Explorer the moment they pulled into the parking lot, and he ambled over with the studied indifference of all seventh-graders. Stuart introduced him to Jane, and they walked into the hangar to meet Shanker and Maggot. But Eric's enthusiasm broke through, and he couldn't stop chattering about the Lightning. Much to the boy's surprise, Jane talked to him like an adult and seemed to share in his excitement. Stuart smiled at the rapport between the two. The smile disappeared when he saw his older brother talking to his father. He made the introductions.

"Call me Maggot," Dwight Stuart said, shaking Jane's hand.

"What an unusual name," Jane replied, falling back into her four-word-response mode.

"Uncle Dwight is a fighter pilot," Eric explained, "and he flies A-10s, that's the Warthog, and everybody's got a special name so they can remember who's who in combat when everything is all confused and Maggot is real famous because he's done lots of fighting and he's a good friend of Matt Pontowski." He ran out of steam and had to take a breath.

"The grandson of President Pontowski?" Jane asked. "The one who was in the news with President Turner?" Eric bobbed his head yes, and she caught the deep frown that flashed across Shanker's face. *What's the story behind that?* she wondered.

"I served under Pontowski for a while," Maggot explained. "I'd follow that man through hell if he asked."

"But not to the White House, I hope," Shanker said pointedly, referring to the rumors of a romance between Pontowski and Maddy Turner, the president of the United States.*

Stuart laughed, trying to defuse the issue. "Pop hates President Turner and can't stand to even talk about her. It sends his blood pressure off the scale."

"Damn woman hates the military," Shanker growled.

"Tell me the threat," Maggot mumbled.

"And I'll tell you my tactics," Shanker snapped, completing the thought. It was one of the rules Shanker had lived by while flying fighters and had passed down to his sons as one of life's truisms.

"Or," Maggot corrected, "I'll tell you my strategy." It was his way of telling Shanker the world had changed and President Turner was forcing the military to change with it. He readily acknowledged that it was a painful task but a necessary one. Facts, however, were the one thing Shanker didn't want to hear.

"What's that supposed to mean?" Shanker barked.

Maggot laughed. "Don't get your shorts twisted around your *cojones*, Pop. It hurts like hell. Matt's a good man and won't do anything stupid."

Jane sensed that Shanker was a cantankerous old curmudgeon and liked the easy way Maggot handled him. There was no doubt Maggot

*Editor's note: Matt Pontowski's relationship with Madeline Turner is told in the book *Edge of Honor* by the same author.

was Stuart's brother—they almost could have been mistaken for twins. But Maggot looked five years older, and there was something about him, a sense of confidence and sureness that escaped most men. There was a look in his eyes and a tone in his voice that eluded her at first. She studied the three as they stood together. Shanker was inordinately proud of Maggot, while he had given up on his younger son. Instinctively she knew the reason. Shanker and Maggot were hunters, sure of their skills, both tested in combat, while Michael was his mother's son, a gentle, introspective man trying to live up to his father's expectations.

"Are you on leave?" Stuart asked.

Maggot gave them his best lopsided grin. "I thought it'd be best if I told you in person. I'm getting married."

"Holy shit!" Shanker roared. "It's about time!"

"Does she know about fighter pilots?" Stuart asked.

Maggot laughed. "Oh, yeah. I wouldn't spring that on her." Shanker and Stuart bombarded him with questions, while Jane fell silent, still studying Maggot. It was obvious he was the father's favorite, and while totally different in appearance from the senior Stuart, Maggot embodied all that Shanker valued. Growing up in Maggot's shadow had to be a painful experience for Michael.

Eric shifted his weight from foot to foot, his feelings hurt because he was cut out of the conversation. He wanted back in and, impulsively, blurted, "Are you sleeping with my dad?"

"Eric!" Michael said.

"Where the hell did that come from?" This from Shanker.

Jane hushed them and smiled at Eric. "Let's go get a Coke and talk." Shanker pointed to the office at the side of the hangar and mumbled something about a refrigerator. Inside the office she found the refrigerator and handed Eric a Coke. "I'll make a deal with you," she said, sipping at a root beer. "I'll answer your question if you'll tell me why you asked it."

Eric hung his head, not sure what to say. But something inside him said he could trust this woman. "Ah, I'm sorry I said it." He looked at her hopefully. "Well . . ." He hesitated. "You go first."

She smiled at him. "No. You go first." They played that game for a few moments. "Okay," she said, "let's play 'Paper-Rock-Scissors' to decide who goes first."

Eric grinned at her, much more confident now. "I've got a strategy," he boasted.

"Do you, now?" Jane replied. "Let's test it." They played a few rounds to warm up, and again his enthusiasm was infectious. "Okay, this one is for real." Eric nodded, and on the count of three she made a scissors with two fingers. As she expected, Eric made a fist, which stood for a rock.

"Rock smashes scissors," he shouted. "I won!"

Jane faked a big sigh. "No, I'm not sleeping with your dad." She gave him a serious look. "Okay, your turn."

He grinned at her, the mischievous seventh-grader in full flow. "I'm not going to tell you, because I won." He bolted from the room with Jane in hot pursuit.

"Wait until I get my hands on you!" she yelled, chasing him out of the hangar. She tackled him on the grass and started tickling him. "Ve haff vays of making you talk," she said, faking a German accent.

He screamed with laughter. "Tick!"

For a moment she didn't get it. Then she rolled off him, shaking with laughter. "Tick-tock, tick-tock." When their laughter died, she became very serious. "Okay, 'fess up. Why did you ask?"

Eric sat up and pulled his knees to his chest. "My mom is always sleeping with someone, and I guess I don't like it."

"I barely know your dad, but I can tell you he's not like that. And I know something very important: He loves you very much."

Suddenly Eric's day got even better.

Shanker walked out of the hangar with his two sons. "I guess we'd better go tell Martha," he said. "I hope she's Catholic," he added.

"She is," Maggot said. "Mom will love her."

"Mom's very religious," Stuart whispered to Jane.

Arlington, Texas

Lloyd Marsten circled through River Legacy Park, looking for the silver minivan. He found it in the far parking area and drove on past, circling back to the entrance. He stopped his gray Jaguar sedan and opened the rear door for Duke, his elderly springer spaniel. The dog emerged from the car and waited patiently for Marsten to snap a lead onto his collar, not that it was necessary. Duke was always the proper gentleman and, at his age, would never do anything as undignified as chasing another dog. A bitch in heat might be another matter, but he would definitely not rush into anything.

"Good boy," Marsten said, giving the dog a loving pat. Duke was his only family, and Marsten feared the day he would die. He headed in the direction of the minivan, another senior citizen out walking his dog on a lovely Sunday afternoon in early October. Joggers moved past him as he walked deeper into the park.

Finally one slowed. "Nice dog. Irish setter?"

"I'm afraid not," Marsten answered. "Duke's a springer spaniel."

"He looks like a real gentleman," the jogger said. He slowed to a walk, his bona fides established. ARA was very careful about maintaining the confidentiality of its clientele. "What can we do for you?"

"Two items. Find out who bombed RTX Farm Supplies outside Miami on the twenty-first of September."

"No problem. I assume the FBI is investigating, so do you want proof leading to a conviction or just information?"

"Information only. But I want it fast. You know how slow the FBI can be, and I'm worried they may hit us again."

"And the second item?"

Marsten carefully considered his words. "A Lieutenant Colonel Michael E. Stuart who works in the Pentagon is probing into our business. I want to find out why and what's going on."

"It's difficult dealing with the military," the jogger said. "We don't have too many options."

"I'm aware of that. But he could make some connections I don't want made."

"Exactly what are these connections?" the jogger asked.

"I don't want him talking to Laser Surveys or Emil Steiner, a French scientist, who you're already watching."

"What exactly does Laser Surveys do?"

"They charter a seismic vessel for offshore oil exploration," Marsten said.

"And if we discover a connection between Stuart, Steiner, and Laser Surveys?"

They were entering dangerous ground, and Marsten needed to be cautious. ARA had no compunctions about operating in gray areas and would do many things. But even they wouldn't do what Marsten was contemplating. Yet Marsten was sure they knew who would. "Then I'll require, shall we say, services of a very specialized nature."

The jogger sensed where Marsten was going. "Services that ARA cannot and will not provide?"

Marsten nodded. "Exactly."

The jogger took a deep breath. The next step was tricky, but the payoff was well worth it. He decided to commit. "I can help."

"I operate in a cutthroat, no-holds-barred world. There are many risks, very dangerous risks. But there are also great rewards."

"I understand perfectly. Of course, it will require some special arrangements." He waited for Marsten's response. A little nod confirmed they were on the same wavelength. "Will these special services be required only with the Stuart connection?"

"It's hard to say at this time," Marsten answered.

Now they had to set a price and work out their cover. "Say, double what you pay ARA, and we agree on bonuses before any difficult operations. And you continue to use ARA to provide a cover for us."

They had a deal. "I believe we understand each other perfectly," Marsten said.

"I'll set up an account in an offshore bank."

"May I suggest Credit Central in Grand Cayman?" Marsten said.

The jogger patted Duke's head. It was just a chance encounter between two dog lovers. Then he was gone, running down the trail. He never looked back as he circled through the woods. After running for thirty-five minutes to be sure no one was following him, he headed for the minivan. A woman was in the back, monitoring the surveillance package. Sophia James was a tall, slender, dark-haired woman who could, when she chose to showcase her looks, be very glamorous. Her ability to change appearance and persona made her an invaluable agent for ARA. "You're both clean," she said.

"Good," the jogger replied, not that he expected anyone to be trailing him or Marsten. But in his business you could never be sure. He stripped off his sweats and rubbed down with a towel.

"I got the conversation on tape," Sophia said.

The jogger stared at her, furious that she had eavesdropped and totally overstepped the bounds. "So?"

"I want in."

"On what?"

"My home is in Miami, and I speak Spanish." She cocked her head as she studied his reaction. He was interested but needed convincing. She ejected the cartridge from the recorder and handed it to him. He stared at her. "I have many contacts in the Cuban community."

"How good is your Spanish?"

"Very good. I was the only *gringa* in the neighborhood where I grew up." She smiled. "In Miami."

"Welcome aboard."

8

St. Louis, Missouri

Ann Silton shifted her weight from foot to foot, feeling very uncomfortable as she waited for L.J. She had never been in a private FBO—fixed-base operations—at an airfield, and she found the masculine atmosphere oppressive. The urge to escape was overpowering, so she retreated to the ladies' room. Inside, she found a very feminine lounge, in total contrast to the conditions outside. It helped ease her discomfort, and she lingered awhile before returning to the pilots' lounge and flight-planning room.

L.J. saw her the moment she entered the room. "Ann!" she called. "I'm so glad you could make it." L.J. rushed up to her and held her at arm's length. "You've lost weight."

Ann looked very unhappy. "It's that damn video."

"I know you're worried," L.J. said. "That's one of the reasons I'm here." She led the way to the ladies' room. "I told them to remodel the lounge the last time I was here. Otherwise I was going to take my business elsewhere." She shut the door behind them, and they sat down.

"What business?" Ann asked.

"They do the maintenance on our Sabreliner, one of our corporate jets. It just came out of an annual inspection, and I'm here to pick it up. It was a perfect excuse to talk to you." She leaned forward and dropped her voice. "We know who did it."

"Who?"

L.J. shook her head. "I'm not so sure I should say."

"Who is it?" Ann demanded. "I'll kill the bastard. Poor Clarissa. She's so young and unsure of herself. This could destroy her."

"I don't think you'll believe me," L.J. said. "If we only knew why."

"Who is it?" Ann shrieked, the lounge echoing with her fury.

L.J. fell silent, timing her answer. "John Frobisher."

Ann Silton stared at her in disbelief. "But why?" Her eyes narrowed as she pictured the executive director of Front Uni in a new light. "He wants us out and his boys in. That must be it. He wants to take over Front Uni."

Again L.J. shook her head. "We can't be sure of that."

"Oh, yes we can. John's scheduled to testify before a Senate subcommittee next week." Ann's face turned hard, her worst suspicions about men reconfirmed. "He needs us out so he can cut a deal. I just know it."

"But why?" L.J. said. "It doesn't make sense."

Ann laughed bitterly. "Of course it does. You haven't heard—few people have—but President Turner is forming a Task Force on the Environment. John wants to be appointed the national director."

"I hadn't heard about that." The lie came easy for L.J. If she was going to make the slow roll work, she had to spread dissension among the environmentalists and split the leadership.

"The bastards," Ann hissed. "Why is it we can never trust a man?"

L.J. patted her hand. "They don't think like we do. But they *are* useful. We have a young scientist working on the benzene problem, and he may have made a breakthrough." Ann's head snapped up. Benzene was high on her personal hit list, and anyone solving that problem would be elevated to the environmental pantheon of saints. "Unfortunately," L.J. continued, "it's going to take money and time for development, and Congress is not very receptive right now to funding major research projects."

"Maybe we can help," Ann replied.

"What I need most right now is time." L.J. shook her head. "I'm afraid John—or Congress, for that matter—doesn't really trust us."

A knock at the door interrupted them. "L.J.," a man said in a loud voice. It was her pilot, Tim Roxford.

"What is it, Tim?" L.J. called.

"There's a message from Life Flight. They need to get a heart to Norfolk for a transplant. It's urgent."

"Tell them we'll take it," she said. "File a flight plan, and I'll be right there."

L.J. touched Ann's hand and lowered her voice. "Please, what I told you about John is confidential. Don't do anything until I do more checking and get back to you."

"We need a woman to head that task force," Ann announced.

"I couldn't agree more," L.J. said, meaning every word. "But please don't do anything rash." She glanced at her watch. "I've got to go. This is important." She hurried out, Ann close behind her.

Tim Roxford was waiting for her at the operations counter, putting the final touches on the flight plan. He was a young man, tall with dark hair. Like many corporate pilots, he wore a short-sleeved white shirt with epaulets, a dark blue tie, dark pants, and black shoes. He was amazingly fit and worked to cultivate an image of sober professionalism, all in the hope of landing a job with a major airline once he'd accumulated enough flying time. It didn't hurt that he was ruggedly good-looking, with bright blue eyes.

"One hour forty minutes to Norfolk," he told L.J. "But most of the area is below landing minimums. Fog and forecast to stay that way for the next twelve hours."

A medical technician hurried through the door carrying a small white-and-red ice chest. "The clock is ticking on this one," he told them. "A little boy has gone critical, and if we don't get this to him . . ." He stopped, not willing to say more.

"How long do we have?" L.J. asked.

"Two, three hours," the med tech said. "That's all."

L.J. signed a receipt for the human heart. "Let's go," she said.

Roxford shook his head. "We'll never get in, not with this weather."

"We won't know until we try," L.J. replied.

"Are you going?" Ann asked, worry in every word.

"I'm the copilot," L.J. said.

"And it's her airplane," Roxford added.

"Can I go?" Ann asked, wanting to be part of the flight and to be with L.J.

L.J. shook her head. "You best not."

Ann took L.J.'s hand, her eyes glowing with pride. "You said you need time with Congress."

L.J. gave a little nod, picked up the cooler, and hurried out to the waiting airplane. Tim Roxford was right behind her.

Over Norfolk, Virginia

The small, two-engine Sabreliner entered the holding pattern exactly one hour and thirty-six minutes after lifting off from St. Louis. At altitude the moonlit sky was clear, but below them a blanket of gray stretched to the horizon. Roxford wired their airspeed at two hundred knots as L.J. copied the latest weather. Nothing had changed, and Norfolk International was still down for fog and forecast to stay that way. L.J. asked for an alternate, but the closest open field was over a hundred miles away and weather conditions there were deteriorating. "We're running out of time," she said. "We land here or the heart will never arrive in time. Let's shoot an approach and take a look."

Roxford was convinced there was no way they could land. "Even the birds are grounded," he told her. She gave him an encouraging look. "What the hell," he said. "It's your airplane." He called for an ILS—instrument landing system—approach to Runway 23 and gave her his best grin. "I don't mind pushing the minimums a bit. But I don't think we're going to see anything close to a hundred and a half." They needed at least a hundred-foot ceiling and a half-mile forward visibility to land.

Roxford broke out of the pattern and intercepted the localizer, the electronic beam that provided an approach path for exact alignment and descent to the runway. He inched the throttles back for the descent, and when their airspeed decayed to 165 knots, called for the gear and flaps. The Sabreliner slowed to 120 knots as they descended into the fog. Roxford's eyes were padlocked on the instruments, and he was sweating. "Call the field," he said, hoping L.J. would see the approach lights. But there was nothing, only dark gray.

"Passing through five hundred feet," L.J. said, her voice dead calm. "Three hundred, two hundred, coming up on decision height, no joy."

"Decision height," Roxford said. "Going around." He leveled off at a hundred feet above the ground, firewalled the throttles, and sucked up the gear and flaps. He never took his eyes off the instruments as they climbed out of the fog, reaching into the clear night air. L.J. announced the missed approach over the radio, and the tower told them to contact approach control on another frequency.

"I think I saw the approach lights just as we leveled off," L.J. told Roxford.

"You got to be kidding," he replied. "In this shit?"

"I think so," she said. "What else could it be? Let's try again."

The look on Roxford's face said he thought it was a crazy idea. But she reached out and touched his arm. "It's important we try." Reluctantly he nodded, and she radioed approach control for vectors back to the localizer to intercept the glide path.

"We make it this time or we divert," Roxford told her. She nodded in agreement, although it was a death sentence for the boy waiting for the heart. Again they intercepted the localizer and descended into the fog. Roxford's shirt was soaked with sweat as he flew the best stabilized approach of his career.

"A hundred feet above decision height," L.J. called. An inner voice told her to go for it. "Fifty feet above. Stay on instruments. I think I see something."

"Decision height," Roxford called, his voice strained, his eyes riveted on the instruments. They were at exactly a hundred feet above the ground and 115 knots airspeed.

"Stay on instruments," she said, "or you'll get disoriented. I've got the approach lights in sight. Don't look up, not yet." She was lying through her teeth and couldn't see a thing, only black. "Looking good. I've got the centerline lights, stay on instruments. We're in and out of it." The wheels touched down with a soft squeak. "Stay on instruments," L.J. said as Roxford got on the brakes. "Come right a tad, that's good, straighten it out. That's good." They came to a halt, and Roxford looked up.

All he saw was black. "Where's the fucking runway?"

L.J. couldn't answer. They had challenged death and won. Slowly her breathing calmed, and her heart stopped its frantic racing. She keyed the radio. "Tower, Life Flight is down and stopped on the runway. Please send the ambulance that's waiting for our delivery. A follow-me would also be appreciated to take us to parking."

"Life Flight," the tower said, "say position on runway."

"We're near the five-thousand-foot remaining marker on Runway two-three," she said. It was a wild guess, as she hadn't seen a single marker in the fog.

"Rog, Life Flight. The ambulance is headed your way. It'll take about twenty minutes in this fog."

Another voice came on the radio. "Life Flight, this is the tower supervisor. Say landing conditions."

Roxford stared at her. "You never saw a thing, did you?"

"I saw you," she said. "That was enough to tell me we could make it." She hit the radio transmit button on the yoke. "Tower, we had a break in the fog at decision height and acquired the runway environment. We went pop-eye on landing rollout."

"Sure you did," the tower supervisor said. "I'm filing a report with Fisdo." Fisdo, or FSDO, was the Flight Standards District Office, the FAA's enforcement arm.

"They'll pull my license," Roxford moaned. He stared straight ahead, his future lost in the fog.

L.J.'s heart melted when she saw the forlorn look on his face. She had to reassure him that everything would be okay and that no matter what, they had done something good. "No they won't," she promised. She came out of her seat, her eyes glowing, and pushed his headset away. Her hands were in his hair as she kissed him again and again. "I'm so proud of you," she whispered. She pulled him back into the cabin, her hands tugging at his belt. "We've got twenty minutes," she murmured.

Dallas

At best L.J. considered frustration a bump in the road that she might slow down to pass over, or if it was big enough and she had to come that way again, have it leveled. But this was the first time in years she had been totally stopped. And she didn't like it. She sat in one corner of the couch in her office and stared at the culprit, a large whiteboard filled with a complex mathematical formula drawn with a black Magic Marker. She pulled her knees to her chest and concentrated. Unfortunately, her calculus had grown rusty from lack of use, and she was stumped.

What's the matter? she raged to herself. She bounced to her feet and attacked the board, circling part of the formula. *Is that the problem?* She returned to her nest on the couch and breathed deeply, her frustration mounting. Her intercom buzzed, and she hit the remote pad on the end table beside her. "Yes!" she barked.

It was Marsten. "Do you have a moment?"

Her voice turned warm. "For you, always." She turned her attention back to the whiteboard, still trying to solve the problem.

Marsten entered without knocking and glanced at the whiteboard. "Ah," he said, hesitating. "I think you should see this." He dropped an eight-by-ten color photo on the coffee table. Artistically the photograph was a gem. Fog misted over L.J.'s Sabreliner as it sat on the runway at Norfolk. Flashing lights from an ambulance cast a prismatic spectrum of color on the fuselage, and a woman was standing in the entrance handing a small plastic cooler to the ambulance driver. Unfortunately, the bare-shouldered woman in the entranceway was wrapped only in a lap robe.

"I do believe that's you," Marsten said. She glanced at the photo, not bothering to pick it up. At times Marsten felt like a Dutch uncle, and he never hesitated to admonish her sternly. It was a twist in their relationship both accepted without questioning. "That was not a smart thing to do."

"Tim was wonderful, landing under those conditions and, and . . ." She pulled into herself, trying to recapture the emotions of the moment.

"And what?" he asked, still the Dutch uncle.

"I was quite excited, and I don't know why I did it. I guess there was a momentary bond between us that I couldn't let go of." She thought for a moment. "Lloyd, I hadn't felt so alive since—since before Eritrea."

Marsten nodded, understanding at last. Eritrea had been a turning point in their lives, forever binding them together and a benchmark to measure their lives. "Basic human instinct will come out," he told her. "When danger and death are all about, Mother Nature tells us to procreate."

She sighed. "The tower said we had twenty minutes before the ambulance could get there. They got there in less than ten."

"Saving that boy's life was a public relations triumph. Even the White House is interested." He tapped the photo with a forefinger. "This would have ended all that. I had to bribe the photographer—ten-thousand dollars to squash it."

"I didn't make that flight for publicity," she said, trying to explain. "How often do we get a chance to save a life?" Marsten didn't answer. "There's another problem," she continued. "The FAA is giving Tim grief about landing below minimums. Can you help?"

"A phone call to Senator—"

She interrupted him. "I don't want to know."

He gestured at the whiteboard, changing the subject. "Steiner's Double Reflection technique?"

She nodded. "It's frustrating. I need a refresher course in calculus."

"It's not calculus," Marsten replied. "Steiner developed a special annotation to deal with the variables he was encountering, or so he told me."

"Maybe I should get someone who understands this type of thing."

"Under the circumstances," Marsten replied, "that might not be a good idea."

She sighed in resignation. She trusted Marsten's instincts and appreciated his penchant for understatement. "You're right, of course. But why do I get the feeling I'm looking at a Trojan horse?"

Marsten caught the reference immediately. "Something, or someone, intended to divert from within." He frowned. "That's because we're dealing with Steiner. He's such a sneaky bastard. But he does excellent work. I'm confident that if we ever have the opportunity to drill, we will find out just how excellent."

"I don't want this blowing up in our faces." Again the sigh. "I'm obsessing, aren't I?"

Marsten sat down beside her. "Considering what's at stake here, it's understandable. Speaking of blowing up, I've been thinking about the bombing at RTX."

"Why am I not surprised?" she said. "I don't want it happening again, and I want whoever did it punished." He heard the suppressed anger in her voice. He had seen her anger in full flow only once, and that was in Eritrea. "If the powers that be can't do something about it, I will. Here."

He handed her the folder that detailed the new security program he had created for the company. She flipped through the pages, focusing on its salient points. "Lloyd," she said, approval in her voice, "this is brilliant. This could be marketed to other companies, it's that good. By all means let's do it." She paused, thinking. "But it will take some time to get this up and running. Until then I want to be sure we're not targeted again."

"I've got ARA on it."

"Good. See if they can get someone on the inside. I wouldn't mind burning them one bit."

He made a note, not arguing. L.J. was a true daughter of Texas, a seething mass of contradictions and a total believer in rough justice and fighting her own battles. He chose his next words carefully. "I've also got them looking at a Lieutenant Colonel Stuart who works in the Pentagon. There might be a connection to Steiner." He explained about the letter from the committee and how Stuart's boat had been in the harbor at the same time as the seismic vessel.

"That is a bit of coincidence, isn't it?" she murmured. "We can't afford to have the government interfering."

Marsten totally agreed. "As it involves Cuba, they will intervene and stop us."

"Is this Stuart going to be a problem?"

"A temporary one at best," Marsten replied.

"Stay on top of it," L.J. said. Marsten nodded and left, throwing the offending photograph into the shredder. L.J. stared at the whiteboard for a few moments, trying to refocus on Steiner's formula. Nothing came to her, and the equations remained as opaque as before. Unbidden, her hand moved slowly and erased the formula. She curled up in one corner of the couch, stared into space, and let her mind wander. *Be honest. You're obsessed with the elephant.* The truth was in front of her. She had never wanted anything so badly, so intensely, that she would risk everything. But how to do it? Suddenly her right hand hit the remote pad on the end table, and the door locked. She reached for the phone and buzzed her secretary. "I'm not to be disturbed unless it's an emergency." Slowly she approached the whiteboard, the way a matador first greets a bull. Using black, red, blue, green, and yellow Magic Markers, she worked as a flow-chart evolved, with arrows connecting little boxes.

L.J. labored well into the evening, erasing, re-forming, and reconnecting the vectors. Finally a decision tree emerged. She stood back and surveyed her handiwork before drawing in a vector labeled "Stuart." *Where in the grand scheme of things do you fit?* He was an uncontrolled variable she didn't need. She drew in a box at the end of Stuart's vector and wrote Marsten's name in it. Doubt assailed her as she stared at what she'd done. With slow precision and in big block letters she wrote the words THE TROJAN SEA at the very top.

She continued to refine her work. When an inner voice said it was right, she committed it to memory. A shiver of doubt shot through her.

Can anyone do this? The audacity, the sheer magnitude of what she had created was staggering. But so were the rewards. The same inner voice that told her Tim Roxford could land in zero-zero conditions told her she had to try.

She wiped the board clean. But the words THE TROJAN SEA were still visible. Then she scrubbed them away. She didn't need to see them again—they were imprinted indelibly on her very soul.

⁕

Duke walked slower than usual as Marsten made his way through River Legacy Park. The temperature was pleasant for the tenth of October but not warm enough for the old dog. "You're too much of a gentleman to complain," Marsten said. Logic told him the walks would soon come to an end, but his heart wasn't listening or able to accept the truth.

The jogger coasted up beside him and repeated the opening protocol even though the two men recognized each other. "Nice dog. Irish setter?" Marsten countered with the proper words as the younger man jogged in place. "Our agent in Miami may have located the terrorists who bombed RTX," the jogger said. "They appear to be a splinter group of Puerto Rican nationalists. No names yet or exactly how they're wired. How much further do you want to take it?"

"Puerto Ricans? How interesting. I'm surprised they're not Cubans." Marsten thought before taking the next step. L.J. had been very specific in what she wanted. "We need to get someone on the inside to monitor the bastards."

The request surprised the jogger, but he never missed an opportunity to make money. "That would require a special arrangement." He named a dollar amount, and Marsten nodded in agreement. "We also have an update on Monsieur Dr. Steiner," the jogger continued. "When he isn't busy abusing young female students, he's telling the Department of Energy about his latest discovery. Something about Seismic Double Reflection."

"The source of your information?" Marsten asked.

"One of the young women."

"Is Steiner talking to Stuart?"

The jogger shook his head. "But Steiner is in contact with DOE, and

DOE has a member on the Strategic Petroleum Reserve Committee that Stuart is serving on."

"So we have a connection."

"DOE and the Department of Defense are pretty big organizations. But a connection is possible."

Does L.J. need to know? Marsten wondered. He made a decision. "Break it."

"Another special arrangement?"

"I see no other alternative," Marsten muttered.

"We're talking in the vicinity of twenty-five thousand dollars."

Marsten jerked his head yes. He spun around and walked quickly away, Duke hobbling after him. He didn't want to know the details.

The jogger ran into the nearby trees and circled through the park. Certain that he was clean, he returned to the minivan where Sophia James, still tan from her recent trip to Miami, was waiting for him. "I got it all," she told him.

"Not on tape, I hope."

"Of course not," she said. "I take it I'm going back to Miami, and you're off to Washington? Freelancing, of course."

"Of course," he replied.

Washington, D.C.

It started in the morning when the automatic coffeemaker's filter clogged and hot coffee spilled over the kitchen counter and drained onto the floor. Stuart cursed eloquently as he cleaned up the mess, not aware he was at the high point of his day. Then he couldn't set the alarm system when he left for work and spent a few extra minutes trying to solve that problem. Giving up, he ran for the Metro station. He arrived in time to see the train leave the platform. That caused him to miss his connection, and he arrived for work an hour late.

Of course, Ramjet wanted to see him immediately. He rushed out of his cubicle only to collide with one of the civilian employees who worked in ILSX. Unfortunately, she was carrying a bag with a spent toner cartridge for a printer. The bag flew into the air, overturned, and dumped a fine black powder over Stuart. The woman was all apologies, but nothing short of dry cleaning was going to clean Stuart's coat.

Rather than send a cloud of dust into the other cubicles, Stuart removed the coat and rolled it up. Already late, he headed for Ramjet's office. Peggy Redman stopped him.

"Go wash your face," she commanded. He quickly explained how he'd been dumped on. "Here, give me your coat. I'll try to clean it up." Stuart did as ordered and was able to enter Ramjet's office in a half-decent state.

"Mike," Ramjet called, obviously glad to see Stuart. "A message from Personnel came down last night. Headquarters USAFE in Ramstein, Germany, needs a plans officer with your qualifications. I recommended you for the job. Wonderful opportunity. They need you ASAP, and I released you for immediate reassignment. They're expecting you next week."

An image of Eric caught in Barbara Raye's clutches flashed in front of Stuart. He panicked. "Sir, I, ah—this is my last assignment before retiring and I've, ah, made a commitment to my family. It would be—"

Ramjet shook his head, interrupting him. "Needs of the service always come first. You know that." He waved his hand, dismissing Stuart. "Good luck, Mike."

Before Stuart could escape, Ramjet stopped him. "Oh, Mike. About your slot on that committee on the, ah . . ." He stopped, as if unable to recall the committee's name.

"Strategic Petroleum Reserve," Stuart said, filling in the thought.

"Yes, that one. Tell General Butler I'll be taking your place."

"I understand," Stuart said, finally making good his escape.

"Colonel Stuart," Peggy called. "General Butler's office called. He's wondering why you're late for a committee meeting. It started five minutes ago." She handed him his coat.

"Ah, shit," Stuart moaned. He ran for the shuttle van that would take him across the river.

Peggy sighed and reached for the phone. "Joannie, Colonel Stuart is on his way. Put in a good word for him. He's having a bad day." She listened for a moment. "Girl, you have no idea how true that is. What would they do without us?"

❄

The meeting was over when Stuart reached the conference room in the Old Executive Office Building. An assistant who was tidying up the room for the next meeting told him that General Butler was waiting for him in the national security adviser's office. Suppressing another "Ah, shit," Stuart hurried to Mazie Kamigami Hazelton's office suite. A pleasant, middle-aged secretary ushered him in. "They're waiting for you," Joannie said.

What did I miss? he wondered. The image of a three-star general and the national security adviser waiting for a lieutenant colonel was not reassuring.

Butler threw him a perturbed look when he entered Mazie's office. "Mike, the uniform."

Stuart nodded dumbly. "Yes, sir. I know. I didn't have a chance to change."

Mazie smiled at him and gestured at a chair. "Has it been one of those days?"

Stuart nodded. "I'm afraid so, Mrs. Hazelton." He sat down.

"We have a problem," Butler said. "The oil companies are digging their heels in on this one and not helping. Not one has been willing to discuss their future plans for exploration."

"Perhaps," Stuart ventured, "that's because they're in a wait-and-see mode and don't know what they're going to do."

"That makes sense," Mazie said. "Also, it keeps their competitors guessing." She leaned across her desk and handed him a folder with the Department of Energy logo on the cover. The word SECRET was stamped in red at the top and bottom, front and back. "DOE received this from a Dr. Emil Steiner. Could this be what they're waiting for? General Butler tells me this is one of your specialties and you can make sense out of the math."

Stuart glanced at the contents. "I've never heard of Seismic Double Reflection before."

"The experts from DOE have looked at it," Mazie said. "They think it's a major breakthrough in oil exploration and may give us the means to break OPEC."

"I can look at it," Stuart said, thumbing through the first few pages. He stopped and frowned. His lips pursed into a tight line. He chose his words carefully. "This will take some work."

"Is something wrong?" Butler asked.

"On the face of it, this is elegant, brilliant. But it feels out of balance. Sorry, I can't put my finger on it. I've heard of Steiner, twice turned down for a Nobel. Always something not quite right."

"When will you know?" Mazie asked.

"In a few days," Stuart answered. "Before I leave for Germany."

"You've been reassigned?" Butler asked.

"It came down last night, and Colonel Priestly released me for immediate travel. He told me to tell you he'll be filling my position on the committee."

Butler's eyes narrowed. "Do you want the assignment?" Stuart shook his head. "I see," the general said. "We'll talk later."

Stuart knew he was dismissed. "Yes, sir."

Mazie waited until Stuart had left. "He's doing good work for us," she told Butler. "What's going on?"

"Office politics. Mike's boss doesn't like him getting all the exposure over here. I'll take care of it and have him frozen in his current assignment."

"We need him," Mazie said. "The president is worried and would like for us to get a handle on this. She doesn't like the idea of other countries controlling ninety percent of the tanker fleet."

Butler looked worried. "I'm not sure what we're seeing, but I fear it's tied to the globalization of the economy. The equilibrium of the system rests on a very fragile balance between states and the market."

"I'm not an economist, Bernie. What does that mean?"

"Neither am I. But I see a system emerging where a nation is captive to the market, which is now beyond its immediate control. So if a country wants to challenge another nation, it first captures a key part of the market critical to that nation."

Mazie nodded. "A form of economic warfare."

"A very sophisticated form of warfare that only a large nation has the resources to pursue."

"Can you give me an example?" Mazie asked.

"Say China decides to challenge Japan and the United States for supremacy in Asia."

"Like during the Okinawa crisis," Mazie added. They both had vivid memories of the early days of Madeline Turner's presidency, when China had blockaded Okinawa in an attempt to drive a wedge between the United States and Japan. It had been a near thing, and Maddy Turner had barely avoided a major war.

"So," Butler said, thinking aloud, "China first gains control of the oil tanker fleet. Then, when push comes to shove, China shuts off the flow of oil, and the U.S. doesn't have the means to supply its forces. In short, the military option is taken off the table."

Mazie's chin came up, her eyes flashing with anger. "And they can also shut off the oil to Japan. I don't think the president wants to hear this."

"Someone had better tell her before it's too late," Butler said.

✳

The yellow chalk dust brought on an itch, and Stuart's nose exploded in a thunderous sneeze, sending his glasses flying. Twice more the small office echoed with a crashing barrage. He wiped at his nose with a Kleenex, picked up his glasses, and stared at the green chalkboard in front of him. "Is your rear-end still attached?" Peggy Redman said from behind him. She was standing in his cubicle's doorway wearing her coat and holding her handbag.

"I hope so," he said.

"Colonel Priestly wants to see you. But I told him you'd left for the day." He gave her a quizzical look, wondering why she'd done that. "Headquarters MPC," she explained, "sent him an e-mail canceling your assignment to Germany. I figured he needed time to cool down." She turned and left, eager to get home.

"Fuckin' Ramjet," Stuart muttered to himself. He turned back to the chalkboard and studied the complicated equation he'd transferred from the file Mazie had given him. "Okay, Dr. Steiner, what's wrong with this picture?" Then he saw it. He circled the same subset that had caught L.J. Ellis's attention four days earlier. "Naw," he said. "I must be doing something wrong. Steiner's too good for that." He sat down at his desk and kicked back, still working the problem. He had always loved math and found an escape in neatly ordered equations and the tight logic of advanced calculus. But this wasn't calculus. *So what is it?* He worked for another three hours, oblivious to the time.

The phone rang, claiming his attention. The flashing light announced it was an outside line and not from Ramjet's office. He picked it up on the second ring. "Mike," Jenny said, her voice tight and a little too loud. "It's after eight o'clock. Don't you ever go home?"

He recognized the symptoms immediately. "What's the problem?"

"Mike, it's just not enough money. We need to buy a car to go to Aspen, and Granny wants a sport utility vehicle with four-wheel drive so we'll have the proper image when we get there, because image is everything in Aspen."

At least I know where Eric's run-on sentences come from, he thought. "You know what I make," he said, hoping that would pacify her.

"Mike!" she shouted. "I don't want to go to my mother!"

And God only knows what will happen then. "Let me think for a minute." Getting Jenny out of Virginia would take the heat off Eric, but Stuart couldn't afford to buy her a new car. *Maybe my Explorer would do the trick. And it's paid for.* "Jenny, I hardly drive anymore, so why don't we switch cars? You take my SUV—it's a four-wheel drive—and I use your car. But I'll need mine back when I retire. In sixteen months."

"That would be wonderful," she sang. "We'll be all set up by then, and you and Eric can come out to get it and visit us."

"Great," he said.

"We want to leave near the end of the month, so we can pick it up at your folks' place then." She hung up before he could change his mind.

Stuart dropped the phone into its cradle and looked up to see Ramjet Priestly staring at him. "I thought you'd gone home," Priestly said, his voice icy cold.

"I stepped out for a few moments," Stuart replied, covering for Peggy. He motioned at the chalkboard. "A major problem."

Priestly glared at him. "That's nothing compared to the bucket of shit you stepped in when you tried to make an end run around me."

Stuart stifled a groan. He wanted nothing more than for Ramjet to be kicked upstairs so a seasoned logistician could take over ILSX. "I'm sorry, sir, I don't understand."

"The hell you don't. You may think you picked up a sponsor in Butler, but I've got friends. And I control the personnel in my division—not you, not Butler. Do you understand?"

"Perfectly, sir."

"Thank God for that. I'd suggest you start packing." Priestly spun around and walked away, his hard heels echoing down the corridor.

Why didn't I hear him coming? Stuart wondered. Ramjet's hard heels were an ongoing joke in the office. Stuart gathered up his coat and hat, turned out the light, and headed for the Metro station. He had to hurry to catch the next train and, as usual, it was almost empty. *With my luck they'll cancel the late trains as soon as I give Jenny the Explorer.* He settled into a seat in the front and let his mind wander. An image of Eric spinning around holding the model of the Lightning flashed in his mind's eye. There was no way Jenny would allow him to take Eric to Germany, and that meant Barbara Raye would win by default. *What do I do now?* he moaned to himself. He glanced at his watch, the memory of the street sweeper still vivid in his mind. Could he catch a taxi for the short ride home? Probably not. *Perfect*, he thought, *an absolutely perfect fuckin' day.*

He walked out of his Metro station in time to see a taxi pull away. For a moment he considered waiting to see if another cab might drive by. But the way things were going, he knew there wouldn't be another one. "What the hell." He sighed, then turned and walked briskly across the street. He passed a few people, all walking confidently, and told himself the neighborhood was improving and perfectly safe. The street sweeper had just been a fluke accident. He turned down his street, less than a hundred yards from his apartment. "Ah, shit," he groaned. The streetlight was out, and he was walking in a dark shadow. Instinctively he hurried toward the next light.

A dark image emerged from the shadows and walked toward him. The man was huge, well over six feet tall, and wore a dark duffel coat that reached to his knees. The hood was up, and his left arm hung at his side as if it were paralyzed. Stuart froze as pure fear sent shock waves through his body.

For a split second Stuart wanted to believe that the apparition bearing down on him was a homeless person begging for money. Indecision tore at him. A primal instinct urged him to run, while his mind rationalized that this couldn't possibly be happening to him. A car turned the corner behind the man, and its headlights flashed on the man's back, setting him in stark relief. A knife dangled from his left hand. *I'm going to get that stuck in my body!*

But Stuart couldn't stop himself from walking. His instincts finally took over. He leaped in front of the car that was bearing down behind the man, desperate to get anything between him and the knife. But he was too close, and the man grabbed Stuart's coat and jerked him back. Stuart twisted and grabbed for the man's left hand in a desperate attempt to stop the knife. Somehow the man's right hand, which was still holding on to Stuart's coat, was jammed against his mouth. Stuart bit down. Hard. The man let go as Stuart twisted away, again jumping into the street.

His assailant's left hand cut an arc, swinging at Stuart's back. The tip of the blade caught in his coat and dragged across his shoulder blades. Stuart fell into the street as another car approached, its headlights flashing across them. For a fraction of a second Stuart had a clear view of his assailant's face under the hood. The driver of the second car stood on the brakes and swerved to avoid hitting Stuart as the man ran into the shadows.

"You okay, buddy?" the driver shouted.

Stuart staggered to his feet. He tasted blood in his mouth. He spit as hard as he could.

9

Miami

The driver deposited the young woman at the entrance to Marsten's hotel at exactly 10:25 Tuesday evening. She was tall and elegant and walked with confidence into the small lobby. She wore a classic little black dress that was on the edge of perfect taste, not too tight but tight enough to tantalize. The night manager came out from behind the counter and buttoned the coat of his tuxedo. "May I help you?" he asked.

"Mr. Marsten is expecting me," she said.

"I see," the manager said, immediately pegging her as a very high-priced call girl. It was a situation the hotel dealt with daily. His only concern was that a guest might make a bad liaison. But as she didn't fit the profile that spelled trouble, he didn't foresee a problem. "Shall I call Mr. Marsten and tell him you're on your way up?"

"Please do," she said, bestowing a beautiful smile on him. She handed him a discreet business card with a hundred-dollar bill folded underneath.

He glanced at the card. "Heather," he read. "And you're with Specialized Associates. I'm not familiar with your, ah, firm."

"We specialize in personal services that require a great deal of discretion," she told him.

"Of course," he said, palming the hundred dollars. He kept her card for a possible referral, should the need arise. He was certain any guest using her services would be most appreciative. He escorted her to the elevator. "Mr. Marsten is on the eighth floor." There was no room number, as each suite occupied an entire floor. He turned a key, and the door slid back. The manager stared at her as the doors closed, trying to estimate what she charged for an evening. He knew that the two other girls currently in the hotel charged two thousand dollars for the night. He decided that "Heather" was worth much more. He didn't know how right he was.

Marsten was waiting when the elevator stopped. "Right on time," he said. "Lloyd Marsten." He extended his hand.

"Sophia James," she replied. They shook hands in a businesslike way. "We have the information you asked for." He nodded and led the way into the study. She sat down at a writing table and pulled a small palm-size computer out of her bag. She plugged in the modern and turned on the computer, all business. "We've a positive make on the terrorists who bombed RTX Farm Supplies. They're a small splinter group of Puerto Rican nationalists who call themselves the Group. The FBI rolled up three of their members in Puerto Rico last August, and until now they've been very quiet."

"Are we dealing with true believers here?" Marsten asked.

"Apparently so," she replied. "While there is always a strong self-destructive element in any group like this, the woman's death was an accident."

Over the years Marsten had developed the ability to take the measure of people quickly, and Sophia James was someone he could use. But he had to probe a little deeper before making a decision. "I'd like to turn this over to the FBI, but you know how slowly they move."

"And only if they believe you. Even then they double-check everything. And that can take forever."

Marsten said, "We're worried this so-called Group may hit us again. We don't want any of our people killed or injured simply because the authorities refuse to act in a timely way." He paused for effect. "We will protect our people and want to be proactive in this matter."

"The FBI won't like that at all," she said.

He nodded. "Perhaps it would be best not to involve them, at least not yet. So exactly who and what are we dealing with?"

Her fingers danced on the keyboard. The screen flashed, and three images appeared. "Luis Barrios is their leader and their only source of money. Neither Francisco Martínez nor Eduardo Pinar works. Prior to her death, the woman known as Carita was the main source of money, which she earned working as a prostitute."

Marsten scanned the dossiers Sophia had compiled, growing even more impressed. "Can we get someone on the inside?"

Sophia instinctively sensed where he was going. "If approached the right way, yes. Barrios is no fool. He knows they need money and information to survive. It's a weakness we can exploit."

"How vulnerable are they?"

"Very," she answered. She hesitated. Did she want to lie to Marsten this early in the game? She decided to be truthful. "You can't believe how easy it was to crack their cover. I know all there is to know about them, including the last time they washed their underwear. It's only a matter of time before the FBI rolls them up." She thought for a moment. "I'll need a cover."

"We can assume they're familiar with the Puerto Rican scene," Marsten said. "You could always be a Cuban freedom fighter."

"That should work," she replied.

Marsten studied Barrios's picture, trying to take his measure. "How does Barrios earn his money?"

"He works for SuperComputers. That's a large chain of computer stores."

"I've never been in one," Marsten told her.

"Interesting place." Her long fingernails clicked as they danced over the keyboard. "For some reason, young males of one ethnic group will take over the staff of a particular store. All of them seem to be wheeler-dealers looking for the golden opportunity. For example, the staff where Barrios works is composed almost entirely of Hindi-speaking immigrants from India. Barrios is the only Latino working there. He specializes in HTML and is the store's Web-site expert."

"Not to mention the token Hispanic," Marsten added. He thought for a moment. "Can you create a Web page?"

"Of course. I can do it now, if you want. Besides, if I left too soon, it would blow my cover."

"We certainly wouldn't want to do that," Marsten replied. He made a decision. "What does ARA pay you?"

"When they use me, four hundred and fifty a day plus expenses. I made forty thousand dollars last year."

It was exactly the kind of problem Marsten delighted in solving. Instinctively he ran the numbers. ARA had used her services eighty-nine days last year. A waste of talent. "How would you like to work full-time for me? A hundred thousand a year, all expenses paid."

She considered the offer. "Very interesting. Does it require, shall we say, certain services of a very personal nature?"

"Absolutely not," Marsten replied.

She smiled at him. "What a pity. I rather enjoy sex. With the right person."

He returned her smile. She was the person he was looking for.

✳

Luis Barrios saw Sophia James the moment she entered the store. The miniskirt to her business suit revealed shapely legs, and her dark hair was pulled back, reminding him of an exotic dancer he had once lusted after. He felt his blood stir as she moved through the displays.

Instinctively he angled her way, hoping to be the first to reach her. But Habib got there first. Normally Barrios would have barged ahead, but Habib was the assistant manager and very conscientious. He would see that she was properly helped. *Not like the others*, Barrios thought. He stood back as he watched them. She glanced at him and held his gaze for a moment. The surge of interest coming from his groin grew stronger. *She's sending signals*, he told himself. There was something vaguely familiar about her. *I've seen her before. But where?* He moved closer and heard her say, "I'm trying to create a Web site for my company. But I think I need to upgrade my computer." She gave a charming laugh. "And I certainly need help."

"Yes, I see," Habib said in his precise English. "You need to speak to Luis. He's our expert on HTML and creating Web sites."

"What's HTLM?" the woman asked, getting it wrong.

"Luis will explain it all to you," Habib said, motioning Luis over. "Luis is an expert Webmaster."

"You're just the man I'm looking for," Sophia said to Luis.

Luis tried to concentrate, fighting the urgent signals coming from his groin, as he led her to the section where a computer station was set up. It was one of Luis's creations, and a big monitor hung from the ceiling to relay to a large audience what was on the computer's screen.

Luis took a deep breath. Everything about the woman excited him—the way she walked, her hair, her perfume. They sat down in front of the computer. Her skirt crept even higher, and he couldn't take his eyes off her legs. "How may I help you?" he asked.

"Well," Sophia said, "I run my own company, and I'm trying to start a Web page. But I'm having trouble with my computer and . . . well, why don't I show you what I already have? We can go from there."

Luis breathed deeply. She was definitely sending signals. "Yes, why don't we do that?" He watched as she typed in www.allaboutyou.com. "What an unusual name," he said. The super-VGA monitor blinked, and he froze. His own photo filled the screen. The monitor blinked again, and Carita's picture appeared, a very dead Carita. That image was quickly replaced by Francisco's and Eduardo's. Then his own picture was back on the screen. His mouth fell open and he gasped, realizing everyone in the store could see what was on the large monitor hanging over their heads.

When Habib was on duty, he never missed a thing. "Luis," he called. "What is going on?"

"Nothing!" Luis said. He bounced out of his chair to see what was on the overhead monitor. At the same time he heard Sophia's fingernails clicking as she worked the keyboard. The large screen went blank, and Habib turned away. Luis collapsed into the chair, his heart still beating fast. "FBI?" he moaned.

"Of course not," Sophia said, switching to Spanish. She stroked the inside of his thigh.

"CIA?"

She laughed. "Never."

"Why are you here?"

"Like I said, you're just the man I'm looking for." This in English.

"Am I?" he replied in Spanish.

She answered in the same language. "We need each other."

"For what?"

"You can do things I cannot. On the other hand, I can supply money and information."

"Who are you?"

"Like you, a freedom fighter."

A fellow traveler, Luis thought. He had seen it before. She was a true believer who had given herself completely to a cause. But which one? Then he remembered. He had seen her at Café Martí talking to the waiter who would sell anything to anyone for the right price. "Cuba?" he asked. A slow blink of her dark eyes confirmed his guess. Again there was an unspoken promise in the way she looked at him. His mind raced with the implications. She was someone he could use, and there was a way to confirm if she was the legitimate article. "I need to think about it."

"Think what might happen," Sophia whispered, moving her hand higher up his leg. She gave a little squeeze and stood up. "I'll be in contact." She pointed at the computer, turned around, and walked away.

A combination of lust, fear, and curiosity cycled through his body, ratcheting up his libido. He wanted to shout, "What's your name?" But Habib was still watching him.

10

Annapolis

Jane drew her paintbrush down the grab rail and gave a last coat of varnish to the brightwork on a wealthy boat owner's sixty-foot Swan. *What a beautiful boat*, she thought. *Too bad it never leaves the marina.* She stood to stretch, feeling very satisfied. A familiar figure wandering aimlessly down the next dock caught her eye. *What's Mike doing here on a Thursday?* she wondered. She watched him for a few moments, sensing that something was not right. *He's sold* Temptress. *Get it over with.* "Mike!" she called. "Over here." From the way he waved back, she knew that something was very wrong. *Don't tell me you're going back to your airhead wife!* She cleaned her brush while he walked back and around the dock.

"Nice boat," he said.

"Real nice," she allowed. *Now, there's a hangdog look.* "What's wrong?"

"Nothing."

"Bullshit." She went back to cleaning up. *Men!* She decided to charge the boat's owner double for the job. He could afford it. Then she relented. *Don't take it out on some poor sap just because he never sails his boat and you're frustrated.* "What brings you here?"

"I took a day off. I had to go to the doctor this morning and, and—" He stared dumbly at his feet.

Her voice was soft. "And what? Mike."

He sat down next to the wheel and looked out across the Severn River. "I was mugged Tuesday night." He told her the story in a flat monotone.

"Did the police catch them?"

He shook his head. "I spent most of yesterday looking at mug shots. Nothing."

Jane became all business. "Let me see the bandage." He turned his back to her and lifted his shirt. She gently touched his skin. "How many stitches?"

"Eight."

"Not good."

"Tell me," he moaned.

"I was cut in a bar fight once," she confided.

He spun around to look at her. "Really?"

She nodded. "I was young and stupid. A bar in San Diego. A bimbo thought I was hitting on her boyfriend—we were talking boats. Later she went after me in the ladies' room. I should have run away. But no, I was a lamebrained idiot and stood my ground. She cut my face with a broken beer bottle. Over two hundred stitches, two layers." She tilted her head so he could examine her left cheek.

The scar was almost invisible. He gently touched her cheek and traced the line. "I never noticed it before."

"I had a good plastic surgeon." She thought for a moment. "I'm surprised they waited until today to sew you up. They didn't waste any time stitching me back together."

"It was the same with me."

"But you said you went to the doctor today."

Stuart didn't answer at first. "I had to see a shrink. There were, ah, complications. Damn! First I get shoved under a street sweeper and now this. Ramjet is dumping on me big time, and Jenny is on my case. Who in the hell did I piss off?" He fell silent, not wanting to sound like a whimpering idiot. But the doubts were there, raging through him.

She recognized the symptoms and took charge. "Bad luck does happen," she told him. "You need some time. How 'bout some lunch? There's a great little place on West Street. Best hamburgers and beer in town."

"Sounds good. Hold on, I got to check my messages. Ramjet is probably having fits." He punched a number into his cell phone and listened for what seemed a long time. His face paled, and he broke the connection. "That was the police. They think they found the bastard who mugged me. They want to see me ASAP."

"Can't it wait until tomorrow?"

"Apparently not. He's dead."

Another thought came to her. "What about your boss?"

"He's only having conniptions today. Fits are reserved for tomorrow." For the first time that day Stuart's back straightened. "Fuck him."

Jane allowed a little smile. "Let's go," she said.

✳

The tension kept building, wrapping Stuart into a tight knot, as they made the drive back to Washington. "I've never seen a dead body," he said.

"Always a first time," she said, back in her four-word mode.

"Thanks for coming." His hand reached out and held hers. They drove in silence to the police station, where they checked in with the desk sergeant. He sent them immediately to Homicide, where a young detective was waiting for them. He handed Stuart two Polaroid photos. "Recognize him?" Stuart shook his head. The detective handed him one more. "This one?" Two very dead eyes gaped at Stuart from the photo. For a moment he was back on the street, staring into the face of his assailant.

"That's him."

The detective handed him another photo, this one of a right hand. "Check the teeth marks. Someone took a good bite out of him."

"That was me," Stuart said. He held his breath, waiting for the next act to play out.

"Thank you Colonel Stuart. We'll be in contact when we have a positive ID."

The tension shattered. "I don't have to identify the body?"

The detective shook his head and stood to escort them out. But Jane wanted to know more. "How was he killed?"

The detective shrugged. "A stupid thing. He tried to rob a woman at an automatic teller machine, held a knife to her throat, probably the same one he used on Colonel Stuart. She broke free and fell to the ground, rolled up in a fetal position, and screamed like hell. An armed security guard heard her and got there in time to stop the perp. Three nine-millimeter slugs, nice grouping, saved the taxpayers a lot of money."

"So the woman wasn't hurt?" Stuart asked.

The detective shook his head. "A minor cut across her throat. She was lucky."

Stuart stared at the floor. "Do you run a lot of tests on the body? Like blood tests."

"Oh, yeah. Everything."

Stuart whispered, "HIV?"

"That, too."

"Will you let me know the results?"

"Certainly," the detective said, making a note on his calendar.

Jane stared at Stuart, at last understanding.

❈

Jane took a quick look around Stuart's apartment, pleased that it was spotlessly clean and neat as a pin. *Just like* Temptress, she thought. "I like your place," she announced. "Bathroom?"

"Down the hall, at the end," Stuart said, rummaging through the refrigerator.

She walked down the short hall, glancing at the small bedroom on the left that obviously belonged to Eric. A framed photo of an extremely pretty woman with long auburn hair sat on the chest of drawers. *That must be Jenny*, Jane thought. She paused at the door to the larger bedroom and looked at Stuart's bed. She had no delusions about herself and accepted the fact that, lookswise, she was no match for the beautiful Jenny. Her spirits soared when she saw the picture on the nightstand. It was a photo of her standing beside the wheel of *Temptress*, looking up, studying the set of the sails. *When did he take that?* She almost floated back to the kitchen. *Don't get stupid*, she warned herself.

"Are omelettes okay?" Stuart asked.

"Sounds good," she replied, thinking not of food but of his bed. Then it all crashed, and she felt like crying. Suddenly she didn't care. Sex might be out of the question for now, but she was going to spend the night with him. Being Jane, she took the direct approach. "Mike, I want to stay here tonight."

She almost laughed at the panicked look on his face. "Jane, you know what I was asking about at the police station. I, ah, I, ah . . ."

She let him off the hook. "That's why you went to the shrink, right?" He nodded, not yet able to talk about it.

Dallas

The jogger put on a burst of speed, pounding along the river walk next to Turtle Creek Boulevard. His breath steamed in the unusually chilly morning air as he passed other runners. The exercise helped control the worry that consumed him like a cancer. *How could anything get so fucked up so quickly?* he moaned to himself. He coasted to a walk when he reached the roundabout leading up to his high-rise condominium. The doorman held the door for him. "Good morning, sir. Nice day for a run?"

"Good morning, Ed. Indeed it is." He rode the elevator alone to the top floor, his anxiety building. He had to tell Marsten, the sooner the better. He let himself into his luxury apartment, wondering how much longer he could afford it.

Sophia James was standing by the big window overlooking Turtle Creek. "A beautiful view," she told him.

Why didn't Ed tell me she was here?

"I let myself in," she said.

How did she get to the elevator? The complex prided itself on its security and hadn't had a break-in in years.

"I came in with a delivery man," she told him, answering his unasked question. "We need to talk. What went wrong in Washington?"

"I hired a fucking incompetent," the jogger muttered. "He screwed it up big time. Stuart got away, and I had to do something. Marsten isn't paying the big bucks for nothin'. Anyway, I figure that was the only shot we had at Stuart. We go after him again and someone gets wise. I decided to break the connection somewhere else. So I went after the woman."

"What woman? You didn't tell me about her."

The jogger flopped down on the couch beside her. "She's Steiner's contact in DOE. I figured no one would make the connection between her and Stuart, since she's not on his committee. I set it up to look like a mugging gone bad at an ATM. My boy tells me he can do it, no problem, and I believed him, figuring Stuart just got lucky. Anyway, a rent-a-cop at the ATM got involved and nailed him before he could get the woman. Dropped him on the spot."

"Dead solves a lot of problems," she said.

"Yeah. But Marsten wants results. I guess I got to tell him. He's gonna cut and run, and we're out of it. Shit! That contract was worth at least twenty-five grand, and it's all down the fuckin' tubes."

"Maybe not," Sophia said. She thought for a few moments. The money was too good to walk away. "Tell Marsten what went down with Stuart, but don't tell him about the woman or your idiot getting snuffed by a cop."

"Yeah, but Stuart's still out there."

"Tell Marsten you'll solve the problem, no extra cost."

"Sure. How?"

An idea started to take shape. "We've got some options. Only this time you do it. No screw-ups. Don't tell Marsten how, just that you'll get the job done. The only reason you didn't try Plan B first was because of the time element. You thought he wanted results fast, and you went for the quickest option. Plan B will take more time."

"And if he doesn't buy it?"

Sophia's face turned into a mask. "He'll buy it."

※

Later that same day the jogger timed his arrival so that he drove up just as Marsten left the veterinarian's office. Duke hobbled painfully behind his master, trying to make a good show of it. The jogger parked next to Marsten's Jaguar sedan and got out. "How is he?" the jogger asked, stroking Duke's head.

"Not too good," Marsten answered. "Arthritis of the hip." They stood beside Marsten's car and talked, for all the world two dog owners discussing their common problems. The jogger outlined the situation with Stuart exactly as Sophia had suggested, while Marsten listened, not saying a word. Finally Marsten opened the rear car door for Duke. The two men gently helped the dog climb inside. Marsten walked around to the driver's side. "Don't cock it up this time."

"Thank you, sir," the jogger said. He watched Marsten drive away. "So what the fuck do we do now?" he grumbled to himself.

⁂

At first it was little more than a rumor, something to gossip about on a Monday morning. Slowly fact changed the buzz to truth, and the offices of RayTex Oil vibrated with the news: *Time* magazine was considering Lee Justine Ellis as their Person of the Year. A surge of telephone calls, faxes, and e-mails erupted from the top floors of the Fountain Plaza Building, and within minutes the entire company knew about it.

The wiser pundits who specialized in such things, attributed the honor to the Life Flight when L.J. had saved the boy's life. Of course, Tim Roxford's role in the amazing landing under zero-zero conditions was almost totally forgotten. As far as Marsten's secretary, Mrs. Shugy Jenkins, was concerned, it was a gross perversion of all that was decent and pure. But as usual, she said nothing and hid her true feelings. So when the phone call from the White House came, she directed it to her immediate superior, Lloyd Marsten. And also as usual, he never missed a beat when the president's secretary came on the line.

"Sorry for the delay," Marsten said. He timed his words to perfection as L.J. picked up the phone. "Here she is. She was in the day care center." Certain that that tidbit of information would be relayed to Madeline O'Keith Turner, the forty-fourth president of the United States, he got off the line. Even he couldn't eavesdrop on that conversation. But he could watch L.J.'s face.

"Madam President," L.J. said. She listened for a moment. "I was the copilot. The real hero was Tim Roxford, the pilot." Silence as she listened. "Well, thank you, I'd be honored." Again she paused. "Yes, of course. We'll be there. Thank you, Madam President." She dropped the phone into its cradle.

She turned to Marsten. "I've been invited to the White House for a special presentation next month. A bit unusual, don't you think?"

"Not really," Marsten said. "Politicians love to have their picture taken with celebrities and you're quite famous now. Besides, you're a very visible, not to mention successful, businesswoman. Turner's facing a tough election in two years, and she needs you to help capture the female vote."

"You make it all sound so cynical."

"Politics is the very embodiment of self-interest. Maddy Turner—or any politician, for that matter—will sacrifice you in a moment if that's what it takes to get them reelected. Never forget that."

"So you think I should go and get my stomach patted?"

"Enjoy the moment. But it's also a golden opportunity for the slow roll and to sidetrack some of the environmental legislation Turner's pushing. We do need to buy time."

"There may be a way," L.J. replied. "Let me work on it." They discussed a few other minor matters before she returned to her office. There she sank into the corner of her favorite couch and gazed out the window. From the soft look on her face, a casual observer might think she was daydreaming. But the observer would have been totally wrong. She reached for the phone and buzzed her secretary. "I need a detailed file on President Turner."

The Pentagon
Colonel Priestly's staff filed out of his office, happy to escape the Friday-morning meeting without being loaded down with crash projects designed to make Priestly look good and ruin their weekend. Only Stuart was shaking his head. "Hey, Mike," a fellow lieutenant colonel asked, "how many projects did Ramjet lay on you?"

"Three," Stuart answered. "All due Monday."

"There goes the weekend," the lieutenant colonel consoled. "Better you than me. What did you do to piss him off?"

"Beats me," Stuart said, really knowing the answer.

He trudged down the hall to his office. The voice-mail light on his telephone was flashing at him. The young police detective from Homicide wanted to talk. Stuart closed his eyes and breathed deeply. It had been seventeen days since he'd been mugged and possibly exposed to HIV. His mouth compressed into a tight line. It was time to learn the bad news. He dialed the detective's number. It was answered on the first ring. *What the hell?* he thought. *Bad news always travels fast.*

"Mike Stuart returning your call," he said.

"Mike, good news. The asshole tested negative for HIV. I thought you'd like to know as soon as possible."

For a moment Stuart was speechless as his spirits soared, the heavy burden finally lifted. "Son of a bitch," he finally managed.

The detective laughed. "That he was. Have a nice weekend."

"Indeed I will" was all Stuart could think of saying. Then, "Thanks." He broke the connection and looked at his notes from the staff meeting. The three research projects Priestly had laid on him had nothing to do with his normal duties. The pettiness and unconscionable harassment ate at him. He would be the only person working in the office over the weekend. The anger he felt was so real that he could taste it. "Fuck you, Ramjet," he said out loud. He grabbed his hat and walked briskly down the hall. But to make his point he deliberately stopped at Peggy's desk to sign out. She gave him a quizzical look. "If Colonel Priestly should ask," he said, "tell him I've got an appointment I couldn't put off any longer."

"Nothing serious, I hope."

"Very serious," Stuart replied. Then it all broke through, and he smiled. "Have a nice weekend." With that he was gone.

Peggy watched him leave. "Whatever got into *you*?"

❋

Jane dragged her tired body back to *Temptress*, anxious for a hot shower and a chance to collapse. She was dog-tired after installing a new diesel engine. Still, she felt good at what she had accomplished and the marina's manager was ecstatic at the business she was generating by word of mouth. She stiffened when she saw the unlocked hatch to the companionway. The word "robbery" flashed in her mind. She relaxed when she saw the open padlock. Only she and Stuart had keys. "Mike?" she called.

"I'm in the galley," he answered.

She clambered down the steps and was ambushed by the smell of baking cornbread and simmering chili, her favorite meal. But she'd never told him. "How did you know?"

"I have my sources," he said, handing her a bottle of Dos Equis, the amber-colored Mexican beer she loved.

She collapsed on the settee and took a long pull at the beer. "You certainly know the way to a girl's heart."

"That's the idea."

The look on his face and the tone of his voice told her all she needed to know. "You're playing hooky, right?" she asked. A nod confirmed her guess. "And you're supposed to be working this weekend?" Another nod. "And you've got good news." The last was a statement, not a question. He grinned at her like the Cheshire cat and didn't answer, wanting to savor the moment. She shook her head in mock disgust. "Be that way." She finished her beer and stood up. "I'm the pits. I need to take a shower."

"That's what you get for working for a living. Go ahead. I'll get dinner ready." She squeezed by him, and he concentrated on cooking to give her some privacy. It had never been a problem when they were sailing in the Caribbean, because one of them had always been on deck.

"Mike," she called, "there's no soap. Check the middle drawer next to the sink." He did and found a fresh bar. He knocked on the door, and a hand and bare arm appeared around the edge. He could also see a bare hip and leg that went with it. He blushed and went back to the stove. When she emerged, dinner was ready. While they ate, they talked about the weather and how it was unusually mild for the first of November. When they finished, he washed the dishes. "Well, are you going to tell me now?"

"Let's go sailing," Stuart replied. "I checked the weather and tide. All good to go."

Jane never hesitated. She loved to sail at night and was out of the companionway and had the sail cover half off before Stuart could come on deck. They moved together like dancers in perfect unison getting *Temptress* ready, and in less than five minutes Stuart was casting off the bowline. He stepped aboard as Jane backed the big boat into the main channel. They idled out of the marina, and as soon as they were clear, Jane headed up into the wind and set the autopilot. Together they raised the mainsail. Jane was back at the helm and spun the wheel to fall off the wind. The sail snapped once, starting to draw, and Stuart unfurled the jib. Jane shut off the diesel, and *Temptress* was in her element, free of the land and all that went with it. Only the natural sounds of the boat working the wind and rushing water broke the silence as they ghosted down the channel in the growing darkness. Ahead of them the moon rose in the east and sent a ribbon of light across the water.

Stuart breathed deeply and was at peace with himself and the world. "It's cold," he finally said. "I'll get your jacket."

"Just a sweater," she called as he disappeared into the cabin. He was back in a moment and took the wheel while she pulled the heavy sweater over her head. She relaxed into the wide seat beside the steering pedestal and savored the moment. The lights along the shore twinkled at them as the cares of the world disappeared into the darkness.

"Almost enough to make you philosophical," Stuart said in a low voice, matching her mood perfectly. Then, "The police called. The tests came back. All negative."

"Thank God," she whispered reaching out for him. Their hands touched as she came to her feet. "I know you were worried about . . ." Her words trailed off. He nodded. Then she was in his arms, her face buried against his chest. "Oh, Mike, I was so worried."

"That's all behind—" He cut his words off in midsentence. He had almost said "us."

"Behind us?" she asked, completing his thought.

"Behind us," he agreed. She lifted her head and kissed him. For a moment they sat there as the moon rose higher in the sky, not saying a word. "Let's go sailing," he finally said.

"Sail hell," she murmured. "I know a great place where we can anchor."

Dallas

The wind was blowing when L.J. came out of church the first Sunday morning of November. She shook hands with the minister and, as expected, he was a shade more effusive with his richest, and now most famous, parishioner. "I understand you've been invited to the White House," he said.

"The president called Monday," L.J. replied. "I was quite surprised."

The minister nodded. In Dallas it was common knowledge that L.J. Ellis and Madeline O'Keith Turner were on opposite sides of the political spectrum. "I know how you feel about her politics," he said. "But she is a good woman."

Now it was L.J.'s turn to nod. She said good-bye and looked for the assistant minister's young wife. She found her in the social hall serving coffee and cake to the Senior Gleaners, the most active group in the church. Under the guidance of the young woman they had accomplished near miracles in providing food and clothing to needy families in the

Dallas–Fort Worth area. L.J. waited patiently until she was finished. "How's everything?" L.J. asked.

"There's a young single mother who's found a decent-paying job but needs a car to get to work. A good car will cost around eight thousand dollars. I know it sounds like a lot, but with reliable transportation she can make it on her own."

"Anything else?"

"There's a teenage boy, he's brilliant but has a terrible family life. If we could get him into a prep school and into the proper environment . . . well, who knows? It'd be taking a chance." She paused for a moment. "A very big chance."

"Is he worth it?"

"Oh, yes."

"Call me with the details."

The young woman beamed. "You know, you give more than the rest of the congregation combined."

"It's only money."

"But you should get credit. They should know what you're doing."

L.J. shook her head. "It must remain anonymous. That's the one condition I insist on."

"God will bless you."

I doubt it, L.J. told herself. "For some reason," she admitted, "doing it this way makes me feel good. I don't try to understand why." She walked hurriedly to her car, hating the wind, and drove to her office, eager to work. As usual, the lights and heat were on, and someone had made coffee in anticipation of her arrival. *Lloyd*, she thought. Marsten cared for her like a father and had the uncanny ability to be there when she needed him. But for the most part his innate British reserve was always in place, seldom intruding. She kicked off her shoes and curled up on her couch. A pile of folders and binders filled the coffee table in front of her, all devoted to one subject: Madeline O'Keith Turner. She spent the next three hours working her way through the mass of material her staff had compiled. Eventually satisfied she had the measure of the president, she leaned back and dozed, setting her subconscious free.

"Don't you ever go home?" Marsten said from the doorway, waking her.

The question wasn't meant to be answered. Instead she said, "I'm worried."

"About the elephant?"

"Of course. The risks are staggering." She would never reveal all that she was thinking, but occasionally she had to vent her anxiety. Marsten alone could provide a sounding board.

"And so are the rewards," he said.

"If I can pull it off."

He almost asked her how she was gaming it, but that would have been overstepping their unspoken boundaries. He looked at his watch. "I need to check on Duke."

"Is he in pain?" she asked.

"Only a little." He closed her office door as he left.

Do what you must, she thought. *Don't let the poor animal suffer needlessly.* An image of her beloved teddy bear came out of its hidden niche. She had been six years old when the family German shepherd had playfully torn it apart when she had left it in the backyard. Afterward, she could find only about half of the stuffed animal, and her father had taught her a painful lesson: She had to let go of something she loved very much. Together they'd buried the remains of the teddy bear in the flower garden. "This is one of those times," her father told her, "when you don't have a choice." She'd been happy then. But that was before she learned about her father's mistress.

The image of the teddy bear changed into that of John Frobisher, the head of Front Uni. *Why does he remind me of Teddy?* she thought. For a moment she wondered what it would be like to cuddle him. "I don't need a teddy bear at my age," she said aloud. *Where in the grand scheme of things do you fit?* It was the same question she had asked about Mike Stuart. But unlike Stuart, John Frobisher was a variable she could control. She closed her eyes and dozed, putting her subconscious back to work.

Newport News, Virginia

Jenny and Grant were waiting for Stuart outside his parents' home when he arrived. As usual, his mother was avoiding Jenny and nowhere to be seen. But the moment Martha saw Jane climb out of the Explorer, she came out of the house to meet them. Eric was right behind her, and he ran up to Jane. He skidded to a stop, not sure what to say.

Jane took his left hand and examined it. "I think you're big enough," she said.

"Big enough for what?" Eric replied.

"To learn to play the guitar."

Eric was interested. "You can play the guitar?"

"A little."

Jenny was anxious to leave and had Grant transfer their baggage to the Explorer while she and Stuart exchanged keys and paperwork. "Eric!" she called, "come say good-bye to Mother." Her son came over and gave her a perfunctory kiss on the cheek before running back to Jane. Jenny gave Jane a quick look and then dismissed her out of hand. All she saw was a short, stocky woman who dressed like a refugee from the Salvation Army.

Grant slipped behind the wheel of the Explorer. "Nice wheels, man," he said to Stuart. Jenny climbed into the passenger seat, and then they were gone.

"Good riddance," Martha said in a low voice.

Shanker walked around Jenny's old car and lifted the hood. He started the engine and listened for a few moments. "This thing is a wreck," he announced. He gave Stuart a hard look. "When are you going to stop letting her run over you?"

"Exactly what am I supposed to do?" Stuart asked.

"When all else fails, select guns," Shanker answered.

Stuart eyed his father sadly. "One of your truisms?"

"It worked when I was flying fighters."

"Sorry," Jane said, "I don't understand." She was back in her four-word-or-less mode of communication.

Shanker studied her for a moment. "In combat the cannon on a fighter, which we call 'guns,' is used for close-in fighting. It's a fearsome weapon and gets their undivided attention. With a little luck you hose 'em out of the sky or your wingman nails 'em." He didn't wait for her to reply and slammed the hood of the car down. "I'll get Chalky and we'll work on this piece of shit. You all go eat lunch."

"I'll help you," Jane said.

"Can I help, too?" Eric asked.

"You bet," Shanker said, glad that at least part of his family had their priorities in the right place.

"You can all work on it after lunch," Martha said, taking charge.

"Sounds like a plan," Shanker grunted, deferring to higher authority.

❄

After dinner Martha herded her family and two guests into the family room to light the first fire of the season in the fireplace. Jane sat next to Wing Commander Robin Seagrave while Shanker taught Eric how to start a fire. "Why the name Chalky?" Jane asked.

"Didn't have much choice in the matter," Seagrave told her. "Hair turned gray in my twenties. If you're in the RAF and have white hair, your name is Chalky. Full stop."

"Full stop?" Eric asked. "What does that mean?"

"It means period," Stuart said. "Like at the end of a sentence." He smiled at his son. "Which you're getting better at."

"Actually," Shanker said, ragging on the Englishman, "Chalky has a fear of flying. That's why the gray hair."

"Listen to the man," Seagrave said, enjoying the good-natured rivalry. "This from the only bloke I know who had a fear-factor gauge installed in his aircraft."

Satisfied that the fire was going well, Eric disappeared. He was back a few minutes later carrying a guitar, still dusty from being in the attic. "That's Maggot's," Shanker said. "Haven't seen it in years."

"About the last time you saw a runway," Seagrave added.

"At least it didn't have any crackpots sitting on it."

"Boys," Martha called, signaling a truce.

Eric handed the guitar to Jane and sat down on the floor beside her. Martha went into the kitchen to get a dust cloth, while Jane tuned the instrument. She took the cloth from Martha and lovingly polished the guitar, making it glow in the firelight. She strummed a few cords and retuned two strings. "I like sea chanteys," she said, starting to sing.

> *What shall we do with a drunken sailor?*
> *What shall we do with a drunken sailor?*
> *What shall we do with a drunken sailor?*
> *Ur-lie in the morning.*

When she had them all singing the chorus, she made up a verse.

Put him in a jet plane, make him a pilot
Put him in a jet plane, make him a pilot
Put him in a jet plane, make him a pilot
Ur-lie in the morning.

The room rocked with laughter. Then she sang "The Sloop John B.," and they heard a soft lament in her voice. Eric asked her to play the chorus again, and in a few moments they were singing. When they finished, she tuned another string, looking into the fire. The golden light framed her face.

"You're beautiful," Eric whispered.

She gave him a sweet smile and started to play an old ballad. Her voice changed, turning soft and pure, and magic captured the room.

The water is wide, I cannot cross o'er,
Nor do I have the wings to fly.
Get me a boat that will carry two,
And both will row, my true love and I.

The phone rang, breaking the spell. Martha answered and handed it to Stuart. Then she sat beside her husband. "Did you see that?" she said in a low voice.

"See what?" Shanker muttered.

"She was singing to Mike." She looked directly at Stuart as he talked on the phone.

"Don't be stupid, woman, she's got too much sense for that."

Stuart dropped the phone and looked at them. "That was the Virginia state police. Jenny's been in an accident." He held out a hand to Eric.

Eric stared at his father, his words barely audible. "Is she . . ." Martha stood and took a step toward her grandson. But Eric turned and found refuge in Jane's waiting arms.

Stuart cursed himself for handling it all wrong. "She's hurt, but she'll be okay," he said. "She's in the hospital."

11

The White House

A young man wearing a dark suit was waiting when the black Cadillac pulled to a stop at the entrance to the West Wing of the White House. He opened the rear door and extended a hand to help L.J. emerge. He immediately caught his breath as every camera and eye focused on her. "Ms. Ellis, this way please." He motioned her into the West Wing as he walked beside her. Tim Roxford climbed out of the Cadillac and trailed along in their wake, completely overshadowed by L.J.

She was wearing a bright red business suit with matching snakeskin pumps. The hemline to her skirt was short, but not too short. The coat snared in at her narrow waist and molded to her body, yet neither the skirt nor coat could be said to be too tight. The way her gold scarf crossed and hid her cleavage hinted that she was not wearing a blouse underneath. In short, the suit had been designed to showcase her figure, leave reporters searching their vocabularies for superlatives, women envious, and men gasping for breath.

A woman reporter who had once been considered for the "Ten Best-Dressed Women in the Capitol" wrote, "Her bright red ensemble is a throwback to the days of Nancy Reagan and best described as the new business chic, part Hollywood, part Paris, and all Texas."

Another veteran White House reporter saw it differently when he said, "Not since the Kennedys has glamour burst on the White House in such abundance."

In his corner office in the West Wing, Patrick Flannery Shaw watched L.J.'s arrival on the security monitor. Officially Shaw was listed as a special assistant to the president, although no one knew exactly what he did. Unofficially he was part mentor, part strategist, part political adviser, all pit bull, and the implacable enemy of anyone who opposed the president. He heaved his bulk out of his chair and shambled down the hall, heading for the Oval Office. He arrived in time for the introductions. He crossed his arms and leaned against a back wall, watching every move L.J. made as she talked to Maddy. Only one thing puzzled him: Why had L.J. brought the pilot along? He worked that problem as the two women chatted amiably. He finally decided Tim Roxford was there as a counterpoint to draw the attention of women away from L.J. and the president. *Very clever,* he thought.

Like the president, the four men in the room were wearing dark, very conservative suits. As a result L.J. glittered like a bright jewel, the only point of light against a dark background. *I know what you're doing,* Shaw told himself. He listened carefully as the two women talked.

"My staff," the president said, "tells me you're active in a variety of causes."

"It amazes me," L.J. said, "how I get drawn in. Sometimes I seem to be working against myself."

"How so?" Maddy Turner asked, sipping at her tea.

"Well, I'm active in the women's movement and support certain environmental issues." She gave Turner a knowing look. "Of course, some are a total anathema to my business, so I avoid those. But I do try to explain our position."

"I take it," Turner said, "that you've heard about my Task Force on the Environment."

"A good friend, Ann Silton, mentioned it to me."

Turner looked surprised. "You know Ann?"

"I met her when she organized the Front Uni convention in Dallas. We hit it off immediately."

"Surely you don't agree with everything she believes."

L.J. sipped her tea, carefully considering her reply. "Of course not. But I do trust her."

Shaw's eyes narrowed. *So you want Silton to head up the task force. Why?* He made a mental note to follow up on it.

There was a slight break as the photographers came in for the photo opportunity and to memorialize the visit. Shaw listened as two women reporters picked L.J. apart. "Look at that spider brooch on her left lapel. I've never seen anything like it."

"Is it a Paloma Picasso?" the other reporter asked.

"I don't think so. But it's exquisite."

Shaw studied the brooch in question. It was a golden spider with long legs. Two diamonds made up its small hourglass body, and the way it perched on her red jacket made it seem almost real. *She's sending a message*, Shaw told himself.

"She's upstaging Maddy," the first woman said.

"No one can upstage her," the second replied.

Wanna bet? Shaw thought. He mentally moved L.J. onto his enemies list.

Shaw waited patiently while Maddy presented presidential plaques for heroism to L.J. and Roxford. Then he followed them back down the hall to the entrance. The black Cadillac was waiting, and the same aide who had met L.J. held the door for her and Roxford. Shaw ambled back to the Oval Office, looking like a bear wearing a rumpled suit. He went right in, not waiting to be announced.

"Well, Patrick," the president asked, "why the sudden interest?"

"The woman's dangerous," he said. "Watch your backside."

The president laughed. "Whatever gave you that idea?"

"The way she was dressed, Madam President." He felt the need to repeat the warning. "The way she was dressed."

"Don't be silly, Patrick. You just don't understand women."

"I understand this one."

The Pentagon

The summons came just after 10:00 A.M. on Wednesday, November 13. At first Stuart was puzzled why the OSI, the Air Force's Office of Special Investigations, would want to talk to him. Later the time and date would be etched in his memory. He told Peggy Redman he had to go to Andrews Air Force Base for the interview and hurried to catch the shuttle bus that ran between the Pentagon and the base.

At Andrews, Special Agent Antonia "Toni" Moreno-Mather was waiting for him. She was a petite, very pretty Mexican-American in her late twenties. She was also pregnant. "Colonel Stuart? I'm Special Agent Toni Mather. Thank you for coming." She led him into a small interview room, where two men were waiting. "This is Sergeant Ledbetter and Sergeant Smatter from the Arlington Police. They want to talk to you." She sat down next to the door and opened her notebook.

Ledbetter was a big African-American who reminded Stuart of a professional football linesman, and Stuart half expected to see a Super Bowl ring on one of his massive fingers. Instead he wore a wedding ring on one hand and a West Point class ring on the other. "Colonel Stuart," he began, "we're investigating the accident involving Jennifer May Wilson Stuart and Grant Woodstock DeLorenzo." His voice was deep and gentle. "We do hope your wife will fully recover."

"Former wife," Stuart said. "Jenny and I are divorced." The three investigators scribbled in their notebooks.

"There is some very bad news," Ledbetter continued. "Mr. DeLorenzo died early this morning from complications stemming from the accident."

"I'm sorry to hear that," Stuart said, surprised that he was sorry. "He and Jenny seemed very happy together." A strange look crossed Agent Mather's face.

"Well," Ledbetter said, becoming more businesslike, "I'm sure you understand that our investigation has changed now, and we do have to ask you some questions. All routine. What exactly is your relationship with Mrs. Stuart?"

Stuart tried to explain in as few words as possible how they had separated and divorced. "Then you were not experiencing any special problems?" Ledbetter asked.

"None that I would call special," Stuart answered.

"Yeah, right," Smatter said. Stuart focused on the other sergeant. He was an older, very wiry, small man who reminded Stuart of a weasel. "We've talked to Mrs. Wilson," Smatter said with the hint of a snarl. "Your ex-mother-in-law. Remember her?" Stuart gave a very audible sigh and tried to explain. It was a mistake. "Now, let me see if I got this one right," Smatter replied. "You've got a rich mother-in-law who only wants to help you, give your kid the best education possible, and you don't like it?"

"The price of her help is too high," Stuart said.

"Yeah, right."

"Colonel Stuart," Ledbetter said, his voice offering protection from the caustic Smatter, "when we examined the mishap vehicle, we found some unusual damage to the brakes that we can't explain. We were hoping you could help us."

"Sure," Stuart replied. Anything to get Smatter off his back.

"Can you provide us with all the maintenance records for the vehicle?"

"No problem. I had it serviced just before I turned it over to them."

"Turned it over?" Smatter muttered. "Let me get this straight. You turned your Explorer over to the guy who was boinking your wife so they could go to Colorado and screw their brains out?"

"They were going to start a business," Stuart protested.

"Yeah, right." Smatter made a show of opening his notebook and flipping through the pages. The sound rippled like gunshots in the quiet of the room. "I want to be sure I got this one straight. On Friday, twenty September, at Dover Air Force Base, your father, who goes by the alias Shanker, threatened to hit Barbara Raye Wilson. Is that correct?"

"It didn't happen that way," Stuart said.

"How did it happen?" Ledbetter asked.

"She had a lawyer and was trying to take my son without my permission. She physically pushed my father out of the way, and he said something like he didn't approve of hitting women but if she touched my son, he'd make an exception. Then he got into a big argument with the lawyer."

Smatter snorted. "And your father threatened him also, right?" There was no answer. "Sounds like you come from a pretty violent family."

"That's not true," Stuart said.

"With a name like Shanker? Gimme a break."

Stuart wanted to be reasonable and tried to explain. "It's his nickname from when he was in the Air Force. His buddies, other pilots, gave him the name."

"Yeah, sure."

"That's the way it works," Toni Mather said. She gave Stuart a look that clearly said he was talking too much.

Ledbetter also got the message. "Well, just a few more items and we'll let you get back to work. We need to know where you were, who you saw, talked to, and what you were doing from, say, a week before the accident up through the day after. Why don't you write it all down and give it to Special Agent Mather here? She can send it to us."

"Is that going to be a problem?" Smatter said.

Stuart's head was reeling. "No, I don't think so."

"Yeah, right. Keep Agent Mather informed of your whereabouts at all times, and don't even think about taking any long trips."

"Well," Ledbetter said, no longer sounding so friendly, "that's all we have. For now." He heaved himself to his feet and opened the door. Smatter popped to his feet and followed him out.

Stuart shook his head. "What was that all about?"

Toni Mather studied him for a moment before making a decision. Her investigative experience was different from Ledbetter's and Smatter's, because the vast majority of personnel in the Air Force were not criminals, only people who did stupid things or got involved with the wrong element. "I think it's obvious," she said. "You're under investigation for the murder of your ex-wife's boyfriend."

12

Miami

Sophia watched the jogger as he ran down the beach. His skin was pasty white, but his muscles rippled with the tone of a superb athlete. She raised herself on one elbow and scanned the crowd lounging on the sand. She stood so the jogger could see her and took another look at the palm-tree-lined promenade next to the street. She didn't see any of the trademark signs of surveillance and decided to chance contact. Still, one could never be sure, not in her business. She pulled on a long T-shirt to cover her thong bikini and walked down to the water in time to meet the jogger. She walked past him and murmured, "In front of the coffeehouse on Collins, tonight at eight thirty-five." He kept on running.

At exactly 8:35 that evening Sophia slowed as she passed the coffeehouse, ready to drive on by. But the jogger was walking toward the curb, the signal that he was clear. She coasted to a near stop and he slid into the front seat beside her. To be on the safe side she leaned over and kissed him. To the unknowing bystander it was either a girlfriend picking up her boyfriend for a little impromptu boffing or a clandestine rendezvous with adultery the prime objective. Both were considered entirely proper forms of recreation on Collins Avenue.

She accelerated into the heavy traffic and reached under the dash to activate the noise scrambler. A low hum filled the car. "This had better be good," he said.

"We've gone critical."

"With our friends the Puerto Rican loonies?"

"They want to believe my cover since I've been so 'helpful.' But they want to verify. It's time for the big test."

"To make your bones," he said. It wasn't a question. "What do they want you to do?" He knew it had to be serious, or she wouldn't have called for an urgent face-to-face meeting.

"They want me to sanction an informant."

"That's it," the jogger said. There was no way he would ask her to cross that line in order to penetrate the terrorist cell. "To hell with the money. We're outa there."

"Why?" she asked.

The jogger looked at her in shock. "We don't do that, that's why."

"If the money's right, we do." She let it sink in. "Tell Marsten it's a go for another thirty thousand."

"Shit-oh-dear," the jogger moaned. She slowed to let him out.

"I need a quick confirm," she said.

"Who's the poor bastard?"

"A waiter at Café Martí. They think he's an informant."

"Is he?" She gave a shrug of her shoulders and waited for him to get out. "I'll call you tomorrow," he told her. "No later than noon your time."

❄

At precisely 10:20 P.M. on Friday evening, Luis Barrios walked into Café Martí and sat at the bar. He was careful to pick a seat where he could observe the sidewalk patio. Three minutes later, and on cue, Sophia walked into the café and found a seat on the patio. Luis caught his breath at the dress she was wearing. It was perfect: skimpy enough to stop traffic and cause heart attacks without getting her arrested. As expected, the waiter moved directly to her table.

"*Señorita,*" he murmured. "How may I serve you?"

She answered in Spanish. "I was here in September, and you served me the best coffee."

The waiter lit up like a neon sign. "Yes, I remember. The lady who speaks our language like a native." *She's the one who thought the Puerto Rican scum were Cuban*, he recalled.

She batted her eyelashes at him. "You remember?"

He was all gallant charm. "How could I forget?" They chatted for a few more moments as she set the hook.

She was waiting in a car when he got off work three hours later. He opened the door and started to hyperventilate. She was wearing a sleeveless sweatshirt that left no doubt that was all she had on. "Where?" was all she asked.

He mumbled a few words and directed her to a deserted street behind a warehouse. Within moments his shirt was open and his pants off as he drew her on top of him. She kissed him over and over as he pulled off her sweatshirt and threw it into the backseat. She scooted under him and raised her legs, guiding him into her. He barely felt the pinprick in his left thigh.

※

Luis Barrios was waiting when she let herself into his apartment. "Well?" he asked.

"The coroner will rule it 'sudden death syndrome probably brought on during lovemaking.' While it is quite unusual in such a young man, it is not unheard of. Of course, he could have been saved had a set of defibrillator paddles been readily available."

Luis was incensed, not that she had killed the waiter but that she had betrayed him and the cause by making love to an enemy. "There must have been a better way to do it."

She reached for him. "I wanted to send him out with a bang," she whispered.

13

Shanker was caged rage as he paced the family room. "Damn! I don't believe this. How could the cops think you had anything to do with jimmying the brakes?" He glared at Stuart as if he were personally responsible for coming under suspicion. "Anything mechanical is totally beyond you."

Martha decided it was time to get her husband back in control. "But the police don't know that, do they?" Shanker turned his scowl on her. "Don't go giving me your steely-eyed aerial assassin look." She fixed him with her no-nonsense gaze.

Jane started to smile but squashed it before Shanker noticed. Seagrave caught it. The Englishman felt uneasy being caught up in a family problem, but as Martha and Shanker's houseguest, it was unavoidable. It had been the only topic of discussion since Mike had called late Wednesday night and told them about the police interview with the OSI. But Seagrave decided early on that the more heads involved in sorting out the problem the better. And he did trust Jane. *She's the levelheaded one*, he thought.

Shanker wilted under his wife's look. "How is Jenny?" he muttered, changing the subject.

"She'll make it," Stuart replied. "She's going to need reconstructive surgery on her face, and Barbara Raye's already lined up one of the best plastic surgeons in New York. But Jenny's got to recover from the accident first."

"Well, William," Martha said to Shanker. She couldn't solve Stuart's problem, but she expected her husband to get involved and do something.

"Okay, we know you didn't do it," Shanker said, "but the police think you did."

"Don't they always look at the husband or boyfriend first?" Jane asked.

Seagrave threw in his two cents. "So you need to get them moving on."

"How do we do that?" Stuart asked.

Shanker paced the floor. "Never forget rule number one."

"Sorry," Jane said, "you lost me." Four words or less again.

"In the fighter business," Seagrave explained, "rule number one is *always* check your six-o'clock position."

"The guy who shot you down was the guy you didn't see," Shanker added.

"Another rule?" Stuart said, not seeing the sense in all the talk.

"Damn right," Shanker shot back.

Stuart's head came up as paranoia shot through him. "What if someone *is* out to get me?" Silence all around as he played with the idea. "Look what happened to me on the way home from work—twice."

"There are better neighborhoods to live in," his mother allowed.

"It's getting better all the time," Stuart replied. "Then Jenny is in an accident driving my car when the brakes fail, and Grant is killed. Tell me it's all coincidence."

"Why would anyone be out to get you?" Jane asked.

Shanker snorted. "Barbara Raye. I wouldn't put anything past that woman."

"But she wouldn't hurt her own daughter," Martha said.

"She didn't intend to," Shanker said. "The accident was intended for Mike."

"It does make sense," Seagrave said. He looked at Stuart. "So who's your wingman in all this?"

"He means who can help you?" Shanker explained.

Stuart shook his head in misery. He had never felt so alone and vulnerable. An image formed at the back of his mind. At first it was indistinct, hidden in a gossamer haze. Then Toni Moreno-Mather emerged. "The OSI agent I told you about."

"You'll need to give her something to work with," Seagrave said.

"Like Barbara Raye's head," Shanker growled.

Andrews Air Force Base, Maryland

Special Agent Toni Mather shifted her weight in the chair, trying to get comfortable. Stuart recognized the symptoms and smiled at her. "Jenny used to say that husbands should have to wear twenty-pound weights around their middle when their wives are expecting."

"What a great idea." Toni paused and groaned. "Ooh! Four more months and he's already kicking field goals."

"Then you know it's a boy?"

"Not really. But only a boy could kick like that." She scanned her notes. They'd been talking for over an hour, and she needed to go to the restroom. But they were almost finished. She frowned as a loose end caught her attention. Was there a connection between the assault on Stuart and the second victim at the ATM who had screamed and fought back? While Toni believed in coincidence, that would have been one too many. "I need the name of the detective you spoke to about the mugger," she said. Stuart gave her the name, and she wrote it down. "Okay, that's it for now. If you think of anything else, give me a call."

"Will do," he said, standing up. "And thanks for listening to me."

When he'd left, Toni called the detective, and they spoke briefly. She jotted down the name Jean McCormick. Then she heaved herself to her feet and walked slowly to the restroom, still trying to put it all in perspective. Was he merely having a run of bad luck? It did happen. And why would anyone be out to get him? The exercise felt good, and she took a little walk on the way back, still playing with the angles, trying to see a pattern. She made a decision. She would go to her commander and get his take. But first she'd talk to Stuart's boss, one Colonel Roger Priestly.

The Pentagon

Priestly glanced at the photo on the ID card and then back to Toni. Her hair was much shorter, but it was the same person. He suppressed a mental groan. He was totally against pregnant women serving on active duty, but it was career suicide to suggest that motherhood and the profession of arms were mutually exclusive. "What can I do for you, Agent Mather?" He waved her to a seat. "Would you like some coffee or tea?"

"No thanks," she replied, taking out her notebook. "As you probably know, Lieutenant Colonel Michael Stuart has been experiencing problems lately that have come to our attention. I was wondering about his job performance and if there's a connection."

Ramjet put on his concerned look. "I am aware of his problems and deeply worried. Frankly, I think it's a combination of personal problems at home, and . . . well, I hate to say this, but careerwise he's a failure." He looked pained as Toni jotted down notes. When she didn't respond, he felt that an explanation was called for. "Stuart is not a team player and is oblivious to the rules." He sighed. "If he remains under investigation, I may have to act. I'm sure you understand my position."

A little jerk of her head answered him. "How did you learn that the police were investigating him?"

Ramjet looked thoughtful. "I, ah, don't recall. Did my secretary tell me? Sorry, I just don't remember."

Without commenting, she made another note. She thought for a moment. "Colonel Stuart said he told you he was interviewed by the police in my presence"—she made a show of checking her notes—"on last Wednesday, November thirteenth." She looked at him expectantly. "Five days ago."

"I, ah . . . why, yes, I believe you're correct. He did tell me. I don't remember when." Ramjet was beginning to feel uncomfortable. "I've been very busy lately."

"The burdens of command," Toni replied.

He breathed in relief. She did understand. "Exactly."

Toni asked a few more perfunctory questions and thanked him for his time. She wrote down "Lying asshole" before she closed her notebook and left.

Priestly's fingers beat a relentless tattoo on his desk as a deep frown crossed his face. Slowly his face relaxed into a pleasant expression. It was time to trash Stuart, and he knew exactly how to do it.

Washington, D.C.

It was dark when Stuart unlocked his garage and raised the heavy wooden door. "Be careful where you step," Jane said. He walked gingerly over the floor and slid behind the wheel of Jenny's car. "Back straight out," she said. "Stay in the same tracks." Stuart did as she said and parked the car in the alley while she turned on the light. "We need a flashlight," she called. He rummaged under the seat and found the flashlight he had stowed there.

"What are you looking for?" he asked.

"I'm not sure," she replied. She squatted down and studied the floor. Like everything in Stuart's life, the garage was clean and tidy as a pin. "Is that oil all from Jenny's car?"

"I'll clean it up," he said.

"No. Don't." Her eyes squinted as she concentrated. "There," she said, pointing to a spot in the center of the floor. "And over there," now pointing to an area where the right front wheel would have been.

"I don't see anything," he said.

She took three careful steps into the garage, picked something off the floor, and then backed out in her same footprints. "Look," she said, showing him a small, oil-covered gray lump. She wiped it clean.

"What the hell is it?"

She rolled it in her fingers. "Ouch." She held it in the flashlight's beam and touched a silver spur stuck in the side. "A metal sliver," she said. She studied it. "I think it's a fiberglass patching material, like Bondo."

"I've never used Bondo in my life," he said. "What's it doing here?"

"Good question. Where does your landlady live?" Stuart pointed to the main apartment of the converted building. Jane walked quickly up the back steps and knocked at the door. A woman in her late seventies cracked open the door and peered out.

"Mrs. Witherspoon," Stuart said, "this is Jane Ryan, a friend of mine."

"Ma'am," Jane said, "has anyone been in Mike's garage lately—when he's been at work?"

The old woman thought for a moment. "A man from the gas company was here about a gas leak. He said he had to look in the garage. That's where he found the leak. Such a nice young man. He fixed it for free, you know. Spoke with a Texas accent. And in good shape physically. Said he jogged."

"Do you remember when he was here?" Jane asked.

"Two weeks ago, something like that."

Jane and Stuart exchanged looks. "That was before the accident," Jane said. Stuart thanked the old lady as Jane went back to lock the garage.

"You can't leave your car in the alley," Mrs. Witherspoon said.

"Don't worry," Jane called. "We won't."

Stuart got into the car and waited for Jane to join him. "What now?"

"Give this to the OSI," Jane said, "and tell them about the gas man." She handed him the chip of Bondo. "And don't go in the garage."

Dallas

Marsten's lips compressed in consternation when he saw the news item on his computer. He hit the print button and buzzed his secretary. "Is Miss Ellis in?"

"I'm afraid not," Shugy replied. "She returned from Washington quite late yesterday evening."

A finger hit the speed dial on the phone console as he rang L.J.'s home. She answered on the fourth ring. "Good morning, Lloyd. What a lovely day."

He recognized the tone immediately. The trip to Washington had been a roaring success, and she was on top of the world, happy and content. "You're taking a leisurely bath, yes?"

"How did you know?"

"A lucky guess." Marsten didn't bother to analyze what was going on inside L.J. She was far too complex for that. He accepted her for what she was: a force of nature who could switch from pirate to saint with the speed of lightning. And when she was happy, she lit up his sky. He hated bringing her bad news and changing all that. "We do need to talk," he said. It was his code for "We have a problem."

A little sigh. "I did want to go shopping this morning. Can it wait?"

He didn't want to ruin her day, but it was urgent. "This afternoon?" he asked. She agreed.

"Until then," he said, hanging up. He drummed his fingers on his desk as he stared at the photo attached to the news clip. He was a very worried man.

Marsten handed L.J. the news clip and the photo he had taken off the Internet. She glanced at it and read part of the caption. " 'The murder victim was a known informant rumored to be working for the FBI.' " She looked puzzled. "How can an informant be 'known' and 'rumored' at the same time? Is this important?"

"We may be involved," Marsten told her.

She arched an eyebrow. "How?"

He sat down on her couch and crossed his legs. "One of my people has successfully penetrated the group who blew up RTX. But our man hasn't gained full acceptance, and this may be the way he proved himself." He hated to lie to her, but it was necessary if he was to build a fence around what he was doing to protect her and RayTex.

The look on L.J.'s face was reassuring. He had not ruined her day, and she knew he was not telling her the whole truth.

"But you're not sure," she said.

"It's a possibility, and the timing is right. We may want to become uninvolved. The sooner the better."

"Why? Especially after going to all this trouble."

Marsten became very alert. Something was on the boil behind her pretty face. But what? He cut to the heart of the matter. "Is there something I need to know?"

L.J. sat next to him and patted his hand. "Poor Lloyd. You have to take so much on faith." She smiled at the sad look on his face. Marsten had given his soul to her years ago, and he was her man, regardless of what she did or where she took them. "We may have need of them once we start drilling for the elephant."

He tried not to sound confused. "For what purpose?"

She suppressed a laugh at his look of total bewilderment. She was really enjoying herself. "To blow up the drilling rig. Of course, there would be plenty of warning to evacuate so no one would be hurt or killed."

"Why would we want to do that?"

"What did the fiasco at Mukluk teach the industry?" she asked.

Marsten had no trouble following her sudden shifts. He thought for a moment, recalling the time he'd been involved in constructing the gravel island on Alaska's North Slope for the drilling rig. "Mukluk had a perfect seismic profile, and it still turned out to be a two-billion-dollar dry hole." His voice grew low. "As for lessons learned, you certainly don't want to shout before you've got it, and it has made the industry very cautious about costly joint ventures."

"So how many companies would be willing to share the risk with us?"

Now Marsten was at his best. "Given the political implications and the fact we're dealing with an unproven technique, I'd say no one."

"So we have to go it alone," L.J. said, "and if we repeat the Mukluk experience?"

"It will most likely bankrupt us."

"Unless what?" she asked.

"Unless," Marsten said, "a disaster interrupts drilling and our insurance underwriters have to pay off."

"Of course, insurance won't cover all of our losses," she said.

"But it would be enough to stem the tide of bankruptcy," Marsten added.

She made another sudden jump. "Have you ever been to Cuba?"

"No. By the way, are you improvising on this?"

She smiled. "Not at all."

✳

Later that same day Ann Silton telephoned L.J. with the news. "Have you heard?" she gushed. She didn't wait for an answer. "The president appointed me to head the Task Force on the Environment! Can you believe it?"

"Congratulations," L.J. replied. "But I'm not surprised. You certainly deserve it."

"I heard what you said to the president. I can't thank you enough."

"All I said was that I trusted you. Which I do."

"Oh, L.J., there's so much I need to learn and don't know. I've got to move to Washington, and I need a new wardrobe and, and—oh, the butterflies!"

L.J.'s laugh rang like summer, full of warmth and promise. "Tim, my pilot, is in St. Louis picking up an airplane. Why don't you catch a ride back with him? I know just the thing to cure the butterflies. A little shopping!"

"Can I bring Clarissa?"

L.J.'s voice turned sad. "Maybe that wouldn't be a good idea, not now." They talked for a few more moments arranging the flight. After hanging up, L.J. thought for a bit. Then she dialed another number.

"Clarissa," L.J. said, "we need to talk about Ann."

❋

L.J. was waiting with a black Lincoln Town Car when the Sabreliner taxied into the chocks at Love Field. The sleek corporate jet seemed small compared to the other jets lined up like princesses awaiting the proper escort to a royal ball. But the Sabreliner glistened with care, and its noisy engines spoke with a lusty impertinence. In a not-so-subtle way the Sabreliner was a perfect reflection of L.J. and RayTex Oil. Her company was labeled a maverick and, thanks to L.J., was considered lean, mean, and highly maneuverable. In the oil industry L.J. and RayTex got things done, just like the Sabreliner.

The entrance door flopped open, and Tim Roxford climbed out to help Ann Silton down the steps. He smiled when L.J. gave her a hug. "You look wonderful," L.J. said. She guided Ann to the waiting car. "We have so much to talk about."

The ride into town was all part of the plan. "There are some wonderful boutiques here that you'll just love," L.J. assured her.

"I don't think I can afford them," Ann said.

L.J. laughed. "Who can? I've got a special arrangement with one in particular, and I get a big discount. Figure one-fourth of what you see on the price tag. But for heaven's sake, don't tell anyone." They giggled like conspirators while L.J. opened a bottle of pink champagne. "This is considered very gauche, but I just love it. Here's to shopping." They toasted the venture and plotted what clothes Ann would need in Washington.

The older woman waiting for them, Elana LaBou, was anything but a normal fashion consultant. Not only was Elana beautiful and elegant, she had a rare sense of style that could find gold on a Kmart clothes rack.

Even more, she was a kind person who liked her customers, as long as they were also kind and polite. More than one Dallas matron, thinking money was the common denominator that gave her the right to be a bitch, had found Elana's services unavailable to her. One customer had threatened to buy the store just to fire Elana. But any thoughts of revenge died when she learned what it would cost to buy out Elana's contract.

"Miss Ellis," Elana said, genuinely glad to see her. "And you must be Miss Silton." She extended her hand in friendship. They shook hands and sat down.

"Elana, I wish you'd call me L.J. like everyone else."

Elana gave her a lovely smile in return. "My mother would die a thousand deaths of embarrassment if I presumed," she said. She turned to business. "Well, Miss Silton, I think we have some little things that may work."

"Trust her," L.J. said, leaning back to enjoy the experience. The first model stepped out wearing a business suit, and Ann gasped. The model was her exact size with the same coloring and hair length.

❋

Ann gazed out the restaurant's window high above the Fort Worth skyline as they ate lunch at the Riata. "I still can't believe the prices," she said.

L.J. looked around to be sure they weren't overheard. "I told Elana what you could afford. Everything you bought came off her back racks." She dropped her voice conspiratorially. "I imagine most of them are returns. You'd be surprised how many women, even very rich ones, buy a dress for a special occasion, wear it once, and then return it afterward for a refund."

"And Elana lets them get away with it?"

"She lets them think they get away with it. They end up paying in other ways. We benefit because Elana refuses to sell returns as new and gives her friends discounts. That's why all the labels are gone. Elana is such a dear."

"I hadn't noticed about the labels."

L.J. reached across the table and touched her hand. "Ann, I can't tell you how much I enjoyed today, but I'm afraid we can't do it again." Ann looked at her in shock. "Once you're officially appointed to head the task force," L.J. continued, "you'll have to be very careful about who you associate with. Many of your old friends, like Clarissa and me, are politically unacceptable. Your enemies will say we're influencing you."

"But I don't have any enemies—" She stopped, her mouth open. "The videotape."

L.J. nodded sadly. "I don't think you have to worry about that. Anyway, I hope I've taken care of it. But that doesn't mean the bastards won't try again. You must be careful."

"What did you do?"

"Don't ask," L.J. replied. Their hands joined for a moment. "We can still be friends, but for now it'll have to be at a distance. Don't be afraid to make decisions that will be unpopular. Above all else, do the right thing. I'll be disappointed if you don't. Whatever you do, don't sell out to anyone. And that includes me."

Ann's eye's glistened with tears. "You're the best friend I could possibly ask for."

L.J. had her friend at court.

14

Dallas

L.J. was in her office talking on the telephone when Marsten joined her. She mouthed the name "Elana" to indicate the caller. "I know. The change is astounding. Ann is so grateful for what you did." She listened for a few moments. "Please, this must remain between you and me. She has no idea what it really cost." Another pause. "Just charge my account with the difference." L.J.'s face lit up with pleasure. "Elana, I can't thank you enough. It was a very sweet thing you did for a very special person." She broke the connection.

"What exactly did you do?" Marsten asked.

"I told Elana to charge Ann only fifteen percent of the price, and I picked up the balance."

"Poor Miss Silton," Marsten said. "First the videotape, now accepting gifts. I take it you'll burn her if you have to."

L.J. sighed. "I don't want to. But the stakes are so high."

"I'm under the impression," Marsten said, "that you like the woman."

"I do," L.J. confessed. "She's a bright and kind person who cares about people and doing the right thing. I know it's a new world, and Ray-Tex has to change. That's not a problem, as long as we're allowed to do so in a reasonable manner. But I will not allow them to do to us what they did to the tobacco companies." She took a deep breath as Marsten smiled gently at her. "I'm preaching to the choir again, aren't I?" He nodded, still smiling. "Well, then," she said, changing the subject, "is your trip all arranged?"

"I leave tomorrow," he replied, "and arrive in Havana Friday afternoon. I should be back next Wednesday. Entering Cuba is no problem, since I travel under a British passport."

"I thought you were a naturalized U.S. citizen."

"I am. I maintain dual citizenship. In this case, I leave the U.S. with my American passport and then travel to Cuba under my British passport. All very legal." He filled in the details. "I'm entering Cuba through Cancún, Mexico, with all the American tourists who think they're being so wicked." He shook his head. "How naïve. Don't they know the CIA tracks Americans going in?"

"Probably not," she replied. "Americans don't really understand heads-on-heads intelligence. Just stick to your cover story that you're on the Hemingway trail."

"Which is true," Marsten said. He was a Hemingway collector and had a library of first editions and memorabilia. "I've always wanted to visit his home and old haunts."

"Where are you staying in Havana?"

"In a *pensión* that caters to the more affluent tourist. ARA will arrange contact." He looked worried. "There is always the possibility that . . ." He didn't finish the sentence, as the memory of Eritrea loomed large. He forced his fears back into their walled niches. "ARA assures me they're the legitimate article."

"I don't think we're being set up," L.J. assured him. "If anything goes wrong, I'll come and get you."

He knew she would. "Take care of Duke while I'm gone."

"I will," she promised.

＊

The phone call from John Frobisher came late that afternoon. The image of the teddy bear was back as he explained how he was in town on business and was wondering if she was free to discuss an important issue that had come up. At first L.J. pleaded that her schedule was full for the day. Then he said that Ann Silton had offered him a job as her vice chairman on the president's task force on the environment. "I'm awfully busy right now," she said, "but if you're free this evening, why don't we meet for dinner?" He agreed, and she asked, "Where are you staying?" He mentioned a hotel in Fort Worth. "The Petroleum Club, say, seven tonight?" She gave him directions before hanging up.

She immediately dialed another number. "Elana, I need something new for dinner at the Petroleum Club tonight." She laughed at Elana's response. "Yes, it's for a man. What's he like? Well, he reminds me of a teddy bear I loved as a child." She paused, deciding what more Elana needed to know. "He's very well connected politically." Again she laughed at Elana's reply. "No, I don't think I'm interested in him romantically."

L.J.'s eyes opened wide when Elana suggested a dress-and-coat ensemble she had bought over a year ago. "Are you sure?" she asked. Elana assured her it was the right dress if she wanted to keep "all" her options open and make a statement.

❊

The elevator stopped at the fortieth floor of the Union Pacific Resources Building. The doors opened silently, and L.J. stepped out. She glanced around and saw Frobisher standing by the big window overlooking downtown Fort Worth. The club was sending the message she wanted—exclusivity and influence. But everything was in balance: secure and established, yet mainstream and in touch with their world of power and decision.

She walked toward him, certain that he saw her in the reflection from the glass. Frobisher turned and for a moment was speechless. Her dress was a simple, low-cut chemise that reached almost to her knees. He wasn't sure what color it was, as it changed color with the light, turning from a dark, very rich brown into a darker shade of golden blue, then back. It was simple, demure, and yet incredibly sexy. Only the matching dress-length coat fashioned of the same material made it acceptable for the more conservative members of the club.

"Impressive," Frobisher murmured. They shook hands.

"I thought you'd like it," L.J. said, fully aware that he was paying both her and the club a compliment. She looked around. "I like it because the decor is so, well . . . old-fashioned. I'm not sure if it's Regency or Empire."

Frobisher gave her his best grin. "It looks more like Old Petroleum to me." Their laughter joined as they strolled toward the dining room.

Curtis, the maître d', was waiting for them. "Good evening, Miss Ellis. Mr. Frobisher, I presume." Frobisher nodded, pleased that he was recognized. "The work you did on saving the whales was truly admirable." Frobisher beamed at the compliment.

"Curtis is one smooth-talking devil," L.J. said.

"I hope *that's* a compliment," Curtis replied.

"It most certainly is," she replied.

Curtis escorted them to a corner table set for two and held the chair for L.J. She sat against the wall under an exquisite painting of a French château, while Frobisher sat at an angle to the big windows, able to see the panorama of lights below them. Since it was a quiet evening, Curtis had not sat anyone at the table next to them, which offered them some privacy while showcasing L.J. "We have a new hors d'oeuvre you must try," Curtis said. "It's leg of quail, deep-fried with a hollandaise sauce, cilantro, and pink peppercorns."

"That sounds absolutely wicked," L.J. said.

"It had better be, or we'll fire the chef," Curtis replied. He handed Frobisher a wine list and disappeared.

Frobisher studied her for a moment. "I take it you like him."

"Curtis is probably the best maître d' in town," she replied, "and I admire anyone who is very good at his—or her—chosen profession."

The hors d'oeuvres arrived and, as promised, were a rare treat. "Now, that's a finger food," Frobisher allowed.

"Only in Texas," she murmured, sucking her fingers clean.

Curtis caught the message halfway across the room and wondered what it was doing to Frobisher's blood pressure. They fell into an easy conversation while he kept a watchful eye, sending the wine steward or a waiter at the right time. He personally took their orders and urged the chef to give their requests special attention.

The evening was drawing to a close when Frobisher reluctantly turned to business. "I was surprised when Ann called me with the job offer," he told her.

"Ann is a wonderful person, but . . . well, very inexperienced in certain aspects. I think you know what I mean." Frobisher nodded in agreement. "You can fill in her weak spots, and I think you should take the position." She could tell that Frobisher was still undecided. "I honestly doubt if she can do it without you," L.J. said.

"Ann can be very difficult to deal with at times," Frobisher confided. "Especially if she thinks a feminist issue is involved. I'm just not sure if I want to put up with all that."

"Keeping her focused may be where you can help the most." Frobisher was almost convinced. She reached across the table and touched his hand. "Think what you can do. It's an opportunity you can't pass up." She paused to let it sink in. "It's been an enjoyable evening, John, but I've got a busy day ahead of me tomorrow." She gave him a lingering look over her wineglass.

"Thanks for the advice," he replied, "and the wonderful dinner. I was impressed."

That was the idea, L.J. thought. She gracefully rose and led him to the elevator.

Curtis was waiting by the entrance to the dining room and bade them a good evening. He watched them as they waited for the elevator. Then they were gone. The wine steward joined him for a moment. "My God! Did you see what she was wearing?"

"Very hard to miss," Curtis allowed.

"She was certainly sending out the signals."

"Actually, I think she was vamping him," Curtis said.

"Did he fall for it?"

"Oh, yes."

L.J. had her second friend at court.

✳

L.J. dropped her dress on the floor of her dressing room and stared into the mirror. *Why am I doing this?* she moaned to herself. *What's wrong with me?* There was nothing wrong with the image staring back at her. She was wearing no bra and only the briefest of panties. Her breasts were still firm and her stomach flat. She looked over her shoulder and examined her derriere in the mirror. Again, as perfect as it could get. She stepped out of her shoes and sat down. Slowly she removed her stockings. Her legs were smooth and taut. She slipped out of her panties and stood up, still appraising herself in the mirror. *John's a nice guy, likable and cuddly and, maybe, under different circumstances . . . ? So why are you doing this to him?* She knew the answer. The elephant.

She kicked the dress into a pile in the corner. She would never wear it again. She walked into her bedroom and slid under the down comforter. She curled up and for a moment felt like crying. Then she turned out the light and went to sleep.

Andrews Air Force Base

Special Agent Toni Moreno-Mather shifted in her chair. Being pregnant, she could never get truly comfortable. But she had work to do. She flipped through her notes before fixing Stuart with a concerned look. "I turned the Bondo you gave me over to the Arlington police, and they sent it to the forensic lab for analysis. It's from the same batch they found on your Explorer."

"What exactly was it doing there?" Stuart asked.

"Best guess? Whoever sabotaged your brake lines used a light coating to hold everything together. A hard or prolonged application of the brakes would cause the Bondo to let go, the brake fluid to drain out, and the brakes to fail." She checked her notes again. "They also disabled the brake-failure warning light. Sounds like the work of a real pro."

"But why me?" he asked.

"Good question," she replied. "Come on. We're meeting Ledbetter and Smatter at your place."

"Why them?"

She shrugged. "That's the way the system works. They were assigned to your case."

"My case?" he said, feeling sick to his stomach.

She gave him a concerned look. "You are their prime suspect."

Stuart fought the panic that threatened to engulf him. Until this moment he had never really believed he was a suspect, sure that it was all a misunderstanding that would go away. "Do you think I did it?"

"I just go with the evidence," she said. "Where's your car?"

"At home. I rode the Metro to work and took the shuttle bus here."

"Do you mind driving my car?" she asked.

He shook his head and felt better. At least she trusted him to drive. He took that as a good sign. They drove in silence to his apartment, and he parked on the street. Ledbetter and Smatter were waiting for them, and neither looked friendly. When he got out, the panic was back. "Wait a minute," he muttered to Toni. "This is Washington, and they're from Arlington. Do they have jurisdiction here?"

"The accident occurred in Arlington," she said. "The D.C. police were more than happy to waive jurisdiction."

Stuart fought the urge to get back in the car and drive away. But it wasn't his car, he was home, and it was late afternoon. He felt like a condemned man as he led the way down the alley and unlocked the garage. "It's been locked since you found the Bondo?" Ledbetter asked. Stuart nodded and raised the door. "Hold on," Ledbetter said. He reached inside his coat and pulled out a folded paper. "Search warrant" was all he said. "Don't go in."

The panic was back, and Stuart's hands shook as he read the warrant. Since he had never seen one before, he handed it to Toni. She glanced at it, and again the shrug. "All in order." His eyes darted from Ledbetter to Smatter and back again as they methodically searched the garage. Smatter bent over and picked something off the floor and put it into a small plastic evidence bag. He carefully noted the time and location on the bag after sealing it. Again, the skinny detective reminded Stuart of a weasel as he worked. *A very dangerous weasel*, Stuart thought.

He couldn't stand to watch the detectives and went inside to change out of his uniform. After a few minutes he wandered back outside to see if they were finished.

"Well, well," Ledbetter said, carefully holding what looked like a big tube of toothpaste. "What do we have here?" He held the tube up for Toni to see. The label clearly identified it as Bondo. "I'm willing to bet that it matches what we found on the Explorer and the floor." A wicked smile played across his broad face. "With a little luck your fingerprints will be all over it."

Something inside Stuart snapped. "How stupid do you think I am?"

"Plenty," Smatter answered. He looked at Ledbetter, who nodded in reply. "Michael E. Stuart," Smatter said, "you're under arrest for the murder of Grant DeLorenzo. Anything you say—"

Stuart didn't hear him say the rest as he watched Ledbetter pull out his handcuffs. "I don't believe this!" he shouted.

"Believe it," Smatter growled after he finished Mirandizing him.

"Why would I show you all this if I had done it?"

"Because you're a smart-ass," Ledbetter said, snapping the cuffs on his wrists, "and you think we're dumb shits."

"Colonel Stuart," Toni said, her voice firm and commanding, "don't say anything else. You need a lawyer."

The panic was back, claiming Stuart's emotions. "A lawyer! I haven't done anything!" He looked at her, pleading his case. "Do you think I've done anything wrong?"

She didn't answer.

❈

Nothing in Stuart's experience had prepared him for the reality of being booked and charged with a crime—not TV, movies, or novels. Experienced criminals learn, often the hard way, to go with the flow and not buck the opening moves of the lockstep sequence called the criminal justice system. But for the average citizen caught up in the process for the first time, it's a devastating ordeal. All the normal courtesies and freedoms taken for granted are gone, and Stuart was never asked to do a thing. Instead he was pushed, prodded, and propelled through the rigid chain of events as if he were a dumb animal being rendered for meatpacking.

But what upset him the most was the fingerprinting process, when a wisp of a woman with small, bony, and incredibly strong hands took his prints. When she was finished, she handed him a small dry paper towel to clean the ink off his fingers. But without any soap, no amount of rubbing could clean off the ink. His dirty fingers were the stain he shared with the other inmates in the holding cell as he awaited arraignment the next morning.

"Hey, bud," a grossly overweight and shaggy cellmate barked, "whatcha lookin' at?"

For a moment Stuart was sure the challenge was the prelude to the rape that popular wisdom held as the informal part of the process. He held up his fingers. "How do you get your hands clean?" he asked.

"Who gives a shit?" another cellmate asked.

"Shove 'em up your ass and swish 'em around," a voice from a corner said.

The shaggy bear stared at him. "What the fuck you in for? Child molestin'?" A dark rumble worked its way around the cell, and Stuart looked for a guard. Would one come if he yelled for help? The mumbling grew louder when he didn't answer, and his panic was back in full force. "Asshole here has a sweet mouth," the shaggy bear said. "Maybe he'd like being on the receivin' end of some man-boy lovin' for a change."

"Yeah," the voice from the corner said. "Don't like no child molesters 'round here."

"I'm charged with murder!" Stuart blurted. The cell fell quiet, and the bear moved away. Murderers were the aristocrats of the criminal class and accorded a special respect, provided the deceased was a criminally correct victim. Even felons had standards.

"No shit?" the voice from the corner said. "Who'd you shank?"

Stuart sensed the change, and for the first time his anger broke through. "I didn't *shank* anyone."

"Yeah. Right." A righteous denial was expected. "So who was the deceased?"

"My wife's boyfriend."

A low murmur of approval worked its way around the cell. If the victim had been a child, Stuart would have discovered what "cruel and unusual punishment" really meant. "Hey, man," the shaggy bear said, "sometimes a man's gotta do what he's gotta do."

The next big surprise was the food. It was terrible and all but inedible. According to jailhouse wisdom, the cooks worked to make it that way, and anything approaching palatability was immediately fed to stray cats and dogs. Astonishingly, most of the men wolfed it down, claiming they had to keep up their strength.

The booking sergeant had warned Stuart that he would be spending the night in jail until he could appear before a judge for arraignment and bail Friday morning. But Stuart didn't know what a night in jail meant. It was a noisy place, filled with shouts and groans as men wrestled with their subconscious and bad dreams. One man two cells down had a screaming fit that required a medic and four guards to control, and even under heavy sedation he continued to moan and grind his teeth.

Finally it was light, and Stuart waited impatiently for a chance to meet with his lawyer before arraignment. Again the process was impersonal and lockstep. "You just say 'not guilty' when the judge asks how you plead," the lawyer explained. "Otherwise don't say a thing. My job right now is to get you out on bail."

"How much will that be?"

The lawyer thought for a moment. "They'll probably hit you with an open-ended murder charge for now. My best guess, with a little luck, two hundred thousand."

"I don't have that much! I know my folks don't."

"That's why there's bail bondsmen. Figure ten percent."

"Twenty thousand dollars?"

"You want to stay another night in jail? Last night was tame. Wait until tonight. And you don't want to be within ten miles of this place on a Saturday night."

Stuart shook his head and joined the line of suspects being arraigned for various crimes. Two hours later he was in the courtroom awaiting his turn in front of the judge. His heart missed a beat when his lawyer walked in with his father and General Butler. "What's General Butler doing here?" Stuart asked in a low voice. His lawyer didn't answer as the clerk read the charge against him.

"How do you plead?" the judge asked.

"Not guilty," Stuart croaked, sounding anything but innocent.

"Bail?" the judge asked.

"This is a charge of murder," the deputy DA handling the arraignment said. "We believe one million dollars is in order."

Stuart almost fainted. "Your honor," his lawyer said, "Lieutenant Colonel Stuart provided the police with the only evidence possibly linking him to this crime. He has a spotless record and is in the Air Force, currently assigned to the Pentagon. Lieutenant General Franklin Bernard Butler is here to vouch for him."

Butler stood up, but before he could say a word, the judge asked, "You'll vouch for him?"

"Yes, sir," Butler answered. "Colonel Stuart will appear as ordered."

"Bail is set at two hundred and fifty thousand dollars," the judge said. "Next case."

"What happened to the two hundred thousand dollars?" Stuart mumbled as he was led away. His next stop was a holding cell as he waited for his father to make bail. Much to his surprise, that was the most efficient part of the process, largely because he was now dealing with the free-enterprise system and was considered a sure thing to appear. But it was still late afternoon before he was released. Shanker was waiting for him outside.

"Your mother is upset," Shanker said, surprisingly calm. Stuart nodded dumbly, not sure what he would say to her. "Damn," Shanker muttered. "How'd you get into this mess?" Stuart stared at the floor, searching for the right words. "Come on," Shanker said, relenting. "Let's go home for the weekend."

"Can I go to Newport News?"

"Why not? That's the address I gave them, and it is your home of record." He led the way out the double doors and into the hall where Barbara Raye Wilson's lawyer was waiting. "Fuck me in the heart," Shanker snarled.

The lawyer looked at Shanker, worry etched on his face. "Mrs. Wilson is concerned about Eric's welfare," he said.

"Then let Jenny talk to Mike about it," Shanker said. "Not the bitch queen of"—he paused, searching for the right words—"of permanently maimed lawyers." He smiled wickedly, enjoying the confrontation. The lawyer jerked his head once and scurried away, glad to escape Shanker's wrath. "Always know when to get out of Dodge," Shanker called. The lawyer walked faster. "Fuckin' commie," Shanker said in a loud voice, using the worst name in his vocabulary. "What's the bitch up to now?"

15

Havana, Cuba

The 1957 four-door Chevrolet sedan rattled and rumbled down Calzada de Infanta, its broken suspension groaning in protest. "Over half a million miles," the driver said with a sigh. "A good car, but parts are so expensive now." He gave a very Cuban shrug. "It's time to end the embargo."

Marsten agreed with him. Everywhere he could see the results of Castro's *revolución* and the economic embargo imposed by the United States. It seemed the entire population of Havana was riding bicycles. Besides those he saw mainly trucks and buses. The vast majority of the buildings were in desperate need of repair, much like the Chevy he was riding in. Yet the people were full of life and the air was charged with a vibrancy that defied Castro's failed Communist dream. Marsten kept looking out the window, wanting to experience the people, feel their pulse, take their measure. Then it came to him. Like the car, the city needed only a chance, and money, to renew itself. Until then both would keep running.

"All the tourists," Marsten said, "that's a good sign."

The driver shrugged. "*Turistas.* They bring money, but it goes to the big hotels, the government, the *jineteras*, not the people."

"*¿Jineteras?*" Marsten asked. His Spanish was good enough to know that was the word for female horse riders or jockeys.

The driver laughed. "*Putas.*" Whores. "Havana has the most beautiful and cleanest *putas* in the world."

"Is prostitution a problem? I thought Castro had ended that."

Again the shrug. "This is Cuba. Sex is a commodity for sale, like food. Besides, how else can a poor girl who only has her youth and her beauty support her family?" On cue he handed Marsten a card. "Very pretty girls." He turned around in his seat and said in a low voice, his lips barely moving, "Your friend the jogger says to ask for Angelica."

The car creaked to a stop in front of a large house near the luxury hotel Nacional and the Malecón, Havana's famous waterfront boulevard. Like most of the houses, which hadn't seen a paintbrush since Castro came to power, little remained of this one's former glory. The tropical climate combined with the sea air was slowly destroying it. "Casa Salandro" the driver said. "A good choice. You will like it here." He got out and opened the trunk to retrieve Marsten's suitcase. "Don't forget the card," he whispered when Marsten paid him.

A handsome young man pushed open the rusty gate and rushed out to carry the bag. "This way, Señor Marsten," the young man said, leading him inside. The gate slammed shut, and Marsten stepped through a time warp and into an open atrium. The decay and poverty of Havana were held at bay, and he was in a well-cared-for home, surrounded by flowers and quiet elegance. A beautiful fountain demanded his attention, and the sound of gently splashing water cast a net of tranquillity and grace over him.

"Beautiful," Marsten breathed. "Absolutely beautiful." The young man led him through one of the doors that opened onto the courtyard. The room was also a throwback to an earlier, more affluent age. A middle-aged couple stood to meet him, and the man extended his hand in friendship.

"Welcome to our home, Señor Marsten. I'm Agosto Salandro. This is my wife, Amelia."

Marsten gently took Amelia Salandro's hand and instinctively raised it to his lips. She was a petite woman in her mid-forties. But the years and the hardships of revolutionary Cuba had been kind to her, and she was still beautiful. "My pleasure," he murmured. For a moment he regretted his bachelor life and the family he never had. It was easy to envision a life with someone like Amelia.

Agosto Salandro smiled. Amelia did have that effect on people. "And you have met our son, Ernesto." The young man who met his taxi nodded. "And may I present our daughter, Rosalinda." A beautiful girl stood up, and Marsten wondered how he could possibly have missed her. She was definitely her mother's daughter, a classic Spanish beauty with dark hair, deep brown eyes, and lips that reminded him of Sophia Loren's. But there was more. The best of Cuba flowed in her bloodlines, and she moved with an inner grace that held the promise of the future. "Rosalinda will be your daytime guide while you're in Havana," Salandro said. "And Ernesto will escort you at night, should you care to go out."

The Salandros led him into another room, and they sat for a few moments discussing his plans. The minutes rapidly turned into an hour, and Marsten soon felt like a member of the family. He was totally enchanted by the Salandros. Finally it was decided that Rosalinda would start his vacation by taking him on the Hemingway tour—first to the Hotel Ambos Mundos where the writer had lived for a time, followed by a walk to El Floridita, his favorite bar, and then by taxi to Finca Vigía, his estate outside Havana.

Later, and much to his surprise, Rosalinda escorted him to his suite on the balcony overlooking the courtyard. "If you need anything special," she said in perfect English, "just ask Ernesto." She studied him for a moment as if she were memorizing every nook and cranny of his face. "Until tomorrow," she murmured.

※

The next two days flew by, bringing Marsten's short vacation to an abrupt end, and thanks to Rosalinda and Ernesto he was beginning to understand the *habañeros* and their city. Now it was Sunday evening, and he had one last task to perform. As agreed, Ernesto was waiting for him by the fountain. "Have you decided what you would like to do for your last night in Havana?" the young man asked. Marsten handed him the card the cabdriver had given him. A knowing grin spread across Ernesto's face.

"Is it open on a Sunday night?" Marsten asked.

"Of course," Ernesto replied. "This is Havana. It's a good choice for your last night here. You will not be disappointed. We can catch a cab on the Malecón." He escorted Marsten outside for the short walk to the seaside promenade. Before they had taken ten steps, a woman burst from her home on the opposite side of the street and hustled toward them.

"The commissar," Ernesto said. "She's the head of the street's Committee for the Defense of the Revolution. She wants money."

The woman walked with self-importance and blocked their way. "The Salandros have not been honoring the *revolución*," she said. "Perhaps it is necessary to take a new census?"

"How much this time?" Ernesto asked.

The woman looked at Marsten. "Five hundred, U.S."

"We are a poor family," Ernesto pleaded.

"So poor that all your family lives under one roof?"

"We will try to find the money," Ernesto said.

"Soon," she replied. "Very soon." She marched back into her house.

"Why do you have to bribe her?" Marsten asked.

"All the homes belong to the people, and we live in ours by the grace of the state and the commissar. Naturally we try to keep our families together, so everyone who lives under our roof is a Salandro. The commissar is responsible for the block census and certifies the members of a household and that the house is fully occupied."

"I thought only your immediate family lives there."

Ernesto grinned at him. "The Salandros who live with us are only ghosts."

"I see," Marsten replied. And he did. The Salandros kept their home by claiming that deceased relatives lived with them, and they bribed the commissar to go along with it.

Ernesto waved down a taxi. "It is the way things are done in Cuba," he explained. "I must interact with many different people, all with different interests." He spoke to the taxi driver, who spun the wheel of the car and headed into Old Havana. He snaked through the side streets and stopped in front of a nondescript house. "Tell the doorman when you want to go home. He will call me."

"You're not coming in with me?"

"It is not necessary," Ernesto replied. "You will be perfectly safe here."

The cabdriver opened the car door, and Marsten took three quick steps into the dark opening. Like the Salandros' home, the outside of this house was a front concealing what was within. Once Marsten was inside, a well-dressed man escorted him to a private suite that reminded him of a luxury hotel. The man sat him in one of a cluster of low chairs in the center of the room and disappeared. An elegant woman in her mid-forties joined him and sat down. "Good evening, Señor Marsten." She smiled at him. "This is terrible, but first we must take care of what you Americans call 'business.' Our basic price is eight hundred dollars. That includes this suite until noon tomorrow, food, drinks, and two girls. If you desire, other extras can be negotiated. We prefer U.S. dollars, but other currencies are acceptable. I'm sorry we do not have the banking facilities to use credit cards, but we soon will."

Marsten handed her eight one-hundred-dollar bills, and she slipped the money into her pocket without counting it. A hard smile flickered across her mouth. "Would you like to meet some of our young ladies?" He nodded, and she raised her right hand, making a beckoning motion. Five girls immediately walked into the room and draped themselves over the chairs. They all wore attractive but revealing dresses that left little to the imagination, and all spoke excellent English. "All our girls speak three or four languages," the woman explained. "Thank God they don't have to speak Russian anymore. Such an ugly language."

"So lovely," he murmured, wondering what he should do next.

The woman spoke a few words in Spanish, and the girls slowly shed their clothes. They were all young, firm, and beautiful. Marsten said nothing, and the girls picked up their clothes and walked away, to be replaced by five more girls. Like the first group, they were young, beautiful, and wore expensive clothes. "If you would prefer to be with one at a time," the woman murmured.

"A friend mentioned Angelica," he said. The woman murmured something in Spanish, and the girls quickly left. Moments later another girl walked in, this time alone. Her hair fell to her shoulders, and her strapless gown was split dangerously high on the left side. He fought to catch his breath as she moved toward him and sat down.

She reached out and took his hand. "Good evening, Mr. Marsten," Rosalinda said.

※

Marsten's eyes were riveted on Rosalinda as she poured him another drink. They were alone in the suite, the lights were turned down low. "I—I don't understand," he stammered.

She gave a soft laugh. "Why I'm doing this? How else can a girl help her family survive?" She gave him a sad look. "Occasionally Ernesto works here. This is how we find the dollars to pay the bribes. But thanks to guests like you, soon my parents will no longer need the money I earn. Then I can save for my dowry and quit."

"How long will that take?" he asked.

"Maybe another two years. Sooner if things change." She sat next to him and held his hand as she spoke in a very low voice. "On Saturday when we were at the Plaza de Armas, I watched your face. And this morning, at the cathedral, I saw you pray. You're a good man." She dropped her voice even lower. "Do you want to help us?"

Marsten had made contact.

A chill swept through him, and for a moment he was back in Eritrea on the edge of a dangerous venture. His hands shook, and he felt the overpowering urge to relieve himself. It was still not too late to cut and run. But what would L.J. say? She would understand and forgive him. But could he fail her again? He knew what he had to do. "I want to help."

She gave him a solemn look. "It is dangerous," she murmured. "Very dangerous."

"I understand."

She touched his lips. "Speak very quietly," she warned. "We must be very careful, and you must do exactly what I say. The secret police are everywhere."

"Agreed."

Rosalinda stood and walked to the door. She spoke to the man who had originally escorted Marsten inside. Then she returned and sat on his lap. "Act naturally," she whispered. She wiggled in his lap as she kissed him, her lips warm and full. The door opened, and a young girl and man entered. He guessed her age at sixteen, the man's at least thirty.

"You wanted a show?" the man said as they sat down.

"Act like you're negotiating the price," Rosalinda whispered in Marsten's ear. "The camera is hidden in the chandelier, but the microphone is too far away to hear us if we speak in a low voice." She moved in Marsten's lap and unzipped her dress. It fell away, and she sat naked as her arms wrapped around him, her lips on his neck. "This is for the cameras," she murmured.

Marsten moved his hands down her bare back, hardly believing they were talking in such bizarre circumstances. Caution told him to go slowly and that he was talking to the negotiator who spoke for the rebels. "I want to see a new show," he told the negotiator. "One that has not been seen in Cuba for years, one that your children can be proud of."

"A free Cuba?"

Marsten gave a little nod.

"Tell me," the negotiator demanded, "why are you so anxious to help us? What's in it for you?"

"Before I answer that," Marsten replied, "who am I dealing with?"

"Don't ask," Rosalinda whispered in his ear.

"Then there's no deal," Marsten said.

The negotiator stared at Marsten for a moment, making a decision. He whispered a few words in Spanish to Rosalinda, much too quickly for Marsten to catch. "We are the Guardians," Rosalinda murmured in English. "We are going to build a new Cuba on the ashes of the old." She nuzzled his ear for a few moments as she told him about the group, her words filled with the idealism of youth.

"Our people are everywhere," the negotiator said, barely audibly. "But Castro is still too strong for us to act. Our time will come when he dies. Then we can capture the government. So for now we prepare. But when we rule Cuba, we will reward our friends and punish our enemies."

"So how can we help?" Marsten asked.

"We need money. It is necessary to organize and survive."

"How much?"

"We are not fools," the negotiator replied. "Nothing is for free, not for you, certainly not for us. May I repeat myself? What's in it for you?" They had come full circle, back to the key question.

Marsten hesitated before answering. "The concessions to develop any offshore oil in Cuba's territorial waters."

The look on the man's face was a combination of surprise and total bewilderment. He spoke in Spanish to Rosalinda. "Does he understand our language?"

"He understands a few words," she answered in Spanish. "But you must speak slowly."

The negotiator's words were machine-gun quick and low, almost a hiss. "I don't believe him. He wants something else."

"Why?" she replied.

"There's no oil. He's an oilman and must know that. The Russians explored every centimeter of Cuba and found nothing. I know, I've seen the reports."

Rosalinda said, "Then give him what he wants."

The man thought for a few moments. "Mr. Marsten," he said in formal English, "the concessions are yours for half a million dollars a month. If you discover oil, we split the gross ninety-ten. Ninety percent to the people."

Marsten shook his head. "Fifty thousand, and we split forty-sixty."

"Impossible," the man said, loud enough for the bugs to record. Then, quietly, "A quarter of a million."

"We know the Russians were very thorough," Marsten said. "They were hoping Cuba was part of the Venezuela shelf. It wasn't, of course. Seventy-five thousand a month, and fifty-fifty."

The negotiator snorted. "Is this the new colonialism? A hundred seventy-five thousand, and eighty-twenty."

"My last offer, *señor*. A hundred thousand a month, and seventy-thirty." Marsten held his breath. He would have taken the last offer but felt duty bound to haggle, as he sensed a weakness.

The man was silent for what seemed an eternity. Then, "Agreed."

"Please," Marsten said, "don't cross us on this. The people I represent are very powerful." A heavy silence came down, and tension split the air.

"We know who you are," Rosalinda replied, desperate to save the deal. The thought of a hundred thousand dollars coming in every month was beyond her imagination. "Otherwise you wouldn't be here. You already hold our lives hostage with what you know. We can only succeed if we trust each other."

Instinctively Marsten knew he could trust them. "And we will succeed," he murmured, sealing the deal.

"Our people will contact you in Miami," the man said. The negotiations were over, and he reached for the young girl's knee. He ran his hand up her dress. "Have the money ready." He pulled the girl to the floor and they started to tear at each other's clothes as they caressed.

"We must play out this charade for those who are watching," Rosalinda said. She kissed him full on the mouth, her tongue reaching for his. Her right hand caressed his crotch, waiting for his response. Nothing.

"Please," Marsten begged. "Don't."

She slipped off his lap and knelt in front of him as she unzipped his fly. Her fingers caressed his flaccid penis, and she reached for his scrotum. Her eyes opened wide as she looked at him in surprise. Then she was back in his lap, her arms around his neck, hugging him. Her tears coursed down her cheek and onto his face. "Oh, my sweet, dear man. I'm so sorry. So sorry." Their tears blended together, and slowly the horror of Eritrea slipped away, finally laid to rest by a young revolutionary.

16

Dallas

It was after seven o'clock on Sunday evening when L.J. pulled up in front of the anonymous house in the midcity area. The front yard needed mowing, and the garage door was in need of paint. She double-checked the address before getting out. It was a world far away from her home in Highland Park, the house where she had grown up and still lived. This was a working-class community, a way of life totally beyond her experience. She had never existed from paycheck to paycheck and worried about making the next car payment or paying a hefty bill from an orthodontist for a child's braces.

She opened the back door of her big BMW and helped Duke out. The old dog licked her hand in gratitude, and she led him up the walk and rang the doorbell. Shugy Jenkins, Marsten's prim secretary, answered almost immediately. "Miss Ellis," she said, "whatever brings you here?" Nothing in her look or voice betrayed her true feelings.

L.J. gave a little smile and motioned at Duke. "Lloyd is still gone, and the kennel called . . ." She took a deep breath. "He's not doing well, and I remember you once saying your husband loved dogs."

The middle-aged woman threw open the screen door and knelt in front of the dog. She tenderly stroked his head. "You miss your master, don't you? You're a good old boy, aren't you?" She glanced up at L.J. "Please come in. But you'll have to forgive the mess; Billy hasn't been well lately." L.J. followed her inside and was assaulted by the smell of urine. A man lay in a La-Z-Boy recliner, his head back and his mouth open as drool dribbled down his jaw. "Billy had a stroke a year ago," she explained. "Billy, look who's here. It's Duke, Mr. Marsten's dog."

The man's head turned, and L.J. saw the glint of recognition and happiness in his eyes. She took in the room. It was as clean and orderly as Shugy's office outside Marsten's corner suite. "Don't you have a full-time caregiver?" L.J. asked.

"Oh, Miss Ellis, I can't afford that, and Billy isn't eligible for Medicare. My neighbor comes in when I'm at work, and her husband helps when I have to bathe him. Billy hates being in bed, so I leave him here where he can watch TV."

"What about the company's health insurance?" Shugy gave her a long look and didn't answer. "Are you telling me our insurance doesn't cover your husband?" A slight nod. L.J.'s mouth compressed into a tight line. "We'll see about that." She thought for a moment. "You stay home tomorrow and take care of your husband." She turned to leave. "Come on, Duke."

"Miss Ellis, I can't." From the surprised look on L.J.'s face, Shugy felt an explanation was in order. "I can't because . . . well, you see, I must be honest. I've never approved of you."

L.J.'s laughter filled the small room. "You think I'm a bitch?"

Shugy looked embarrassed. "Well, sometimes you do things that are not"—her head came up, and she looked L.J. directly in the eyes—"well, they're just not Christian. And I know your father taught you better." Tears streamed down her cheeks. The truth was out, and she would pay the price. But her conscience was clear. She had done her Christian duty.

L.J. reached out and held her hand. She was back in time with her spinster aunt, a woman she had loved for her honesty and kindness. And like her aunt, Shugy was a pillar of strength who accepted whatever fate handed her, never losing her faith or complaining. She deserved better. "You didn't know my father like I did. But that's the way I am, part Jekyll, part Hyde. I can't help myself, and to tell the truth, I don't want to change."

Shugy wouldn't let it go. "I, we, can't take your charity Miss Ellis. I'll be at work the normal time tomorrow."

"And I'll fire you if you are. You take care of your husband until we can make the proper arrangements. Then you come back to work."

"How can you say that, knowing how I feel about you?"

"I also know you never let on or told anyone. Or let it get in the way of your work. Besides, you're an excellent secretary, one of the best." She looked at the dog. "Duke, come."

"Miss Ellis, please leave him. He likes being near Billy." It was true. The old dog was curled up on the floor, and Billy's hand had dropped, resting on his head.

"You take care of them, hear?" L.J. said.

The Pentagon

Peggy Redman looked up, her eyes wide with surprise, when Stuart walked into his office at exactly eight o'clock Monday morning. "Colonel Priestly wants to see you immediately," she said. Her voice carried all the warning he needed.

Stuart tried to grin, but it just wasn't there. "The beginning of a perfect day." He did the mental equivalent of stiffening his backbone and knocked on Ramjet's door.

"Come," Ramjet barked. Stuart marched in and started to salute, the routine way of reporting in. Before his hand reached his eyebrow or he could say "Reporting as ordered," Ramjet snarled, "Don't bother sitting down." Stuart lowered his hand. Ramjet kicked back in his chair and fixed Stuart with the look he had practiced in front of a mirror for twenty minutes that morning. "I think it's safe to say, Stuart, that your ass is grass in this man's Air Force."

Stuart didn't know how to respond. "It's not what you think, sir."

"Bullshit. It's exactly what I think. You're facing a murder charge and have certainly disgraced the Air Force." He threw a copy of the *Washington Post* across his desk. "You made the news, Stuart. Page six."

"And here I was hoping for page one," Stuart quipped, immediately regretting it.

Ramjet stood and paced his office, his hard heels clicking and echoing in the small space. The staff had always laughed about it, calling him an authoritarian goose-stepper. But now the humor was gone. "I've pulled your security clearance, and you're outa here. Admin will keep you busy doing whatever, or they can put you on administrative leave until your case is resolved—their call. But make no mistake, I'm going to do everything in my power to see that you're kicked out of the Air Force. The sooner the better."

"Sir, I've got fifteen months to go to retirement. I'm in the safe zone."

Ramjet glared at him. Once anyone in the Air Force was within two years of being eligible for retirement, they couldn't be separated in place of retiring. "Not if you're court-martialed," Ramjet barked.

Panic drove a spike into Stuart's heart. He was forty-one years old and had spent his entire adult life in the Air Force. Without retirement pay to fall back on, he'd be broke and starting all over. And what chance would he have of landing a decent job with a court-martial on his record? "Court-martialed for what?" he asked, desperation behind every word. "I haven't been found guilty of anything."

"I can think of a few things the state of Virginia will never consider. Like conduct unbecoming, bringing disgrace on the Air Force. Try those on for size. Clear your desk and get out of here. Dismissed."

"But, sir . . ."

"Are you hard of hearing? I said 'dismissed.'" Stuart spun around and opened the door to leave. "I'd suggest you render a proper salute before retiring," Ramjet barked. Stuart turned back around and saluted. "Very good," Ramjet said. "Military courtesy is not beyond you. Now you're dismissed." He waved his fighter-pilot salute at Stuart.

Outside, Stuart beat a hasty retreat to his cubicle, aware of the heavy silence and that all eyes were on him. Even with the door to Ramjet's office closed, they had heard every word through the thin partition. He dropped into his chair and held his head in his hands. "Christ, what's next?" he moaned. He went through the motions of emptying his desk, surprised that there were so few personal effects. There was an engraved pen set from a previous assignment, a framed photograph of Eric on *Temptress*, and an ornate desktop nameplate announcing his name and rank. *Is this all?* he thought. *Eighteen friggin' years in the Air Force, and this is all I have to show for it?*

Despair crashed down like a huge wave as he wallowed in a sea of confusion. He had never felt so alone, not even after his divorce. He gasped for air, fighting for survival, but no matter where he turned, there was only disaster. Twice someone had tried to kill him, first by shoving him under a street sweeper and then with a knife. When the direct approach didn't work, they tampered with his Explorer's brakes and managed to kill Jenny's boyfriend. The irony of it all drove him even deeper into his despair. What they—whoever "they" were—couldn't do, the police would. And Barbara Raye Wilson and her high-priced lawyers were like sharks lurking in the sea, always ready to go into a feeding frenzy at the smell of blood. Now Ramjet was going after his career, his last anchor in a raging storm.

He swore to himself. *They wouldn't do it if I were a pilot!* But an inner voice told him that wasn't true. He shook his head to force the blackness away. For the first time in his life he understood why people chose suicide over living. Another voice that sounded suspiciously like Jane's said, "That's a permanent solution for a temporary problem."

"Colonel Stuart," Peggy Redman said, bringing him back to the moment. "Colonel Priestly wants the files for the Strategic Petroleum Reserve committee. He's going to take your place."

Stuart's head snapped up. "Is this what it's all about? Serving on some damn committee?"

"Apparently so," Peggy answered.

He gestured at a filing cabinet. "Most of them are in there." He scribbled the combination to his safe on a piece of paper and handed it to her. "The classified files are in the top three drawers of my safe. He's welcome to them."

She glanced at the safe and the filing cabinet. "That much? Might as well leave it all here." She fingered the piece of paper with the combination. "You know, nothing is going to get better until you stop feeling sorry for yourself." She spun around and walked back to her desk.

Stuart stared at his hands for a few moments before he snapped open his briefcase and scooped in what was left of his military career. He marched out of the office. Outside, he took a deep breath. Then he walked back in and stopped in front of Peggy's desk. "Thanks for everything. I'll miss you."

"And I'll miss you, Mike." It was the first time she had called him by his first name.

Dallas

The three men who handled risk assessment and insurance for RayTex Oil stood when L.J. entered their office first thing Monday morning. It was a short walk down one flight of stairs from her office to theirs, but the only time they saw her was when a major disaster had hit RayTex or its subsidiaries. Since nothing unusual had happened over the weekend, they assumed there was a screw-up somewhere, of monumental proportions. They had no idea of how right they were.

"Who negotiated our employees' health-benefit package?" she asked.

"Actually," the team chief answered, "it was a compromise we hammered out with the employees' representatives and our office."

"What would it have cost us to provide catastrophic medical coverage for spouses, to include full-care nursing in case of a stroke?"

The three men sat down and pounded on their computers. They had an answer in less than a minute. "Approximately sixty-one dollars more per employee per month," the team chief said. "As we insure two thousand employees, give or take a few, that would equate to a hundred and twenty-two thousand dollars per month, or one million four hundred sixty-four thousand per year."

"And what would the tax offset do to our bottom line?"

The team chief was sweating. "We can safely assume the company would have recouped thirty percent of that expenditure, or approximately four hundred thousand per year in tax credits." His fingers flew over the keyboard. He paled when he saw the answer. He gulped. "We would have reduced our tax load by—" He ran the calculation again to be sure and gulped even harder. "We would've received a tax credit of almost a million and a half per year."

"Let me see if I understand this correctly," she said, her voice dripping with honey. "We would have paid out a million four sixty-four and saved a million five in taxes, for a net gain of thirty-six thousand by properly insuring our employees." She stared at them for a moment. "Negotiate a revised health-care package immediately and include Mrs. Jenkins's husband, who had a stroke, in that coverage."

The team chief was sweating. "But that's a preexisting condition! No carrier will do that."

"Then you had better negotiate the best possible deal you can to maximize the tax offset. Because that's how we're going to pay for his care. If y'all can't squeeze out enough, you'll make up the difference out of your salaries. And if you don't like that, I'm sure other companies will be glad to hire you."

She tilted her head and smiled. "Get to it, fellas." She turned and walked out, leaving a stunned silence in her wake. Halfway out, she stopped and came back in. "Forget the salary thing. I came down too hard on you. Part of this was my fault. I should have made sure you were talking to other players, like the comptroller."

The three men watched her leave, relief on their faces. "What do we do now?" the junior man asked.

"It's pretty obvious," the team chief said. "Start talking to every other division in the company. I don't think she's gonna give us a second chance."

Washington, D.C.

The plaque hanging on the wall of the lawyer's office was not reassuring.

> Most of my clients are in jail or going there.
> —*Samuel B. Broad*

"A grateful client made that in prison," Samuel B. Broad said when he saw Stuart read it for the third or fourth time. The lawyer was a small, wiry African-American with bushy white hair. His suit hung on his skinny body, and his neck stuck out of his shirt's oversize collar like an ostrich's.

"Grateful?" Stuart asked, convinced he was talking to the wrong lawyer. But all his neighbors said Broad was the best defense lawyer inside the Beltway.

"Grateful he wasn't on death row," Broad said. He laughed at the crestfallen look on Stuart's face. It was a high-pitched, giggling laughter that made Stuart think again of a bird.

"I hope I'll have more than that to be thankful for," Stuart mumbled.

Broad leaned across his cluttered desk and folded his hands. "These things do take time, so meanwhile, don't worry." The lawyer leaned back. "There are many defenses open to you. Besides, I know Ledbetter, he's a good cop, and Smatter will self-destruct on the witness stand. So you just go home for now and enjoy your vacation. I'll be in contact."

"We haven't talked fee," Stuart said.

Broad adjusted his half-frame reading glasses and scanned the folder in front of him. "We'll start with a fifty-thousand-dollar retainer. For a case like this, that should cover most of it. Of course, there could be complications. But we'll cross that bridge when we come to it."

"I just paid twenty-five thousand for bail. That wiped me out. I'll have to sell my boat, but I only have maybe forty thousand dollars' equity in it."

"Then you need to find another ten thousand," Broad said. "Of course, I can carry a loan for you at, say, eighteen-percent interest for the balance."

"Of course," Stuart muttered, wondering what he had gotten into. Still, the lawyer did come with the highest recommendations from people who should know. That was one of the side benefits from living in his neighborhood.

Broad tried to be reassuring. "I don't think this case will ever go to trial."

"I wish I had your confidence," Stuart said.

"Not to panic," Broad said.

Easy for you to say, Stuart thought.

Outside, Stuart sat in Jenny's car and leaned his forehead against the steering wheel. *What now?* Without thinking, he started the car and headed for Annapolis. He drove on mental autopilot, and reality only kicked in when he turned off Highway 50 for the short drive into town. *Will Jane understand?* He hoped so. He ran some phrases through his mind, but they all sounded trite when he said them aloud.

Since it was about the time Jane broke for lunch, he was surprised when he found *Temptress* locked. He looked around, half expecting to see Jane working on a nearby boat. But there was no sign of her. He walked the docks to the marina office, where the manager said she was working at O'Brien's Oyster Bar at the foot of Main Street. "Tell her to get her pretty butt back here. We've got a shakedown." Stuart said he would relay the message. He smiled as he walked. He had never thought of Jane as having a pretty backside. But when he considered it, she did.

He pushed through the door to O'Brien's and immediately saw her taking an order at a nearby table. He sat at the bar waiting for a chance to talk to her. " 'Ey, sailor," she finally said, putting on her best Cockney accent. "Got a light?"

This was Jane, straightforward and down-to-earth, all that he wanted in a woman. Suddenly everything felt better. "I wish I did. Bad news. I've got to sell *Temptress*. Lawyer's fees."

The bad news was like water off a duck's back. "No problem, I'll buy her. I've been saving, and now I've got two jobs. That should make any banker happy."

"I need pretty much top dollar," he told her.

"She's worth it." She studied his face for a moment. "Bad day?" He nodded an answer. "I know the cure. Let me finish here, and I'll meet you on *Temptress*."

"You've got a shakedown cruise," he said.

"Perfect. We'll do it on someone else's dime. Go get the boat ready." The way she walked away sent his libido off the Richter scale.

It was one of those perfect afternoons for sailing that happens two or three times a year. Even though it was the end of November, the weather was unseasonably warm, sixty-five degrees. The wind was blowing out of the east at a constant twelve miles an hour, and the water was calm, with only a little wind chop. Puffy clouds chased each other across a blue sky, and the weatherman predicted more of the same and a full moon for that night.

The boat that needed a shakedown was an old forty-five-foot wooden ketch that had just come out of the yard after a complete refit. Her brightwork gleamed with care, and the cabin had been completely redone. Stuart had the sail covers off and the boat ready to sail when Jane arrived. She threw a bag of food on board, along with two blankets and heavy jackets. "Start the engine," she commanded, and within moments she was aboard and at the wheel as they backed out of the slip. They had barely cleared Spa Creek when she headed up into the wind to raise the sails. Stuart worked the halyards, enjoying the physical exercise. Jane played the helm as the boat fell off the wind and the sails snapped, starting to pull.

She cut the engine, trimmed the sails, and turned the helm over to Stuart as they headed into the Chesapeake. For the next two hours she checked every system on the boat and poked into corners he never knew existed. At one point she threw a pack of condoms out the companionway. "Put 'em in the abandon-ship bag!" she called.

"That's my kind of emergency!" he yelled back.

She stuck her head out the companionway and gave him a patronizing look. "They're good for protecting wounds on a finger, storing stuff, or protecting equipment like a handheld radio or GPS. In a pinch they can even be used as a canteen, like a water balloon." That was Jane, supremely practical. She came on deck and adjusted the standing rigging. Finally she returned to the cockpit and retrimmed the boat. Stuart could feel it respond, sailing in perfect balance and moving faster through the water. She darted back into the cabin and came back with two Dos Equis beers. She sat down beside him, a look of contentment on her face.

"Now I know why people love these old boats," he said.

"She is lovely," Jane murmured.

And she was.

Late that evening they anchored ten miles south of Annapolis in a cove near Curtis Point. The ketch rode easily with a gentle rocking motion as Jane cuddled next to Stuart in the cockpit. She listened without saying a word as he recited all that had happened. "Ramjet is such an asshole," he said. Silence from Jane. "I've done nothing wrong, and I'm getting hit with shit from every side." She got up and disappeared down the companionway. She was back in a moment with a blanket. She dropped it on the seat beside Stuart and straddled him, her knees locked against his hips.

"Talk later," she murmured, pulling at his shirt.

※

Jane was lying on top of him, the blanket pulled over them, their clothes in a pile on the cockpit sole. Her cheek was against his neck, and he could feel her heart beat against his chest. "Does it get any better?" he asked.

"It always gets better," she said, back to four words or less.

Then, "Will you marry me?"

She rose up and stared at him. He held his breath, waiting for her answer. "I love you," she said. "No."

He couldn't believe what he was hearing. "Why not?"

"Because I love you."

"That doesn't make sense."

She had to explain. "Mike, bad things happen to people all the time. It's not their fault, but they have to cope. That's what life is all about. You're the sweetest guy I know. I love the way we fit together when we're making love, and I feel safe with you. I want to be with you, but I want the Mike Stuart I saw when we were running for safe harbor in Cuba, not what I see now." It was the longest speech she'd ever made.

"What do you see now?"

"A beat-me boy. Believe it or not, you've led a charmed life. Now, for the first time, you've hit a real rough spot. Learn to cope." She got up and dressed. "Time to go back."

"Jane, I love you."

"I know."

"Does this mean we're finished?"

She gave him a look he couldn't read. "No. I'm still with you."

The Old Executive Office Building, Washington, D.C.

General Franklin Bernard Butler, better known as Bernie to his friends, came to his feet when Special Agent Toni Moreno-Mather waddled into his office. He felt a surge of fatherly instinct at the sight of the pregnant woman and smiled. "Thank you for coming over so promptly," he said, wanting to apologize for her drive from Andrews Air Force Base and the hassle of finding a parking spot. "I hope you didn't have to walk too far."

She settled into a chair. "There's a garage on G Street about a block away. I needed the exercise."

"Your first?" he asked.

She nodded. "I'm due in March."

"Are you going to stay in?"

Toni shook her head. "My husband wants me to go the mommy track. We don't need the money, and it's what I really want to do." She didn't mention how difficult her pregnancy had become and how the walk from the parking garage had tired her.

Butler nodded. "Trust me, it's worth it." He leaned back in his chair and folded his fingers. "You are the agent heading the investigation into Lieutenant Colonel Michael Stuart?" She nodded in answer and fished a notebook out of her handbag. The bag clunked when she dropped it on the floor from the weight of her semiautomatic nine-millimeter Glock. "As you probably know," he said, "Colonel Stuart has been a key player on a special committee formed at the direction of the president." He stared at his hands, wondering how much he should tell her. "I'm worried about possible security implications."

She flipped the pages of her notebook. "I did wonder about that," she said. "Isn't he a bit low-ranking for such an assignment?"

Butler felt like grinding his teeth. "He was selected because he's our resident expert in the area."

She glanced at her notes. "I was under the impression that the Strategic Petroleum Reserve was managed by the Defense Logistic Agency."

"It is," he replied, not willing to say more.

"Further," she said, "you seem to have taken a special interest in Colonel Stuart. You kept him on the committee when Colonel Priestly wanted to replace him."

"Colonel Priestly is a fine officer, but we needed a technician."

"Right. And you canceled Colonel Stuart's assignment to Germany." No answer from Butler. She checked her notes. "And you appeared at his arraignment hearing to speak on his behalf."

Butler stood up and walked to a window overlooking the White House. "You don't miss much. Tell me, do you think he's guilty?"

"I just go with the evidence."

"You didn't answer my question."

Toni took a deep breath. "Possibly." She tried to gauge his reaction. But there was nothing, not even a slight tensing of his shoulders. She decided it was time to turn up the heat. "General, why's an old spook like you involved with the procurement, supply, and delivery of POL?"

A hard silence came down between them as he stared out the window. After what seemed like an eternity, she thought he made a little chuckle. "What have you heard about me?"

Again she consulted her notes. "You speak Russian like a native and have drifted in and out of the Air Force for years, always reappearing at a higher rank. You were one of the 'Boys in the Basement' during the Reagan years, a mover in the Intelligence Support Agency until it was disbanded, led 'Bernie's Boys' during the Kosovo crisis—"

"That was fun," he allowed.

"And the founder of Checkmate. What's going down, General?"

"Like I said, you don't miss much. We've had hints from many sources that our Strategic Oil Reserve is destabilizing. Perhaps it's due to the globalization of the oil companies, the shift of power to the producers, the way international finance functions independent of national control, a combination of all the above, who knows? But the bottom line is that our government is losing control." She jotted down a short note. "What we're discussing is classified," he said. "May I see what you wrote?"

She blushed brightly. "I'd rather you didn't, General." He held out his hand and she reluctantly handed him her notebook.

" 'Lying asshole,' " he read. He scowled at her, putting all the force of his rank into his voice. "Agent Mather, disrespect toward a senior officer is a serious offense." He stopped when he saw her smile.

"You called me, sir. And I know a cover story when I hear one."

He handed back the notebook. "You were taught well."

"My mentor was the best. Harry Waldon."

"I knew Harry," Butler said, his face softening. The pieces fell into place. "You worked on the Jefferson court-martial at Whiteman." She nodded in acknowledgment. "That was a good piece of work."*

"Can we cut to the chase, sir?"

"Harry did teach you well. What I told you was true enough, as far as it went. The size of the Strategic Oil Reserve is predicated on certain factors, such as the number of producing oil wells in the continental U.S., the capacity of our refineries, the number of oil tankers available, things like that."

"So what's Colonel Stuart's role in all this?"

"He discovered that we could lose access to ninety percent of the tankers we need to supply our forces in the event of a crisis."

"So who controls the tankers?"

"Good question. When we took a good look, we couldn't find an answer."

"There's more you can't tell me, right?"

"Correct. Let's just say we're trying to head off a potential problem, and what Colonel Stuart discovered may just be the tip of the iceberg."

*Editor's note: Special Agent Toni Moreno's investigation into the Jefferson affair is detailed in the book *Against All Enemies* by the same author.

"See one rat and you know there's more in the woodwork," she said. "So you're involved because the president is worried that a foreign power is taking a run at our basic infrastructure."

"Very good, Agent Mather."

"So that raises the question of who has the resources to do that?"

"You sound just like Harry," he said. "If you were me, where would you look?"

Toni never hesitated. "China. Remember that spy fiasco at Los Alamos a few years ago and before that the campaign-contribution scandal? How much coincidence do you believe in?"

"I don't believe in coincidence," he told her. He held up a hand before she could protest. "Okay, I know it happens. But I don't like it when it happens to people around me. Stay on top of this. I want to know if any of Stuart's problems are linked to his work on the committee."

"His problems with Colonel Priestly are," she told him.

Butler sighed. "I didn't need to hear that. Is there anything else?"

Toni consulted her notes. "Do you know a Miss Jean McCormick?"

"I never heard of her. Why?"

"She was mugged at an ATM by the same man who assaulted Stuart and almost killed him."

Butler frowned. "There's the man you need to talk to."

"Unfortunately, he was killed by a guard when he mugged Miss McCormick."

"There's still the lady."

"I'll get on it. Is there anything else, sir?"

"Mike Stuart is a good man, and I happen to like him. Help him if you can."

"Will do, sir." She stood carefully and walked slowly out of his office. She was riding the elevator down when the first pain hit her in the back. "Damn," she moaned, holding on to the man next to her. He hit the emergency call button and summoned help.

17

Dallas

"How was Cuba?" L.J. asked.

Marsten looked up from his desk. "Most rewarding." He hit the intercom. "Shugy would you be kind enough to bring tea for Miss Ellis and myself?" L.J. smiled. He was the only person she knew who spoke in sentences constructed like stained-glass windows. "I did make contact," he told her. "The option for the concession will cost us a hundred thousand dollars a month until our partners can faithfully deliver. If and when we strike oil, we split the gross seventy-thirty."

"My God! That's a steal. Well done, Lloyd."

"I thought you'd be pleased."

The door opened, and Shugy wheeled in a tea cart. Without a word she poured Marsten a cup and stirred in the normal two teaspoons of sugar and a dash of warm milk. Then she handed L.J. a cup. "I believe you prefer just one sugar and lemon," she said. "Will there be anything else?"

"No, thank you," Marsten said as L.J. shook her head. The secretary left, closing the door behind her. "Most unusual," Marsten said. "She never did that before." He gave L.J. a suspicious look. "What have you been up to?"

"We talked when I asked her to take care of Duke, that's all."

Marsten sipped his tea. "He's doing much better. It seems that being with Billy helped."

"Maybe it gave him a reason to live," L.J. suggested. She thought for a few moments, "Lloyd, we need to talk. My office."

Marsten took a final sip, set his cup down, and followed her along the hall to her much smaller office. She locked the door behind them, pulled the curtains, and turned on a high-frequency jammer that would scramble any eavesdropping device. "My," he said, "this must be serious."

"It is." She pulled out the big whiteboard against the back wall and picked up a Magic Marker. Slowly she wrote The Trojan Sea across the top. Without a word she outlined a flowchart with arrows and boxes. "Here's what I've been thinking." She filled in the boxes, explaining as she went. She sat down next to Marsten and studied the chart, which was still incomplete. Her brows knitted in concentration. "Currently I see three problems: Stuart, Steiner, and activating the concessions."

"ARA," Marsten said, "tells me Stuart has been sidetracked and won't be a problem."

For L.J., Stuart was a faceless nobody and she didn't need to know the details, only that he was no longer a problem. "And Steiner?" she asked.

"We know he's told the Department of Energy about Seismic Double Reflection."

"So DOE knows about the elephant," she said.

"Apparently not," Marsten replied. "I assume he's keeping its existence a secret until he believes it's safe to approach another company."

"To do that he needs us out of the way. Well, that's not about to happen. I'll render the little bastard first." She paused, deep in thought. Marsten recognized the signs and waited. She was about to make a critical decision. L.J. erupted from her chair and took four quick steps across the office to the whiteboard. "Watch." She picked up a red marker and drew another vector that connected three boxes. She left the first and last box blank and wrote the words Castro Blamed in the middle box. The vector's arrow touched the empty third box and then pointed at the words New Government in Cuba. Marsten gasped at her audacity, for the first time completely understanding where she was going. Then she picked up a yellow marker and made a series of connections.

"My God," he whispered. "The money—" He couldn't finish the sentence. "But the risks." The words came slow. "No. You can't do this."

"Why not?"

"It's totally over the top."

"Not if we get the concessions. We'll never have another opportunity like this one. We can break out, become international."

"But the potential for"—he was sputtering—"disaster."

"Think of the payoff. It will work. Every company will want a piece of the action in order to survive. And if we hold the concessions, we can auction off blocks in return for company stock." She dangled the possibilities in front of him.

Marsten saw it immediately. "They assume the risk and we become key shareholders in every major oil company that wants to be a player."

"We'll be bigger than BP or Exxon," L.J. announced.

"It's not worth the risk if something goes wrong. It could mean the end of RayTex."

She paced the floor with long strides. "Lloyd! We'll go down in the history books." More pacing. Marsten had seen L.J. in many moods, but seldom one like this. She was total concentration and focused energy. The image of a caged tiger he'd seen as a youth in the London Zoo flashed in his mind. The same relentless pacing, the beauty concealing the strength within, the will to hunt—all were there. Like the tiger, L.J. was a force of nature to be reckoned with, a power unto herself. *When was she last like this?* he thought. He couldn't remember.

"The industry will never be the same," she said. The same intensity was caught in her words, and he was fascinated, drawn to her like a moth to the flame, unable to resist its fate. "We've got to try." She was alive with the challenge, resolute, convincing. Then he remembered. It was in Eritrea, when he lay in a fever near death. It was much different then, yet it was the same; she had been there, pacing the tent, claiming the moment. Then she had gone out and won their freedom.

"Is it the challenge?" he asked.

"It's always the challenge," she replied. "All we have to do is start a revolution in Cuba."

Marsten shook his head. "William Randolph Hearst may have been able to do it in 1898, but it's not possible now. One message came through loud and clear while I was there: For all their problems, the vast majority of the people love Castro and are very proud of the *revolución*. I don't see it happening until he dies."

"Until he dies," she repeated. She thought for a moment. "Like in assassination?"

"Definitely not. If that happened, the Cubans would make him a martyr and turn the *revolución* into a holy crusade."

L.J. stood in front of the whiteboard and contemplated her chart. "There has to be a way," she murmured.

Marsten came to his feet, his knees still a little wobbly from what L.J. had shown him. He waved a hand at the board. "Don't even think about this. Too dangerous."

"Keep all our options open. All of them." She watched him leave and returned to the board. "Here's to the revolution," she said. Another thought came to her, and she buzzed Marsten's office. "Lloyd, tomorrow's Thanksgiving. Why don't we send everyone home at noon and come back Monday?" He agreed, and she resumed pacing the floor, glancing at the empty blocks in her flowchart. She darted to the third, and still empty box, and wrote "Castro removed in disgrace." She sat down and savored her handiwork. Only one block remained to be filled in.

All she had to do was find something that could make it happen.

Newport News

A rare feeling of contentment worked its way through Jane. Normally she felt so at peace only at sea following a rough night when a vibrant sunrise cracked the horizon with the promise of another day of God's grace. She was not a religious person and seldom thought about spiritual matters, but there was an order in the universe that was with Stuart's family as they gathered for a traditional Thanksgiving dinner. She held Stuart's hand as Shanker murmured a blessing. He ended his prayer with "And please save us from that misguided creature in the White House."

Martha, Stuart's mother, gave her husband a warning look and told him to start carving the turkey. "What was that all about?" Jane asked in a low voice.

"Dad hates President Turner," Stuart answered. "I don't think he can handle the idea of a woman being the commander in chief of the armed forces." Jane mentally categorized Shanker as an old grouch with nothing better to do than complain. She dropped the subject, remembering how her grandfather would go on endlessly about President Nixon, until finally they couldn't take the old man anywhere.

Across the table, Chalky Seagrave, the English Lightning pilot, was thoroughly taken with Maggot's fiancée, a pretty, vivacious, but slightly overweight woman from Missouri named Mary. Maggot sat on the other side of his bride-to-be and just smiled a lot. Stuart's son, Eric, kept wiggling in his chair, excited about what Friday might bring.

"Do you think the weather will be okay?" he asked for perhaps the tenth time.

"Eric," Stuart said in exasperation, "we've been over this I don't know how many times."

"It's okay," Seagrave said. "I remember my first flight in a jet. I didn't sleep for two nights." He looked at Eric. "There's a weather update at eighteen hundred hours. We'll check it then." His bright blue eyes twinkled. "My guess is that you won't be sleeping much tonight."

"Then we're going, we're going!" Eric shouted.

"Don't get your knickers in a twist," Seagrave told him. "I want at least a five-thousand-foot ceiling and ten miles visibility before we take off."

Maggot cocked his head, thinking. Federal aviation regulations called for a thousand-foot ceiling and three miles forward visibility under VFR, visual flight rules. "Are those your personal weather minimums?" he asked.

"Which are the highest in the world," Shanker kidded. "It makes you wonder how the blokes ever crawled out from under the rocks and built Stonehenge, much less took off in an airplane."

"I'll think about that," Seagrave said, giving as good as he got, "when I buzz the field. Of course, you *will* be watching from your normal position on *top* of the rocks, yes?"

"Boys, boys," Martha said, warning the two to stop.

Seagrave, always with an eye for a pretty woman, explained it all to Mary. "Since we're flying for fun and not to frighten ourselves, I want decent weather. No need to challenge the gods of flying." He winked at Eric. "Right?"

"Right!" the twelve-year-old answered.

Jane squeezed Stuart's hand. "Eric will be in good hands," she whispered. Stuart gave a little nod, accepting the truth of it. However, he was still worried about his only son going up for a ride in the Lightning. But Eric had worked hard as member of the ground crew and had been there for every takeoff and landing when others had gone up. Now it was his turn.

"It'll be all right," Shanker said. "Chalky's a damn good pilot."

Seagrave laughed. "This from Shanker? Will wonders never cease?"

✳

Eric was up early the next morning and checked the weather. Disappointment crashed over him like a tidal wave when he heard that there was a heavy cloud deck at four thousand feet moving in off the Atlantic. "Not to worry," Shanker told him. "It often lifts, and we should have five thousand feet by noon." Martha went along with the amateur forecast and packed a picnic lunch for them to take to the hangar. "I love cold turkey sandwiches," Shanker announced. The four men—Shanker, Seagrave, Maggot, and Stuart—allowed Eric to hustle them out to the car. Jane stayed behind with Martha and Mary to work on details for the wedding, which was scheduled for late January.

The hangars on the general-aviation side of the airport were alive with activity that morning as the men who called themselves the Gray Eagles gathered. They were an odd collection bound together by a love of old airplanes and their latest acquisition, the Lightning. But they were not alone and shared the hangar complex with an Experimental Aircraft Association chapter, whose members built their own aircraft. There was a lot of good-natured kidding and rivalry between the two groups, but they always worked together, sharing advice, tools, building skills, and lies.

When the Stuart family and Seagrave arrived that Friday morning, there was a rush of activity around the hangar. They watched as the Lightning was tugged outside between two hangars and parked next to a white Legend, a small kitplane that bore an uncanny resemblance to a World War II P-51 Mustang fighter. But unlike its famous predecessor, the Legend was much smaller, just under twenty-six feet long with a twenty-eight-foot wingspan. While the Legend sat on tricycle landing gear and was not a tail-dragger like the famous Mustang, there was no doubting its heritage. Hidden under the sleek cowling was a Walter 657 shaft horsepower turbine engine, which gave it a performance rivaling the old fighter.

The owner and builder of the Legend was a solid person, in both physique and reputation. He was a family man, a respected member of the community, and active in the Rotary Club. As a young man he had dreamed of flying high-performance fighters, but family pressure and an early marriage had forced him into the family business, where he had acquired a large fortune and a small potbelly. Nearing retirement, he had finally pursued his dream and built the Legend. He was a good pilot, safe enough, and knew his limitations. But deep inside, Hank Langston was a teenager who had never grown up, only old, and still dreamed of fighting the good fight. Consequently, and lacking a son of his own, he had semi-adopted Eric, and the two had become good friends.

"Is today the day?" Hank called when he saw Eric. The twelve-year-old boy gave him the traditional thumbs-up. "Well," Hank said, "whenever you want to fly in a real airplane, give me a call."

A TV reporter and cameraman drove up to shoot a special on Hank for a local TV station. When the reporter saw the two aircraft sitting side by side, he wanted to contrast the Legend against the overpowering Lightning. The Gray Eagles readily agreed, and soon the reporter was interviewing everyone in sight. He faked a deep envy when Eric told him he was going up for a ride in the Lightning, if the ceiling would only lift. The cameraman maneuvered to record Eric being strapped into the passenger seat while Shanker explained how the electrically operated seat had plenty of adjustment to accommodate even a boy who was just over five feet tall.

Eric was still sitting in the cockpit when Seagrave climbed into the seat next to him. "The weather is cooperating, and we've got five thousand feet," he announced. "Let's do it before Mother Nature changes her mind." He laughed at the smile on Eric's face. The Gray Eagles sprang into action and tugged the jet out to the main taxiway, where it was safe for engine start. Even at idle, the jet thrust reached back over a hundred feet and could do harm. The TV reporter followed as Harry gave a running monologue on what Eric must be feeling or, at least, what *he* would be feeling. The starting whine of number one, the engine mounted on top, drowned out any further conversation.

They all walked to the edge of the parking ramp to watch the Lightning take off. Shanker tuned his handheld radio to the tower frequency for the TV crew as Stuart shifted his weight from foot to foot. He envied his father and brother their cool calm as worry nagged him, eating away at his confidence. *Eric is my only child,* he thought, now sorry that he'd let him go. *I should be worried.*

"Did you see that kid smile?" Shanker said.

Maggot laughed. "See it? I heard it all the way over here."

The TV camera dutifully recorded their remarks. "Can you tell me what's going on?" the reporter asked.

Shanker shrugged as if only an idiot wouldn't know what was happening. "They've taken the active runway, and we should hear the tower clear them for takeoff." On cue, the tower cleared them. "Chalky's running the engines up and should release brakes about now." The Lightning started to move, slowly accelerating. A sharp crack echoed over the small group when Seagrave lit the afterburners. "He's stroked the reheats," Shanker explained as the Lightning rapidly accelerated. "Reheat is bloke talk for the afterburners. At a hundred and fifty knots he'll pull smoothly back on the control column—there he goes—and come unstuck between one seventy-five and one eighty knots." The men watched in silence as the jet lifted off and the flaps and landing gear came up.

Shanker nodded in approval, his face a study of envy, pride, and remembrance. "Watch this," he said. The Lightning pitched up into a steep climb and disappeared through a big hole in the clouds. "He's climbing out at four-fifty knots, point nine Mach." With the Lightning out of sight, the cameraman focused on Shanker's face. "His initial climb is probably around fifty thousand feet a minute, but he'll lose that real quick. He'll level off around thirty-five thousand feet in about four and a half minutes."

"I'm impressed," Maggot muttered under his breath, also a little envious. He flew A-10s, and while he loved the jet, the Warthog did nothing fast.

They listened to the radio as the tower cleared the Lightning to switch frequencies to Norfolk Approach Control. "What happens now?" the TV reporter asked.

"He'll head out over the ocean, perform a few flight checks, probably give Eric a little stick time, and then come back down for some pattern work before landing."

"How long will they be up?" the reporter asked.

Shanker ran the numbers. "We topped off the internal and wing tanks, no external fuel tanks, so that's ninety-one hundred pounds of fuel. Probably be on the ground in forty to forty-five minutes with sixteen hundred pounds of fuel remaining."

"That doesn't seem like a lot of time," the reporter said.

Shanker gave him a condescending look. "This isn't an airliner."

I've got to trust them, Stuart thought. He scanned the sky and frowned. The high ceiling seemed much more ominous than just a few moments before. "Maggot," he muttered, "the clouds seem thicker. How're they gonna get back down?"

"No biggie," Maggot said. "If he can't find a break to descend, he can call for an instrument approach with Norfolk Approach. Piece of cake." The cameraman never swung his Betacam around, but he did record the conversation.

❋

The Lightning tipped and rolled as Seagrave put the jet through its paces, never flying straight and level for more than a few seconds. The old skills came back with a rush and, for a few moments, he was in a fighter pilot's heaven. "Wow!" Eric shouted over the intercom when the horizon was finally where it should be.

"You want to try it?" Chalky asked. Eric nodded, and Seagrave turned the controls over to the boy. "I'll talk you through an aileron roll."

"Can I do that?" Eric asked.

"Sure, why not? You're not an airline pilot, are you?" Eric shook his head, his smile a mile wide under his oxygen mask. "It's real easy," Seagrave explained. "Hold the stick lightly, that's it, and snap it smartly to the right, always holding a little back pressure to keep the nose up, but don't hold it over, and you need to center it back up so the old girl will stop rolling. Okay, you do it."

Eric moved the control column to the right, and the Lightning performed as advertised. "I can't believe I did it! It was so easy!"

"That's because the Lightning is very maneuverable," Seagrave explained. "It's like we're balanced on the point of a needle."

"Doesn't that mean it's unstable?" Eric asked.

"Instability is the handmaiden of maneuverability." He hoped the boy understood.

"I get it," Eric said. Before he could say more, Seagrave held up a hand, cutting him off. The generator caption light was glowing red on the standard warning panel. The TURB, AC, and GEN warning lights on the auxiliary warning panel flicked on, then off, then on again. Seagrave throttled back smoothly and flipped the generator switch to standby. Now the CPR—cabin-pressure warning—caption on the standard warning panel caught his eye.

"We have a burst air duct," he told Eric. Nothing in his voice indicated his worry. He immediately switched the generator to the emergency position, knowing this would tell him where the air duct had burst. Fortunately, the inverter had gone to standby, so his MRG—master reference gyro—was still on-line. He selected the inverter to its standby position, hoping that it would continue to function.

"Well, Eric, like the astronauts say, 'Houston, we have a problem.' Let's just say it's semi-serious. But we don't panic. While I sort it out, would you take a look at the flip cards I gave you? Then we can double-check all my actions." Eric reached for the packet of Flight Reference Cards in his flight-suit pocket while Seagrave ran the emergency checklist from memory, one of the abilities that mark a fighter pilot.

The generator light on the standard warning panel had gone out, which confirmed his gut reaction that they had a burst air duct. Checking, he noted that after switching the generator to emergency, he still had TURB, AC, and GEN warnings on the auxiliary warning panel. This was bad news, for it meant the reheat nozzles would be fully open, giving him a power loss of some 40 percent. While this was no sweat with both engines running, it was something he could have done without. Now he took action for the AC failure: pressed the AC reset. *Damn, no joy.* The warnings remained.

The inverter and pitot heater were set to the standby position. He didn't want the ASI—airspeed indicator—to fail due to icing when he penetrated the cloud cover below them. Off with the autopilot master switch, radar off, and now scan the standby ASI. At least that was working. *What else?* No speed strip, Tacan lost, IFF failed, fuel-vent heaters not working, no windscreen heaters. The canopy blower for demisting was out, along with the JPT—the jet-pipe temperature controllers that automatically regulated the exhaust temperatures. *Must keep a careful eye on engine temperatures,* he reminded himself.

When he was done, Seagrave had Eric read the checklist from the flip cards just in case he had missed an action. But he'd gotten it right the first time. "You're the cool one," he told Eric, paying the boy a true compliment.

Seagrave was about to key the radio when the generator light on the standard warning panel flashed on. The doll's-eye warning indicator for the inverter flickered, and the master reference gyro tumbled. He immediately pressed the generator reset, but there was no response. Now they really had problems—just battery power to get them home. He immediately dumped all the main electrical loads, the DC fuel pumps first, and switched the pitot heater to standby power.

Now Seagrave made his only mistake. He should have declared an emergency with Air Traffic Control. But his experiences with the British Civil Aviation Agency had made him distrustful of all bureaucrats, and he didn't want the U.S. Federal Aviation Agency using this emergency as an excuse to ground the Lightning. He owed the Gray Eagles at least an effort to avoid that. Besides, if the situation got any worse, he could declare an emergency then. And his being a fighter pilot, there was no doubt in his mind that he could safely land with minimal assistance.

He keyed the radio. "Norfolk Approach, Lightning One RTB at this time for a precautionary landing."

※

Shanker turned up the volume of his handheld radio the moment he heard Approach Control answer Seagrave's radio call announcing he was returning to base. Because of the range, he could hear only Approach's transmissions and not what Seagrave was saying. The TV reporter caught it immediately and told his cameraman to focus on Stuart. "This could be hot," he said under his breath before moving next to Shanker so he could pick up the radio calls.

"What's wrong?" Stuart asked.

"We don't know yet," Maggot answered.

The radio squawked at them as the approach controller asked for the nature of the problem. "Copy you have a burst air duct and AC turbine failure," the approach controller repeated.

Stuart was almost screaming. "What's that mean?"

"Electrical problems," Maggot answered. "Take it easy. Happens all the time. Chalky can handle it." He looked at Shanker and motioned him to step away to where they could talk in private. The cameraman zoomed in on them, wishing he could pick up the sound.

When they were out of microphone range, Maggot asked, "What's he lost?"

"He's lost his AC bus," Shanker explained, "which means all his nav aids and the IFF." He ran down the list of AC-powered electrical systems the Lightning had lost. It was extensive. "The generator has picked up some of the load."

Maggot shrugged, a perfect reflection of his father. "No sweat."

Shanker's lips compressed into a straight line. "We've been having generator problems lately. It checked out okay last time, but if he loses the generator, he'll lose the master reference gyro."

"Which means he'll lose his altitude indicator, right?"

"Yeah, and he'll be on battery power."

"Not good," Maggot said. "What systems will he have to shut down?"

"He'll shut off the main radio and DC fuel pumps first thing," Shanker said. "They really suck up the power, and he has to conserve power for his basic instruments. There's another problem: With the DC fuel pumps off, he's gravity-feeding the engines."

"Fuckin' lovely." Maggot muttered. He looked at the sky. "He'll be okay if he can get below that cloud deck so he doesn't have to rely on his instruments."

"The quicker the better," Shanker said. The two pilots scanned the sky, neither one liking what he was seeing. "Langston's Legend is a real hot rod," Shanker said, hoping Maggot would catch his meaning. He did.

Maggot ran over to Hank Langston, who was standing next to the TV reporter. "Hank, I need to borrow your body and the Legend." Hank looked at Maggot, his eyes wide, not knowing what to say. "We need a chase plane to bring them down."

To Hank's everlasting credit, he never hesitated. "Let's go." He and Maggot ran for the Legend.

"What's happening?" the TV reporter shouted.

"The Lightning needs a shepherd to get him down," Hank called back.

"Can my cameraman go in the backseat?"

"Not unless he can fly formation," Maggot shouted.

Hank felt his stomach flip-flop at the word "formation." But he never stopped running. He was panting when they reached his plane, and he paused to catch his breath. "You ever flown formation?" Maggot asked. Hank shook his head. "Dual controls?" Hank nodded this time. "Good," Maggot said, giving him a push onto the wing. "You fly in the front seat." Hank slipped into the seat as Maggot crawled in behind him. "*Go-go-go!*" he yelled.

Hank reached up and pulled down the canopy, flicking the latches to the locked position. His fingers hit the battery switch and flew over the front panel. In less than two minutes the turbine engine was on-line, and they were fast-taxiing for the runway. Maggot worked the radio and requested an instrument departure to VFR on top. "We're going after Lightning One," he advised the tower.

The tower controller was aware of the Lightning's problem and cleared them for an immediate takeoff. "Climb runway heading and contact approach for radar vectors to on top."

"Cleared for takeoff," Hank radioed. He moved the prop lever to full pitch and fed in the power. The Legend sprang forward like a Thoroughbred racehorse out of the starting gates. It took only six hundred feet to reach seventy-five miles per hour and Hank pulled back on the stick. He immediately sucked up the gear and climbed out at thirty-five hundred feet a minute. Unfortunately approach control wasn't as fast as the tower and delayed their instrument climb through the clouds.

"Maintain runway heading and VMC," approach ordered.

"Rog," Hank answered. He climbed straight ahead and punched into the clouds at exactly five thousand feet.

"Jesus H. Christ," Maggot said over the intercom, his voice amazingly calm, almost conversational. "VMC means visual meteorological conditions. I can't see shit."

"Your eyeballs ain't my eyeballs," Hank answered, now well into the clouds. But the cloud deck was much thicker than Hank had expected, and when they didn't punch out in a few hundred feet, he broke out in a dead sweat. He started to pant heavily.

"Keep your instrument scan going," Maggot said, his voice a cool fountain of reassurance. "Control your breathing. Don't hyperventilate. You're looking good. Don't fixate on one instrument. Lookin' good. Ain't no one else flying around in this crap. Think big sky, little airplane.

You're doing fine." After what seemed an eternity, they broke out on top at fifteen thousand feet. Hank kept the climb going, and exactly eight minutes after he'd hit the battery switch for engine start, they were level at seventeen five and headed for the Lightning.

✳

A sixth sense told Seagrave he had to really conserve his battery and keep radio transmissions to a minimum. "Norfolk Approach, I need to descend below this undercast as soon as possible. Radar vectors, please."

He gritted his teeth when Approach uttered the inevitable: "Stand by, clearing airspace below you."

Maggot's voice came over the radio. "Approach, Legend Five-one-five-one requests vectors to join up on Lightning One."

"Roger, Legend Five-one," Approach answered, shortening the Legend's call sign. "Fly heading one-one-zero. Lightning One is on your nose at fifty-four miles."

"Copy all," Maggot replied.

"Your uncle to the rescue," Seagrave told Eric. "My guess is that Hank's in the front seat and wetting his knickers."

"Hank can be cool," Eric replied, defending his friend.

Seagrave patted him on the knee, pleased with the boy. "You're helping, and I'm glad you're here." Eric beamed, for he knew it was the truth. His self-esteem shot over the moon.

"Legend Five-one," Seagrave radioed. "How read?"

"Copy you five-by," Maggot answered.

"You might want to get the thumb out. I'm on battery power."

"Rog," Maggot answered.

✳

"How fast can this puppy go?" Maggot asked Hank.

"Time to find out," Hank answered, firewalling the power lever.

The three-bladed prop bit into the air, and Maggot watched the indicated-airspeed needle touch 290. He mentally converted the indicated-airspeed readout to a true airspeed of 380 knots. He gave a low whistle of approval. They were traveling at 440 miles per hour. "She's a real screamer," Maggot allowed.

"Performance Aircraft," Hank said, "the people who build the kit, redline it at four hundred and fifty miles per. I think it'll go faster."

Hank moved up in Maggot's estimation. He may have been a paunchy fifty-five-year-old man, but he had walrus-size balls, and his attitude was in the right place. "This will do just fine," Maggot said, not willing to push the flight envelope any further.

Seagrave's voice came over the radio. "Legend Five-one, I do not have a tallyho. Do you have me in sight?"

"No joy," Maggot replied.

⁕

The TV reporter had gone live and was talking to his anchor in the station. "A real-life drama is unfolding here at Newport News–Williamsburg International Airport as Hank Langston, a local business-man, attempts a daring rescue of an aircraft in distress."

"Get with it," a voice said in his earpiece. "We're live on national TV, and that's the third time you've said that. We need something new."

The TV reporter gulped. "Right now, like the family, we can only wait." The cameraman zoomed in on Stuart and Shanker, who were hud-dled over the radio. "Why is a twelve-year-old boy flying in an antiquated jet fighter? Regardless of the answer, the heroism of the two men attempting to intercept and lead the stricken aircraft to safety cannot be questioned. But why should their lives be in danger in the first place?"

The voice in his earpiece said, "Heroism versus stupidity. Play that." The reporter swallowed hard, his mouth dry, and tried to think of some-thing more to say. Then it came to him. "Isolate on the father," he told his cameraman. He walked quickly over to the men and shoved his microphone in Stuart's face. "Colonel Stuart," he said, "is it true your brother is up there with Mr. Langston attempting to rescue your son?"

Stuart nodded dumbly at the reporter, not sure what to say. Shanker grabbed the microphone. "That's a true statement. Mike here is not a pilot. He works in the Pentagon." He gestured at the sky. "My older son, Dwight—they call him Maggot—he's a fighter pilot and flies the A-10

Warthog. He knows what he's doing and it's no big deal, just a precautionary landing. Besides, fighters have electrical problems all the time."

It wasn't what the reporter wanted to hear. "So the situation is quite safe."

Shanker gave him a look that seriously questioned his intelligence level. "I didn't say that. I said it was a precautionary landing, just in case. We're playing it safe, that's all."

"I would like to hear from the father," the reporter said, fighting with Shanker for the microphone. He finally wrestled it out of the older man's grasp and turned to Stuart. But Stuart had moved away and was standing on the grass between the parking area and the runway, his eyes locked on the clouds above him.

The voice in the reporter's earpiece was talking. "We got a hot one here. We can turn it into a special—old men chasing youthful fantasies and putting a boy in danger."

※

"Tallyho!" Maggot called.

"Where?" Hank shouted, not seeing a thing.

"On the nose, six miles."

"I don't see it."

"I got the aircraft," Maggot said, taking control. Hank started to protest, but there was an authority in Maggot's voice that told him to let go of the stick. "Sweet," Maggot said, feeling out the controls. He jerked the Legend to the right as he made a radio call. "Chalky, we've got you in sight. Hold your heading, descend to sixteen-five. Say airspeed."

"Three seventy-five knots indicated."

Now Maggot had to get them both in the same flight envelope while converting to the Lightning's stern. Fortunately, the Legend's indicated-airspeed indicator was calibrated in knots per hour like the Lightning's. But the Lightning could slow down only to around 220 knots indicated before handling became delicate, which was something they wanted to avoid while flying formation. On the other hand, the Legend's indicated top speed was around 300 knots indicated, a much better airspeed for the Lightning. While 80 knots of airspeed may seem like a lot, it is a narrow window for two such dissimilar aircraft. Maggot split the difference. "Set two sixty knots indicated." He radioed.

✳

Hank tried to be cool when Maggot tucked in next to the Lightning. But it just wasn't there. "Oooh, shit," he muttered. He was looking directly across at Seagrave, a little more than twenty-five feet away. But it looked much closer, and he could swear the Lightning's left wingtip was in his lap.

"He's on battery power," Maggot told Hank, "so he'll keep off the radio to save the juice. He'll be fine once we get him through the clouds." Maggot reached around and patted his right shoulder with his left hand, the universal signal for Seagrave to fly on his wing. Seagrave tucked in closer and matched his speed.

"Oooh, shit," Hank repeated, thinking what it would be like descending through clouds with a thirty-eight-thousand-pound fighter welded onto his wing. "Can we do this?" he wondered.

"Piece of cake," Maggot assured him. He keyed his radio. "Norfolk Approach, Legend Five-one. Lightning One is on my wing. Descending to four thousand feet at this time."

"Legend Five-one, you are cleared to ten thousand feet."

"Norfolk," Maggot replied, "that will put us directly in the soup. Not the best place to fly formation. Leaving sixteen-five for four."

"Legend Five-one, you are cleared to ten thousand, repeat, ten thousand. I will clear you lower as soon as possible."

"Sorry, Norfolk," Maggot replied, "your transmissions are coming through broken. Leaving sixteen-five for four."

"I can hear him perfectly," Harry said over the intercom.

"No you can't," Maggot said. "He can divert traffic. He doesn't want to because that will upset the traffic flow into Washington. Which will tick off some senator who thinks the system exists for his benefit."

"But we got to do what the controller says."

"Only if we hear him. Besides, his only purpose in life is to help us, not the other way around." Maggot edged the Legend slightly forward of the Lightning as they dropped closer to the cloud deck below them.

Now they were skimming the top. Suddenly the Lightning's nose pitched up seven degrees. Hank gasped. "Not to worry," Maggot said. "He's shut off the fuel pumps to save the battery, and the fuel-collector boxes are gravity-fed. He's just refilling them before we enter the clouds."

Seagrave gave him an okay sign and tucked back in. "Here we go," Maggot warned. Hank sucked in his breath as Seagrave moved in even closer, and this time he was sure they were going to collide. "No lost wingman today," Maggot murmured, almost praying. Hank knew that if they lost sight of the other aircraft, each would turn away fifteen degrees to give them separation. But without an altitude indicator, a directional gyro, and a vertical velocity indicator, the Lightning was in a world of hurt. But Hank had no way of knowing that he was in the presence of two consummate pilots. They were aggressive to a fault and believed in meeting any challenge head-on. Both were more than willing to pit their skills against the odds, and Hank was about to learn what that really meant.

The two aircraft punched into the clouds, welded tight.

The cloud enveloped them like a soup sandwich as Maggot flew a stable descent, maintaining a constant rate of descent and speed. His heading was locked on 283 degrees, and the heading indicator never budged. Traces of turbulence rocked the airplane, but Maggot held the descent constant. Hank's eyes darted from his instrument panel to the Lightning as it misted in and out of sight. His breath came in rapid pants. "Don't hyperventilate," Maggot warned him again. Maggot's eyes moved in a fixed pattern, scanning the instruments before looking outside to check on the Lightning and then back inside. He never moved his head, and the stick was in constant motion as he made minute adjustments.

"I can't see him!" Hank shouted. More than anything he wanted the Lightning away from his aircraft, the baby he'd spent over two years building and sunk $165,000 into. Finally he couldn't stand it any longer. "We're gonna have a midair! Go lost wingman!"

"Your eyeballs ain't Chalky's eyeballs," Maggot gritted, throwing Hank's words back at him. He, too, had lost sight of the Lightning. "We gotta trust him. He ain't got much in the way of instruments. We're his main attitude reference."

The Lightning emerged out of the mist. It had never budged from its position on their wing. "Oh, God," Hank whispered, not able to take it anymore. He closed his eyes.

※

Seagrave's eyes were padlocked on the Legend as it drifted in and out of view. When it disappeared, he would start a mental countdown from five. If he reached zero, he fully intended to turn away fifteen degrees for fifteen seconds before resuming his original heading. But that would have meant relying on the standby airspeed indicator, the turn-and-slip indicator, and the RPM gauges. Not a lot. Fortunately, he never reached the count of two.

"It's getting lighter," Eric said. "I think I saw the ground."

"You've got keen eyesight," Seagrave said. But his words were labored as the Legend momentarily disappeared. Then it was there again, still leading them down.

"I see ground," Eric said.

They dropped out of the clouds and leveled off at twenty-five hundred feet. Seagrave moved away from the Legend and took a deep breath. "Well done, Maggot," he murmured.

"We never panicked, did we?" Eric said.

Seagrave peeled away his oxygen mask and let the cool air wash over his face. He smiled at his copilot. "No we didn't."

※

The TV reporter stood so his cameraman could frame him in the same scene as the Lightning landed in the background. But the cameraman had a better sense of the dramatic and focused on the two aircraft as they came down final in a loose formation. At exactly five hundred feet Maggot firewalled the power-control lever and pulled up and out of the pattern while the Lightning touched down in what looked like a routine landing. Since he had no indication showing residual brake pressure, Seagrave decided he had taken enough chances for one day and stopped on the runway. Stuart was the first to reach the aircraft and looked up to see his son smiling down at him from the cockpit.

"It was cool, Dad! I got to do an aileron roll and we flew formation with Maggot through the clouds." Stuart didn't know what to say and could only look at his son. "And we never panicked either."

The TV reporter arrived with his microphone. "That's a good question, Colonel Stuart. Why should they have panicked?" Stuart didn't answer.

Shanker helped place the crew boarding ladder against the jet. "Hey, Chalky, don't you ever taxi back in on your own?"

Seagrave stood up in the cockpit, his face lined with fatigue. "Why should I when so many of you blokes are willing to do it for me?"

"Why didn't you declare an emergency?" Shanker asked.

"What emergency?"

For a moment there was silence between the two men as they grinned at each other. Then, "Thanks, Chalky. I owe you."

The Englishman climbed down and stood beside Shanker as Hank piloted his Legend to a picture-perfect landing on the cross runway. He taxied in to a forest of thumbs-ups as shouts of approval from his friends washed over him. He lifted the canopy as the propeller spun down. Slowly he stood up, surprised how tired he was from the short flight.

"You did good, Hank," Maggot called from the backseat, loud enough for everyone to hear.

More shouts of approval echoed over Hank as the cameraman zoomed in on his face. He hopped down from the wing and ran his hand lovingly over the fuselage, a quiet look on his face. Then he declared, "Cheated death again."

Hank Langston and his Legend had met the challenge.

18

Miami

What a crazy business, Sophia James thought as she waited for the traffic to move off the Causeway and into Bal Harbour. She hit the retract button and lowered the top of her new Jaguar convertible. A gentle evening breeze ruffled her hair as the top slipped into its hiding place. She smiled contentedly. The car was made for Miami Beach and was a statement about who she was and that she had definitely arrived. The traffic moved, and she savored the moment. She was aware of the image she cast for the tourists and wondered if she should charge the chamber of commerce for advertising. She laughed at the thought of Miami Beach's stodgy burghers paying beautiful women just to be seen. It would never happen.

Fortunately she didn't need the chamber of commerce's money to live in the style she had always dreamed of. Between the hundred thousand a year that Marsten was now paying her, the parsimonious 40,000 or so that ARA kicked in, and the money she skimmed off the top of what she was funneling to Luis Barrios and his group of crazy Puerto Rican loonies, life was indeed good. But how much longer would it last? She didn't care and would find something else when it dried up. *What a crazy business,* she repeated to herself as she accelerated off the Causeway.

The man from ARA whom she now only thought of as Jogger was waiting for her at the corner. He slipped into the passenger's seat and they kissed, a perfect scene for the snowbirds and elderly shuffling by on the sidewalk. He handed her an envelope. "Twenty thousand dollars, as promised. Our man in Dallas hopes he's getting his money's worth."

"They haven't blown up any more of his businesses," Sophia replied.

"He needs them to blow up an offshore oil platform."

She sucked in her breath. "So that's his game. Eliminate the competition."

"I think it's one of his."

"I see," Sophia murmured. "Insurance."

"That's what I figured. Get them working on it."

"It won't be easy," she warned.

"That's what we're paying you for."

She nodded. *How much further can I ride this?* she wondered. She wasn't ready to give up her new lifestyle. At least not yet. She coasted to a stop, and he got out. She pulled into traffic and headed south into Miami Beach. When she was safe in her new condominium, she opened the envelope and extracted five thousand dollars. The remainder was more than enough for Luis and the Group. She reached for the telephone.

❋

The contact had gone wrong from the very first, and Sophia cursed herself for breaking with their normal routine. They should have met on neutral ground, and she should never have gotten into his car. The word "overconfidence" flashed in her mind. "Where are we going?" She asked. Luis Barrios only stared straight ahead and crossed a double set of railroad tracks. She calculated they were on the western side of Fort Lauderdale, but she couldn't be sure. The convertible in front of them slowed and turned down a side road. As the car turned, the woman in the passenger seat pulled off her T-shirt, revealing a well-tanned body.

"That's a nudist resort," Luis said, also seeing the woman.

"How boring. Where can you go without clothes?" Sophia murmured, more to herself than to Luis.

Luis turned onto a county road and headed west, away from Fort Lauderdale. They drove in silence for twenty minutes before he turned off onto a dirt road that led to a dilapidated mobile home set on cinder blocks. A mangy dog barked at them. Luis yelled at the dog in Spanish, and it shut up. They got out, and she followed him inside, where Eduardo Pinar was sprawled on a couch watching TV. He was wearing boxer shorts, and, as usual, his dreamy eyes were half closed. His mustache seemed even more limp than normal. "Where's Francisco?" Luis asked.

"At the supermarket," Eduardo replied.

Luis jerked his head in acknowledgment and disappeared into the small bedroom at the far end. He was back in a few moments and, like Eduardo, was only wearing boxer shorts.

Sophia's inner alarm bells were all ringing. "Luis, I have an important appointment this afternoon. I do need to get back."

"As soon as Francisco returns," Luis replied. He opened an overhead cupboard and pulled out a cloth-wrapped bundle and a shoe box filled with rags and a gun-cleaning kit. He sat at the kitchen table and slowly unwrapped a submachine gun. It was spotlessly clean and gleamed with care. Luis carefully disassembled it as he lovingly touched each part. "This is a Heckler and Koch MP5 nine-millimeter submachine gun." He stroked the silencer, his eyes gleaming. "Such a beautiful weapon," he murmured. "It has an incredibly smooth roller-locking bolt system and never jams."

She became increasingly uneasy as he played with the submachine gun. Finally a car pulled up outside. Eduardo stood up. "That's Francisco," he said. "Help us unload." She followed him outside and stared in amazement. The car was filled with shopping bags. "This is the last," Eduardo said. She helped the two men carry the bags into an aluminum shed behind the trailer.

"My God," she said, "you could supply an army here." The two men didn't reply as they finished unloading the car.

Luis came out and looked in the shed, apparently satisfied with what he saw. They all filed back inside. "We're ready," he announced. "From this moment on we have absolutely no contact with the outside world. We talk to no one, we make no phone calls, we only listen and wait for our moment." Eduardo and Francisco nodded in understanding.

Sophia fought the panic that threatened to engulf her. "What is the moment you're waiting for?" she asked.

Luis didn't answer her question. "We must watch each other," he said, "to make sure no one makes a thoughtless or accidental slip that could be our undoing."

"Undoing of what?" Sophia asked loudly, almost screaming.

"Of our plans," Luis replied. "We must support each other and give of our understanding. Each must do his or her part for the common good. We must all sacrifice."

"Look, I don't know what you're planning, so how can I accidentally reveal it?" There was no answer. "Besides," she said, "you need someone on the outside to help if there's an emergency. I'm that person."

"We may be here a long time," Luis said. "And we all have our needs." She shivered at the way he looked at her. "You must do your part."

"What do you want me to do?"

"For now, take off your clothes.

"Why?"

"We are men," Eduardo said, "and have the needs of men that must be satisfied."

"Where can you go without clothes?" Luis said, an echo of her comment in the car.

She started to undress. "So what are we all sacrificing for?" They watched her as she shed the last of her clothes.

Eduardo stood up, his languid look gone and his face hard. "We're going to—"

Luis cut him off. "No! She doesn't need to know."

19

Stuart and Jane worked at the kitchen table on Sunday morning, transferring the ownership of *Temptress* to Jane. As usual, Stuart had everything organized—a detailed inventory, an equipment list, the location of all the spare parts, instruction manuals, and all the necessary documentation that went with a long-range cruiser. "I feel guilty about what you're paying," Stuart said.

"Forty-two thousand is a fair price for your equity," she told him. "Trust me, with the way you equipped *Temptress*, I'm getting a good deal."

"It does get me off the hook. Thank goodness the Air Force is still paying me. I just might survive all this—if they let me retire. Until they make a decision, I'm on administrative leave. It's almost like house arrest, since I have to call in every day and can't go anywhere."

"That's too bad. I'm starting a charter business, and you could help. There's a couple who wants to sail to Bermuda and see if they're cut out for cruising. They want to leave next week. We're shooting for Wednesday."

"Isn't December a bad time to make a Bermuda run?" he asked.

"It can get rough, but they want to see if they can hack it." She touched his cheek. "Just like you wanted to see if you could do it."

"Will you be back for Maggot's wedding?"

"I plan to," she said.

Behind them, Martha and Eric did the breakfast dishes. "I really liked it, Grandma," Eric said, still bubbling over with excitement from Friday's flight in the Lightning.

"Well, I don't know," Martha said hesitantly. "It seems like that plane is a lot of trouble."

Chalky Seagram wandered in from the family room to refill his coffee mug and heard her comment about the Lightning. "I wouldn't call it troublesome," he said. "It certainly requires expert maintenance, but given that, it's probably no better or worse than any other complex military machine."

Eric joined in. "And we're getting better at maintaining it, aren't we?"

"If you mean the Gray Eagles," Seagrave said, "you're absolutely right."

"A bunch of silly old fools, if you ask me," Martha mumbled under her breath. A loud shout echoed from the family room. "What's upset him now?" she asked.

"He's watching one of your Sunday-morning talking-pundit shows," Seagrave said. "Some discussion about President Turner's new gun-control legislation."

"Oh, Lord," Martha said. "That will set him off."

"Why does Gramps hate President Turner so much?" Eric asked.

Another shout from Shanker. "You dumb bitch! Didn't you read the Constitution!"

"I'm not sure why," Martha answered. "And I've been married to the man for forty-six years."

Shanker stomped into the kitchen, his face beet red. "That crazy woman," he growled. "She wants to outlaw all semiautomatic weapons." He poured himself another cup of coffee. "Congress will hand her her head on this one."

"We're going to church," Martha announced. "All of us. You go get dressed."

"Ah, what for?" Shanker groused as he headed for the bedroom to change.

"To pray for a little understanding," Martha said to his back.

Jane held Stuart's hand. "Can I come, too?"

"When Mom says 'all,' she means 'all,'" Stuart said. No one disobeyed Martha Stuart in her own home.

"You Yanks do take command and control seriously," Seagrave mused, also going off to change.

❋

A man was waiting in a parked car in front of their home when they returned from church. He got out as they did and walked directly up to Stuart. "Michael Stuart?" he asked as he handed him a white envelope.

"What's this?" Stuart asked.

The man walked rapidly away, looking over his shoulder at Shanker. "I believe it's a subpoena," he said, thankful when he reached the safety of his car.

Shanker rushed up. "You step on my property again and I'll blow your ass away!" he shouted.

"So much for church," Seagrave muttered.

Stuart read the subpoena. "It's a summons to appear in family court and show cause why Eric should not be immediately returned to his mother's sole custody." He looked forlornly at Eric. "What do I do now?"

"Honor the threat," Shanker said.

"And how do I honor the threat here?" Stuart grumbled.

"You can start by getting in her face," Shanker shot back.

Annapolis

Stuart and the marina's manager cast off the dock lines and watched as Jane backed *Temptress* out of the slip. The middle-aged couple chartering the boat stood in the cockpit and waved at the friends and family who had come to see them off. As usual, Jane was all business and only turned to wave good-bye at the last moment. An inner voice warned him that she was a sea gypsy and now she was gone, returning to the sea and following her heart. A loneliness welled up inside of him. "Damn," he whispered to himself, certain that he would never see her again.

"You shouldn't let that one get away," the marina manager growled.

Dallas

Shugy saw the two FBI agents on the security monitor the moment they entered the Fountain Plaza Building. She immediately buzzed L.J.'s office as her fingers flew over her computer, calling up Marsten's schedule. "The two FBI agents who interviewed Mr. Marsten on"—she hesitated while she pinpointed the exact date—"Thursday, October third, of this year, are downstairs waiting for the elevator."

"Why did they talk to him, and where was I?" L.J. asked.

Shugy called up a confidential file on the computer. "They interviewed Mr. Marsten about the bombing of RTX Farm Supplies, and he gave them access to RTX's personnel files." She checked L.J.'s schedule. "You left that day on the Sabreliner for Houston and then on to St. Louis for the weekend."

"Where's Lloyd?"

"Mr. Marsten is taking Duke to the veterinarian and will be gone the rest of the afternoon."

"Do a slow roll for a few moments before you show them in," L.J. replied.

The elevator doors opened, and the two FBI agents stepped out. Shugy deliberately called Marsten's voice mail and carried on a businesslike conversation while the two agents cooled their heals. "Yes, Mr. Marsten does understand," she said. "Please tell the senator thank you for his cooperation and we are most appreciative." She paused. "Yes, I'm quite sure they didn't mean to overstep their bounds. Yes, I assure you Miss Ellis also understands and is not angry." Another long pause. "Thank you again." She hung up and smiled at the two agents. "How may I help you?"

The two agents presented their identification cards and said they were there to see Lloyd Marsten. "Mr. Marsten is out of the office for the afternoon, but I can see if Miss Ellis is free. She's the president and chairperson of the board, you know." They said that would be fine as Shugy buzzed L.J. "Please, go right in," she said, rising to escort them. The two grateful agents trailed along like puppy dogs.

L.J. came around from behind her desk and played the perfect hostess for the two agents. She joined them on the couch and flashed her long legs, distracting the junior agent. Shugy hurried out to bring coffee and tea. "How may I help you?" L.J. asked.

The senior agent dug out his notebook and flipped pages. "Are you aware that Mr. Marsten was in Cuba for four days just before Thanksgiving?"

"Yes, I am," she said.

"Travel to Cuba is restricted," the senior agent said.

"Unless I'm mistaken, can't he travel under his British passport, since he maintains dual citizenship?" No answer from the agents. "Also, Lloyd is an admirer of Ernest Hemingway and has one of the best Hemingway collections in the United States. He has wanted to follow the Hemingway trail in Havana for years. Before it's too late." She lowered her voice to speak in confidence. "His health has not been the best, you know, and he *is* sixty-four years old."

"Are you aware that he also visited a house of prostitution?"

"I didn't know that," L.J. said, looking very concerned. Marsten hadn't told her, and she suspected that was how he had made contact with the Guardians. But if the FBI learned about his physical condition, they might become suspicious and start asking the wrong questions. She needed to get them looking in another direction. "Oh, the poor man. I know he's very lonely. That must be it, you know." She made a show of thinking. "I'll look into it and make sure he hasn't been harassing any of the staff. You can't be too careful these days about this type of thing. I would appreciate knowing if there's anything wrong so I can take action. Lawsuits, you know."

Problems with sexual harassment were very low on the FBI's agenda. "There's another item," the senior agent said, flipping more pages and turning to a problem worth their time. "Do you know a Dr. Emil Steiner?"

"Of course. He's one of our independent contractors."

"What is the exact nature of your relationship with Dr. Steiner?"

L.J. never hesitated. "He's developed a new exploration technique for us."

The younger agent consulted his notes. "What exactly is Seismic Double Reflection?"

"I'd rather not discuss it. Trade secrets, you know. If our competitors learned of it, we'd stand to lose millions of dollars."

The senior agent took over. "In conversations with the Department of Energy, Dr. Steiner accused Mr. Marsten of physically threatening his life when he was negotiating with RayTex."

L.J. leaned forward, letting her blouse fall open to reveal her cleavage. "That's ridiculous." Her soft Texas accent was more pronounced. "Lloyd would never do anything like that. I was involved in those negotiations, and while we had a major disagreement over the dollar value of Dr. Steiner's process, I assure you no threats were made. Dr. Steiner has an overactive imagination."

The two agents exchanged glances and, as one, closed their notebooks. They stood up. "Thank you for your time," the older one said. "Would you have Mr. Marsten call us to set up an appointment? We need to talk to him before forwarding our report."

"Of course," she murmured, walking them to the door.

After they were gone, she paced the silk Persian rug in front of her desk. She strode back and forth, her arms clasped to her breast. Her chin was down, her eyes half closed. Suddenly she locked the door and turned to the blank whiteboard that had become a permanent fixture in her office. She quickly filled it with a series of arrows linking information boxes. The final vector she labeled "Steiner." Then she picked up a red marker.

She kept repeating, "You bastard! You bastard!" as she slashed a series of X's across the vector. Her anger spent, she started drawing new connecting lines, trying to bypass the void left by Steiner. Slowly an idea came to her as she drew in a new vector with a new set of connected boxes. She stood back and stared at what she'd created. "It might work," she murmured to herself. She called her comptroller, a glamorous CPA she had shanghaied from Sacramento, California. "Marcia, what would it cost to obtain a lease option on every deep-water drilling ship? I want to have the right of first call whenever one comes available." She listened for a moment. "That's more expensive than I thought, but it is doable." She walked to her bathroom and dampened a towel to scrub the whiteboard clean.

She kept thinking about the FBI agents. *They'll be back.* Then she buzzed Shugy. "Will you please call Lloyd and tell him I need to see him as soon as possible? Then please come in. We need to talk."

Shugy was in her office two minutes later. "I called Mr. Marsten. He should be here in a few minutes."

"Please close the door," L.J. said. They sat down on the couch next to each other. "Has Lloyd ever made an inappropriate comment or suggestion to you or to any other woman in the office? Of a sexual nature?"

Shugy shook her head. "No. Absolutely not. He's always been a perfect gentleman."

"I can't tell you how relieved I am to hear that. Those two FBI agents kept asking the most embarrassing questions." She lowered her voice. "About sex." Then, angrily, "Those idiots! Sometimes men get fixated on sex just because they're men." The two women clasped hands.

"I know." Shugy sighed. "I could tell you things about Billy . . ." Suddenly she felt the need to talk, to confide in someone. "He used to beg me to give him, well, you know, use my mouth."

L.J. suppressed her amusement at the thought of the prim Shugy giving her husband a blow job. "Men!" she consoled. "We've got to protect Lloyd from those perverts."

"I'll pray for him," Shugy said through tight lips.

"And I," L.J. promised. They stood and walked to the door in time to see Marsten get off the elevator.

Shugy brushed past, her head up. She was a ferocious gatekeeper when she gave her loyalty, and as far as she was concerned, the FBI and its agents were now the barbarians at the gate.

"What's gotten into Shugy?" Marsten asked.

"She's just chosen sides," L.J. said. She came right to business. "Those same two FBI agents dropped by today to see you. It seems that when Steiner talked to the Department of Energy, he accused us of some unsavory things."

"Of which we are totally innocent," Marsten added in a deadpan tone.

"Exactly. They also asked about Seismic Double Reflection. I imagine everyone in the government knows all about it."

"Which means," Marsten said, "the industry will know about it in a matter of days."

"I don't care about that," L.J. said, surprising Marsten with the anger in her words. "I want that concession."

"I don't know what we can do," he said.

"We're going to make something happen," she told him.

Washington, D.C.

Jane's departure had left Stuart depressed, and, certain that he had lost her, he was deep into his beat-me mood when he stopped in at the law offices of Samuel B. Broad. As before, he had an overwhelming impression of a scrawny chicken wearing a suit. He handed the lawyer a check for fifty thousand dollars, the required retainer fee. "I love cases like this one," Broad said.

"Why's that?" Stuart asked.

"It's weak because of the evidence."

"And because someone is out to get me."

"We don't have to suggest alternatives," Broad said. "We work the facts. At the right time I'll talk to the DA and show her where the case will fall apart. I'll tell her you're a nice guy and never even got a parking ticket. Also, you have an alibi."

Stuart was confused. "Alibi?"

"Certainly. You drove the car some two hundred miles before turning it over to your wife. Further, you were with a witness the entire time, who will testify she never saw you work on the car. What reasonable man is going to drive a car with brakes that he's sabotaged? That hole of reasonable doubt is so large I can drive a truck through it." He studied Stuart's face for a moment. "And there is always the option of a plea bargain."

He doesn't believe me, Stuart realized. He was back in the road, run over by the street sweeper. Despair overwhelmed him and for a moment he was further back in time, trapped in *Temptress*'s cabin in the hurricane. Now, as then, something inside him snapped. His words were slow and deliberate. "No . . . fucking . . . way."

Broad leaned back in his chair and nodded. "Good. I needed to know my marching orders. I'll go straight for it and make it go away. But it will take some time." He fingered the check. "Please give this to my secretary on your way out."

"One more thing," Stuart said. He quickly outlined the subpoena he had received and his problems with Jenny and her mother.

Broad's advice came quick. "Don't take a lawyer into a family court on the first appearance. Plead for time, tell them how happy and well adjusted your son is, that your ex may still be suffering post-traumatic shock from the accident. Tell them don't listen to the lawyers, listen to Eric."

It all made sense to Stuart. "Thanks," he said.

Broad stood up and extended his hand. "You're a good man," he said. "It's my pleasure."

Stuart felt better as he left the lawyer's offices. He decided it was time to quit feeling sorry for himself and get on with his life. He sat in Jenny's car and called her on his cell phone. "Jenny, can we talk?" He listened for a moment. "Sure, I can be right there." He wrote down the directions to her new home before breaking the connection. "Where in hell is Occoquan?" he wondered aloud. He started the car and drove south, heading for Fredericksburg on Interstate 95. Forty minutes later he turned into a neighborhood that shouted affluence, family, soccer moms, and good schools. *The perfect place to raise a kid*, he thought. *All thanks to Barbara Raye.*

He parked in the driveway behind a brand-new silver Lexus and got out. Hesitantly, he rang the door bell. There was no answer, so he rang again. Still no answer. *That's Jenny. Make an appointment and then go some-place else.* He was about to leave when the door opened. Jenny was standing there barefoot, wearing a tight T-shirt and jeans. Her belt and the top button of her jeans were undone, revealing her flat tummy. "I was almost in the shower," she said. She held the door open, and he walked inside.

"Nice," he said. "Very nice. Barbara Raye?" She nodded, tears in her eyes. Her right hand came up and touched the fresh scars on her face from where she had gone through the windshield. "I can hardly see them," he lied.

"My doctor says they'll be almost invisible after a year." He could hear the old insecurity in her words, now magnified a hundred times. For Jenny, her looks had been everything, and now, with her beautiful face scarred, there was nothing left for her to fall back on.

"He did a good job. You'll be fine." He gave her an encouraging smile. "This will all go away. But it will take time."

"Who'll ever look at me again?" she whispered.

They had been down this road before. He gave a little laugh. "Who won't?"

"Will you?"

He searched for the right words to reassure her and restore her fragile sense of confidence. He had to do it, for Barbara Raye used Jenny's insecurity as a way to control her. Without it Jenny would turn to her mother for support, and that meant trouble. "You're as beautiful as always."

She was in his arms, crying. "Oh, Mike! Are you sure?"

"I'm sure," he murmured in her ear. Her mouth was on his, her tongue exploring. He pulled free. "You don't have to prove anything." He had to explain. "Jenny, bad things happen to people all the time. It's not their fault, but they have to cope. That's what life is all about." He was sounding like Jane, and he knew it.

"Oh, Mike, we've always been able to work things out." She kissed him again, her right arm around his neck as her left hand rubbed his crotch. She broke the embrace and stepped back. She pushed her jeans down with both hands and stepped out of them.

"Jenny, you don't have to prove anything," he repeated. He turned toward the door, but she threw her arms around his neck, clinging to him.

"Please, Mike. Please. For what we meant to each other." She pulled off her T-shirt and led him into the bedroom.

20

The woman was politeness personified as she escorted L.J. and Marsten from the meeting with two Department of Justice lawyers. "Thank you for your time," she said as she held the door to their waiting limousine. She closed the door and watched the limo pull into traffic before returning inside.

It was a short ride from the Department of Justice on Constitution Avenue to the Department of Energy on Independence, and the jaws of tension and anxiety still held Marsten tight. "Are we in trouble?" he asked.

"I don't think so," L.J. replied, hiding her anger. "If we were, they'd have sent a formal letter notifying us that we were the target of an investigation. No, I think DOJ is on a fishing expedition."

"How can you be so sure?"

"I'm not. I'm guessing the FBI simply up-channeled their report, and it landed in the Environment and Natural Resources Division."

"Lovely," Marsten muttered. "With only five days before Christmas."

"Our imperial masters must be obeyed."

"Why are they looking at us now?" Marsten asked, fully aware that he would have a hard time explaining some of his activities.

"Probably because of what Steiner told them," L.J. said. "But why did Steiner tell *our* government about Seismic Double Reflection and not his own? It doesn't make sense."

"Perhaps his own government knows him too well," Marsten observed dryly.

L.J. thought for a moment. "It's an attempt to discredit us. If I ever get my hands on that little . . ." Her voice trailed off as she enjoyed the image of all the women the French scientist had abused descending on him like a flock of vengeful banshees. The limousine pulled up in front of the entrance to the Department of Energy, and L.J. got out. "I'll meet you back at the hotel," she told him.

"Are you sure you want to do this alone?" he asked.

"I wouldn't do it any other way." She fought her way past a horde of government employees knocking off early on the last Friday before Christmas. She stopped at Security. "L.J. Ellis to see Ann Silton."

The guard checked her ID and called for an escort. "Have you heard?" he asked. "The president appointed Miss Silton as the assistant secretary for Environment and Safety yesterday afternoon."

"After only one month?" L.J. mused, surprised that the environmentalist had made such an impression in so short a time.

The guard said, "Here's your escort."

L.J. turned to face Clarissa Jones, Silton's young friend. "Clarissa!" L.J. sang. "I didn't know you were in Washington."

"Ann needs all the support she can get," Clarissa said coldly. She signed L.J. in and led her to an elevator, not saying a word. They rode in silence to the top floor, and Clarissa walked with quick strides into Ann's new office.

"Very nice," L.J. said, looking out the window. Ann Silton stood but did not come around her desk. L.J. studied her, surprised by the change in her demeanor. There was an aggressive confidence she had not seen before. *Maybe clothes do make the woman*, L.J. thought. Or had the sudden acquisition of power brought out a hidden side of Ann's nature? She didn't know.

"Thank you for coming on such short notice," Ann said, sitting back down. "Since you were in the city, I wanted to take advantage of the moment. There are some things we need to discuss." She motioned at Clarissa to leave.

"Please," L.J. said. "I'd like for her to stay." She sat down in a straight-backed chair next to Ann's desk and felt herself slip forward. "Oh," she said. It was an old trick, shortening the front legs of a chair to make a visitor very uncomfortable. She moved over to the couch and sat down beside Clarissa. "Really, was that necessary?" Ann only gave her a cold look in reply. "I'm puzzled," L.J. said. "How did you parlay the appointment as the director of the Task Force on the Environment to an assistant secretary's slot so quickly?"

"The position has been vacant for some time, and the two were a natural fit. I thought it was common knowledge."

L.J. was very impressed and gave Ann high marks for political maneuvering. *I underestimated her.* She smiled at the woman, seeing her in a new light. "I missed that one."

Ann hit the intercom on her desk. "Would you please come in? Miss Ellis is here." The door to a side office opened, and John Frobisher walked in. "John is now heading up the Task Force on the Environment," Ann explained.

"Just like old times." L.J. said, still smiling. She hoped the reference to the convention in Dallas struck a nerve.

"What exactly is the slow roll?" Ann asked, all business.

Who told her that? L.J. wondered. "A delaying tactic," she answered. "It's very useful when faced with rapid change that can hurt business."

"And you thought you could do it to us?"

"As I recall, it was never discussed. But I was up-front from the very first. I'm in this business to make money."

"And you're causing incalculable damage to the environment."

"Am I?"

"Yes, you are, and we're going to stop you."

"So," L.J. replied, "you used me to get appointed as head of the president's Task Force on the Environment, knowing that would give you the inside track for this position."

"I used you no more than you intended to use me."

L.J. conceded the point. "What do you want to talk about?"

Ann said, "We've learned that in the last three weeks you've obtained lease options on every available deep-water drilling ship."

Not quite, L.J. thought, *but close enough.* "Why should that concern you?" she asked.

"Let me ask you this," Ann replied. "Does it have anything to do with Dr. Steiner's new discovery?"

L.J. was enjoying the moment. "Again, why does this concern you?"

Ann spoke in her best bureaucratic voice. "Because we're going to stop all offshore drilling until the oil industry makes all such drilling ships, platforms, and rigs environmentally safe."

L.J. arched an eyebrow. "Obviously you're not familiar with modern drilling procedures. The oil companies are doing a good job as it is. Do you have any idea what that would do to the oil industry?" *Or to me financially?* she added mentally. Then it hit her. Hard. They *did* know. It was the last time she would ever underestimate Ann Silton.

"We don't really care," Ann said.

"May I ask how you intend to enforce such a ban, especially beyond the territorial limits of the United States?"

"We prohibit any U.S. company from engaging in offshore drilling," Ann replied, still speaking in bureaucratese. "Further, anyone or any company doing business with a country or business doing such drilling will be barred from the U.S. market."

L.J. worked hard not to laugh at the simplicity of their thinking. They didn't have a clue how the oil business worked. Still, it was a complication she didn't need. She tried to be reasonable. "Regardless of what you believe, the computer chip has not made oil just another commodity. Take oil out of the equation, and our economy and political system will crumble. Unlike the computer chip, oil generates real wealth, not speculation on the stock market."

Ann snorted. "We've heard this all before."

"I'll be the first to admit," L.J. said, "that oil is a two-headed monster, capable of both great good and great evil."

"You've got that one absolutely right," Ann said. "That's why we're going to control it, not you or any oil company."

"I know some Eritrean rebels you need to talk to," L.J. replied.

"What does that mean?" Ann snapped.

"There's a whole Third World out there that fully intends to reap the benefits of an oil-driven economy."

"Really, Ms. Ellis," Ann said, her voice patronizing, "you must stop believing your own propaganda. Our brothers and sisters in the Third World know how to live in harmony with the environment. Their understanding and sophistication are much greater than ours in that regard."

L.J. sighed and pulled off the gloves. "I've never heard such unadulterated bullshit in my entire life. But since that seems to be the commodity of the day here, let me pitch some of my own and we'll see what sticks." She looked around the room, fully aware that it was probably bugged. *Why is John being so quiet?* she wondered. *Time to test the waters to find out exactly where they are.* "First there's the matter of the videotape of you and Clarissa."

"We think you made that tape," Ann said.

L.J. waited to hear more. But Ann's silence was proof that she had no intention of suggesting John may been involved in making the tape. *She still isn't sure about him!* L.J. thought. *I can use that!* Again she had to suppress her elation. She fired her second salvo. "There's the matter of your new wardrobe. You really didn't think it cost so little, did you?"

"But I was led to believe—"

"You were led to believe nothing, Ann. That was a bad mistake on your part." L.J. turned her sights on John to see if there were more cracks in their façade that she could exploit. But before she could launch another round about RayTex's underwriting of Front Uni's convention in Dallas, the intercom buzzed.

Ann picked it up, and her face went white. "Turn on the TV," she gasped. "CNC."

Clarissa rushed over to the big TV built into a bookcase. The face of Elizabeth Gordon, CNC-TV's political correspondent, filled the screen. "I repeat," she said, "a missile apparently shot down the president's helicopter, but President Turner is unhurt." The camera zoomed in on a crash wagon driving away from the scene. Then it panned to the burning wreckage of a helicopter as sirens and screams echoed in the background.

Suddenly the crash wagon slammed to a halt, and Madeline O'Keith Turner climbed out the back. Gordon and her cameraman ran toward her in time to hear the president shout, "Get out of my way!" as seven Secret Service agents surrounded her. "Back off! Give me room!"

"Madam President," an agent shouted, "we've got to get you to—"

"I don't give a damn what *you* have to do! There are injured people out there." She pushed clear of the cordon and started pointing, issuing commands. For a moment there was utter chaos around her. Then there was order.

Liz Gordon faced the camera. "We have witnessed a miracle here. President Turner is totally unscathed." The cameraman panned to the burning pillar of flame reaching into the sky. "All others on board perished in the crash."*

In Ann Silton's office, silence bound the four people as they stared at the TV. Clarissa started to cry, and John sat down, his hands shaking. Ann rushed over and put her arm around Clarissa to comfort her. L.J. stood in the center of the room, her own arms crossed across her chest, her face a mask.

"Who could do such a thing?" Clarissa gasped.

A very good question, L.J. thought.

Newport News

Shanker hunched over the computer in his den, picking at the keys, while Stuart sat on the couch and read. Shanker grunted in satisfaction at what he was finding. "Right on. That'll fix the bitch."

"Who's the bitch?" Eric said from the doorway, fresh from school. He was still carrying his backpack.

"None of your business," Stuart told him, "and you shouldn't use that word. Any homework?"

"Naw. Today was the last day before Christmas vacation, and the teachers gave us a break." The boy walked over to help his grandfather with the computer. He read the screen. "Boy, somebody really hates President Turner," he said.

Stuart's head came up. "What are you doing?" he asked his father.

"We're getting organized to stop her dead in her tracks," Shanker explained. "No way we're going to let her outlaw semiautomatic weapons. The Gray Eagles are all against her, and we're going to do something about it. That dumb-ass bill will never get through Congress. We'll see to that. Besides, it's plain unconstitutional."

"My social studies teacher," Eric said, "hates guns, and he's really upset, too. He says he's writing his congressman and wants him to vote against it, too."

"Even a stopped clock is right once a day," Shanker grumbled.

---

*Editor's note: The attempted assassination of Madeline Turner is described in detail in the book *Edge of Honor* by the same author.

Stuart looked at his son while he tried to fold a chart. "Did your teacher say why he was against the bill?"

"Well," Eric said, trying to appease his grandfather, "he says it's all wrong because everyone who already owns a semiautomatic weapon gets to keep what they already got. He says that won't solve anything, and the government ought to outlaw all guns."

"Another friggin' liberal," Shanker grouched.

"Is that true, Dad?" Stuart asked. "You can keep your weapons?"

"Supposedly," Shanker replied, his voice loud and angry.

"Sounds to me like she's pissed off both sides of the argument," Stuart said. "Who knows? She might be onto something."

Shanker glared at his youngest son. "Lee Harvey Oswald, where are you now that we need you?"

"Who's Lee Harvey Oswald?" Eric asked.

"Dad," Stuart said, "that wasn't called for, and you know it."

The two men stared at each other for a moment. "This is my goddamn home!" Shanker shouted. "And I can say anything I want!" He stormed out of the room just as his wife rushed in.

"Turn on the TV," Martha gasped. Eric grabbed the remote control and flicked it on. A picture of a burning helicopter filled the TV screen. Tears filled Martha's eyes. "Oh, no," she moaned. "How could anyone do such a terrible thing?"

"The reporter says she's okay!" Eric shouted.

"Look at her," Stuart said, wonder in his voice. "She's taking charge."

Shanker stood in the doorway, a grim look on his face. "What would you know about taking charge?"

"I can only guess, since I've never been in a situation like that," Stuart replied. "And neither have you."

Shanker didn't reply because it was true. He had faced real danger and real bullets many times in combat. But neither he, nor his wingmen, had ever been hit. He had never lived through the terror of a crash. He glared at his youngest son. It was the first time Stuart had ever stood up to him.

21

Sophia James stood at the kitchen sink of the grimy mobile home and scrubbed at the three men's dirty underwear. She pulled her hands out of the hot water and studied her fingernails. They were all broken and in need of a manicure. *You miserable bastards!* she cursed silently She peeled off the cheap red T-shirt Luis had given her to wear and threw it in the hot water. "Let's see how you like pink shorts," she hissed to herself.

She walked past the three men, who were watching TV, and into the single bedroom at the back. They were so used to seeing her naked that they took no notice. She slipped into a clean T-shirt and sat on the edge of the bed, half listening to the TV. *At least I only have to fuck one of you a day*, she thought. That and the T-shirt had been the only concessions she'd wrung from Luis. Rather than let herself fall into another round of despair and self-pity, she seriously contemplated murder.

The sound of the woman's voice on TV didn't register at first, and Sophia had to concentrate on what she was hearing. She walked to the door and listened. As one, Luis, Eduardo, and Francisco were leaning toward the TV set. "We have witnessed a miracle here," the woman reporter said. "President Turner is totally unscathed. All others on board perished in the crash."

All three men started yelling at once in Spanish. They spoke so fast that she had a hard time understanding. Slowly the pieces came together. They were angry because someone had tried to assassinate the president of the United States. And failed.

"They bungled it!" Eduardo shouted.

"Amateurs," Francisco said.

"That's why they failed," Luis said, flopping back onto the couch. "The Secret Service will be on full alert and much more dangerous now."

"How can they call themselves men?" Eduardo said. "Protecting a *puta*." Sophia assumed the *puta* was Madeline Turner.

"Is it still possible?" Francisco asked.

"It will be even a greater honor because of the danger," Luis told him. "The cause of our people is sacred, and we do not run from danger. Always remember, we live and die as men."

Sophia caught her breath, at last fully understanding. That explained why two of them would disappear for long periods of time into the shack behind the trailer while one guarded her. That was why they would order her into the bedroom, turn up the TV, and then sit at the kitchenette table and talk for hours at a time.

They were plotting to assassinate the president of the United States.

❉

Eduardo rolled off her and fell asleep. Sophia waited until he was snoring loudly before she got out of bed and went into the bathroom. She took a quick shower and wrapped a large towel around herself. She padded quietly into the kitchen, careful not to wake the two men asleep in the small living room, reached into the freezer, and pulled out the small paring knife she'd hidden there the day after Luis had sealed them in. Since they hadn't missed it, she assumed it was safe to move it to the bedroom. She knew exactly where to hide it: under the pile of dirty clothes they expected her to wash. She walked quietly back into the bedroom and hid the knife before lying back down.

Then she lay awake, forcing herself to think and not give in to the panic that threatened her sanity. There was no doubt they would kill her, either before they moved or immediately afterward. *Probably before*, she decided. She ran possible scenarios through her mind. One fact stood out: She had to make herself indispensable to them until she could escape. But how? What did she have to offer that had value to them? Being Latino, they would never take her into their plans, which was just as well, since it was such an absurd idea. Pointing out the flaws in any plan they could come up with would only make them angry at her. *Divide and conquer*, she thought. She liked that idea.

She thought about the three men, trying to visualize them in different situations. It had to be Eduardo, the dreamer. But first she would have to do something about the shorts she'd stained pink.

22

Newport News

It was a military wedding, complete with an honor guard and mess dress uniforms as Maggot and Mary exchanged their vows. As the best man, Stuart stood back and crossed his hands when the priest turned to the congregation. "Let me introduce Colonel and Mrs. Stuart." Maggot lifted his bride's veil and swept her into his arms in the best fighter-pilot style. Stuart tried not to look embarrassed and smiled at Jenny, who was sitting with Eric in the first pew. Movement at the back of the church caught his attention as Jane slipped into the last pew. She had made it back from her charter cruise as promised.

The organist played "We've Only Just Begun" as the couple retreated down the aisle. As it was raining and spitting snow outside, the honor guard was at the back of the church, forming an arch with their swords. As the couple approached, the first two swords dropped, blocking their way. Maggot kissed Mary, and the guardsmen raised their swords to let them pass. The second set of swords dropped, again barring the way. Again the couple kissed before the swords were lifted. Twice more they repeated the rite, kissing their way free of the arch. As tradition dictated, the last guardsman tapped Mary's rear end with the broadside of his sword, sending them on their way.

Jenny's laughter rang over the church. "They never did that at our wedding," she sang out.

Stuart caught the funny look on Jane's face and made his way to the rear, anxious to talk to her. Eric joined him. "I'm glad she made it," Eric said. "Me, too, son. Me, too."

※

Because of the weather, the guests were slow to gather at the reception at the Officers' Club at Langley Air Force Base. Shanker pulled at the tight-fitting jacket of his mess dress uniform, feeling very uneasy next to the dapper Chalky Seagrave, whose old RAF mess dress uniform still fit perfectly. The two men smiled when eight pilots from Maggot's old A-10 squadron marched in wearing gray-green flight suits and yellow bow ties made out of the squadron's neck scarves. "Why do I sense this is going to be quite the reception?" Seagrave asked as Jenny descended on the pilots.

She was wearing a low-cut, skintight black dress that reached to the floor and was split dangerously high up the side. "I do hope she's wearing knickers," Seagrave murmured as the pilots surrounded her. "Ah, there's Jane." He wandered over to speak to her. "May I escort you to a table?" She held his arm as they found places next to the head table.

"I feel so out of place," Jane said, looking at the other guests. She was dressed in a bright spring dress with beige shoes, the best clothes she owned, and was in total contrast to the other women, who were wearing winter ensembles.

"You look lovely," he told her. "A breath of sea air." It was just the right thing to say, and she brightened.

The dinner and toasts proceeded normally, although an eager antici-pation hung in the air as the guests waited to see what might happen. The disc jockey started the music, and Stuart slipped away from the head table to finally join Jane and Seagrave. "It's been a madhouse," he told her. She listened and smiled at all the right times as Stuart and Seagrave recalled the preparations for the wedding. "I'm glad you made it," he told her.

"We had rigging problems," Jane said, "and made for Norfolk. Docked there this morning. My charter didn't mind and jumped ship. I'll single-hand *Temptress* back to Annapolis." Behind them the dance floor filled and voices rang out.

A woman's voice shouted "Dead Bug!" and all the men in uniform, including Stuart and Seagrave, fell to the floor on their backs, their feet and arms upright and waving helplessly in the air. Jane stared at them in disbelief. On the dance floor a lovely pair of bare legs kicked in the air. "It's a drinking game," Stuart explained from the floor. "The last guy to make like a dead bug gets to buy the next round of drinks."

"Are all Air Force weddings like this one?" Jane asked.

"I hope not," Stuart replied.

"Pity," Seagrave murmured.

"Do women play, too?" Jane asked.

Stuart came to his feet to see who the bare legs belonged to. "No." He looked at the dance floor. "Jenny."

"She called Dead Bug," Seagrave said.

"Oh, no," Stuart muttered.

"Is that bad?" Jane wondered.

"The generals don't allow singing or games in the bar anymore," Stuart explained. "It's not professional."

"He means," Seagrave added, "that it's not politically correct." Along with everyone else, he stood. "I do hope the generals are all safe in their beds when the shooting starts." At the bar, two male voices bellowed the final stanza of "The Balls of O'Leary" with gusto.

> *The women all muster, to see that great cluster*
> *And they stand and they stare*
> *At that bloody great pair*
> *Of O'Leary's balls.*

"That broke the ice," Stuart said. "It's going to get wild. I better get Eric home."

Before he could leave, Jenny hurried up, anxious to talk and out of breath. "Oh, Mike," she breathed, "thanks for inviting me. It was just what I needed." She gestured at the group of fighter pilots wearing flight suits. "They're so cute and cuddly."

"Jenny," Stuart warned, "they're all certified aerial assassins. They fight hard and play hard. They're not kittens."

She reached out and caressed his cheek. "You were right, I didn't need to prove anything." She didn't draw her hand away. "You were there when I needed you." She kissed him, lingering a moment. Her tongue flicked at his lips as she pulled away. "Thanks, Mike." She turned and walked back to the waiting pilots.

Jane turned and walked away. For a moment Stuart didn't move, stunned by the events. "Go after her," Seagrave urged. Still Stuart didn't move. "Jane, you dolt."

Stuart ran into the foyer, desperately looking for her. Then he saw her through the entrance windows, walking through the blowing rain and sleet. He ran after her, slipping and sliding on the sidewalk. He fell once and caught her as she slid into the driver's seat of her rented car. "Jane, what's the matter?"

She clutched the steering wheel and looked at him. "What's the matter? The matter is that I'm stupid. Why did I ever think that . . ." Her voice trailed off.

"I don't understand," he bleated.

"You slept with her!" She jerked the door closed and gunned the engine. The wheels threw up a wave of slush and mud, drenching his pants.

He stood in the rain as a desolate wind blew through him.

※

Stuart turned up the heater in the hangar's office as gusts beat at the big doors. He gazed at the Lightning parked in the big bay while an Air Force lieutenant colonel outlined his proposal to the Gray Eagles. "Someone finally got a clue at ACC," the eager young LC said. ACC was Air Combat Command, headquartered at Langley Air Force Base. "We've been concentrating on avionics and missiles, assuming we'd kill the enemy before the merge."

"Which means," Shanker said, "your pilots can't yank and bank worth shit."

"I think," Seagrave said, trying to smooth any ruffled feathers, "that my friend means you need to return to basics."

"Exactly," the lieutenant colonel said, "and that's where your Lightning comes in. It's perfect for DACT." DACT was Dissimilar Air Combat Training, or dogfighting. The generals hated DACT because it involved two very different fighters maneuvering against each other in mock combat. It was inherently dangerous, and success all came down to pilot skill. "As a third-generation fighter," the officer explained, "it will give our pilots a taste of what they'll be up against in a conflict with

China. Also, by denying the F-15s use of their radar, we can simulate an engagement with a stealth fighter where visual contact is everything. Congress, in all its wisdom, has finally decided it was time to get serious about training and has given us the money to do something worthwhile."

"Train like you plan to fight," Shanker muttered.

"We couldn't agree more," the officer said. He laid out the details of a lucrative contract in which the Lightning would simulate a MiG-21 type aircraft and fly DACT against F-15s and F-22s based at Langley. To make the training more realistic, the Air Force wanted to hang training missiles on the Lightning.

"If you think the Lightning is a MiG-21," Seagrave huffed, "you chaps need to spend more time in aircraft recognition."

"There is a resemblance to the untrained eye," the officer said.

Stuart's attention wandered as he half listened to the men discuss the contract. *Damn*, he thought. *I blew it with Jane. How could I be so stupid?* He was looking directly at the side door when it banged open. The men all glanced up. "It's Jenny," Stuart told them. "I'll take care of it." He stepped out of the office and headed for his ex-wife. Halfway there he regretted it. Barbara Raye and the lawyer who was a permanent appendage to her hip came through the door. From the way Jenny paced back and forth, he knew there was trouble.

"We came for Eric," Jenny said.

"Why?" Stuart replied. "He's still in school. What's the problem?"

"The problem," the lawyer said, "is the environment he's in." He gestured at Jenny. "Mrs. Stuart objects to the influences he is being subjected to."

"What are you talking about?" Stuart said.

"Your brother and his pilot friends," Jenny snapped. "They're nothing but a bunch of perverts. Which I found out at the wedding."

"It looked like you were enjoying yourself," Stuart said.

"All they think about is sex, sex, sex," Jenny wailed.

The look on Jenny's face told Stuart what had happened. "One of the pilots dumped on you, and this is your way of getting back, right?" She didn't answer. "Maybe *you* were sending the wrong signals," Stuart said.

"There is also the matter of the boy's safety," the lawyer said. He pulled a videocassette out of his briefcase and handed it to Stuart. "Have you seen this?" Stuart shook his head, not knowing what the man was talking about. "This," the lawyer explained, gesturing at the Lightning, "is a tape of a special TV program which hasn't aired yet. It documents your son flying in that airplane under very dangerous circumstances. Which, I might add, the court will not view favorably."

Stuart looked at Jenny. "I thought we had put all that behind us."

"Not hardly," Barbara Raye snapped. "Because of your careless disregard of Eric's safety, we think it best if he's in Jenny's care. Permanently."

The lawyer said, "You have joint custody, and Eric has been in your care since September. You cannot deny Mrs. Stuart's rights any longer. She has a home and the means to care for him in a proper and safe manner."

"All thanks to Barbara Raye," Stuart countered. "Look, he's happy and doing well in school. Wait until summer before moving him."

"Under the circumstances," the lawyer said, "I can't allow that. His safety is paramount. And there is the matter of your impending trial for the murder of Mr. DeLorenzo."

Stuart knew when it was time for damage control. "Drop the court hearing and he can move during the semester break, which is in two weeks."

Jenny, Barbara Raye, and the attorney huddled together for a few moments. From the way Barbara Raye stomped her right foot, Stuart could see there was a problem. The lawyer spoke in a low tone so Stuart could not hear. Then there were nods all around. "Agreed," the lawyer said. "You deliver Eric to Jenny's care immediately after the semester ends, and we drop the court hearing."

"And he can be with me over spring break and during vacation," Stuart added.

Again the brief huddle. "Agreed," the lawyer said. They turned to leave.

Barbara Raye gave Stuart a look of pure hate. "You're nothing but a poor, pathetic—"

The lawyer interrupted her. "Not here, Mrs. Wilson." She bit off her words, and they marched out of the hangar.

※

"Fuck me in the heart," Shanker rumbled as the video played out. "That reporter made us look like a bunch of idiots and the Lightning like a flying accident looking for a place to happen."

The TV reporter's face filled the screen as the Lightning was towed clear of the runway. "Only the quick and heroic action of Harry Langston in his homebuilt aircraft saved Eric Stuart from certain death."

"That asshole hasn't got a clue," Shanker said heatedly.

"The power of the media," Seagrave murmured.

"Do you think the Air Force will cancel the contract to fly DACT?" Stuart asked.

"Who knows?" Shanker replied. The phone rang in the other room. "Honey," Shanker called to his wife, "will you get that?" He rewound the tape. "I wonder if Hank has seen this?"

"What difference would that make?" Stuart wondered.

Martha came to the door. "Mike, it's for you. The Coast Guard. Something about an emergency on *Temptress*."

Stuart hurried to the phone. A voice on the other end asked if he was the owner of sailing vessel *Temptress* bound between Norfolk, Virginia, and Annapolis, Maryland. "I recently sold it to Jane Ryan," he replied. "I guess the paperwork hasn't caught up yet."

The voice said, "We received a Mayday from *Temptress*. There's an injury on board, and we've dispatched a cutter."

"That's Jane," Stuart explained. "She's single-handing it. How bad is she hurt?"

"We don't know the full extent yet."

Stuart said, "Please let me know."

"What shall we do with the boat?" the caller asked.

"Can you tow it to the city docks at Annapolis? I'll meet you there." The caller agreed and rang off.

"What's happening?" Shanker asked.

Stuart explained the situation. His eyes narrowed. "That accident was meant for me."

"Yeah, sure," Shanker said. "Everybody's out to get you." He stopped at the sound of his words. There *was* too much wrong in his son's life. "You know, Mike, you may be right."

"What do I do?"

"When something goes wrong," Shanker intoned, "get aggressive."

For the first time Stuart understood what his father was telling him. But he didn't know *how* to get aggressive.

Dallas

The phone call came before the close of business on Friday, January 24. Marsten sensed there was trouble the moment he heard the Jogger's voice. "I've lost contact with Sophia."

Marsten paused before answering. "When was the last time you saw her?"

"Friday, the twenty-ninth of November."

Almost two months! Marsten raged to himself, But nothing in his voice betrayed his anger. "When you delivered the package?" Both men knew that the package was twenty-thousand dollars destined for the Group.

"Correct."

"Has she done a flit?" Marsten asked. It was not unusual for mules to take the money and run.

"I don't think so. I checked out her condominium and found her car. No trace of Luis and the Group."

"Find her," Marsten ordered, "and get back to me. Monday at the latest." He broke the connection. *Damn! Maybe we should cut and run. Only two people can connect us to the Group—the Jogger and Sophia. If Sophia's dead, he'll be more than glad to sever the connection.* Was it time to tell L.J.? Maybe she didn't need them anymore. He hit the intercom to her office. "L.J., a moment please."

"Now's good," she answered.

Marsten made the short walk to L.J.'s office and passed Marcia, Ray-Tex's glamorous comptroller, as she left. From the stern look on her face, he sensed another problem, this time money. He found L.J. pacing her office deep in thought, a sure sign something was wrong. She came right to the point. "We've got a cash-flow problem."

"With the elephant, no doubt."

"Of course," she replied. "We have to make something happen. Soon."

"Perhaps, it's time to cut our losses and withdraw."

From the set of her jaw, he knew that the advice was premature. "Not yet," she said, telling him the obvious. "But I don't know how much longer we can hide it, not with Steiner talking to DOE. Sooner or later he *will* tell them."

"The industry does feed on rumor," Marsten said. She gave a little humph of disgust. "Perhaps we can turn it to our advantage," he suggested.

"Perhaps," L.J. allowed. She sat down and visualized her decision tree. Was a radical change called for? She had succeeded in the cutthroat oil industry by being flexible, always ready to exploit a change in circumstances without losing sight of the objective. But she was on new ground and feeling her way.

"If we can no longer hide it," Marsten said, "flaunt it. Get everyone watching us so that when we start drilling, they'll want a piece of the action. We can sell off enough blocks to cover our investment. They assume part of the risk."

"If we can start a feeding frenzy—"

"Which has been known to happen," he said.

"Do we need to crank up the rumor mill?" The oil industry fed on rumors as the companies watched each other. "Wentworth?" she suggested. Wentworth Country Club outside London was considered hallowed ground by European oilmen, and more information was exchanged, rumors spread, and deals cut on its golf links than in any boardroom.

"It's winter," he reminded her. "But there is the professional-amateur golf tournament in Palm Springs next weekend. I had accepted, but perhaps some of those hours you've spent on the links could be used to advantage." They talked for another twenty minutes before he left. The subject of Sophia and the Group never came up.

23

Palm Springs, California

L.J. wired the Sabreliner's airspeed at 165 knots and called for the gear and flaps. Ahead of them, Palm Springs Regional Airport shimmered in the morning sun as they came down final. "Very nice," Tim Roxford said from the copilot's seat. "You've a slight left-quartering crosswind. No problem." Their airspeed decayed to 125 knots as L.J. inched the throttles back and crossed the runway numbers at 115 knots to touch down at 110 knots. "Sweet," Roxford allowed. He radioed the tower when they were clear of the active runway and ground control guided them to parking.

The ramp was full of sleek corporate jets that had brought in the professional golfers and business executives for the Pro-Am Golf Tournament. But of all the players, only L.J. had piloted her own jet. A silver Bentley convertible was waiting for her. "I'll see you Sunday evening," L.J. told Roxford. "Departure around six in the evening. Back to Dallas."

"We'll be good to go," Roxford assured her. He placed her bags and golf clubs in the Bentley. "Ah, L.J.," he stammered, "I've been offered a job with Delta, and they want me to report in two weeks."

"That's wonderful," she said. It was no surprise, for she had spoken to a friend at the airline about hiring Roxford. But all the same, she was sad to hear that he was leaving. "You've been a wonderful instructor, and I'll miss you." With that she slipped into the driver's seat of the Bentley and drove to the resort where she was staying during the tournament.

❊

The two men were chatting amiably when L.J. joined them at the starting tee for the first round. "Felix," L.J. called. "What a pleasure."

The tall, gray-haired Scotsman who bore an uncanny resemblance to Sean Connery smiled at her. Felix Campbell was the epitome of the European oilman—educated, sophisticated, and politically adept. His credentials, as well as his manners, were impeccable, and he looked great on TV. "L.J., so good to see you." They shook hands, for all the world the best of friends. He introduced his partner for the tournament, the current leader of the PGA tour. "And how is Lloyd?" Campbell asked.

"Doing quiet well," she replied. "How are things at BP?" Campbell was the president of British Petroleum and rumored to be making a move to buy out Exxon. If the merger went through, it would effectively re-form John D. Rockefeller's Standard Oil.

"Moving right along," Campbell replied.

L.J.'s partner walked onto the course and waved to the spectators. He was considered the grand old man of the PGA, and he worked the crowd like a master. They shook hands all around and posed for the cameras. The formalities dispensed with, the starter motioned them onto the green, and L.J. stepped up to the tee. Tournament rules allowed her to use the red ladies' marker, which was the shortest distance to the pin. However, she moved to the white middle marker normally played by men. The two PGA professionals had to play the blue marker set thirty yards farther back. The signal was unmistakable: She was playing Campbell as an equal. No quarter would be given, and she didn't expect any in return. A hush fell over the crowd as she addressed the ball and swung. The two pros followed her ball as it sailed down the fairway for 225 yards. It landed in the middle and rolled another twelve yards. "I think we're in trouble," Campbell's partner whispered.

Campbell shook his head. "All show and no go."

"A lightweight?" the golfer asked.

"In my business, the lightest."

As Campbell had intended, L.J. overheard the exchange. She smiled sweetly at her partner.

On the third green L.J. stood beside Campbell while his partner sank a four-foot putt for an eagle, two under par. "How's the merger going?" she asked.

"Rumor, merely a rumor," Campbell told her.

"I was talking to Justice and Energy before Christmas," she said, using the rumor mill to full effect. She was fairly certain the industry was buzzing about her summons to Washington. "They're not treating it like a rumor." This last was a blatant lie. Now it was Campbell's turn to putt. But he wasn't concentrating. BP's lobbyist had reported that she and Marsten were in Washington and talking to the departments of Energy and Justice before Christmas. Now he knew why. He muffed his putt, sending it across the green.

L.J. studied her lie, a twenty-foot downhill putt from the cup. She addressed the ball and gave it a gentle tap. But she hadn't hit it hard enough, and it was running out of momentum. The crowd held its collective breath. But the ball had legs and kept rolling. For a moment it held on the edge of the cup. Then it dropped in for a birdie, one under par. The crowd broke into applause.

"I thought you said she was a lightweight," Campbell's partner moaned. Even though it was a charity tournament, he hated losing.

Campbell had not become the president of British Petroleum by being either stupid or slow. "Rumor has it she's an indifferent golfer."

"That's not an indifferent rumor we're playing."

"She'll tire on the back nine," Campbell predicted. "She always fades in the stretch."

His partner grimaced as L.J. teed off on the fourth hole, driving the ball well over two hundred yards. "She plays like a man."

Campbell waited until the seventh fairway before counterattacking. He spoke quietly as L.J. took a practice swing. "You're not really involved with Steiner, are you?"

She didn't answer and addressed her ball. Her swing was a study in perfection, but she deliberately hit it fat, leaving the ball well short of the green. "We've talked to him." She pitched her voice just right, sounding nervous. "How did you hear about it?"

The muffed shot and her voice told him what he needed to know. "The rumor mill, how else?" Actually his Washington lobbyist had a highly placed source inside the Department of Energy.

L.J. chose the ninth hole to retaliate. "By chance, your rumor mill wouldn't happen to be John Frobisher?" She saw his jaw tense. She used a five-iron to hit the ball 160 yards to the green. It rolled to within a yard of the pin.

"Great shot," her partner said.

"By chance," Campbell said, "would you be interested in a side bet?"

"It depends what the stakes are," she replied.

The two pros overheard the exchange. "Would I like part of that action!" Campbell's partner said, not thinking of golf or betting at all.

"She'd eat you alive," the old master replied, knowing exactly what he was thinking.

Campbell spoke in a low voice to L.J. as they walked to the back nine. "Have you tested Seismic Double Reflection?"

"What's the bet?" she asked.

"Next hole. I win, you answer."

"Make it the fifteenth hole, and if I win," L.J. said, "you give ten thousand to the charity of my choice."

Campbell thought about it. He had played this course before, and the fifteenth hole was a killer. "Done," he said.

L.J. hated losing but forced herself to miss a putt on the fifteenth that allowed Campbell to win by a stroke. "We've tested it in the field," she told him.

"What were the results?" Campbell asked.

A smile flickered at the corners of her lips. "That wasn't part of the bet."

"Right," Campbell said, enjoying the game. "Same bet on the sixteenth?"

L.J. agreed, and Campbell played the best hole of golf of his entire life, beating her honestly. "It works," she told him.

"But was it significant?" he asked. She gave him the sweet smile but didn't answer. "Okay," he said, "same bet on the seventeenth." L.J. played it perfectly and matched him stroke for stroke, again allowing him to win by deliberately missing a putt.

She frowned before answering. "It's safe to say the results were significant."

Campbell's eyes opened wide. "Where?" Again no answer. "Same bet on the eighteenth?"

"No," she told him. "Fifty thousand if I win."

Campbell gulped. Hard. But he was hooked. "Done."

L.J. stepped up to the white marker and teed off, driving the ball 240 yards down the fairway.

"So much for fading in the stretch," Campbell's partner said sotto voce. "She could turn pro."

"Where I come from," Campbell muttered, "a pro is a hooker." He stepped up to the tee, took a practice swing, and then executed a picture-perfect swing, driving the ball farther than ever before. But it was too much, and it landed in the rough.

"Jesus H. Christ," his partner said.

L.J. suppressed a real groan when her shot from the fairway landed in a sand trap short of the green. Campbell was out of the rough with one stroke and onto the green with a long five-iron shot for three. The pros were both on the green in two with decent lies close to the pin.

L.J. took her time lining up the next play. This had always been the weakest part of her game, and it normally took her two strokes to get out of a sand trap. Her caddie handed her a sand wedge. She studied the ball and tried to get a decent stance, but it wasn't going to happen. "I think I'll try a nine-iron," she said. The caddie shook his head and made the exchange. She walked up to the ball, set her feet, and swung. The ball rose out of the bunker in a shower of sand and cut a graceful arc over the green to stop two yards off the fringe on the far side for three.

Even though he was on the green, Campbell's ball was farther from the hole than hers. Technically he should have played first, but he wanted to keep the pressure on. "Your shot," he said to L.J., deferring to custom among American amateurs where the player still off the green plays first.

L.J. set her stance and started to swing. But she pulled up short. "Sorry, I think the rules call for you to go first." She stepped back from the ball, effectively putting the pressure back on Campbell. She smiled apologetically.

"The smiling assassin," the old master whispered to the other pro.

Campbell carefully lined up his shot. "You shouldn't play with the big boys," he told her. He planted his feet and stroked the ball. It rolled straight for the hole, sure and true. But it slowed and stopped less than an inch from the cup. A loud groan swept over the spectators as Campbell willed it to drop. Nothing happened. He shrugged and tapped it into the hole for a bogey five.

The old master's eyes followed L.J. as she took a few practice swings with a nine-iron. The pressure was off. "Five hundred says she sinks it," he said to Campbell's partner.

"You're on."

L.J. swung, and the ball lifted out of the grass, hit the green, and rolled six feet into the cup for four.

"Yes!" the old master shouted.

Campbell's eyes narrowed into slits as L.J. walked over to shake his hand. "Well done," he said, hiding his anger. Then, "You didn't find anything, did you?"

She fixed him with a steady look. "Let's just say you're merging with the wrong company." She deliberately sashayed off the course, fully aware that every eye was on her.

The rumor mill was primed.

Newport News

Eric stood in the doorway as Stuart loaded his bags in the car. "It's time," Stuart said. He felt like crying when Eric turned to his grandmother and gave her a hug. Eric walked manfully to the car and got in, hiding his tears.

"Dad, I want to say good-bye to Commander Seagrave."

"You want to see the Lightning, right?" Eric nodded, and Stuart started the car. "You'll be back during spring break. Then there's this summer to look forward to."

Eric gave him a look he had never seen before. "If Mom sends me to Grandma Barbara's, I'll run away."

"That's not going to happen, son. I promise." They drove in silence to the airport. Stuart wanted to tell his son that everything was going to be okay. But saying it wouldn't make it true.

It started to rain as they pulled into the general-aviation side of the airport, and Stuart turned on the windshield wipers. He was surprised by the large number of cars parked around the hangars and had trouble finding a parking place. When he did find a spot, he and Eric had to run a fair distance through the rain. They pushed through the side door into the hangar and came to a dead halt. The hangar was full of people, most of whom Stuart had never seen before. A small group of active-duty Air

Force maintenance NCOs were clustered around the Lightning with Seagrave while four senior airmen and a staff sergeant assembled a blue air-to-air missile.

In the large open area off to one side, Shanker was surrounded by approximately fifty men. All were about his age, gray-haired, and wearing black baseball caps with gold lettering announcing they were members of the National Rifle Association. "What's going on, Dad?" Eric asked.

"I don't know," Stuart answered. They stepped into the side office where Hank Langston, the owner of the homebuilt Legend, was watching the videotape of the TV program that claimed he was a hero and had saved Eric from certain death in the Lightning.

"That shit-for-brains hasn't got a clue!" Hank shouted. "He never mentioned Maggot, even though I told them he was at the controls when it counted."

"That's the media," Stuart said. "Not much we can do about it."

"We'll see about that!" Hank roared.

"What are you going to do?" Eric asked.

"No idea. But when things go wrong, get aggressive." He stomped out of the office.

"I think he's been listening to your grandfather," Stuart told his son. They followed him out to the hangar bay and joined the men gathered around the Lightning.

"There you are," Seagrave said to Eric. "These men are from Langley and want to fit the Lightning with a training missile so we can fly against their jets." He explained how the blue missile being assembled was the training version of an AIM-9 Sidewinder. The latest version of the Sidewinder was the best short-range, heat-seeking, air-to-air missile in the world. But the training missile was inert and didn't carry a warhead. They needed its guidance head only so they could tell if a simulated launch during training was within the tracking and firing parameters of a real missile. It was the way they kept the pilots honest during the debrief after a training mission.

"It's not going to happen," the senior NCO said. "There's not enough room to mount a launch rail in the missile wells. He pointed to the indented areas on the forward part of the fuselage just under the leading edge of the wing root.

A loud "Squad-ron, a-ten-hut!" echoed over the hangar, stopping all conversation. It was Shanker forming up the Gray Eagles. At the command of attention, they all straightened up and did their best to appear military. "Dress right, dress!" Shanker shouted. The men extended their right elbows to take pacing and shuffled their ranks. The senior NCO shook his head at the sight of the retirees drilling. "You may be able to dress 'em up," he said, "but you definitely don't want to take 'em out." He turned back to work and ignored the Gray Eagles.

Stuart studied the missile and the launch rail. His college degree was in engineering, but he hadn't used it in years. Yet this was exactly the type of problem he enjoyed solving. He bent down and looked under the wing. "Did you mount a pylon here?" He pointed to a teardrop-shaped panel on the underside of the wing.

"Correct," Seagrave said. "We could carry a thousand-pound bomb or rocket pod under each wing."

"Is the wiring still intact, and do you have the pylons?" Stuart asked.

"Yes and yes," Seagrave replied. He led them to the back of the hangar, where all the spare parts were carefully stored and catalogued. The two pylons were wrapped in protective foil.

Stuart pulled away the foil and carefully examined the streamlined attachment that bolted to the underside of the wing. "I've got an idea." He led them into the office and sat at the table. "Here's how it works." He sketched a diagram of the bomb pylon hanging under the Lightning's wing. "The problem is mounting the missile launch rail on the bottom."

"They're incompatible," the senior NCO said.

"True," Stuart replied. "But in the mobility kits you maintain for deployments, you've got universal wing-tank adapters so you can mount NATO fuel tanks on our pylons." The NCO nodded in agreement. Stuart sketched the clamps that were part of the universal adapter. "You take the mounting clamps off the adapters and bolt them here and here." He drew arrows to the underside of the Lightning's pylons. "Then you mount the missile rails to the new clamps. It should work."

Eric was looking at his father, admiration in his eyes. "You know all this stuff, Dad?"

"Yeah. Anything to do with fuel. You name it, I've been involved."

"Your dad is a vital part of the team," Seagrave said. "Without him nothing happens. I do have a question: How do I jettison the missile in case of an emergency?"

"The same way you jettison a Sidewinder," the NCO replied. "You launch it off the rail. Just be sure to point it so it won't hit anything."

Seagrave shrugged. "If all you need is a firing signal, why not? I'm quite sure the Eagles can jury-rig the wiring." Another thought came to him. "Of course, I'll need a pylon and missile on the other wing. Aerodynamics, weight and balance, that sort of thing."

"Sounds good to me," the NCO said. "Let's see what my bosses have to say."

"Sorry, folks," Stuart said. "We've got to go." He looked at his son who was beaming with pride. "Say good-bye. We've got to hit the road."

Eric marched up to Seagrave and stuck out his hand. "Good-bye, sir. I'll always remember the ride."

"My pleasure," Seagrave replied, shaking the boy's hand.

Eric bobbed his head and walked over to Shanker, who was still drilling the Gray Eagles. Again he extended his hand to say good-bye. But the cantankerous old man wasn't having any of it. He gathered his grandson in his arms and gave him a big hug. "Always check six, hear?"

"I will, sir," Eric promised. He took a last look at the Lightning and walked quickly out of the hangar.

"You need to straighten that woman out," Shanker groused.

"I'm trying," Stuart replied. "By the way, what's this all about?"

"We're goin' to Washington and we're gonna protest," Shanker said. "That woman and her goddamn stupid gun law."

Stuart shook his head and followed his son into the rain.

Occoquan, Virginia

"It's a nice place," Stuart assured Eric as they turned down the lane leading to Jenny's new home. The weather had finally broken, and the sun had come out.

"Yeah," Eric muttered, oblivious to his new surroundings.

Stuart turned into the driveway. "Damn," he said softly. Barbara Raye's black Cadillac and a BMW he didn't recognize were parked in front of the garage. "Her lawyer, no doubt."

"I'm not going in," Eric said.

For a moment Stuart didn't know what to do. But he couldn't blame Eric for not wanting to be here. "Let me go grease the skids."

"Make them go away," Eric told him.

Stuart nodded and went inside while Eric walked down the street. Jenny took him into the family room, where Barbara Raye and her lawyer were waiting. "Where's Eric?" Barbara Raye asked.

"He's waiting until you leave," Stuart told her.

"I'm his grandmother. Don't you forget that."

Something hardened inside Stuart. "Then I'd suggest you start acting like one."

Barbara Raye glared at him. "You little weasel. You've poisoned him against me."

"I think you did that yourself," Stuart calmly replied.

Barbara Raye jutted her chin at her lawyer, bringing in her reinforcements. "Colonel Stuart," the lawyer began, "we have determined that it's in Eric's best interests to modify the custody agreement. We have two choices: We can either be civilized or do it the hard way." He handed Stuart another summons.

Stuart glanced at the summons, read the court date, and flared. "Hold on! I agreed to bringing Eric here only if you dropped the court hearing."

"I changed my mind," Barbara Raye snapped.

"You don't have a thing to say about it," Stuart said, his voice deadly calm now.

"Mike," Jenny pleaded, "what's gotten into you? You've always been so reasonable, and I do want to be with him."

"Maybe I've stopped being reasonable," Stuart said. But she had a point. She was Eric's mother, and he couldn't deny her access to her son. "For now Eric can stay with you as long as the crocodile here—"

The lawyer interrupted him. "Name-calling will not help matters."

Stuart turned on the man. "Wanna bet, fuckface?" He was an echo of his father, and the lawyer blanched. "Let's get a few things straight. First, Barbara Raye will not have access to Eric without my permission. Second, either you leave now or Eric and I leave. Third, see you in court."

"That we will," the lawyer said. He retreated to the front door. For a moment Barbara Raye glared at him. Then she followed him out.

"Mike," Jenny said, rebuke in her voice.

Stuart waited until he heard the two cars drive off. "I'll get Eric. Jenny, he loves you, but he can't stand your mother. You'll lose him if you're not careful. And he's a great kid." They went outside and found Eric standing by the car talking to two pretty girls his age. "Seems he's discovered girls," Stuart said.

Eric waved at them. "I think I'm going to like it here." He paused. "I heard what Grandma Barbara said to her lawyer about you when she got in her car. Thanks, Dad. You were cool." He wore the same expression Stuart had seen in the hangar.

Annapolis

It was late Saturday afternoon when Stuart arrived at the marina where *Temptress* was docked. He took a deep breath when he got out of the car. The gate was open, and he walked slowly down the dock. *Will she listen?* he wondered. He had called Jane three times while she was in the hospital, but she would talk only about *Temptress* and Eric. When he'd tried to visit her, the duty nurse had given him a hard look and said that Jane was not receiving visitors. He'd sent flowers, but they'd been returned with a note saying she'd been released.

He recognized the signs before he reached the boat: The dinghy was stowed on the foredeck, jerry cans of diesel fuel were lashed to the port side of the cabin trunk, and the sail cover was off. Jane was preparing the boat for sea. She looked up from the cockpit and waited, not saying a word. "I didn't know you were leaving," he said, looking at the bandage on her face.

"I've got a charter," she replied. Four words or less once again.

"But you're not healed yet."

"I've been hurt before," she said.

"What happened?"

She pointed to the aft shroud on the port side of the mast. "Rigging problems. It snapped. Hit me in the face."

He was stunned, and for a moment he couldn't speak. The shrouds were the stainless steel cables that supported the mast. They were under tremendous strain when the sails were driving the boat, and the thought of one breaking and whipping across the deck was frightening. She was lucky to be alive. "How badly were you hurt?"

She shrugged. "Lost an eye."

"Oh, my God! You can't go anywhere." No answer. "Jane, you're in no condition to go sailing." Still no answer. In the silence another thought came to him. "That was no accident."

She whirled on him. "Stop being paranoid. It *was* an accident, pure and simple."

He was stunned by the anger in her words. Then, slowly, "How do you explain the brakes on the Explorer?"

"I can't."

"Jane, don't go." He was pleading. "I was incredibly stupid. Please give me another chance."

"Why?"

"Because I love you."

Her face softened. "And I love you. Earn it." She pointed at the dock lines. "Help me cast off."

He did as she commanded and watched as she motored out of the marina. Jane headed *Temptress* into the wind and alone, hoisted the mainsail. The wind was freshening, and she set the first reef before unfurling part of the jib. Even from a distance he could see that the boat was in perfect balance as the sails started to draw. He didn't move until she was out of sight.

He walked back to the car. He sat behind the wheel as a fine mist settled over the marina. He had never felt so alone. "Damn!" he raged, pounding on the steering wheel. His eyes narrowed into slits as something deep inside him turned to steel. "Time to get aggressive," he said aloud to himself. He started the engine and headed back to Washington.

24

The panic was back, eating at Sophia as the three men talked endlessly and cleaned their weapons again and again. The pressure kept building until she screamed, *"Do something!"* The men only stared at her and went back to whatever they were doing. She sat next to Eduardo and whispered. "Can you forgive me, my love? I'm only a woman."

"We understand," he murmured. "The waiting is hard." She whispered in his ear that she would show the proper gratitude that night in bed. He gave her his dreamy look and nodded. Her campaign to divide and conquer had finally borne results, however small.

She wasn't sure, but she thought it was the Wednesday or Thursday of the first week in February when their training routine changed. They all sat in the car, and Luis drove slowly around the compound. Without warning he slowed even more and shouted, "Go!" Francisco rolled out the rear right door holding his AK-47 submachine gun across his chest. The car accelerated away as he came to his feet and tried to bring the AK-47 to a firing position. But the combat vest he was wearing got in the way, and he fumbled with the weapon. They tried it again, but this time he hit the ground wrong and jammed the AK-47 against his sternum, knocking his own breath out.

"It's too big," Sophia told them. "He needs a smaller weapon, like the MP5." The Heckler and Kock MP5 was Luis's prized weapon, which he treated like a child. The men discussed her suggestion for a moment, and Luis reluctantly handed Francisco his submachine gun. Again they drove

around the compound. This time Francisco executed the maneuver perfectly. He came to his feet smiling and swung the submachine gun around
in a clearing motion.

"How did you know?" Luis asked.

"You forget who I am," she said. "Cuba trains its fighters well." Luis
nodded in agreement. "Your enemy is our enemy," she told him. "Use
me. Let me share the honor."

✳

She was cleaning up after dinner that same night when Eduardo
brought a large wooden cross into the trailer and set it in the corner next
to the TV. *Are they going to pray?* she wondered. She went back to the
dishes. *Why can't I get Eduardo to talk? He thinks I worship him and will do
anything for him.*

Luis spoke quietly to her. "Why do you favor Eduardo?"

"Why does the sun shine?"

"He says you are one of us."

Her spirits soared. She was making progress! "We are the few against
the many," she said. "We are the weak against the strong. We are the pure
against the impure."

Luis took up the chant. "We are the few against the many. We are
weak against the strong." He ran outside and was back in a few moments
carrying a Cuban flag on a short staff. He propped it next to the wooden
cross. "Do you truly wish to die for Cuba?"

"It would give my life meaning," she replied. She stood beside the flag
and touched it. "This stands for all I cherish most dear." *Am I laying it on
too thick?* She touched the cross and drew her fingers down the coarse
wood in reverence. *Don't overplay it.*

The three men were pleased with her answer, and Eduardo joined her.
He took her hand and held it to his cheek. "Do you wish to be with me?"

"With all my heart." *Careful!*

Again it was the right answer. Luis nodded, and Francisco stood up
holding a combat vest. But this one was different. *Where did that come
from?* she wondered. She stepped back into the kitchenette with Eduardo
as Francisco draped the vest around the cross.

The vest hung there, its wires and explosives fully exposed.

"Francisco es cagado," Eduardo whispered, calling Carita's ghost from its shadows.

She couldn't take her eyes off the cross and its grotesque burden. Then it hit her. The cross was her exact height, and the vest was meant for her. Her panic was back, washing over her like a giant wave, driving her down into the depths of darkness.

25

The uniformed Secret Service agent and the park ranger crossed Seventeenth Street and walked across the grass with measured steps. Ahead of them the newly refurbished Washington Monument rose with majestic simplicity in the cold February sun. Behind them the two commemorative arches of the World War II Memorial framed the Reflecting Pool with the Lincoln Memorial at the far end. The two men headed for what looked like a military formation that was participating in the WWII Memorial's dedication ceremonies. But up close any semblance of military spit and polish dissolved into a ragtag band of fifty-four retired veterans wearing ill-fitting uniforms. Old age and a sedentary lifestyle had expanded most of their waistlines, and a few loose belt buckles dangled in the air. About half had undone their coat buttons to escape the straitjackets from an earlier age and were wishing they had bought a new uniform for the occasion. Still, they all sported trim haircuts and polished shoes. To a man, they were the proud survivors of an earlier generation that had fought in Vietnam.

"I can't believe you're letting them get this close," the ranger muttered.

"President's orders," the Secret Service agent replied. "She isn't worried about demonstrators as long as they cool it during the dedication ceremony." He gave a little snort. "Besides, what can a bunch of old geezers do? They run thirty steps and it's heart attack time."

"Baby-sitting the geriatric crowd is not my idea of observing Washington's birthday," the ranger groused as he studied the men. "What about the seven guys with the rifles?"

"The firing squad?" the agent replied. "Luckily they're firing blanks. Otherwise one might shoot his toe off." The agent pointed at the new monument to the men and women who fought in World War II. "We put 'em over here outa sight so they wouldn't scare anyone." He swung his metal detector from its strap. "But we'll check 'em out and make sure they're only shooting blanks."

"At their age what else can they shoot?" The park ranger glanced at his clipboard and called in a loud voice, "May I speak to Colonel William D. Stuart?" Shanker broke free and walked over to the two men. "Are you the organizer?" the ranger asked.

"My name's on the parade permit," Shanker said. "Why can't we get closer?"

"Security," the Secret Service agent said.

"Look," Shanker said, "we got rights—"

"Indeed you do," the agent said, interrupting him. "Which is why you got this far. So here are the ground rules: First, you all must remain in this area from now until the dedication ceremony is over. Second, while the president is on the Mall, the rifles and all blank shells are in my possession."

"Fat chance," Shanker said. "You ever heard of the Second Amendment?"

"You ever heard of Leavenworth?" the Secret Service agent replied. "Don't play silly-ass games with me, Colonel Stuart." Shanker's face froze in a grim mask. Thanks to his years in the Air Force, he recognized authority when it was about to run over him and knew when to keep his mouth shut. The agent took his silence as agreement. "Good. Finally, you will not disturb the dedication ceremony in any way, and that includes your bugler over there. After the ceremony is concluded and the president has left the area, you can do whatever you came to do."

Shanker couldn't help himself. "Fuckin' Communist state," he grumbled.

The agent motioned Shanker aside and spoke in a low voice. "Sir, we don't need any problems here. Exactly eight weeks ago tomorrow, the president was almost assassinated. It's not going to happen again—not today, not on my watch. As far as I'm concerned, you're a problem we don't need. Unfortunately, the president's a strong-willed lady who fully supports your right to peaceably assemble. I can't change her views on that, no one can. But you gotta understand one thing: I'm the guy who's going to make sure you *stay* peaceably assembled. Now, if you think for one moment that I'm out here alone, you got another think coming." He pointed to the Washington Monument. "I'll be over there if you have any questions."

Shanker watched him walk away. He snorted once. "Okay, boys," he called, pointing to a spot near the junction of Seventeenth Street and Independence Avenue. "Let's dig the grave right there."

✳

Eduardo wheeled the rented minivan onto Independence Avenue and tried for the third time to head west, toward the Lincoln Memorial. But a traffic cop motioned him to turn north onto Fourteenth Street. Frustrated, he crossed the Mall and drove past the sprawling Department of Commerce building. He tried to punch a number into his cell phone, but the combination of so much traffic and driving an unfamiliar vehicle defeated him. Sophia grabbed the phone out of his hands and dialed the number, then handed the phone back to him. "They've blocked off Independence," he said. "I can't get any closer than Fourteenth."

"Park and walk," Luis replied. "I need you in place in thirty-one minutes."

"Ten-four," Eduardo replied, mimicking the dialogue from an old TV show.

Sophia sighed and gave him a patronizing look. "This isn't going to work," she told him. "Security is too tight. Break it off while we still can. There will be a better time."

Eduardo glared at her and turned right on Pennsylvania to loop back to the south side of the Mall. "The time is now. We're not cowards."

"Neither am I," she retorted, "but I'm not stupid." She reached for the door handle, more than willing to take her chances with traffic.

But Eduardo was ready. He slapped her, hard, and jammed on the brakes. Traffic piled up behind them as drivers hit their horns. Eduardo ignored them as he lay across her, pinning her into her seat. Sophia saw a traffic cop walking toward them and held her breath as Eduardo fumbled with a set of handcuffs. The cop was twenty feet away when Eduardo finally managed to clip one onto her right wrist and the other onto the door handle. "Luis warned me," he said, sitting upright. He was looking directly at the cop, now less than ten feet away. "Sorry, Officer," he called. The cop stood aside and motioned them forward.

He was able to turn south on Seventh Street and again crossed the Mall. He jerked the minivan onto C Street and pulled into a reserved parking spot behind the Department of Agriculture. He jumped out and buttoned his knee-length trench coat, making sure the vest underneath was totally hidden. But the explosives and wires gave him a bulky look at odds with his slender frame. He ran around the van and jerked Sophia's door open. But he had forgotten about the handcuffs, and she spilled out onto the ground. "Get up." He glanced at his watch. Time was running out. He unlocked the cuff on the door and transferred it to his left wrist, tying them together. Then he threw away the key.

Sophia followed the key as it arched across the other cars. "This is crazy," she told him.

"Think of Cuba," he told her.

"I'm thinking of now!" she shouted. He pulled a six-foot staff with a rolled-up flag out of the van and threw it over his right shoulder. Then he grabbed her hand and walked quickly away, half dragging her after him.

※

The final strains of "The Star-Spangled Banner" drifted over Shanker as he watched the two men dig the grave. "That's deep enough," he told them. The men climbed out, thankful they didn't have to dig down to the regulation six feet. "Okay," he told another group, "start calling." As one, eight men dug out their cell phones and called every TV station, newspaper, and media organization in the city. Shanker dialed the *Washington Post*. "News desk? Look, I just thought you'd like to know a group of veterans are digging a grave between the Washington Monument and the World War II Memorial while the president is talking." He listened for a moment. "No, I don't know what's going on. But they got an honor guard with rifles, a bugler, and a folded flag. It looks like they're gonna bury someone. Maybe you wanna check it out." He punched the call off. "That got their attention," he announced.

He buttoned the coat to his uniform, thankful that Martha had let out the seams as much as she could. But it was still tight. He carefully adjusted his wheel hat, making sure the bill was exactly the regulation two finger-widths above his nose. He came to attention. "Squad-ron! Fall in!" The men organized themselves into five ranks of eight men each while the seven-man firing squad, minus their rifles, lined up on the far side of the grave. An honor guard of five men bearing the Stars and Stripes flanked by the flags of the four armed services wheeled into position behind Shanker. The lone bugler took his position opposite the firing squad, his brass trumpet gleaming in the sun. The squadron was formed.

The Secret Service agent and park ranger walked over to Shanker. "What in the world are you clowns up to?" the agent asked.

"You ever been to a military funeral before?" Shanker asked. He turned to face the men. "Stand easy!" They all relaxed in place. Again coat buttons were undone and belt buckles loosened. Now they had to wait.

※

Eduardo kept checking his watch as they hurried along Independence Avenue toward Seventeenth Street. A few latecomers to the dedication ceremony gave them wary looks but moved out of their way. Off to their left a policeman saw them but was preoccupied with a drunk who had passed out on the grass. "At least tell me what we're doing," Sophia pleaded. She pulled up. "My foot!" she wailed, faking a cramp. She bent over and pulled at the top of her boot.

At the same time the cop looked up from the drunk. He saw a very pretty woman bending over next to a handsome young Latino. "Hold on," he called, not moving. "What's the flag?" Eduardo waved at him and unfurled the flag. Sophia didn't hesitate. She slid her fingers into the top of the boot and palmed the paring knife she had taken from the kitchenette in the trailer. She slid it up her sleeve as Eduardo gave her a long, lingering kiss. The cop waved back, not recognizing the flag with the white star in a red triangle next to the blue and white stripes. "Honeymooners?" he called. Eduardo hugged Sophia in answer, still holding on to the flag. The cop motioned them on.

Eduardo was careful not to walk too fast, lest he draw attention. He glanced at his watch. "We're late. Way too late."

Sophia heard the worry and indecision in his voice. "I want to help," she said. "But I don't know what to do."

Eduardo spoke in a low voice. "There's only three ways for the *puta* to return to the White House. She can use a helicopter, and Luis will shoot her down with a Stinger."

Sophia was appalled. During all her time in captivity, she had never seen the deadly American-built, shoulder-held antiaircraft missile or heard them talk about it. But that did explain some of their long absences. "What are the other two ways?" she asked, fearing the answer.

"She can go by car directly north, up Seventeenth Street toward Luis and Francisco, or south on Seventeenth."

"And if she comes our way?"

"Then I will be there, waiting for her."

"Why do you need me?"

"So the world will know we stand together." He started to chant. "We are the few against the many. We are the weak against the strong."

Fear clutched at her, holding her tight as he dragged her toward the monument. Like the three men, the plan to assassinate the president of the United States was simplicity itself. So simple that it just might work. But thanks to her cover identity as a Cuban fellow traveler and freedom fighter, she was caught up in a suicide mission.

She slipped the knife into her hand.

❉

The handheld radio was glued to Shanker's ear as the speaker updated him on the ceremony. Still holding the radio in his left hand, he turned to the men. "The ceremony's over," he told them. "She's leaving." Behind the men he saw two TV crews and what looked like three or four reporters leave the monument and walk their way. The phone calls to the media had worked. Shanker drew himself up and sucked in his stomach. "Squad-ron! A-ten-hut!" As one, the men came to attention. Out of the corner of his eye, Shanker saw the TV crews start to shoot. It was time to tell the world why they were there. "Order of the day!" he shouted, hoping the cameras were picking it up. "In protest against an unlawful act by the president of the United States, Madeline O'Keith Turner—namely, the outlawing of all semiautomatic weapons—we hereby renounce the medals awarded to us by the United States government for the defense of our country and freedoms. Squad-ron, by ranks, pass in review!"

The first row of eight men did a half-decent right-face as Shanker took his place at the front of the line. Then, loudly, "Forward—March!" Shanker led them in lockstep toward the freshly dug grave. As he approached, his right hand grabbed the medals on his chest and he ripped them off, throwing them into the grave. One by one, each man threw his medals into the grave. Tears streaked the faces of two as they struggled to match Shanker's example. It wasn't quite what they had planned, but without the firing squad, it was as close as they could get.

Shanker spoke in a loud voice as the second rank of men filed by the open grave. "Firing squad, come to attention and salute each group as they pass by." The seven men lined up on the far side of the grave did as commanded. "Bugler," he ordered, "play 'Taps.' " Off to the side the bugler came to attention and raised his trumpet to his lips. The first haunting refrains of the melody echoed over the park, and the TV cameras were recording it all.

"Ah, shit," Shanker moaned. A young couple carrying a Cuban flag and walking hand in hand down Seventeenth Street were in the way. As one, the TV cameras shifted their focus. At the same time a burst of machine-gun fire echoed in the distance. "What the hell?" he wondered. He keyed his radio. "What's going on?"

"Beats me," the voice responded. "But the Secret Service is going apeshit. Hold on! Oh, my God! I think someone's shooting at the president!"

A sudden fear grabbed Shanker. If some crazy tried to assassinate the president a second time, the FBI and Secret Service would take the Gray Eagles apart, ride them hard, and put them up wet. They were at the wrong place at the wrong time, doing the wrong thing. He yelled into the radio. "Where's the president?"

"Her motorcade turned around and is heading your way," came the answer.

Shanker looked toward the road. The couple holding the Cuban flag were standing next to the curb. Then he saw it. They were handcuffed together. He never hesitated. "Follow me!" He led the charge, heading straight for the couple as the Gray Eagles converged on him like a collapsing amoeba. The man holding the flag looked up as the woman's free hand reached for his neck. In the distance Shanker heard more gunfire as the Secret Service agent and the park ranger ran into the street, motioning people to clear the road. Unfortunately, the mass of people leaving the ceremony effectively blocked any exit. The line of cars came to a halt as Secret Service agents set up a human shield while other agents tried to clear a path through the crowd that was running away from the gunfire.

Shanker was puffing hard and had almost reached the couple when the man collapsed, dragging the woman to the ground. He saw a knife in her hand. At first it didn't make sense. Then he saw the blood gushing from the man's neck. She had cut his throat. "He's got a bomb!" the woman screamed as she pulled open the man's coat. Shanker skidded to a halt at the sight of the wires connecting the vest pockets. "He hit the timer when he saw you!" She sawed at the man's wrist with the knife.

More gunfire coming from the direction of the White House filled the air. Shanker grabbed the flag and threw it away. He started to lift the body. "Help me!" he shouted. Two Gray Eagles grabbed the body and lifted. "The grave," Shanker shouted. They scrambled for the grave site with their grisly burden, dragging the woman after them. "Everyone down!" Shanker shouted. "Take cover!" The uniformed Secret Service agent was running toward them, his weapon drawn.

The men reached the grave and threw the body in. But the woman, still attached by the handcuffs, almost went in after it. Shanker pulled her back as they fell to the ground beside the grave. The woman's arm dangled over the side as the Secret Service agent loomed over them. Shanker reached into the grave and pulled on the handcuffs, bringing the man's hand to the edge. "Shoot the chain!" he yelled. The agent hesitated. "Shoot the fuckin' chain!" Now the agent reacted and placed the muzzle of his gun against the connecting links of the handcuffs. He fired once, and the woman rolled free. Shanker came to his feet, pulling her with him. "Run!" The agent grabbed the woman, and they ran from the grave just as the ground erupted in a volcano of flames and dirt.

Shanker lay on the ground and tried to breathe. He sputtered and sucked in a gulp of air. But an acrid stench from the explosion made him cough. He came to his hands and knees, still sputtering. He shook his head, driving the cobwebs away. The Secret Service agent lay on the ground next to the woman, who was sobbing loudly. Four men in dark suits rushed up, submachine guns at the ready. One spoke into his whisper mike, and Shanker was vaguely aware of the president's motorcade driving past.

"Is she okay?" Shanker asked.

There was no answer. The uniformed Secret Service agent slowly stood, his knees weak. "Colonel Stuart, you just may be a goddamn hero."

Newport News

Martha Stuart was glued to the TV set as she surfed from channel to channel, trying to discover what was behind the cryptic phone call from her husband. He had told her not to believe what she saw on TV and that he was okay. As a result, it took a long time to piece together the complete story. On CNN a reporter was speaking in front of a wrecked car with the White House in the background. "In a well-timed maneuver, the two would-be assassins drove this car through a police barricade and south on Seventeenth Street, which had been cleared to expedite the president's return to the White House. When the assassins crossed E Street, the car slowed, and one man dove out with a submachine gun. He came to his feet and fired indiscriminately into the crowd, killing over twenty bystanders. Because the car accelerated ahead, initial speculation is that the gunner was a diversion designed to create confusion and draw the attention of the police and Secret Service."

Martha switched channels to NBC. A very upset woman reporter was standing at the newly dedicated monument. Her hands were shaking, but her voice was calm and measured. "The presidential motorcade had just left the dedication ceremonies and was headed toward the White House when gunfire broke out. The motorcade immediately reversed course and headed away. But the press of people running from the gunfire impeded its progress."

Click. Martha changed channels to Fox News at the White House. The Fox White House correspondent was standing in front of the West Wing. "The White House press secretary has just released a statement confirming that President Madeline Turner was not hurt and is safe in the residence with her family. When asked why the delay in leaving the dedication ceremony when the shooting erupted, the press secretary replied that the president had ordered the driver to proceed cautiously through the crowd and not hurt anyone."

Click. Back to CNN, where the same reporter was still talking in front of the wrecked car. "A quick-acting Secret Service agent used his car to ram the assailant's car, stopping it here, well before the president's motorcade arrived. The driver jumped out with an AK-47 and fired. The Secret Service agent then returned fire and killed him."

Click. She turned to CNC-TV where her favorite reporter, Liz Gordon, was standing beside a fresh crater behind the new memorial. "Two other assassins, a young man and woman waving a Cuban flag and handcuffed together, attempted to block the presidential motorcade as it headed this way. As the man was wearing a vest wired with explosives, my sources suspect it was a suicide mission. We are still not sure what a group of veterans were doing here, but they had dug a grave and were conducting a mock funeral for some purpose. When their leader, a retired Colonel William Stuart, saw the two assassins, he attacked them and, realizing that the man was wired with explosives, dragged him and the woman to the grave and threw the assassin in. He managed to free the woman from her handcuffs before the bomb exploded. She is now in custody." Martha stared in amazement at the screen.

Liz Gordon paced off the hole dug by the explosion. "Judging by the size of the crater, the man was wired with enough explosives to destroy every car in the motorcade."

Click. Martha cycled to the cable channel where Shanker's favorite political commentator was holding forth with his usual bombast. "Wake up, America! Why were the assassins waving a Cuban flag? It doesn't take a rocket scientist to figure out who was behind this attempt on the president's life. Once again it raises the old question of who was behind Lee Harvey Oswald and the assassination of JFK? How much longer are we going to cave in to the liberal left wing and their slavish adulation of Fidel Castro?"

Martha punched him off with a sigh of relief when a car pulled into the driveway. She hurried to the door. A dark-suited man was holding open the rear passenger door of a black limousine as Shanker climbed out. The man shook Shanker's hand and, then, slowly, Shanker walked toward his wife, his body protesting in pain at every step. Martha waited at the door. Her arms were folded across her ample breasts, and her face a soft reflection of all she was. When he reached the door, they stood there looking at each other and not saying a word.

"I suppose I'll never hear the end of this," he finally groused.

Tears filled her eyes. "I'm so proud of you," she murmured, taking his hand and leading him inside.

26

The White House

Lieutenant General Franklin Bernard Butler stood against the side wall in the cabinet room early Tuesday morning and read the initial report. It was hot out of the copying machine, and he was surprised by the amount of detail so early in the investigation. "Interesting," he murmured, rereading a particular section three times. It was the one thing he didn't want to think about, much less see in a report detailing a conspiracy to assassinate the president of the United States. He looked around and mentally checked off the men and women filing into the room. Every high roller in the nation's law enforcement and intelligence communities was in the room, and he was the lowest-ranking person present. He leaned against the wall and crossed his arms. This was going to be a very interesting meeting. The door opened, and Sam Kennett, the vice president of the United States, walked in. Mazie Kamigami Hazelton, the national security adviser, was right behind him.

Kennett stood beside the president's empty chair. "I cannot tell you," he began, "how thankful I am not to be sitting in this chair." He looked around the room with a steady gaze. "What happened yesterday at the dedication ceremony will not happen again." Every head in the room nodded in agreement. "Mazie, it's all yours." He sat down.

Mazie stood at the end of the table. "I don't think I need to remind you that exactly eight weeks ago today the president narrowly escaped an assassination. The fact that an attempt was made yesterday tells me we're in deep trouble." She glanced at her notes. "As of now, we have identified the three dead assassins: Luis Barrios, Francisco Martínez, and Eduardo Pinar. We also have in custody one Sophia James, who cut Pinar's throat. She claims she was a hostage held by the three men, and so far her story checks out. The FBI is still investigating other details she provided, and there's more to come. But according to James, the men were members of a secret Puerto Rican cell called the 'Group.' "

"Mrs. Hazelton," the director of Central Intelligence said, "we rolled up and rendered that bunch of loonies last August."

"Well," Mazie said, "apparently they're back."

"Why the Cuban flag?" Sam Kennett asked.

"We're checking that out," the director of the FBI replied. "But we think it was part of their cover."

"That's dumber than dirt," a voice said.

"The initial interrogation of the James woman," the director of the FBI answered, "indicates we're dealing with three imbeciles. God only knows what they were thinking. But for now we're assuming nothing. Also, given their level of support, we're confident they were part of a larger organization, or at best a splinter group of Puerto Rican nationalists."

"So they were not Cuban?" Kennett said.

"To the best of our knowledge," Mazie replied, "no."

Butler took a deep breath. Better to raise the issue now, at the earliest possible moment. He raised his hand. "Mrs. Hazelton?"

"For those of you who don't know Bernie Butler," Mazie said, "he's one of the Pentagon's 'Boys in the Basement' and a survivor of more successful covert intelligence operations than I care to remember."

"Don't discount the Cuban connection," Butler said. Mazie arched an eyebrow, an unspoken "why?" "During the Angolan operation in the 1980s," Butler explained, "we tagged a batch of Semtex plastic explosive with a trace element that left a unique acrid stench when it exploded. We then sold it to the Cubans operating in Angola as a way to identify who was doing what to whom and to make a little money. But they never used it." He held up his copy of the initial report. "That Semtex showed up yesterday."

Washington, D.C.

Samuel B. Broad glanced at the summons to appear in family court and dropped it with a flick of his fingers. "I'm not that well versed in family law," he told Stuart. "But I do happen to know the Honorable Loretta Calhoun, who will be hearing your case."

"Is that good or bad?" Stuart asked.

"It all depends on what you do," Broad replied. "First, don't go in with a lawyer. She doesn't like lawyers. Take witnesses, but not your father—she doesn't like men like him. Too macho. Think about calling this Hank Langston, the pilot of the homebuilt aircraft that's on the videotape. By the way, did that story ever air?"

Stuart shook his head. "Hank spoke to the TV station. I don't know what he said, but they canceled it."

"Good. Also take your mother. But whatever you do, do not try to deny your wife access."

"What about Jenny's mother?"

"Sidestep that issue," Broad counseled. "Argue that the current agreement is in your son's best interests and doesn't need changing."

"What about my case? How do I sidestep that?"

"That is a problem," Broad allowed. "I would suggest you argue there are developments that may cause the case to be dropped."

"What developments?" Stuart asked.

"I'd suggest you supply some."

"I don't even know where to start looking," Stuart replied.

"Always follow the money trail."

"Nothing I do has anything to do with money. So how can there be a trail?"

Broad shook his head. "I'd suggest you take another look. If that fails, *cherchez la femme.*"

Stuart shook his head. "Yeah, right. Get serious."

Broad gave him a long look. "I'm being very serious, Colonel Stuart. Take away money, sex, and drugs and I'd be out of a job."

※

"Cherchez la femme," Stuart muttered to himself as he walked toward his car. He snorted and stepped off the curb to cross the street. A car

came around the corner, making a right-hand turn against the light, and forced him to jump back. But his reactions were a little slow, and the car grazed him, pushing him back against the curb. He sat down hard, hurting his tailbone as the car accelerated away. "Son of a bitch!" he shouted. "Not again!" He tried to get the license number, but mud and snow hid the last four digits. He watched as the car disappeared around a corner. Much to his surprise, a police car surged past in pursuit, its siren wailing and lights flashing.

"You'll never catch him," Stuart said to himself. He waited for the police car to return and confirm the obvious. "Just another coincidence?" he said. *I've got to stop talking to myself,* he thought. He didn't have to wait long.

"Sorry, sir," the young patrolman said. "I lost him."

"I'm not surprised," Stuart said.

"Did you get the license number or make?"

"Only the letters ALO. Virginia, I think. A red compact sedan."

"That's enough," the policeman said. "We'll get him."

"Yeah, right." Stuart gave him his name, address, and phone number before returning to his own car. He wondered if the cop were even old enough to drive. "*Cherchez la femme,* my ass."

Dallas

"Thank you, Matt Drudge," L.J. said for perhaps the hundredth time as her fingers flew over the keyboard in her search of every major news channel on the Internet. Thanks to a highly placed leak, the cyberspace columnist had broken the story that the explosives used by the assassins had come from Cuba. The capital had exploded with the news, and the media, not to mention Congress, were in an uproar. Finally. L.J. couldn't contain her jubilation and hit the intercom. "Lloyd, are you free?"

"I'll be right there," Marsten answered.

"I'll come to your office," she told him, needing the activity to calm down. She forced herself to walk slowly as she made her way past the secretaries in the outer office. "Good morning, Shugy," she sang. "How's Billy?"

"Oh, Miss Ellis," the secretary replied, "not good. He's had another stroke."

L.J. stopped. "How bad?"

"He's worse than before," she answered.

"I'll send some flowers. Where's he staying?"

"He's still at home."

"Billy needs to be in a full-time nursing home," L.J. said. "The company will pay for it."

"Thank you, but we're managing. Besides, you've already done so much, I can't ask for more."

"Shugy," L.J. said, "yes you can, and we're going to help. Now, go find him a nursing home. And don't come back until you do. Hear?"

"Thank you, Miss Ellis."

The look on Shugy's face was all that L.J. needed. "There's nothing to thank me for. Go take care of your husband." She gave the secretary an encouraging nod and walked into Marsten's office, closing the door behind her. "Have you heard the latest about the terrorists?"

Marsten's face was grim. He had to tell her. "They were the same lot who blew up RTX Farming Supplies."

L.J. made the connection immediately. "And the woman?"

"She's the agent I hired to get on the inside. She's very bright, so I don't think she'll reveal that connection."

"Because of the murdered waiter," L.J. added. Marsten nodded in confirmation. L.J. paced the floor. "But sooner or later they'll trace her to ARA—and that means us. Sooner, I imagine, than later."

"True," Marsten replied. "But they'll never connect us, specifically me, to the James woman. I was very careful about that."

L.J. breathed in relief. "So when the FBI does come knocking, we keep our story simple. We had hired ARA as part of our new security plan to protect ourselves from terrorists. We may have been paying for their services, but we had no idea what was going on." She sat down. *What will happen when the FBI starts to take a hard look at us?* she thought. *Will it mean the end of the elephant?* A feeling of unbelievable loss swept over her. It was more intense than when she had lost her parents. The decision tree she had so carefully constructed flashed in her mind. *What's changed?* She had only lost the option of using the Puerto Ricans to blow up a drilling rig to collect insurance money to cover their losses. But thanks to the Puerto Ricans and Sophia James, there was now a connection to Cuba, a totally unexpected development she could exploit. They were still in the game. "Actually, I think we're ahead in all this."

Marsten was with her. "Because of the Cuban connection."

"Precisely. Castro is being blamed for it, and Congress is in an uproar." She fell silent. Long experience had taught Marsten to be patient. He poured himself a cup of tea and waited as she reexamined every aspect of her game plan. It was decision time. Either cut their losses now or go for the elephant. It wasn't really a decision.

"Lloyd, I think we have a very narrow window of opportunity here."

Marsten had been running his own decision matrix while waiting for L.J. and was not surprised. "To secure the concessions." It wasn't a question but a statement of fact. He also understood the hazards as well as L.J. But he couldn't help himself. Not since Eritrea. "Whatever we do, at least one major must get on board," he told her.

"I imagine that both BP and Exxon are burning with rumors."

"But do they want part of the action?" Marsten asked. "They haven't exactly been chasing us down the street and throwing money at us."

"They will. It's just a matter of convincing them we have the concessions. Then they'll move fast to get in on the ground floor."

"So how do we do that?"

"First, exercise the options on the drilling ships. I want three positioned in southern Florida and ready to move at a moment's notice."

"Why three?"

"At forty thousand dollars a day per ship, the industry will know we're serious."

He pointed out the obvious. "But that doesn't give us the concessions."

"That's why you're going back to Cuba."

"To scare my contacts silly, no doubt."

It was a classic understatement, and she laughed, breaking the tension. But more important, they were on the same wavelength. "They know you're from Dallas, right?" He nodded in answer. "So you tell them that because of this assassination attempt on Maddy Turner, a witness has come forth who links Castro to Lee Harvey Oswald and the JFK assassination."

"They know that's not true," Marsten said.

L.J. shook her head. "The question is not if it's true or not, but what does the U.S. believe? Emotions are running extremely high in the States over what happened to Turner. Tell your contacts that the Castro-JFK link is the straw that will break the camel's back, and it means invasion. So if they want to save Cuba, they had better act now. Otherwise Maddy Turner will be choosing the next government of Cuba."

"The FBI will eventually sort all this out," he said.

"That's why we have to act now. Hopefully we'll have the concessions and be drilling by the time the penny drops and the Cubans realize what's happened. But by then our people will have benefited from all the turmoil and be running Cuba. A win-win situation for everyone."

"Everyone but Castro," Marsten added. "My cover story for going to Cuba this time?"

"A combination of business and romance," L.J. replied. Marsten arched an expressive eyebrow at her. "You're exploring business possibilities," she explained. "In the event the embargo is lifted."

"Not that," he replied. "The other."

She laughed. "Well, men your age have been known to become involved with young foreign girls."

"I'll leave as soon as I take care of Duke."

An image of the old dog lying at the feet of Shugy's husband flashed in L.J.'s mind. "I'll take care of him," she promised.

"One thing," Marsten cautioned. "We do have a cash-flow problem. Hold off on the drilling ships as long as possible."

"Speaking of cash flow," she said, "take lots of money. I'd suggest gold Krugerrands."

Newport News

The Gray Eagles tugged the Lightning out of the hangar and positioned it on the taxiway for engine start while Shanker and two Air Force sergeants ticked off a checklist. Hank Langston stood in his hangar bay and watched the preparations, impressed with the thoroughness of the ground crew. "You boys are really serious about this," he said to Stuart.

"Dissimilar air combat training is a demanding mission," Stuart replied, parroting his father's words. He didn't have a clue what that meant, but it sounded good. "Chalky is over at the base briefing with the two F-15 pilots he'll be flying against today." He checked his watch. "He better hurry if he's going to make his takeoff time. By the way, I've got a favor to ask." He quickly explained about his upcoming court date and how Langston could help when Barbara Raye's lawyer used the videotape of the TV program to prove they had placed Eric in danger. Harry said he would be glad to help. "One question," Stuart asked. "Why didn't the TV station ever show the tape?"

"Because," Langston replied, "I told them it was a bunch of bullshit about Eric being in danger, and if they showed it, I'd buy the station and fire every one of their asses."

"Can you afford to do that?"

"Hell no. But *they* don't know that." He grinned. "When you can't win it in the air, win it in the debrief."

"You sound just like my dad," Stuart said as a car drove up. Seagrave got out wearing a flight suit. He pulled a G suit out of the back and quickly zipped it on. "Your chaps do get carried away with briefings," he told the men. "Covered about everything under the sun—except the sun's position."

Shanker grinned. "Sounds like a mistake to me."

"Absolutely," Seagrave replied. "Especially when you're going back to basics."

"What's happening?" Langston asked.

"They can't use their radars to find me," Seagrave explained. "They've been assigned to roam an area and deal with whatever happens."

"It's Red Baron time," Shanker chortled. "All else is rubbish."

"Jesus H. Christ," Langston muttered. "I'd trade half my sex life to go along."

Seagrave pulled on his helmet and climbed the boarding ladder. "Sorry. No passengers on this one." He checked his watch. "Shanker, call ground control for engine start and coordinate with the tower for a fast taxi and immediate takeoff."

"Why all the fuss?" Hank asked.

"Fuel is a real problem in the Lightning," Shanker explained. "Any delay cuts into the mission. He's only got maybe fifty minutes max before he's got to be back on the ground." Shanker made the radio calls and gave Seagrave a thumbs-up. The Gray Eagles sprang into action as Seagrave gave them the signal to crank engines. Less than a minute later he was taxing for the runway.

The quiet after the Lightning had cleared the hangars was deafening.

One of the wives who'd come along to make sure their husbands stayed out of trouble emerged from the hangar office. "Mike, a phone call for you. The Washington police. Something about catching a hit-and-run driver."

"I'll be damned," Stuart said, hurrying to take the call. The boom of the Lightning's afterburners echoed over the hangars as Seagrave took off. Stuart picked up the phone. The caller identified himself and quickly explained the situation. The police had found the driver, a teenage girl who was driving her parents' car without a license or their permission. She was scared to death. Did he want to press charges? He told the caller no and turned it back over to the police. He thanked them and broke the connection. "I'll be," he said to himself. *Maybe Jane was right. Maybe I'm just having a run of bad luck. That explains everything but the car brakes.*

He pulled into himself, thinking. *What did Broad say? Follow the money trail? What money?* Then it hit him.

He dialed his parents and told his mother he was returning to Washington. He had work to do the next few days. "Over the weekend?" Martha asked.

"That's the only time," he replied.

❈

Seagrave leveled off at eighteen thousand feet and checked his fuel. It was a long way to the training area over the Atlantic Ocean, and fuel was going to be a problem. He radioed ATC requesting clearance into the training area and was immediately cleared in. He spoke into the microphone in his oxygen mask so his tape recorder could document for the debrief what was happening. "Crossing western boundary of training area." According to the rules of engagement, they could engage in DACT only inside the training area, and anything outside was considered as sanctuary for the Lightning. It was a rule Seagrave intended to use to his advantage. He scanned the sky, looking for the distinctive planform of the F-15 Eagle. The Eagle is a big fighter, but its air-superiority gray paint job makes it hard to see.

Fortunately there was nothing wrong with Seagrave's distance vision, and he saw two dots on the horizon at his ten-o'clock position—exactly where they were supposed to be. He fell in behind them and nosed over, never losing sight of the two Eagles. It got even better when he confirmed he was following them. "Tallyho two bogeys, twenty-four thousand feet, heading one thirty-five degrees into the sun. I'm seven miles in trail descending to the deck." He maneuvered through a low marine layer of clouds that covered about 50 percent of the sky. He dropped out the bottom of the clouds at nine hundred feet and leveled off. He checked his fuel. He never flew straight, weaving back and forth to keep a clear patch of sky above him so he could keep the F-15s in sight. Again he needed the clouds. His neck ached from constantly looking up, but that would soon change.

"Bogeys reversing course now, heading approximately two-sixty degrees, away from the sun, directly toward me." He called up the Sidewinder missile mounted on the left pylon just under the leading edge of the wing root. He fully intended to have the F-15s for lunch.

"Partially obscured by clouds. Bogeys haven't seen me yet." He wasn't surprised, since the Lightning's dark gray paint blended perfectly with the gray ocean and clouds. He checked his fuel. "Come on, chaps, get the finger out. Haven't got all day." He waited for what seemed an eternity as the jets converged. But age and experience had made him a patient man—when required. "F-15s passing overhead at approximately twenty-four thousand feet. Reheats now." He stroked the afterburners and sat the Lightning on its tail, heading straight up. He punched through the clouds, directly beneath the F-15s.

The tone of his voice changed as his fangs came out. "Confirm bogeys are F-15 bandits. I'm engaged." He passed directly behind the two Eagles, still going straight up. He pirouetted ninety degrees so he could look over his left shoulder as he climbed above the Eagles, which were still going away from him. "Check six, old chaps, or you buy the farm."

He was about to slice down behind the Eagles when they finally saw him. Seagrave had never flown against the Eagle and was astounded by the violence of their maneuver. One pitched back left, the other right, as they turned back into him. For all appearances it looked as if they were hinged at the tail and flopped backward. In a fighter like the Lightning that maneuver would have killed all its airspeed, but the Eagles came out accelerating—climbing thirty degrees and headed straight for him.

At this point enemy pilots had been known to reach for the ejection handle in a last-ditch attempt to survive. Seagrave laughed and sliced down into the attacking F-15s, which were now looking directly into the sun. A loud growling sound filled his headset as the Sidewinder's infrared guidance locked on and told him he had a shot.

He made a radio call, as required by the rules of engagement. "Lightning has bandits in sight. Fox Two on the right Eagle." Fox Two was the brevity code for employing a Sidewinder. The Eagles had no choice and honored the threat. Again both maneuvered violently to avoid the simulated missile heading their way. In the confusion Seagrave nosed over and stroked his afterburners, heading for the cloud deck below him. Now it was a race for sanctuary before the F-15s found him and maneuvered into a firing position. His altimeter unwound like a sprung clock, and he was relying on pure skill and instinct to know when to pull out. He racked the throttles full aft and pulled on the stick. For a fraction of a second he was sure he had delayed too long and wasn't going to make it. The nose came up, and he shoved the throttles full forward, engaging the afterburners and killing his sink rate. He skimmed along above the ocean's surface at 600 knots, partially hidden by the cloud deck above him. "Tallyho, the fox," came over the radio. The F-15s had him in sight. "Blue One's engaged."

Seagrave keyed his radio before he heard a Fox Two call. "Lightning One is outside the area." It was a lie, and he still had two nautical miles to go, another ten seconds away. He squeaked the Lightning down another fifty feet and checked his fuel. It was going to be close. Another voice came over the radio. "Blue Two confirms bandit still inside the area. Take the shot!"

Seagrave laughed and hit the transmit button. "Sorry, chaps. But I am outside the area now." And he was. The engagement was over.

He turned to the west and zoomed, trading his airspeed for altitude. He throttled back and radioed ATC. "Lightning One RTB at this time. Declaring minimum fuel, request priority handling."

✳

The Gray Eagles paced the ramp as they waited. To the man, they were trying to act cool and unconcerned, but their relief was obvious when the Lightning touched down and taxied back on one engine.

They marshaled the jet into the chocks and gave Seagrave the cut-engines sign. He popped the canopy as the engine spun down. "Maintenance problem?" Shanker called, expecting another mechanical difficulty.

Seagrave pulled away his mask and rubbed his forehead. The outline from the mask etched his face, and he was exhausted. But he hadn't been so alive in years, and he laughed at the signals coming from his groin. "Other than a bit short of fuel," he answered, "she's absolutely perfect."

Shanker gave him a thumbs-up. The Lightning was fully operational and up to speed. "We got to get your ass over to Langley for the debrief," Shanker said. "They're hopping mad."

"Can't say I blame them," Seagrave replied. "They had a very bad day."

"What did you do?"

Seagrave climbed down the boarding ladder. "Cheated."

Shanker smiled. "What the hell, a kill's a kill."

"My thoughts exactly."

❄

The small briefing room was packed with bodies when Seagrave and Shanker walked in. The two F-15 pilots were locked in a serious discussion with their squadron's ops officer as a lieutenant colonel and colonel, both wearing blue uniforms and not fight suits, listened. The men all fell silent as Seagrave sat down at the head of the table. "Shall we begin?" he asked. His blue eyes sparkled in anticipation.

"This was, without doubt," the lead F-15 pilot said, "the most fucked-up mission I've ever flown."

"How is that so?" Seagrave asked.

"First, we weren't allowed to use our radar to find the bandit."

"Can your radar find a fighter with stealth characteristics?" Seagrave asked. There was no answer. "The reason you were denied use of your radar was to simulate engagement with a stealth fighter where your radar will be of limited use."

"Second," the pilot protested, "you jumped us out of the sun. We couldn't see you."

Seagrave almost laughed. "That's the way it's done. If you recall, it was agreed in our earlier briefing that either aircraft could engage as long as it had the other aircraft in sight and came no closer than two nautical miles. I had you both in sight and never entered your bubble."

"Third, you cheated. I was about to take my shot, when you—"

Seagrave interrupted. "Assuming my first shot didn't kill you."

"You can't document that," the pilot replied, trying to be calm.

"I agree any missile shot is always problematic," Seagrave said. "But still, I had a steady growl in my headset, indicating the missile head was tracking."

"I honored the shot and turned away!" the pilot shouted. "But that radio call that you were outside the area was a fuckin' lie!"

"It did cause you to hesitate. Are you assuming an enemy will not cheat?" A hard silence came down.

The squadron ops officer stood up. "This mission was a waste of time, fuel, and our training resources. It was a very bad idea to begin with, and it got worse when we did it."

"Was it?" Shanker said from the back of the room. "I was with the Triple Nickel when it deployed to 'Nam." Everyone in the room but Seagrave knew that the 555 Tactical Fighter Squadron had earned the title "MiG Killers" during the Vietnam war. "But we had to relearn some hard lessons before we got good. You just relearned a few of 'em today."

"What exactly were those lessons?" the colonel in the blue uniform asked.

Seagrave stood up and wrote on the whiteboard in big red letters CHECK SIX. "I was down on the deck and followed you into the area at your deep six-o'clock. I never once saw you perform a belly check."

"Shit," the colonel moaned.

"Further, when you reversed course, you flew right over me. Once your tail was to me, I zoomed into the sun." The colonel's moan turned into a growl. "The next time you engage someone coming out of the sun," Seagrave said as he diagrammed the engagement, "split-plane maneuver so one of you is very high, looking down on the engagement like God, or go low to look up and not into the sun. That way you take away any up-sun advantage the bandit may have and force him to split his attention. Finally, you allowed me to talk you out of a good missile shot. When you have a shot, take it. Sort out the rules of engagement on the ground."

"But what if the bandit has reached sanctuary for real?" the pilot protested.

Shanker guffawed. "A kill is a kill. Take the shot and say you're sorry later. Otherwise the goner will come back the next day and hose one of your buddies out of the sky. Your wingman will thank you, even though the REMFs will hang you out to dry."

"REMFs?" Seagrave asked.

"Rear Echelon Mother Fuckers," Shanker told him.

"Ah," Seagrave replied. "We have a few of those in the RAF." He looked at the two seated pilots. Both were superb fliers who only needed seasoning. "Always remember, when all else fails, cheat."

"It's the British way," Shanker confirmed.

The blue-uniformed colonel looked at the two pilots. "Gentlemen, if this debrief is over, we need some privacy." The pilots and their ops officer left the briefing room and closed the door behind them. "Commander Seagrave," the colonel said, "I work for the inspector general. I think we can use you and the Lightning."

"How so?" Seagrave asked.

"We've reinstituted no-notice Operational Readiness Inspections," the colonel explained. "I want to throw some real stressors at our fighter wings, and I think you can do that. If nothing more, it will force a return to basics."

"What exactly did you have in mind?" Shanker asked.

"As you probably know," the colonel said, "the Air Force has reactivated Homestead Air Force Base south of Miami along with the thirty-first Fighter Wing."

Shanker said, "The Thirty-first flies F-16s, right?" The colonel nodded in answer. "All things considered," Shanker muttered, "a good move."

"This is close-hold information," the colonel added. "We're hitting the thirty-first in about six weeks with a no-notice inspection. We want to use you in much the same manner as today."

"It won't work if we fly out of the same base," Seagrave said.

The colonel thought for a moment. "You can launch out of Navy Key West. That's near the training areas, which will help with your fuel problems."

"Yeah!" Shanker said. "You can play like you're a defecting Cuban MiG."

"Or a hostile one," the colonel added.

Shanker shook his head and looked at Seagrave, deeply envious. "How'd you get so lucky?"

"I ate my veggies," Seagrave replied.

27

The young FBI special agent pulled up in front of the elegant building late Friday night and checked the address. He was at the right place. The words "money," "class," and "Italian Renaissance" flashed in his mind. Another young man came out to park his car. "I'll only be a few minutes," the agent said, waving his ID. "Is the night manager in?"

"He came on duty a few minutes ago," the valet replied.

The agent got out, dog-tired. The agency had been pushing everyone to the limit since the attempted assassination on the president and was demanding results. He had never seen the tree shaken so hard. Even the ACLU was backing away, afraid to get in the way of the steamroller. He made a mental note to phone his pregnant wife in Virginia after this interview and see how she was doing. The night manager came out of his office and buttoned his coat. "May I help you?" he asked.

"Special Agent Mather, FBI." Again he waved his ID. "I'm following up on your phone call." He checked his notes. "You called us yesterday morning at seven oh-five A.M."

"Yes, that's correct. I would have called sooner, but I didn't recognize her at first."

"The woman, Sophia James." Agent Mather said.

"Yes, that's correct. Of course, she was much more glamorous when I saw her."

"She was staying here?"

"No. She had an appointment with one of our guests." The manager handed Mather a business card.

Mather read the card. " 'Heather. Specialized Associates.' What exactly does Specialized Associates do?"

"She was—or is, I believe—what you might refer to as a 'call girl.' A very expensive one, I might add. The going price for a girl like her normally starts at twenty-five hundred dollars."

Adrenaline shot through Mather. If this lead checked out, he might have made a breakthrough. "I'll need the details," he said, jotting down notes.

The manager led the way into his office and checked his log. "She arrived at ten twenty-five P.M. by taxi—I didn't get the number—on Tuesday, the fifteenth of October, last year. She left at two-ten in the morning."

"And her client?"

"A Mr. Lloyd Marsten, representing RayTex Oil out of Dallas, Texas."

Mather felt the adrenaline crash. Sophia James was just out making a buck, or in this case a lot of bucks. He closed his notebook. "And he wore a big silver belt buckle, no doubt."

The manager was incensed to think someone like that would stay at his hotel. "As a matter of fact," he said huffily, "Mr. Marsten is quite the gentleman. English, I believe."

A warning signal tickled the back of Mather's mind. If he hadn't been so tired, it would have been a Klaxon at full alert. "Anything else you can think of?"

"Well, the time she was here, less than four hours, was very unusual. Normally the girls stay the night." He checked his log. "Also, the phone was in constant use."

"Phone sex, no doubt."

"*I* doubt it. I can provide you with a printout of the phone calls, if you wish."

"I wish. Anything else?"

The manager typed a command into his computer, and the printer whirred. "I also saved the tape from the surveillance monitor." He pulled a videocassette out of his desk and inserted it in the TV. The image was not the normal one seen on TV of a thug holding up a convenience store late at night but a high-quality color image.

Mather sucked in his breath. "My God!"

"Very beautiful, yes?" The manager handed Mather the tape and the computer printout of Marsten's phone calls.

The agent scanned the printout. "Over two hours on one call. Any idea who they were calling?"

The night manager drew himself up at the suggestion that he would eavesdrop on a guest. But this was the FBI, and they would soon know. "I believe," he replied, "that they were creating a Web site called 'All about you dot com.'"

Mather finally heard the Klaxon. "Thank you very much. We'll be in contact." He ran from the hotel and called for his car, his wife totally forgotten.

The Pentagon

Stuart stopped at the security checkpoint on the main concourse and signed in. "I forgot my badge," he said, showing his ID. The civilian guard shoved a temporary pass at him and went back to reading the Saturday newspaper. Even on a weekend the Pentagon was a busy place, and Stuart joined the line of people filing through the checkpoint. He walked briskly to his old office complex and tried the main door. As expected, it was unlocked. *Sleep safe, America,* he thought. He closed the door and locked it. *No need to take chances.* He turned on the light in his cubicle and sat down at his old desk, still unoccupied. He placed his hands flat on the green blotter and took a deep breath as Samuel B. Broad's advice kept ringing in his ears: "Follow the money trail." So far he hadn't done anything wrong. But that was about to change, since this was the only money trail he could think of. It was time to cross the line.

He tried the top drawer of the file cabinet. Locked. He turned his attention to the four-drawer safe where he had stored all the classified files from the committee working on the Strategic Oil Reserve. If Ramjet or Peggy Redman had moved the files, he might as well go home. He spun his old three-number combination into the lock. Nothing. Peggy had probably changed the combination. He thought for a moment. "Got it," he mumbled. Like many people who worked around classified material, Peggy gave each safe a name. And that was the clue. So what did she name this one? "Stuart," he said aloud. He looked at the number pad on the telephone sitting on the desk. The letter *S* in his name equaled the number 7 and *T* equaled 8. He had a first number, 78. He rapidly decoded the *U* and *A* to 82, and the *R* and *T* to 78. He spun the three numbers into the lock and heard a satisfying click. That left the file cabinet.

He walked down to Peggy's desk and opened the bottom right-hand drawer. At the very back was a plastic cup with odds and ends, including three spare keys. He tried each of the keys in her locked file cabinet. The third key worked. Then he found the key ring he was looking for at the back of the top drawer. He walked quickly back to his cubicle and unlocked the file cabinet. He returned to Peggy's desk and made sure everything was exactly as he'd found it. He turned on the copying machine to let it warm up.

Back at his desk he took another deep breath and opened the top drawer of the safe. All the files were there, just as he'd left them. Next he went to the file cabinet and quickly opened every drawer. Again everything was there. Now to go to work.

Stuart had always been a conscientious staff officer, working diligently on whatever project he was assigned, and he spent the next three hours going through each file with a fine-tooth comb, looking for anything that could possibly be linked to a money trail. Finally he collapsed back in his chair and rubbed is eyes. *Where is it?* he raged to himself.

Okay, start at the beginning. What's the first step in making money from oil? Striking oil. Wrong. Exploration. His eyes snapped wide open. "No way," he muttered. He heard a faint click and came even more alert. Someone was unlocking the outer door. He turned off his light and tried not to breathe. The door opened, and he heard the click of hard heels on the floor tiles. The overhead lights came on. It had to be Ramjet! He hoped not, but who else wore shoes with such hard heels? He waited, afraid to move. *I left the copying machine on!* Suddenly he felt an overpowering urge to urinate. He crossed his legs, but that didn't help. The person was walking again. Now he stopped. *Go into your office!* Stuart urged.

Ramjet was moving again, coming down the narrow passageway. Stuart closed his eyes and took a deep breath, trying to think of a good lie to explain what he was doing. *Be creative*, he told himself. *Tell the truth.* The clicking grew louder, then stopped. He opened his eyes and looked directly into the face of Peggy Redman. His eyes glanced down at her shoes. They were brand-new with narrow high heels, the latest fashion rage. For a moment the two of them stared at each other. Then she turned and, without a word, walked back to her desk. Stuart waited, fully expecting to hear her call for security. He heard a desk drawer open then close. More clicking heels. He was so keyed that he felt the slight change in air pressure when she opened the outer door. He could sense her pause.

"Mike, turn off the Xerox machine when you leave." The door closed behind her.

Stuart picked up a file and raced down to the copier. His hands flew as he fed the pages into the machine. But it seemed to take forever. Finally he was done. He turned off the machine and hurried back to his office. He made himself slow down as he replaced all the files, making sure everything appeared undisturbed. He wasn't worried about leaving fingerprints, as he had worked on all the files before Ramjet relieved him of duty. But just to be sure, he wiped down the file cabinet, safe, telephone, and desk with his handkerchief. Satisfied all was in order, he turned off the light and walked out of the office carrying his copy of the file labeled "Steiner" in his briefcase.

Havana

Marsten broke out of the sweating crowd packing into José Martí International Airport and breathed the cool night air in relief. He made his way to the taxi stand and waved down an empty cab. The driver gave him a gesture of dismissal and sped away empty. "Impertinent bugger," Marsten mumbled. He tried again, with the same results. Taxis were streaming into the airport and depositing tourists anxious to leave the country. But none were waiting for a return fare to the city. That made sense, as aircraft were arriving almost empty. Behind Marsten a loudspeaker blared something about invasion and Yankee imperialism. "Of course," he said to no one. The real money was at the major resort hotels, where worried tourists would pay exorbitant amounts in hard currency to reach the airport. Fidel Castro's version of a socialist society was breaking down under stress, and the age-old principles of supply and demand were reasserting themselves with a vengeance.

It was a phenomenon he understood perfectly, and the gold Krugerrands hidden in his belt and shoes had quadrupled in value. When four taxis arrived at once and a group of German tourists piled out, Marsten stepped under a streetlight and held up a hundred-dollar bill. The first taxi slammed to a halt and he got in. "Casa Salandro," he said. "Near the Hotel Nacional." It was exactly where the driver wanted to go.

"English?" the driver asked. Marsten confirmed his guess. "This is a bad time to come to Havana, *señor*. The damn Yankees are going to start a war."

"I find that hard to believe," Marsten said, deliberately urging him to talk.

"That attempt to kill Turner. All a CIA plot to give the Yankees an excuse to invade. But we will resist and drive them into the sea, just like the Bay of Pigs." It was exactly what Marsten wanted to hear. The driver ranted and waved his hands as he drove, cursing the United States until he reached the street corner nearest the Salandros' house. The car jerked to a stop. "Another hundred dollars, *señor*." Marsten laughed and paid him. The cab roared away, leaving behind a strange silence. Marsten walked down the darkened street until he reached the heavy barred door of Casa Salandro. He pulled on the doorbell and waited. Nothing. He pulled again. Still no response.

"Damn," he cursed. Then the door cracked, and a shadow materialized on the other side. "I'm Lloyd Marsten. You're expecting me." The door slammed shut. *What now?* he wondered. He picked up his bag and hurried for the Nacional, three blocks away. He felt his skin grow prickly as he walked, a sure sign of danger. He turned and looked down the deserted street. Nothing. He kept walking and turned the corner. Ahead of him he could see the luxuriant foliage surrounding the Nacional. Behind the trees the mass of the hotel rose in darkness, all its lights out. He never slowed his pace. Suddenly he heard footsteps. Again he turned and looked. Nothing. He walked faster. A patrol car turned the corner, and its headlights flashed down the street. Marsten breathed a sigh of relief and stepped to the curb to be seen. The car stopped, and two soldiers jumped out, their weapons drawn.

The older was all of eighteen years old and looked like a boy playing at war with a helmet two sizes too large. "Your papers!" he barked in Spanish. It sounded so ridiculous that at any other time or place Marsten would have laughed. But not now. He fumbled for his passport while the boys twitched. He handed it over. The older boy thumbed through it. He spat something in Spanish, much too fast for Marsten to understand.

"CIA!" the younger of the two shouted.

"Don't be silly," Marsten replied. "I'm English." The boy shoved Marsten's passport into his shirt pocket. "That belongs to me," Marsten protested. The other boy clubbed him to the ground with his pistol butt. He took a step forward and jammed the muzzle against Marsten's head.

All at once a burst of submachine gun fire echoed over Marsten, and the boy collapsed, his blood washing Marsten's face. Another burst of gunfire and the second soldier crumpled to the ground. Marsten was afraid to move and played dead as running footsteps surrounded him. "Are you hurt?" a woman's voice asked. He looked up into the muzzle of a submachine gun. Was he next? Rosalinda Salandro extended her hand and pulled him to his feet. "You knocked at the wrong door."

"Lovely," he muttered, feeling the back of his head.

※

He flinched when Rosalinda dabbed iodine over the cut on his head. "What did you do with the bodies?"

"We'll bury them." Her fingers gently probed the wound. "The bleeding has stopped."

"And the patrol car?"

"It's being salvaged for parts. The blood has been scrubbed off the sidewalk, so there is no trace of what happened. The army will treat them as deserters."

"But someone must have heard the gunfire and looked out a window. Won't they talk?"

Rosalinda taped a bandage across his head. "During times like this it is better to know nothing." She handed him some old clothes and a worn pair of sandals. "Put these on." She turned away while he changed clothes and didn't see him hide his shoes with the Krugerrands concealed in the heels. It was one of the paradoxes of Cuba. In the brothel where he had made contact with the Guardians, she had never blushed at being naked. But here, in the home of her parents, she became the modest daughter any father would be proud of. The tan dungarees and short-sleeve print shirt were well worn and patched, yet they were freshly laundered and very comfortable. "Don't tuck the shirt in," she told him. He cinched the belt, holding the rest of the Krugerrands, and slipped on the sandals. Like the shirt and pants, they had been mended many times. He looked at himself in the mirror. The image staring back at him had changed. He had become Cuban.

She gave him a battered straw hat to cover the bandage. "Try not to show your teeth. They are too perfect."

"They are mine, you know."

She shook her head. "This is Cuba. Come, it's daylight. We can walk. Remember, Cubans are macho, so walk like a man. Do not slouch like an American or march like a German. Don't be afraid to look at a woman, especially if she is alone."

"Where are we going?"

"Mass. It's Sunday." Another contradiction. They stepped outside, and she took his arm.

It was a long walk, almost two miles. At first the streets were deserted, ghostly quiet, as if Havana were holding its collective breath. But as they neared the Plaza de la Catedral, the street filled with people. Rosalinda held his arm tightly and brushed against his shoulder in a way that suggested she was not an attentive daughter. A man murmured a few words under his breath as they passed. "Did he say what I think he said?" Marsten said.

"It was a compliment." She laughed, enchanting him. "He said you must be hung like a donkey to be with me. A very big donkey." They joined the people streaming into the cathedral and found seats near the front. The memories came surging back, and he was young again, a Catholic boy in a Protestant town in England. Near the end he looked at Rosalinda, struck by her beauty. A black mantilla framed her face as she prayed, reminding him of a Madonna. But this Madonna had killed two men less than twelve hours before and worked as a prostitute in an expensive bordello.

When the Mass ended, they joined the crowd filing out. But she pulled him aside into the southern transept. A man was waiting for them and led them to a small wooden door. He unlocked the door and handed her a flashlight. Rosalinda clicked on the light and led the way down a spiral stone staircase that descended into the crypt. The door closed behind them, and Marsten heard the key turn, locking them in. "What's going on?" he asked. She didn't answer. A musty smell assaulted him as they passed through piers reaching into the darkness over their heads. Ahead of them he saw light streaming through a small opening at street level. Dust drifted aimlessly through the narrow shaft of sunlight and made him think of all the lost souls who had lost their way. A man stepped out of the shadows. "Señor Marsten?" It was the Guardian he had met and bargained with in the bordello while Rosalinda sat naked on his lap.

The man pulled Rosalinda aside, and they spoke for a few moments. Then they were back. "This is dangerous," the man said. "Very dangerous."

"It's also very important," Marsten said. "Otherwise I wouldn't be here."

The man spun around and retreated into the shadows. Rosalinda gently guided Marsten after him and, after a few steps, pulled him to a halt. Marsten couldn't see a thing but had the feeling he was surrounded by living, breathing bodies. "What is so important?" an unfamiliar voice said from the shadows.

Every nerve in Marsten was on edge, and in the darkness his senses came alive. A slight odor caught his attention. Then it was gone. What was it? Then it came to him—gun oil. Rosalinda pressed his hand, and there was no doubt he was on trial for his life. And Rosalinda's. "It's about the assassins who tried to kill Turner," he said in English. Rosalinda translated for him. Silence. "There is evidence linking them to Cuba."

"Cubans would not have failed," a voice said from the darkness.

"It's a plot by the CIA," a woman's voice said. "The Yankees want an excuse to start a war."

"I have a highly placed contact in the government," Marsten said.

"Who?" the man asked.

Rosalinda's hand pressed his more tightly. A warning. Thankfully, it was a question he had expected, and he had carefully framed an answer. But it had to be just right, technical enough to convince them it was authentic and at the same time reinforce their version of reality. Another question loomed large in his mind. *How sophisticated are they?* "My contact is the FBI's RAC in Dallas."

"Rack?" another voice asked. "What is rack?" It sounded like Ernesto, Rosalinda's brother.

But Marsten couldn't be sure. "RAC stands for 'resident agent in charge.' The FBI knows how the CIA operates, and my source tells me the FBI is not treating it like a CIA plot." More whispering in the shadows, and Rosalinda's hand relaxed.

"Why should this RAC tell you this?" another voice asked.

Marsten held up his left hand and rubbed his thumb over his fingertips, the age-old sign for money. Could they see it? "I'm a businessman. How do you think I stay in business?" From the tone of the low murmuring, they believed him. "There's more. He tells me a witness has come out of hiding with evidence, very hard evidence, that Castro was behind the assassination of JFK." An audible gasp in the darkness.

"That's a lie," a new voice said.

Now he had to drive it home and plant fear in their hearts and minds. "It doesn't matter if it's the truth or not. It's what they believe is the truth. And they believe this." Rosalinda translated, and he could tell from her tone that she believed him. "You need to act now, or Madeline Turner will pick the next rulers of Cuba."

❀

Marsten paced back and forth, wearing a path in the flagstones surrounding the fountain in the Salandros' small courtyard. He came alert at the sound of gunfire and gave Rosalinda's mother, Amelia Salandro, a worried look. "When will Rosalinda return?" he asked. An expressive shrug answered him. More pacing. But at least there was no more gunfire. He glanced at his watch and did a quick mental conversion. It was seven o'clock Sunday evening in Havana—6:00 P.M. in Dallas. He needed to call L.J. and tell her he was okay. Now a new sound echoed over the courtyard. A heavy vehicle with a diesel engine lumbered by.

"An armored personnel carrier," Amelia Salandro told him.

"What's going on?" Marsten asked. No answer. He continued to pace as the minutes dragged, slowly ticking away. It was after midnight when Rosalinda returned. She was wearing dark clothes, and her face was haggard.

"Where is Ernesto?" Amelia asked, worried about her only son.

Rosalinda didn't answer. Instead, "Castro has declared martial law and ordered a twenty-four-hour curfew."

A cold, hard panic held Marsten tight. "Why?" he blurted.

"He says it is because the Yankees are going to invade. But he fears a revolution."

"Why should he fear a revolution?" Amelia asked.

"Because Ernesto told them about the Guardians," Rosalinda shouted.

Amelia collapsed to the floor. "My son, an informant?"

Rosalinda crouched beside her mother and pulled her head to her breast. Together they rocked back and forth, tears streaking their faces. Finally Rosalinda helped her mother to stand and led her inside. Marsten felt his heart turn in pity at what Amelia was going through. After what seemed an eternity, Rosalinda came back. "I'm so sorry," Marsten said.

"It is not your concern," Rosalinda said, her voice cold and flat.

"I need to make a telephone call," Marsten said.

"The phones are out," she replied.

"I have a satellite telephone. It was in my briefcase, but I can't find it."

Rosalinda disappeared into the house and returned a few moments later carrying the handheld global satellite telephone. She studied it carefully. "You can talk to anyone in the world?"

"If they have one or subscribe to a service that links them into the system."

"You can tell them the revolution has started. Tell them a new government will rule Cuba by Wednesday, or we will all be as dead as Ernesto."

"Ernesto, dead?"

She stared at him. "*Sí.*" There was a finality in her voice he had never heard before.

"Are you sure?"

Nothing in her voice changed. "I killed him." She threw the phone to the ground, venting her anger. "He was alive until you came." She kicked the phone, and it skidded across the flagstones to Marsten, breaking off the antenna.

He held out his hands in supplication. "It's not my fault."

She jerked her head yes, accepting the truth of it. "Do not leave the house," she ordered. "It's too dangerous."

28

Dallas

Vivaldi normally helped.

L.J. turned up the music and gave herself over to "The Four Seasons." That didn't work. The buoyant, rushing virtuosity of violins announcing the arrival of spring carried a sense of rebirth that grated on her nerves. *Maybe Beethoven's* Pastoral? She thought. She slipped the CD into the player, turned up the volume, and lay back in her chair. Nothing. "Where are you, Lloyd?" she said to no one, deeply worried. She glanced at her calendar. It was Monday morning, and he should have been out of Cuba twelve hours ago.

A knock at the door of her office gave her an excuse to turn the volume down. "Come on in," she called. Shugy Jenkins wheeled a tea cart through the door. "Shugy, how nice of you," L.J. said.

The secretary poured her a cup of tea. "I know you're worried about Mr. Marsten."

"He should have called by now." She touched the satellite phone on her desk. Shugy handed her the teacup. "Thank you. I hate the waiting, you know."

"Does the music help?" L.J. shook her head in answer. "May I?" the prim secretary asked. L.J. nodded. Shugy turned to the elaborate sound system and dialed an FM station. The sounds of country-western music filled the room. "Give it a moment," she said. She pushed the tea cart out of the office and closed the door behind her.

Much to L.J.'s surprise, the blatant emotionalism of the lyrics and simple melody touched her in a way she had not expected. Her father's words from a time long past came back. "You can never have enough country-western bands in Dallas." *Why did I send Lloyd?* she thought. The demon in her answered. She could no more stop herself than refrain from breathing, it was that elemental. Kenny Rogers's "The Gambler" came on, and for a moment the demon was grinning at her. She forced it away. Her intercom buzzed. "Were you expecting Dr. Steiner?" Shugy asked.

L.J. stiffened at the mention of the French scientist. "No, as a matter of fact, I'm not. Please schedule an appointment if I'm free tomorrow." There was no doubt that Shugy would have him out of the building in a few minutes.

"He says it's very important and can't wait. It's about Mr. Marsten's trip to Cuba."

L.J. cursed to herself. *How did he know about that?* "I'll see him." She reached to turn the music off. She changed her mind and turned it down. The door opened, and the dumpy little scientist walked in wearing a very smug look. "What can I do for you?"

"Aren't you going to ask how I learned about Marsten's trip to Cuba?"

"No."

A little smile flicked across his lips. "Always in control. I appreciate that." He sat down and glanced at his watch. "I asked Ann to call you at this time."

"Ann Silton?" L.J. asked.

Another glance at his watch. "We have many areas of mutual interest."

The intercom buzzed. "The Department of Energy is on line one," Shugy announced.

"I'll take it," L.J. said. A look of triumph flashed across Steiner's face when she punched at the button connecting her to the caller. A voice told her to please hold for the undersecretary. "No," L.J. replied and hung up. "A pity," she said, "that might have been an interesting call." She smiled sweetly. "Is there anything else?" Before Steiner could answer, the phone rang again. "Yes, Shugy."

"Miss Silton is on line one."

"Much better. Thank you." She casually shifted the receiver to her other hand and glanced at Steiner. "Would you like to hear this?" Steiner's nod was a little too eager. She punched the monitor on. "Good morning, Ann. How are you?"

Ann's voice filled the room. "Don't ever hang up on my secretary again."

"I'm afraid we made a bad connection," L.J. replied. "By the way, Professor Steiner is listening with me and is most interested in this call."

"I take it you've heard the news coming from Cuba?"

"They do seem to be having a few problems down there," L.J. replied.

"After talking to Dr. Steiner, I spoke to the secretary of state. He apprised me of the situation there, and I, of course, explained your interest in Cuba."

"Based on what Emil told you no doubt."

"Of course."

"He is under contract to RayTex, you know. I do hope that DOE is not interfering in that relationship."

"Not at all," Ann replied. "But I did want to tell you that we have enjoined all offshore drilling rigs and ships from drilling until they are certified to be in compliance with all applicable directives governing the environment."

"Enjoined? You make this sound so legal, Ann. May I ask who signed the directive enjoining us?"

"I did, of course. It's totally within my purview to do so."

"I see. Well, thank you for calling. I appreciate the personal touch. It does inspire confidence in our government."

"I'm glad you understand," Ann said. "We'll be in touch."

"No doubt," L.J. replied. She broke the connection and turned on Steiner. "Was this why you came here?"

He giggled. "I wanted to see the expression on your face. I told them everything. They know why you're interested in Cuba and why you've chartered the drilling ships."

"Pure conjecture," she said. He stood up to leave, his face flushed with triumph. "Is there anything else?" she asked.

"Oh, yes." Then he was gone.

"A very bad mistake," she muttered. When it came to revenge, she was an extremely patient woman. Without thinking, she ran her hand along the first rack of CDs and plucked Richard Wagner's *The Ring of the*

Nibelung from its slot. She dropped the disk in and cycled the forward button to the third act of *Die Walküre*. She turned up the volume as the heavy strains of the Ride of the Valkeries filled her office. This time the music worked perfectly.

In the outer office Shugy Jenkins looked up, overwhelmed by the sound. "Oh, dear Lord!"

Reston, Virginia

Stuart turned up the long drive that led to a house set well back from the road. "Someone's got money," he said to himself. He seriously doubted he had the right address, but there was only one Mather listed in the book. He parked in an area obviously meant for guests and walked up to the front door. *What OSI agent could afford this place?* he thought. He rang the doorbell. A handsome Mexican-American woman in her late fifties came to the door. "Excuse me, I'm looking for an Antonia Moreno-Mather. I'm Lieutenant Colonel Mike Stuart, U.S. Air Force." The woman studied him for a moment, and he could see a definite resemblance to Special Agent Toni Moreno-Mather.

Without a word the woman held the door open. He followed her inside. "Very nice," he murmured. The woman ushered him into a sunroom off the family lounge, where a very pregnant Toni was propped up on a couch. The woman spoke in Spanish. "It's okay, Mom. I know him." She gave her mother a warm smile. The woman murmured a few words and retreated back into the family room, leaving them alone. "Mom's here taking care of me," Toni explained.

"I had a heck of a time finding you," he said. "Are you on maternity leave?"

"No. I started having trouble carrying the baby, and Brent, my husband, said it was time to quit. So here I am." She gestured at their surroundings and said something about "his family" that Stuart didn't quite catch, but it was obvious that their money had bought the house. She struggled to an upright position. "Mom flew in from California to take care of me when the FBI sent Brent on a special assignment to Florida. Something to do with the attempted assassination at the memorial." She pushed pillows around until she was comfortable. "Another month to go. So what brings you here?"

"The investigation," he said. "But I thought you were still on it." She shook her head, telling him the obvious. "Do you know who's handling it now?" he asked.

"I seriously doubt the Air Force will stay involved," she told him.

He looked so forlorn, that she wanted to hug and comfort him. "I know it sounds stupid," he said, "but I think somebody's out to get me."

"Why do you think that?"

He told her about everything that had happened to him and Jane. He concluded, "That accident on the boat was meant for me, not Jane."

"But why?" she asked, coming to the heart of the matter.

Stuart carefully considered his answer. "That's what I need to find out."

"So that's why you came looking for me?" He nodded. "I don't know what I can tell you," she said. A heavy silence came down. "There is one thing: I never had a chance to interview a Miss Jean McCormick. She was the one lead I didn't check out."

Stuart shook his head. "I never heard of her."

"The guy who assaulted you was killed attempting to rob her at an ATM."

Stuart's head came up. "Do you think there might be a connection?"

"That's what investigations are all about. I need to check my notes. Mom!" she called. Her mother immediately reappeared. "Upstairs in my office is a white cardboard file box in the far corner next to the bookshelves. My notebooks are in it. Would you bring it down, please?" The woman turned and left. Toni made small talk while they waited. "Are you related to the Colonel Stuart who saved the president at the memorial?"

"He's my father."

"I thought I saw a resemblance." She rearranged her body and groaned. Her face paled.

"Are you okay?"

"I will be. My doctor says he doubts I'll go full term." She took a few deep breaths, but it was obvious the pain wasn't going away. Her mother returned carrying the file box. Toni gave her a wan smile. "You better call Lois, Mom. I think we need to go to the hospital." Her mother dropped the box and ran for the telephone. "Mom doesn't drive, and Lois is my next-door neighbor who's helping."

Her mother rushed back into the room, obviously panicked. "Lois has gone shopping."

"Call a taxi," Toni said. She bent over in pain, gasping for breath.

"I'll take you," Stuart said. "Let's go." He helped Toni to her feet while her mother ran ahead to gather up their coats and open doors. Within moments Toni was in the backseat and they were moving down the long drive. It was starting to snow. Stuart handed Toni his cell phone. "Call the hospital and tell them we're coming. Then dial the police for me." Toni did as he commanded, and when she was connected to the police, handed the phone to Stuart. He explained the situation and asked for an escort. When the dispatcher questioned the need, Stuart's voice hardened and filled with command. "I've got an emergency here, it's starting to snow hard, and I need backup. Are you going to do your job or not?" He listened for a moment. "Thank you." He broke the connection and dropped the phone in his lap. "Help's on the way."

※

Stuart was sitting in the waiting room with Toni's mother when the doctor came out. "Congratulations, Mr. Mather. You have a son, and your wife is fine. You got them here just in time."

"I'm a friend, not the father," Stuart explained. "This is Mrs. Moreno, Toni's mother."

"Your grandson is premature, but he'll be fine," the doctor said. "Would you like to see them?" Mrs. Moreno nodded and followed the doctor inside. Stuart waited until she returned to drive her home. When he saw her, the smile on her face told him all was well.

"Toni says thank you. She also said to show you the . . ." She fumbled for the right word.

"Notebooks?" Stuart said.

※

Toni's writing was small and cramped but easily understood. *She was very thorough*, he thought. He read her notes from their first interview and the follow-up phone call to the police detective about the name of his assailant's second victim at the ATM. He had found what he had come for and committed the name of Jean McCormick and her phone number to memory. He was about to drop the notebook back into the box and leave when on impulse he flipped to the next page. It was the interview with Ramjet. *I shouldn't be reading this*, he told himself. He read it anyway. He swore eloquently when he saw Ramjet's statement about not knowing exactly who'd told him about the police investigation of the car accident that killed Jenny's lover. *I told the son of a bitch!* Then he laughed when he saw Toni's note, "Lying asshole."

He flipped to the next page and froze. It was her interview with Lieutenant General Butler. "My, God," he whispered. He ripped out a few blank pages and furiously copied her notes. He shook his head when he saw the same comment about "Lying asshole." *She doesn't cut anyone slack*, he told himself. "Not a bad idea," he said aloud.

Havana

Sweat streamed down Marsten's face as he sat at the table by the window. He was sweltering in the noonday sun, but he didn't have a choice. He needed the light and clear access to the sky to uplink. He worked carefully as he reattached the antenna to his satellite telephone. Unfortunately he didn't have much to work with and had used a set of fingernail clippers from his shaving kit to strip copper wiring from a lamp cord. Lacking a soldering gun, he resorted to chewing gum to hold the fragile wiring together. Outside, the street was empty, and it had been over three hours since he'd last heard gunfire. The only disturbance was when the woman who commanded the neighborhood Committee for the Defense of the Revolution walked the street pounding on doors to summon the faithful to guard duty. But no one answered her, and she stomped off in frustration.

He meticulously wiped the sweat off his face and dried his hands. It was now or never. A low rumbling sound reverberated down the street. He ignored it as he punched in the number to L.J.'s satellite phone. *Come on!* he urged. The sound outside grew louder.

"Lloyd!" L.J. said, her voice clear and strong. "Where have you been?"

"Sorry, I'll explain later." He took for granted that they were being monitored, and he had to be cautious. "Suffice it to say, this has not turned into the ideal vacation. Things here have become very interesting, and I'm trying to get out. But I was wondering about our last conversation. I assume the three doctors you hired are ready to move to their new location."

In her preoccupation with Marsten's safety, L.J. missed the message. "We can worry about all that later. After you're back."

"Dr. Steiner, Silton, and Drill may not be available if we delay," he replied, trying once more. The noise coming from the street turned into the deep-throated sound of a diesel engine with the unmistakable clanking of steel tracks. It had to be a tank. But even that did not prepare him for the sight of the old Soviet-built T-62 main battle tank grinding and jerking as it turned the corner. Nothing in his experience—movies, TV, books, nothing—had prepared him for the reality of the steel monster coming his way, and raw fear shot through him. "What's that noise?" L.J. asked.

"I believe it's a tank," Marsten said. He fought to control his panic.

"For God's sake, Lloyd, get out of there!"

"Believe me, I'm trying." Marsten watched the tank as it clanked to a stop. The turret hatch swung open, and the tank commander's head emerged. He glanced at a piece of paper as if he were checking on an address. The woman from the Committee for the Defense of the Revolution came out of her house and spoke to the soldier. "I forgot to tell you," Marsten said, laboring to keep his voice normal, "that I had arranged for them to start work this Wednesday. I do hope they're ready. If they can't, you'd best cancel their contract."

"Stop worrying about business and come home, okay?"

Marsten's heart raced when the woman raised her hand and gestured in his direction. He couldn't hear what she said, but from the way the tank commander looked directly at him, there was no doubt that the subject was Casa Salandro. *Did he see me?* There was no way of telling. The tank commander disappeared down the hatch, and the cover banged closed. "Oh, dear," Marsten said, calling up the last of his British reserve. The tank started to move. "Can I call you back later?" He scooped up the telephone and dropped it into his shoulder bag, along with his passport, shoes, and belt with the Krugerrands. He ran from the room as the clanking grew louder. He was racing down the stairs when the tank ground to a halt. A loud whirring sound echoed over the courtyard with its beautiful fountain as he ran for the back of the building. It was a sound he had only heard in the movies: a tank turret traversing on its track. Amelia

Salandro, Rosalinda's mother, came out of the kitchen. "Run!" he shouted. For a moment she hesitated, confused. He grabbed her and jerked her out the rear entrance, still running.

The explosion was deafening. Marsten kept running as dust and debris rained down on them. A second explosion rocked him. Now he was sure the source was the tank's cannon. He looked back as a heavy machine gun barked. Plaster and chips blew out the rear wall of the house in a horizontal cascade. Then the machine gun stopped, and the flying debris died away. The unmistakable sound of a house crumbling in on itself echoed down the narrow alleyway. Amelia Salandro fell to her knees weeping hysterically. He had a brief impulse to run away, leaving her behind. Instead he pulled her to her feet. "Come," he said, leading her down the alley.

Dallas

The phone clicked, and L.J. heard a dial tone. She started to redial Marsten's number but thought better of it. Obviously he was caught up in the middle of a revolution and didn't need a phone going off at the wrong time. She reran the entire conversation through her mind. "Of course," she groaned to herself, finally getting the message. "Dr. Drill. How stupid can I get?" Cuba's fate would be decided by Wednesday. Her fingers beat a relentless tattoo on her desk. The three drilling ships were in southern Florida and ready to go. But unfortunately they were all in harbor, and that meant under Ann Silton's injunction. RayTex held a lease on a foreign ship, but getting it into position and drilling would take weeks. And she had only days.

More fingers drumming. Her hand flashed out and picked up the phone. "Shugy, please contact Mr. John Frobisher at DOE." Automatically, she checked her watch—1:35 P.M. Dallas time—and made the conversion to Washington, D.C., time. John Frobisher came on the line. "John," she sang.

"Good afternoon, Ms. Ellis. What can I do for you?" His voice was cool and reserved.

"I'm going to be in the city this evening, and I was wondering if we could chat?"

"And the subject?"

"John, we do have some unfinished business from the convention."

"Really?"

She pitched her tone just right. "I'll be staying at the Four Seasons. I do hope you're free."

"As a matter of fact, I am free this evening."

"Wonderful. Shall we say eight o'clock?" He readily agreed, and she let her contentment show. "Until then," she said. She punched off the connection and buzzed her secretary. "Shugy, call Love Field and get the Sabreliner ready for a flight to D.C. Have them file an IFR flight plan to Ronald Reagan International, departure at three P.M."

"Yes, ma'am. But won't you need a copilot? Tim Roxford has left, and I don't know who's available."

"Have them find someone."

"I'll try," Shugy promised.

❋

"I'm sorry, Ms. Ellis," the dispatcher at Love Field said, "but we don't have any qualified copilots available on such short notice." He handed her the completed flight plan that needed only her signature.

"Not a problem," L.J. said. She wrote in the name "S. Jenkins" as her copilot, signed the flight plan, and handed it back. She gathered up the paperwork and hurried out to the flight line. "Shugy," she called, "have you ever been to Washington, D.C.?"

"Oh, Ms. Ellis. I couldn't possibly go on such short notice."

"Why not? What's waiting for you? Billy's in the nursing home, and he won't miss you for one night. We'll buy anything you need, and we'll be back tomorrow by noon. It'll be fun." Shugy started to weaken. L.J. gave her an encouraging smile.

"Well, all right."

"You'll love it, and you can sit up front with me and play copilot."

29

Over Virginia

The approach controller cleared the Sabreliner for the approach to Ronald Reagan International Airport. L.J. read the clearance back. "Cleared for the ILS to Runway Thirty-six." She did a quick review. The radios were all set up, the ILS tuned and identified, the GPS selected as a backup, and she had the inbound course, altitudes, decision height, and missed approach procedures memorized. She took a deep breath and punched off the autopilot before lowering the gear and flaps. Approach cleared her to the tower frequency. "Washington Tower," she radioed. "Sabreliner four-four-two Kilo, outer marker now, ILS Runway Thirty-six." Simultaneously she started the timer and checked the compass heading and gear-down indicators. She picked up her instrument scan as light turbulence rocked the jet.

"Sabreliner four-four-two Kilo," the tower replied. "Cleared for landing. Be advised the last two aircraft ahead of you went missed approach and diverted."

"Copy all," L.J. replied. The turbulence increased as the airspeed indicator fluctuated from five to six knots. She stabilized the airspeed and kept her instrument scan going. They had a left-to-right crosswind, and she shaded the heading to the left. She turned farther to the left. Slowly the CDI—course deviation needle—on the ILS centered. The turbulence spiked and rocked the Sabreliner. For a fraction of a second the aircraft was out of control.

"Dear me," Shugy said from the right seat. She clutched the arms of her seat.

"Make sure you're all strapped in," L.J. said, her voice labored with strain. Even in the cool cockpit her face glistened with sweat. She rechecked the gear. Down and locked. Another gust rocked the jet, but not as bad. Airspeed good. Coming up on decision height. Ten seconds to go on the elapsed timer. "Where are you?" she shouted. The altimeter touched the decision height, and she looked up from the instruments. The approach lights were at her one-o'clock position and not in front of her! She fought the impulse to alter heading. She inched the throttles back and crossed the runway numbers at 115 knots, still holding fifteen degrees of crab for wind correction. Just before touchdown she kicked the rudder and lowered the left wing.

The left main gear touched down as a sudden gust of wind hit the Sabreliner. She blipped the throttles and cranked in more aileron to keep the jet on the runway. Instinctively she eased off on the ailerons as the gust bled off. The right main touched down just as the nose wheel came down. Another gust of wind skidded them to the right. She corrected with rudder and nose-gear steering, fighting to stay on the runway. Finally they stopped on the right side of the runway with two thousand feet remaining.

L.J. bent over the yoke and breathed deeply, for the first time fully appreciating what she had done to Tim Roxford on the Life Flight into Norfolk. "Oh, Tim. I'm so sorry."

"My!" Shugy said. "That was certainly exciting."

Washington, D.C.

The young man looked up from the computer screen. "Good evening, Ms. Ellis. Welcome to the Four Seasons." The limo driver had called ahead and primed reception for her arrival. "Your suite is ready." He motioned for the bellhop to take her small bag to the Presidential Suite. L.J. paused and motioned at Shugy. "My companion came along at the last moment and will need to do some shopping." She thought for a moment. "Perhaps a new outfit and makeover this evening? Put it all on my bill."

"Certainly, Ms. Ellis."

She walked with Shugy to the elevator. "I've asked them to spoil you this evening," L.J. said. "Now, don't you go telling them no. You're to enjoy yourself, hear?"

"I can't," Shugy protested.

L.J. laughed. "Oh, yes you can! Especially after what I put you through. I'll call you in the morning."

✳

John Frobisher relaxed into the sofa's deep cushions as he watched L. J. pour the wine. She was wearing a simple, floor-length sheath that moved and flowed over her body in ways that set his nerves jingling. A CD played softly, setting the mood. "Who's the artist?" he asked.

"Charles Aznavour," she replied, handing him the wine. "I like his interpretation of 'My Way.' Much better than Sinatra's."

He sipped the wine. It was excellent. He looked around the hotel suite. Like the wine, it made a definite but quiet statement about elegance, good taste, and wealth. It was a quantum leap from the Regency Hotel in Dallas where they had first met at the Front Uni convention. Now, as then, she dominated her surroundings. He tried to take her measure, but she was beyond him. Rather than lose his focus, he simply accepted her as an elemental force of nature. "I don't think you asked me here to talk about the relative merits of French and American recording artists."

She sat beside him and sank into the corner of the sofa, looking at him over the rim of her glass. "No."

"You're concerned about the latest regulations stopping offshore drilling," he said.

"Aren't you?"

"Is there a reason I should be?"

She moved closer to him. "John, you didn't think it through. Anytime you, or any other government agency, changes one of the ground rules, the rest of the system changes with it. You're not dealing with a static situation. The entire dynamic shifts." It was obvious he didn't understand. "I make hundreds of decisions every day based on the existing rules. For example, if the tax code is altered in any way and it's to my benefit financially, I can take RayTex outside your jurisdiction with a few computer keystrokes. That's the nature of the global economy."

"Yes, but you'll leave most of your capital investment behind."

She gave him a look he couldn't read. "Will I?" She doubted he understood the complicated system of ownership, financial mirrors, and leaseback arrangements the oil industry employed. She certainly wasn't going to explain it to him.

"Then why are we having this conversation?"

"Because in the long run it's to my benefit to remain in the system. Take that away and RayTex is gone. Besides, I care about the people who work for me." She turned her back to him and slipped a shoulder strap onto her arm. "Can you rub my right shoulder? It's been a terrible day." He gently massaged her shoulder, feeling the bone structure underneath. "Perfect," she murmured.

"But you want something."

"Of course," she said. "The other shoulder, please." He did as she asked, now rubbing both shoulders. The dress slipped lower and exposed her back. "Can we do this in the Jacuzzi?" She heard him sharply inhale. "Come. Bring your glass." She stood, picked up the wine bottle, and walked into the huge bathroom. She set down her glass and the bottle and stepped out of her dress.

Frobisher stared at her as she stepped into the Jacuzzi. He wanted to possess her so badly that it hurt. But he wasn't a fool. "L.J., this isn't going to work."

"We're just going to talk," she said. She sat down and laid her head on the edge to watch him undress. She appraised his body as he slipped into the water. Like so many of the inhabitants of the Imperial City, he was pudgy and out of shape. "You do know why my company is interested in Cuba, don't you?"

He chose his words carefully. "According to Dr. Steiner, there's the possibility of a large offshore discovery."

"An elephant," she said.

Frobisher shook his head. "Our geologists tell us that's impossible."

"That's why they work for you and not me." She sat up and turned her back to him. "Again, please." He dutifully massaged her shoulders as she sat between his legs. She gave a little wiggle and scooted against his groin. She felt his erection turn to granite. "I've a narrow window of opportunity to act—by Wednesday at the latest—if a U.S. company is to develop those reserves." She bent over and held her hair back. "Lower, please." He did as she asked. "That's good."

Frobisher wasn't thinking too clearly. "So you're saying if you lose, we all lose."

"No, John, that's not what I'm saying at all. "The United States loses. I'll still be a player, because an offshore corporation of RayTex, which is beyond your control, holds the concessions for the elephant." It was a lie, but there was no way he could verify it.

"How in the hell did RayTex get the concessions?"

She leaned back into his hands. "By having my man in Havana at the right time, talking to the right people."

He fought to control his voice. "What exactly do you need?"

"The injunction lifted, so my ships can do what I'm paying them for."

He moved his hands down her arms and said, "Ann probably overstepped her authority when she approved the new standards. I can always raise a few legal questions that need to be resolved. We might have to delay implementation until the secretary's chief legal counsel signs off."

She turned around in his arms and faced him. With an easy motion she straddled him, locking his thighs with hers. Her arms were around his neck. "That would be wonderful."

His words were deep and husky. "There's something I've got to know. Who made that video of Ann and Clarissa?"

"No idea."

"Oh, my God," he whispered, understanding at last. "You want to keep it hanging over their heads for leverage."

"Can we stop talking about business?" She shifted her weight on his lap. "A promise made is a debt unpaid," she whispered in his ear.

Newport News

The silver Lexus pulled up to the hangar, and Eric jumped out. He waved at Stuart and Seagrave as he waited for the two young girls in the backseat to pull on their heavy coats. Jenny got out from behind the wheel and walked over to Stuart. "Thanks for bringing him," Stuart said. "I know you didn't have to."

Jenny shot a look of disapproval at the two twelve-year-old girls.

"The way he got on my case, I didn't really have a choice, not since their school is having a day off for a teacher's conference."

Stuart followed her look. "Aren't those your neighbors?" A curt nod answered him. "You look at them the same way your mother looked at me."

Jenny snorted. "Little tramps. They call him constantly. I had to get him his own telephone."

"Still, I do appreciate your bringing him to say good-bye. By the way," he ventured, trying to make a peace offer, "do we really need to go to court? We've always been able to work things out before."

Jenny ignored the offer. "He's not allowed to fly while we're here. Don't even mention it—or we leave immediately."

"I won't. But flying's not dangerous."

"You forget I saw the videotape that reporter made."

"They never aired that program because it wasn't true."

Jenny watched Eric show the two girls around the Lightning. Her eyes narrowed into tight lines. "My lawyer says it's relevant." She immediately regretted saying it.

Stuart deliberately passed over the remark but mentally filed it away for later use. He grinned at Jenny's discomfort when Eric introduced the girls to Seagrave and Shanker, who were wearing flight suits. "Dad's flying down to Key West with Chalky," Stuart told Jenny. "That should be some flight."

"How long will they be there?"

"The contract calls for six weeks," Stuart answered. He smiled when Eric brought the two girls over to introduce them. Jenny was growing more agitated by the minute.

"Dad," Eric said with great solemnity, "I'd like you to meet two friends, Becky and Andy." Stuart shook their hands, and both girls giggled. Eric pointed at the two external fuel tanks mounted on top of the wing. "Are those fuel tanks?" he asked. "I thought drop tanks were hung underneath."

"Not on the Lightning," Stuart explained.

Eric wanted to impress the girls and asked, "So how do they jettison them in combat?"

"I don't know. You'll have to ask Commander Seagrave. By the way, your grandmother is in the office. Go introduce your friends before she leaves."

"Martha's leaving, too?" Jenny asked.

Stuart shrugged. "A lot of wives are driving down to keep an eye on things."

"I see," Jenny said. It was her turn to file away that bit of information.

It was time to launch the Lightning, and Eric helped the ground crew while the two girls joined Stuart and Jenny. "Isn't he cute?" one of the girls whispered. Jenny glared at them. Engine start and taxi went smoothly, and Stuart herded them into the crew van to drive out to the runway to watch the takeoff. He parked on a taxiway three thousand feet down the runway, where he estimated the Lightning would lift off. They all piled out and stood by the van. The air behind the Lightning rippled like a mirage, and the jet started to move. Then a loud crack echoed over them when Seagrave lit the afterburners. The two girls watched transfixed as the jet hurtled down the runway toward them. The nose gear came up, and the Lightning lifted over them, still in full afterburner. The noise washed over them, pounding their bodies with a basic, primeval message pulsating with energy.

"Oh," Jenny gasped, her face flushed. As it had in so many before her, the Lightning had touched a deep sexuality.

"Exciting, yes?" Stuart said.

＊

Martha Stuart came out of the kitchen and set a bowl of hot soup in front of Stuart. "I saw you talking to Jenny at the airport. Is she still going ahead with the hearing?"

"I'm afraid so, Mom. Next Wednesday, March fifth."

"How bad is it?"

"It's not good, Mom."

"What does your lawyer say?"

"Don't use a lawyer."

"Mike, don't be foolish. Barbara Raye's lawyer will be there and, and . . . well, you can't go in there and face someone like that."

Stuart patted the chair beside him for her to join him. "I'm not going in unprepared, Mom. What does Dad always say? 'The guy who shot you down is the guy you didn't see.' Well, Mom, you're the guy who's going to shoot them down. Jenny thinks you're in Florida with the other wives, so you're going to blindside them." He opened his briefcase and pulled out a yellow legal pad full of notes. He outlined his strategy and what he had to learn in the next few days.

"Can you do all that?" Martha asked.

"I've got to try."

Dallas

The elevator doors to the top floor of the Fountain Plaza Building ghosted open. The two women stood there and took in the scene. For all appearances it was a normal Wednesday morning as the staff went about their work. "Go ahead," L.J. told Shugy. "You look wonderful." The new Shugy saw her reflection in the elevator's polished bronze. She was wearing a very stylish pantsuit with matching Italian shoes. Her hair had been cut and styled to frame her face, while makeup highlighted her eyes and accentuated her high cheekbones. She straightened her shoulders and marched resolutely to her desk. For a moment the staff was silent. "Mrs. Jenkins!" one of the secretaries gasped. "I didn't recognize you!"

L.J. smiled but inside, a sadness touched her. She wished she could have given her spinster aunt a moment like this one. She went into her office and turned on the TV. As expected, the news was dominated by Cuba. Her phone buzzed, but she hesitated, wanting to hear what the commentator was saying. "Havana is in chaos, and Fidel Castro has disappeared. The rumor currently on the lips of every resident of this neurotic, jittery city is that he has returned to his revolutionary headquarters in the Sierra Maestra mountains." She picked up the phone.

"Felix Campbell is on line one," the old Shugy said.

L.J. punched at the button. "Felix," she said, "how are things at BP?"

"You know damn well how things are," Campbell replied. "I hear your drilling ships are on their way to Cuba."

"They sailed this morning."

"Do you have the concessions?"

The intercom buzzed, and she glanced at the caller screen. Dutch Shell was on line two. "Not yet," she answered. She would lie to Frobisher, but never to Campbell.

"We need to talk."

"Are you making a preemptive offer?" L.J. asked. Silence answered her.

"Felix, you need to put something on the table. Sorry, I've got to go. Amsterdam is on line two." She didn't wait for his answer as she broke the connection. Before she could punch up the line with Amsterdam, the caller screen flashed. A name she did not recognize was calling from Miami. *How did he get this number?* she wondered. She punched up that line.

"Miss Ellis?" a voice with a heavy Spanish accent asked. She confirmed her identity and he said, "I represent the provisional government of Cuba and have been directed to speak to you about certain concessions."

30

"In the name of God," Amelia Salandro begged, "don't do this. We're cousins. We played together as children. Please, let us stay." The man shook his head and pushed her toward the door. Again she pleaded with him. "Please, Agosto said to meet him here."

Her cousin sneered in contempt. "Your husband left."

"How long ago?" Marsten asked. Before the man could answer, gunfire echoed down the street. The man jerked in fear and yelled at Amelia. Marsten caught something about Agosto's being *una mierda*—a real shit—and not helping the family.

"He said a few minutes ago," Amelia answered.

"Tell him I can make him a wealthy man," Marsten said.

"He says we must leave now," Amelia said. "He says the soldiers will kill everyone if they find us."

Marsten started to unbuckle his belt to bribe him with a Krugerrand. But he thought better of it and handed him his Rolex watch. Amelia's cousin snatched the watch and slipped it on. He fumbled at the snap, finally securing it to his wrist. More gunfire echoed in the next block, and he looked up, a very frightened man. He shook his head and grabbed Amelia, dragging her to the door. "Where are we supposed to go?" she wailed.

The man rasped, "Follow the shit!" Gunfire rang out, much closer now, and he hesitated before opening the door.

"The soldiers will kill us!" Amelia shouted. Her cousin opened the door and shoved Amelia into the dark street. But she held on to his shirt and kept pleading. He turned his back to Marsten and beat Amelia to the ground, yelling something in Spanish about *putas* and Rosalinda.

"She's my daughter!" Amelia wailed. The shouting and gunfire grew louder. Marsten quickly unbuckled his belt and pulled it free. He twisted an end around each wrist, feeling its heavy weight, and looped it over the man's head. Then Marsten jerked hard, garroting him. The man tried to fight and grabbed at the belt as Marsten dragged him back into the house. Amelia staggered into the house and banged the door closed. "He's my cousin!" she wailed, beating on Marsten with her tiny fists.

Marsten ignored her and kept pulling. He had never killed a man before, and it seemed like an eternity before the man quit twitching and lay still. "I didn't have a choice," Marsten said, breathing deeply. Outside, the gunfire stopped. "Blow out the candle." Amelia extinguished the candle as Marsten dragged the body into an alcove under the stairs. "What now?" he wondered aloud. Amelia gasped at the sound of boots pounding down the street and ran into Marsten's arms. He held her tight, surprised that she was so thin and frail. They froze at the sound of someone banging on the door across the narrow street. *What would L.J. do?* Marsten thought. The answer was unbelievably simple: take care of Amelia. He released her and chanced a look out the heavily shuttered window.

A pack of soldiers was breaking down the door on the opposite side of the street. The door collapsed, and a soldier sprayed the interior with a burst of submachine-gun fire. Two ran inside and dragged a man out. Marsten sucked in his breath. It was Amelia's husband, Agosto Salandro. He watched in horror as the two soldiers twisted and straightened Salandro's arms behind his back, forcing him to his knees. A burly sergeant pulled his automatic, thumbed the safety off, and jammed the muzzle against the back of Salandro's head. *"Traidor!"* he yelled. A single shot rang out, and Salandro slumped onto the pavement facedown in a pool of his own blood. Marsten turned away and took Amelia's hands, relieved that she hadn't witnessed the execution. "We must hide. Is there a back door?" Amelia pointed down a side hall. He pulled her after him, hurrying into the back, desperate to escape. A loud banging at the door sent fear jolting through him. He found the back door and jerked it open. The banging grew louder.

He forced himself to think. He was doing exactly what the soldiers expected him to do. *Give them what they want!* he thought. He left the door open and pulled Amelia back to the alcove where he had hidden her cousin's body. He dragged the body out and propped it up against the side of the stairs, its back to the front door. Then he stepped into the alcove, still holding up the body. The door crashed open, and the beam of a flashlight swept the entryway. Then a burst of automatic gunfire deafened him. At the same time, Marsten pushed the body away as hard as he could. It fell against the opposite wall as a second burst of gunfire rang out. The body jerked as round after round tore into it, the force of impact tumbling it toward the kitchen.

Marsten fell back into the alcove, his body shielding Amelia. He closed his eyes as soldiers crashed into the house, mere inches away on the other side of the thin boards framing the alcove. Footsteps pounded over his head as two soldiers ran up the stairs. Another pair ran into the kitchen and shouted. They had found the open door. Soldiers streamed into the house and out through the back door. Now the two soldiers who had run upstairs returned. The first one down paused over the dead body. He reached down and pulled the Rolex watch free, trying to hide it from his partner. The second soldier yelled that he wanted to see the watch. "It's for the people!" the thief shouted in Spanish, following the others out the back door. The last soldier ran after him.

Marsten leaned against the wall as Amelia collapsed into his arms. "We've got to leave," he told her. "Out the front." But he had to warn her. "Don't look at the body. It's very bad."

She nodded, and he led her out the front, fully intending to head in the direction the soldiers had come from. But Amelia saw the body and recognized her husband. She fell to her knees and cried, unable to go on. Marsten scooped her up, not sure how far he could carry her. Then he stopped. The neighbor's door was back in place as if nothing had happened. Still holding Amelia, he kicked at the door. No answer. Twice more he kicked. It cracked open, and he saw a dark shadow. Then it flew open full wide, and Rosalinda rushed out. "Mama! Mama!" she shouted, taking her mother in her arms.

※

Marsten drank, surprised at how thirsty he was. Then he set down the bottle and looked around the room. It was packed with people he recognized: the cabdriver who had first given him the card and told him to ask for Angelica, two servants from the Salandro household, the madam from the whorehouse where Rosalinda worked, and finally the negotiator from the Guardians he had cut a deal with on the concessions. "Who's winning?" Marsten asked.

"The Guardians are in control," the negotiator answered.

Marsten glanced at the people crowded around him. "It certainly looks like it."

"We control the radio and the government. But the army is in revolt."

"So you control about half."

The negotiator gave him a hard stare. "The important half."

"And the concessions?" Marsten asked. The negotiator said he had no news. "Well," Marsten said, "let's find out." He took the pieces of his satellite phone out of his shoulder bag and carefully patched them together. He stood by a window and dialed L.J.'s number. She answered on the first ring.

"Lloyd! Where are you? Are you okay?"

"I'm okay," Marsten said. "For now. What's happening?" The irony struck him. He was in the middle of a revolution, and he didn't have a clue what was going on.

"I'm in contact with the provisional government's representative in Miami, and we've got the concessions. The ships are on station and drilling."

"The army is still loyal to Castro," he said. "What about the Cuban navy?"

"I bought them, lock, stock, and leaky boat."

"Money's a wonderful thing," he said.

"You haven't heard?"

"Heard what?"

The signal was fading and the "battery low" light flashed at him. Just as the phone died, he could have sworn he heard her say, "The Guardians captured Castro."

Seven minutes later the soldiers returned, and again Marsten was running for his life with Amelia still in tow. He pulled her into a dark alley, and Rosalinda crashed in behind them. She slung her submachine gun onto her back and gave her mother a hug. "You can bribe Rogelio, if you can find him. Do you have any money?" Amelia shook her head.

"I do," Marsten replied.

"Go," Rosalinda urged. She unlimbered her submachine gun and ran into the street, firing on the run. This time Amelia led the way down the dark alley.

Dallas

L.J. laid the satellite phone on the desk in her library and walked out onto the flagstone veranda overlooking her garden. The cold air bit at her, and she shivered. She threw back her head and let the wind stream through her hair as she clasped her arms under her breasts. Relief flooded through her. Lloyd was safe, at least for now. The phone rang, and she breathed deeply. It should be Felix Campbell from BP with a new offer. She walked back inside, glanced at the Caller ID, and picked up the phone. "Yes, Felix," she said.

As always, Campbell's unruffled accent made her think of the Scottish Highlands and bagpipes. Nothing in his voice betrayed the fact that he had not slept in over thirty-six hours. "Good evening, L.J. I understand it's quite cold in Dallas."

She countered with her thickest Texas drawl. "You are the smooth one, Felix. It's colder than a polecat's ass swimmin' across Loch Ness. It's almost midnight here. Don't you ever sleep?"

He didn't answer. Instead, "I do think we have something you might be interested in. We want to make a preemptive offer."

"Preemptives are expensive," she murmured. "Are we talking a seat on the board of directors? Perhaps a vice presidency with stock options?"

"Please, L.J. For an unproven reserve?"

She could almost hear the bagpipes droning in the background. "The ships are drilling," she said. "Shell and Exxon are knocking at the door. They want in bad." Campbell casually mentioned a large dollar amount and a larger amount of stock in British Petroleum in exchange for 50 percent of the oil concessions. "I think our polecat drowned, Felix." He doubled the stock number, absolutely stunning her. "Our polecat is showing new signs of life."

"I should think he is," Felix replied. "That will make RayTex the tenth-largest shareholder in BP. However, there are conditions."

"Because Dr. Drill hasn't spoken," she said.

"Exactly. In the event there is no oil—"

She interrupted him. "That's the chance you're taking, Felix."

"If we experience another Mukluk, RayTex will, of course, keep the money—"

"And half the stock," she said.

She heard him take a deep breath. "I can't justify that. Not unless BP acquires sixty percent of your stock in RayTex as a quid pro quo." He paused. "A gamble, yes?"

L.J. knew he was baiting her, exactly as she had baited him on the golf course. She needed the money desperately. But was she willing to take the chance? An inner voice spoke to her. "Arranging that will be tricky," she said, edging toward the offer.

"There are means through offshore holding corporations," he told her. "Please remember, with that amount of stock in British Petroleum, RayTex is going to be a very rich company—"

Again she broke in. "Which, with sixty percent of my stock, you'll shortly control."

"We're all assuming risks here," he said. "But no matter what happens, you'll be a very wealthy woman."

They had a deal. "Our polecat just made it to shore," she said.

⁕

L.J. collapsed into her bed after signing a letter of intent and faxing it to Campbell. But the numbers kept swirling in her head, all to the accompaniment of bagpipes. Slowly she drifted off to sleep.

Five hours later she woke with a start. She sat bolt upright, her back rigid, her face streaming with sweat. She had been dreaming, and her subconscious had sent her a message. Even now the image was clear and vivid. She was standing at a blackboard in a college classroom working a calculus problem as the professor's voice droned in the background. But it wasn't a calculus problem, it was Steiner's Seismic Double Reflection matrix. The professor said, "As you can see, it's a gambit, a deliberate mislead. Brilliant, yes?" L.J. gasped. It was Steiner's voice, laughing with glee.

She ran for the bathroom and collapsed by the toilet, throwing up. When there was nothing left, the dry heaves started. Again and again convulsions racked her body. She clutched at the commode and laid her cheek against the cool porcelain. Like a spotlight snapping on to catch the hidden action, her subconscious had worked through Steiner's math. Seismic Double Reflection was a total fraud. Lloyd had warned her. But she hadn't listened, and in her mad drive for power she had lost RayTex.

"Get a grip," she told herself. It was a dream. She was obsessing. She went back to bed, confident she could always back out of the deal with Campbell.

Fairfax County Courthouse, Virginia

Stuart silently cursed himself for taking Sam Broad's advice and not retaining a lawyer for Eric's custody hearing. The Honorable Loretta Calhoun was not a sympathetic judge in the least and had bombarded him with questions while listening politely to everything Barbara Raye's lawyer said. Calhoun was a tall, severe woman in her mid-sixties. Her gray hair was pulled back in a tight bun, and her skin sagged under her bright blue eyes. After the first twenty minutes Stuart labeled her a man-hater. She seemed to enjoy watching Barbara Raye's lawyer eat him alive on every point he had spent hours preparing to make in court. He had a vision of judges and lawyers in short black robes with bare feet and knobby knees dancing around a boiling cauldron chanting legalisms as they dumped him in for a judicial rendering. He scribbled "legal cannibalism" on his notepad as the lawyer slowly tore Hank Langston's testimony apart on cross-examination. "Then," the lawyer said, glancing at Jenny and Barbara Raye, "you admit that Eric was in a life-threatening situation when this jet fighter, an old Lightning, experienced electrical failure."

"It had the potential to be dangerous," Hank replied.

The lawyer studied his notes for a moment. "Thank you, Mr. Langston. That's all I have."

Stuart stood up for redirect. He had worked hard to represent himself, but so far he was striking out. He couldn't quit now, though. Not with Eric's future on the line. He framed a question in the best legalese he could muster. An inner voice that sounded like Jane told him just to be himself. "Mr. Langston, would you have let your grandson go on that flight with Wing Commander Seagrave?" The lawyer objected to the question. "Your Honor," Stuart argued, "if Mr. Langston is qualified to determine if the flight was dangerous, he's qualified to determine if it was safe enough for his own grandson to go for a ride."

Calhoun studied Stuart for a moment. Did he see a twinkle in those startling blue eyes? "I'll allow it. You may answer Mr. Langston." Stuart couldn't believe it. He had won a point!

"Yes, I would," Hank answered.

"Knowing what you know now," Stuart said, "would you go for a ride in the Lightning?"

"In a heartbeat," Hank replied.

"One last question: Why didn't the TV station air the tape shown to this court?"

"When I pointed out all the errors to the producers, they canceled it."

"Thank you," Stuart said. "That's all I have." He glanced at the lawyer.

Barbara Raye whispered furiously in his ear. "Tear him apart," she ordered sotto voce.

The lawyer nodded and stood up. Calhoun actually smiled in anticipation. The lawyer sat down as Barbara Raye glared at him. "We'll reconvene in chambers to interview Eric. My clerk will show you in when I'm ready." The judge stood and left.

*

Calhoun's chambers were not what Stuart expected when he ushered his mother in. Barbara Raye's head snapped up at the sight of Martha Stuart, and she spoke fiercely to her lawyer, demanding, "I want her out of here." The lawyer whispered something and shook his head.

"Is this your mother?" Calhoun asked. Stuart introduced them, and the judge spoke to her clerk. Stuart looked around. The room was utilitarian to a fault, and hanging on the wall, amid a constellation of degrees in jurisprudence, honorable doctorates, citations from three presidents, and civic awards, was a simple plaque.

> Most of my clients are in jail or going there.
> —*Samuel B. Broad*

Calhoun caught Stuart reading the plaque, and her eyes sparkled with mischief. She waited until he looked at her. "At one time I was an assistant district attorney. Mr. Broad and I clashed on many occasions."

Stuart fought an urge to escape. *What did Broad say about Calhoun?* He couldn't remember. Then it came to him: She didn't like lawyers. In the middle of the room Calhoun's clerk placed six chairs in a semicircle facing two chairs. The judge sat in one of the two empty center chairs. "Well," Calhoun said, "shall we get started?" She pointed to one side of the semicircle. "Colonel Stuart, would you and your mother sit there and leave an open chair between you. Mrs. Stuart, would you and your mother do the same on this side?" She looked at Barbara Raye's lawyer. "You may sit against the back wall with the court reporter. But while Eric is in the room, you will remain absolutely silent. Any questions you have will be answered when we reconvene in open court. If you say a single word, you'll be held in contempt and you will spend the night in the county jail."

You'll love that, Stuart thought.

Calhoun hit the intercom and told another clerk to bring in Eric. The door opened, and the clerk motioned Eric to enter. "You may sit wherever you want," Calhoun told him.

"Come here," Barbara Raye said, patting the chair between her and Jenny.

Eric hurried to the open chair between Stuart and Martha. He sat down and held his grandmother's hand. He had made his choice, and Calhoun's eyes sparkled. Stuart's spirits soared. He'd won! Barbara Raye realized what had happened, and her jaw clenched. She twisted around in her chair and glared at the lawyer.

"Your Honor," the lawyer said, "I object strenuously."

"I hope you brought your toothbrush," Calhoun said.

The lawyer breathed in relief. "Thank you, your Honor."

Stuart's mouth fell open. *He'd rather go to jail than face the wrath of Barbara Raye. What the hell goes on in that household?* He listened as Calhoun asked Eric a few questions. It was obvious she liked him and the way he conducted himself.

Finally she was done. "I would prefer to finish this in here," she said. "Eric, you may stay if you wish and hear what I have to say."

"I'd like to stay, ma'am."

Calhoun smiled, and Stuart saw the beauty underneath. "Colonel Stuart, I am concerned about your problems with the police." She paused, waiting for him to reply.

"Your Honor, my lawyer thinks the district attorney will drop the charges—"

"We'll see about that," Barbara Raye snapped.

"Would you care to join your lawyer tonight?" Calhoun asked. Barbara Raye threw Calhoun a hard look but rapidly wilted and looked away as Calhoun stared her into submission.

"As I was saying," Stuart continued, "my lawyer thinks the charges will be dropped or a judge will dismiss them if we are forced to go to trial." He looked at Calhoun, all his worry and love for his son written plainly on his face. "Your Honor, what harm will be done by leaving the current custody agreement in effect until my case is resolved? If I *am* tried and found guilty, then it should be changed. But not until then."

Calhoun spoke to Eric. "Where would you prefer to go to school?"

"At Grandma Martha's," he said. "But, but—"

"You like being with your mother?" Calhoun said, finishing his thought.

"Well, most of the time. But I don't like the arguments and all the shouting."

"Between your mother and Mrs. Wilson?" Calhoun asked.

Eric nodded unhappily.

"I'm ready to rule," Calhoun said.

✳

Stuart floated out of the judge's chambers with his mother, still not believing what had happened. It was a slam-dunk! Calhoun had simply left the current custody agreement in place pending the outcome of Stuart's trial. Then she had cautioned Jenny to keep all contact between Barbara Raye and Eric to a minimum, and even then only after Stuart had agreed. Barbara Raye rushed past on her way out. "You're dog meat!" she shouted.

"Woof, woof," Stuart said. She spun around and glared at him. For a moment their eyes locked, hers filled with pure hate, his with a determination he had never felt before. She broke contact and stormed away. "Have a nice day," he said to her back.

"You sound like your father," Martha said.

"Is that bad?"

She thought for a moment. "No, it's not bad, just a different side of you."

Eric wandered up while Jenny followed a few steps back. "Eric," Jenny said, "why don't you wait for me in the car?" Eric scampered off, like the kid he really was.

"I really didn't want to be here today," Stuart said by way of a peace offering.

Jenny nodded in acceptance. "Are you going to let Barbara Raye see Eric?"

Stuart considered it for a moment. "Yeah, but only at your place and as long as you two don't argue when he's around."

"I'll try," Jenny said. "I love my mother, you know. I want us to see a counselor, and she's agreed."

Stuart was pleased. "Sounds like a plan. There may be hope for us all yet."

Jenny extended her hand in friendship. "Thanks. I'll make it work." She hurried after her son.

"She's finally growing up," Martha allowed.

"You've raised a fine son," Calhoun said from behind them.

"Thank you," Stuart said, wondering how long she'd been watching them.

She laughed. "There are two things you need to know. Sam gave you excellent advice, and I don't hate men. I just haven't trusted anyone in years. Now, go fix your other problem so you can focus on that wonderful son."

"You can count on it," he said, never so sure of anything in his entire life.

31

Dallas

Shugy Jenkins was worried. L.J. had been in a deep depression for over a week, and the buoyant, eager attitude that had made RayTex such a successful company and a happy place to work was gone. Everyone was slinking around the corridors, and most office doors were slammed shut as the staff ran for cover in their confusion. For Shugy it was one of life's lessons as she personally experienced how one person made all the difference. She did her best, mollifying the staff in the hope L.J. would snap out of it. But, if anything, L.J. became more withdrawn. Finally Shugy decided she had to act. She prepared a tea cart, wheeled it resolutely to L.J.'s office, and knocked. No answer. She pushed the door open and saw L.J. curled up in one corner of the couch. "Tea?" Again only silence. "Is it Mr. Marsten?" A little nod from L.J. "I know you haven't heard from him for a week, but he'll be okay."

"I wish I had your faith," L.J. replied. A long pause. "I did a very stupid thing."

Shugy assumed she meant sending Marsten to Cuba. "We all make mistakes. Pray for forgiveness."

"I may have put everyone's job at risk," L.J. said.

Shugy was shocked but quickly recovered. She had come to accept L.J. for what she was, faults and all. "Well, if you did, you didn't mean to. Do what you must. I know you'll do the right thing."

L.J. shook her head. "I wish I had your confidence."

"We trust you," Shugy said.

L.J.'s head came up, and she saw tears on Shugy's cheeks. Then it hit her. Regardless of what she had done, they still needed her. And knowing that was exactly what *she* needed. "Thank you. I appreciate that more than you know." She stood up. "I'm going home to wash my hair and change. Schedule a staff meeting for two o'clock this afternoon. It's time we got back to work."

Shugy returned to her desk and made the necessary phone calls.

The feds arrived exactly forty-three minutes later.

Shugy first saw the men on the security monitor when they filed onto the elevator on the ground floor. They were all wearing blue windbreakers with yellow lettering on the back she couldn't read and carrying a variety of cases and boxes. At first she thought they were a team of cleaners that had come during normal working hours and not at night. She didn't know how right she was. Then the elevator doors opened, and the first of fifteen men trooped off. That was when she could finally read the yellow letters that said "FBI." The team leader handed her a search warrant and presented his identification. He dropped a list of the team members' names on her desk with a curt "I can vouch for them."

"One moment, please," Shugy said, her voice cool and calm. She buzzed the legal office and left a message that the FBI was in the office with a search warrant. Then she called L.J. at home with the same news. Finally she turned to the team leader. "*You* may be able to vouch for your team, but *I* can't. Please have them each show their identification." It was Shugy's version of the slow roll. One by one the team filed by her desk, presenting their identification cards. She carefully studied each one. "I'm sorry," she said, "this man has a beard on his identification card, and he's clean-shaven."

"As I said before, I can vouch for him."

"Of course," she replied. "But please note it on your list here." She pointed to the offending name. The team leader grabbed a pen and did as she requested. "Now, how may I help you?" she asked.

"Please stay out of our way," the man said.

Shugy watched as the team went to work. They were like a giant vacuum cleaner, sucking records and documents out of the offices and cart-ing them down the elevator. Not once did she hear a snide remark, and they were very businesslike and polite—which made it worse. A search warrant was not meant to be punitive, but it was a catastrophic blow to RayTex and would effectively put them out of business.

The team leader stopped by her desk and handed her the first inventory sheet. "May I get you some coffee or tea?" she asked. The team leader shook his head. "Perhaps I can direct your search," she said.

He was interested. Often a disgruntled employee led them to exactly what they were looking for. "We're looking for anything to do with ARA—Action Research Associates."

"Ah, yes. That was Mr. Marsten." She typed a command into her computer. "Here's what you're looking for." She swiveled the monitor toward the agent. He read the list of Marsten's phone calls to ARA. "Of course, I don't know what they discussed." She typed another command. "Here's his appointment schedule for the last twelve months, but I don't see any reference to ARA." Her fingers flew over the keyboard. "There's nothing in the correspondence file. I don't have access to accounting, but they would have any record of billing."

"And Miss Ellis?" he asked.

"Oh, she had nothing to do with ARA," Shugy said. "That was Mr. Marsten's area of responsibility."

"We'll have to take your computer and all your backup disks," the agent said.

"Of course," she said.

The agent sensed an opportunity. "What exactly was Mr. Marsten's relationship with ARA?"

"I believe it had to do with security."

"And Miss Ellis had nothing to do with security?"

"No. Other than normal business, she concerns herself with health care, the children's day care center on the floor below, and that type of thing. In fact, she even discussed our day care program with the president. But you probably all ready know that."

The agent scribbled in his notebook. "Where is Mr. Marsten?"

"In Cuba."

"Really?" the agent said, even more interested. "Do you know why?"

"I have absolutely no idea."

Washington, D.C.

Stuart circled the big apartment complex on North Sixteenth Street looking for a parking place. On the third circuit he managed to squeeze in between two cars. He got out and buttoned the coat to his uniform, surprised by how loosely it fit. He was definitely losing weight. A cold wind whistled down the street, and he pulled on his overcoat for the long walk to the apartment building. A pretty woman walking by stopped to ask if she could help him. He smiled and said, "No thank you." *That hasn't happened in a long time*, he thought.

He reached the entrance as snow started to fall. He buzzed the number, and a woman's voice answered. "I'm Lieutenant Colonel Stuart. I called earlier." He looked up at the monitor camera so she could see his face. The door clicked open, and he walked inside. He took off his overcoat as he waited for the elevator. The same woman he'd passed outside joined him in the elevator.

She smiled at him and shook her hair free prettily. "Hello again. No human should be out on a night like this."

He returned her smile. "That's the truth." It was all he could think of to say.

"Well, if your car gets snowed in, you can use my phone." She handed him a card with her address and telephone number.

He glanced at the card before pocketing it. "Thank you," he said, not sure what to make of the offer. The elevator stopped at his floor, and he got off. Jean McCormick's door was six steps away, and she answered on the first knock. He handed her his military ID card. "Thank you for seeing me," he said. She smiled and asked him to come inside. Jean McCormick was a middle-aged woman about his height and on the slender side. She had a pleasant smile and beautiful hazel eyes. Her hair was cut short, and the way she moved reminded him of a runner. The trophies on the mantel confirmed the impression. "I see you run," he said, making small talk.

"The triathlon, actually. You look quite fit. Are you a runner?"

"I sail whenever I get the chance."

"Can I get you some coffee or tea?"

"Tea would be wonderful," he replied. "It is freezing out there and starting to snow."

"Well, if you get stuck, don't hesitate to use my phone."

What's with all the phones? he wondered. She stepped into the kitchenette and put the water on to boil. "I don't want to take too much of your time."

"Oh, it's no problem."

Stuart blinked, finally realizing what was happening. Women were taking an interest in him. "It seems we have a mugger in common, and I was wondering if there might be some connection."

"I don't really think so. But who knows?"

There was little doubt that she wanted to explore backgrounds. "I'm assigned to the Pentagon," he said, "and work in logistics. I'm what they call a ground-pounder in the Air Force."

She smiled at him. "That's good. I was married to an Air Force pilot. What a jerk." She hesitated for a moment. "Are you married?"

"Divorced. One kid. A twelve-year-old boy." He took in the room while she made tea. Books were piled in the corners, and she had made a coffee table by stacking big picture books as a pedestal and setting a sheet of glass on top. He looked at the dust jacket of the top book through the glass. The title *Exploring Our World* was printed across the photo of a ship. Jean carried the tray in and sat down next to him. Her leg brushed against his. "I like what you did with the books," he said, "using them for a coffee table."

"We get a lot of books like that at work. No one seems to want them, so I try to find a way to use them."

"May I ask what you do?"

She poured him a cup of tea. "I work for the Department of Energy. My specialty is environmental pollution. But it seems like I do everything but that."

"It's the same with me. In fact, lately I was serving on a committee with DOE. We were working on the Strategic Oil Reserve."

She shook her head. "That's way above my pay grade." They chatted for a few moments, but it was obvious the only thing they had in common was a random mugging. They laughed about that, and Stuart stood to leave.

"Thanks for seeing me," he said.

She handed him his overcoat. "It's too miserable out there to drive."

Stuart ignored the offer to stay. "Well, I've got to get going." They shook hands, and he left. Once he was outside, he regretted not staying. *Get a grip*, he told himself. *You don't need to get involved.* He reached his car and fumbled with the keys. But before he could get the door open, a man stepped out of the shadows and barreled into him, smashing him against the car.

"Gimme the fuckin' keys," he growled.

"Oh, shit!" Stuart moaned. "Not again!" The man drove his fist into Stuart's stomach. But there was no strength behind the blow, and Stuart's heavy overcoat helped protect him.

"Don't fuck wid me!" his assailant shouted. "I cut you fucking throat." He reached into his pocket.

Stuart's basic instincts took over, and he stomped on the man's foot. The man grunted. Stuart stepped back and kicked him in the knee as hard as he could. The man collapsed to the sidewalk in pain as he jerked his hand out of his pocket. He was holding a switchblade knife. The click of the blade opening was like a cannon shot. But he fumbled in the bitter cold, and the knife fell to the ground. He scrambled to pick it up. Stuart stomped on the man's hand. He felt the bones give as the man screamed. Then he kicked the knife into the gutter. "Big mistake," he muttered. He climbed into his car and started the motor. Should he call the police? "Freeze, asshole," he said. He pulled away from the curb.

The same brief feeling of elation he felt when he'd made safe harbor in Cuba captured him. But this time it stayed.

The revelation hit him like a bolt of lightning, jangling his nerves and setting him on fire. He slammed on the brakes and skidded to a halt. He shook his head. It couldn't be. He found another parking space and ran for Jean McCormick's apartment entrance. She answered on the first buzz and let him in. The elevator door was open, and he raced for it. It seemed as if it took an eternity for the elevator to reach her floor. When the doors opened, she was waiting for him. "I'm glad you came back," she murmured.

"Your coffee table, the book—" He fumbled for the right words.

She looked confused and led him inside. Stuart shed his overcoat in an easy motion and reached under the glass top of the coffee table. He carefully extracted the top book from the pedestal. "You got this at work?"

"Companies send them out."

He quickly thumbed through the book, finding the pages he wanted. It was the same ship as on the cover. "Do you know what kind of ship this is?"

"It's a special-built ship used for offshore oil exploration. It has to be very wide because it trails as many as twelve streamers of geophones in the water. Each streamer can be up to eight thousand meters long."

"The geophones—seismic reflection?"

"That's correct."

For a moment he was speechless. A name flashed in front of him. "Dr. Emil Steiner?"

"That's classified information and I can't talk about it."

"That's okay. One more thing: In your work, do you deal with oil companies?"

"All the time."

He felt like kissing her. He closed the book. "Can I keep this?" She nodded. "Thanks. I can't tell you what this means."

A tentative smile. "Maybe you can try."

"I'll call you. Dinner?"

"I'd like that." They said good-bye and he ran for his car.

I'm not paranoid! he shouted to himself.

※

Lieutenant General Franklin Bernard Butler thumbed through the book. "So you're telling me that this is the ship you saw in Cuba."

"The same, or one like it," Stuart said.

"And there's a connection between this survey ship, Steiner's Seismic Double Reflection, and the mugger who attacked you and Mrs. McCormick?"

"Correct," Stuart replied. "And when he failed, they sabotaged the brakes on my car. But there's a kicker: Seismic Double Reflection is a fraud, a total con. When I first looked at it, all I saw was the elegance of the mathematical logic behind it. But on examination it's totally fallacious. Here, let me show you." He jotted down the critical part of Steiner's matrix and started to work the problem.

"Don't even try," Butler said. "It's totally beyond me. Okay, let's assume what you say is true. Given that, why should you and Miss

McCormick be targets?" He knew the answer, but he wanted to see if Stuart was on the same wavelength.

"Because someone discovered a major oil field and wanted to keep it a secret, since U.S. companies can't do business with Cuba. The government would step on them hard."

Butler shook his head. "There's one problem. Steiner contacted us about his new seismic technique."

Stuart felt as if he'd just been kicked in the stomach. "True," he admitted. "Besides, Jean McCormick and I are too low on the feeding chain to be worth messing with."

Butler considered Stuart's dilemma from his unique perspective. He had been in counterintelligence so long that nothing surprised him, and he was a firm believer that the best way to solve a problem was to attack it at the low end. And Stuart and McCormick were definitely on the low end. "Mike, I don't believe in coincidence. Let's assume someone made a major oil find off Cuba."

"But why would anyone even bother with me?"

"To keep it a secret," Butler answered. "You have no idea what's involved in a major oil discovery. Countries start wars for less, much less, and that's what made you a target."

"Normal people don't do things like that."

"You're not dealing with normal people, Mike. To survive in the oil business, you've got to be a shark. I have no trouble believing that some of the most civilized people you've ever met would kill you in a nanosecond if you got in the way of a big oil discovery."

"So how do I find out who it is?"

"The key is the ship you saw in Cuba. Find out who it belonged to and you've found the link."

Stuart shook his head. "If I've learned one thing in all this, it's that no oil company is going to tell anyone squat-all about where they've been surveying or what they've found. It's easier to steal the crown jewels."

"Keep digging, and I'll tap my sources. Who knows what may turn up?"

"But where does Steiner fit in all this?"

"That is a conundrum," Butler allowed.

Stuart knew when he was being given the bureaucratic slow roll. "I'll see what I can find. Thanks for listening." He gathered up his notes and left.

Butler pulled into himself, fitting what Stuart had told him into another, much more complicated scenario. The more he thought about it, the more promising it looked. He picked up his secure phone and dialed the Director of Central Intelligence in Langley, Virginia. Butler quickly outlined what Stuart had told him. "It's one more link to RayTex Oil in Dallas," he said. "It could be critical. I think we should let him run with it and see where he leads us."

The Director of Central Intelligence agreed and told him that the investigation into the Puerto Ricans was stalled. They needed to make something happen. The sooner the better.

"I'll build a fire under Stuart," Butler said.

32

Dallas

L.J. walked through her ransacked offices with Shugy and her comptroller, Marcia. She was infuriated by what she saw. RayTex's chief legal counsel trailed behind her, his short legs hard-pressed to keep up with her. "Mizz Ellis," he protested, "you shouldn't be here. If they return, they can still search your personal belongings, your briefcase, your purse, and confiscate whatever they want."

L.J. ignored him. "I can't believe this!" she raged. "What didn't they take?"

Marcia took the question very seriously and consulted her clipboard. "The furniture and the supply cabinet."

The lawyer spoke up. "It was definitely a punitive raid."

"So what can we do about it?" L.J. demanded. "We can't do business with all our records confiscated."

Before the lawyer could answer, Shugy said, "We have backup records." L.J., Marcia, and the lawyer stared at her in disbelief. The lawyer held up his hand. "I can't hear this. If the FBI learns about a second set of records, they can confiscate those. Please excuse me." He scurried away, leaving the three women alone.

"You have a backup?" Marcia asked, still not believing it.

"Well," Shugy explained, "Mr. Marsten has me make a set of backup records every day before I go home. Everything is so interconnected and date-sensitive that it only takes a few moments to do it."

"How complete is the backup?" L.J. asked.

Shugy motioned at her new computer, which had been only delivered that morning to replace the one the FBI had taken. "We have everything except what happened yesterday morning—before the FBI came."

"Computers are a wonderful thing," L.J. said. "What do you do with the disks?"

"They're not on a disk. I download to our computer site in the Bahamas."

"I didn't know we had an offshore computer site," L.J. said.

"Oh, yes," Shugy replied. "It's part of Mr. Marsten's security program in case terrorists bomb our office. I need special codes to activate the encryption circuits and open the files. Do you want me to show you?" She sat down at her computer.

L.J. shook her head. She held a finger to her lips, urging them to be silent, and grabbed a notepad. She wrote furiously.

1. Don't talk. The FBI may have left bugs behind. Write notes and destroy them later.

2. Send everyone home like we're shut down for business. Have the staff meet at my house Monday morning.

3. Have Security sweep the office for bugs, then do same for my home.

4. We're going to war—and those bastards are going to lose.

The two women were seeing a new side of their employer. But Lloyd Marsten would have recognized the L.J. he saw in Eritrea.

Varadero, Cuba

Amelia Salandro was sound asleep, her head cuddled against Marsten's chest as the truck bounced over the rough road. Amelia stirred, and he held her close. They had been on the run for eight days, constantly moving, always one step ahead of the army or secret police, as chaos swept Cuba. At first Amelia was his passport to the Guardians and their sympathizers. But their relationship quickly changed when she showed him how to make the best use of his Krugerrands. Without her he would have never made contact with the man known simply as Rogelio. The short, heavyset Cuban was one of the new entrepreneurs who was willing, once the right amount of money had changed hands, to take them to safety in one of his trucks.

Suddenly the road smoothed, and the truck accelerated. Marsten pushed the canvas covering the back aside and chanced a glance outside. It was night, and they were racing down a street fronted by darkened luxury hotels. In the moonlight he could see gentle waves breaking on a beautiful beach. He dropped the canvas. "Where are we?" Amelia murmured.

"I'm not sure. I saw a beach and counted three or four luxury hotels. No lights."

"Varadero," she said. "It's a resort for foreigners. When the Soviet Union collapsed, Castro went after tourist gold." The truck ground to a halt behind a hotel, and willing hands helped them climb down. Both were stiff from the ride, and they walked slowly together, very much a pair. Rosalinda was waiting for them inside.

Mother and daughter fell into each other's arms, both crying and talking at the same time. "Thank you, thank you," Rosalinda kept repeating over and over to Marsten.

"It was the least I could do."

"Come," Rosalinda said, "you can stay in my room," she said. She used a flashlight to lead them up the stairs to a room on the fourth floor. "You can take a bath," Rosalinda told her mother.

Amelia disappeared into the bathroom while Marsten walked out onto the balcony. It was a gorgeous night, and Rosalinda joined him. "What's happening?" he asked.

"It's chaos," she replied. "About one third of the people are loyal to the revolution and support the army. Another third are behind us, and the rest are neutral, waiting to see who wins."

"So who *is* winning?"

Rosalinda shook her head. "Who knows? The Guardians hold key positions in the government, all public utilities, and the airports. Most of the police and the navy are with us. The air force is switching sides constantly, and no one knows which side they're on at any moment. I think it depends on where the army is. People are flooding in from all over the world bringing money and weapons to help both sides."

"How are they getting here?"

"Mostly by boat, because the air force has shot down many planes."

"Maybe we can bribe a captain to take us out?"

"I must stay," she said.

"I was thinking of your mother."

"It's possible, if you have enough money."

He allowed a tight smile. "How do you think we got here?" He decided not to tell her about the gold Krugerrands he still carried in his belt and shoes. Another thought came to him. "What happened to Castro? The last I heard, the Guardians had captured him."

"We have. We're putting him on trial."

"Where?"

"Here."

Washington, D.C.

Stuart had turned his apartment into a neatly ordered war room. Two flowcharts on the wall tracked every lead he had pursued, while one of his personal computers automatically searched the Web for leads. The new search program he'd "borrowed" from the Pentagon could dig deeper than any commercial search engine and was producing some results. The printer whirred, and another hit printed out. He read it, annotated the flowchart, and dutifully filed it in the correct folder. He made a cup of coffee, sat back in his swivel chair, and took stock of where he was.

"Stymied," he muttered to himself. It was true. It was a relatively simple matter to probe the basics of offshore oil exploration. But the detailed information he needed was more closely guarded than Critical Nuclear Weapons Design Information, one of the numerous top-secret clearances he'd once held. "Maybe a process of elimination?" he mumbled. He shook his head, trying to clear the cobwebs. He'd been at it for over eighteen hours and needed some sleep. He set his coffee cup down and dozed.

Next thing he knew, the phone was jolting him awake. *How long have I been asleep?* A quick look at the master clock on the wall. *Less than thirty minutes*, he decided. He hit the speaker button on the phone. It was Sam Broad, his lawyer.

"I'm afraid I've got bad news, Mike. I just came out of a meeting with the DA, and she says they're going ahead with your trial."

"Tell me I'm still asleep and having a nightmare."

"You're awake, but it is a nightmare. Apparently she got a phone call from someone saying they wanted to see a positive resolution in the matter."

"After the custody hearing Barbara Raye said I was dog meat."

A long pause. "I don't think it was her," Broad finally said. "This call was from someone with smack. Any idea who it might be? I could use it in a motion to dismiss."

"Will that work?"

"Probably not," Broad conceded. "We'll need to go to a SODDI defense."

"What the hell is a shoddy defense?" Stuart asked, expecting the worse.

Broad spelled it. "S-O-D-D-I. Some other dude did it."

"I might be able to find something," Stuart said.

"The sooner the better," Broad said. "The DA's asking for an early trial date."

"Why?"

"Like I said, the phone call was from somebody with smack." He broke the connection.

Stuart punched off the speaker and fought the panic that loomed over him like a tidal wave. His mind raced with possibilities, but he always came back to one inescapable fact—the survey ship he saw in Cuba was the key. But no oil company was going to reveal where they'd been shooting seismic. What he needed was a name. Once he had that, Broad could subpoena the ship's log and charter, which would lead him to the so-called other dude. But how could he find the name? "Jane," he decided. He grabbed the phone and dialed the number for the satellite telephone aboard *Temptress*. He heard it ring. "Come on, answer." He counted the rings.

On eleven, he heard her voice. "Jane, it's Mike." No answer. "Please don't hang up. I need the name of the ship we followed into Cuba during the hurricane."

"Ask the port captain." Four words or less. Not good.

"How are you?" he asked.

"Fine."

"Where are you?" She broke the connection.

He dropped the phone into its cradle. "Damn." The phone rang almost immediately, and he punched the speaker on, hoping it was Jane calling back with a change of heart.

It was Smatter, the Arlington police detective. "You're on a short leash, Stuart. Don't leave town, and report in every morning before ten A.M. or we'll revoke your bail."

"Does this count for today?" Stuart asked.

"Yeah," Smatter replied. "Don't fuck with us on this one or you're back in the slammer." He broke the connection.

Stuart turned to his computer and searched for the telephone number for the port captain in Cienfuegos. He had it in less than a minute and was dialing the number. But the international operator told him all lines were down. "Shit, fuck, hate," he spat, surprised at how much he sounded like his father. He searched the news channels to see how bad the situation was in Cuba, and an item caught his attention: Brothers to the Rescue was flying messages, supplies, and people into Cuba. They were operating out of Marathon in the Florida Keys because it was close to the part of Cuba that was held by anti-Castro forces. He tacked a map of Cuba onto the wall and circled Marathon. The airport was a hundred miles north of Cuba. Because he was tired, it took a few minutes for him to realize that Cienfuegos was another sixty-five miles away on the southern coast of the island.

He called up the State Department to check on the travel warnings. A special warning urged all people to avoid trying to enter Cuba by either air or boat. *Why the warnings unless people are trying?* he thought. He went back to the Web. Little by little he was able to divide the country into areas held by the army and the Guardians. But which side held Cienfuegos? Another report claimed that the entire south coast was calm and free of fighting. It was all he needed. "When things go wrong, get aggressive," he said, repeating one of his father's favorite rules. He shut his computers off, walked into the bedroom, and packed. The last thing he did was to take down the map of Cuba and shove it into his shoulder bag.

Newport News–Williamsburg International Airport

Hank Langston was surprised to see a car parked outside the Lightning's hangar so early on a Saturday morning. As far as he knew, the hangar was empty and the Gray Eagles and Lightning One were still down at Navy Key West having the time of their lives. He sighed, wishing he were with them. Life had been remarkably dull since the day he and Maggot shepherded the Lightning down through the weather. At least he still had the Legend to occupy his weekends. He parked his car outside the hangar and pushed the big doors open. As always, he smiled when he saw his Legend.

Stuart got out of his car and stretched. " 'Morning, Hank."

"G'morning," Hank replied. "What brings you out here?"

"You," Stuart answered. "I've got a favor to ask." Hank looked interested. If nothing else, being around the Stuarts was never boring. "Any chance you can fly me down to Marathon in the Florida Keys?"

"Why do you want to go there? Your dad and the Gray Eagles are at Key West."

"I want to hook a flight with Brothers to the Rescue into Cuba."

"You lost a screw?"

Stuart grinned. "A long time ago."

"Shee-it!" Langston exclaimed, feeling his juices start to flow. "Only an idiot would want to go into Cuba now." He walked over to his Legend and checked the fuel. "How far to Marathon?"

"Exactly seven hundred seventy-seven nautical miles," Stuart said.

Langston snorted in disbelief. That was the Legend's exact range at maximum cruise speed. "Sounds like you've done your homework—or you're trying to con me."

"I hope so," Stuart replied.

Langston thought for a moment. "We could single-hop it down in less than three hours, and I could be back in time for dinner. The wife wouldn't even know I'd been gone."

"You'll do it?"

"Sure, why not? A man's got to have some fun before Alzheimer's gets him. Help me push her outside, and we'll crank and go before my brain kicks in." The two men pushed the aircraft outside, and Stuart used his cell phone to check in with the Arlington police. Eleven minutes later they lifted off and turned to the south. Neither of them saw the dark gray sedan and the lone driver who had followed Stuart from Washington.

33

Hank flew low over the Florida Keys as Stuart gazed out the window. In less than three hours they had left the winter of the Eastern Seaboard behind and were flying in an unbelievably blue sky laced with small white puffy clouds that reached to the horizon. Below them the chain of islands linked by a causeway stretched into the blue waters of the Straits of Florida like a string of pearls. "It's beautiful," Stuart said. "No wonder you love flying."

"Yeah," Hank replied, "it kinda gets to you." He dialed in the frequency to announce their arrival. "Marathon Unicom," he radioed. "Legend five-one-five-one five miles north for landing. Request traffic advisories."

A voice answered, "Legend five-one-five-one be advised the FBI has closed all airports in the Florida Keys, and transit aircraft are not allowed to land."

"Since when has the FBI controlled airports?" Hank groused. He glanced at his fuel gauges. The needles confirmed what his watch told him: They were into their reserve fuel. Hank didn't hesitate. "Legend five-one-five-one is declaring minimum fuel at this time." For emphasis he added, "If the FBI doesn't want us to land at Marathon, they can get clearance for us to land and refuel at Navy Key West."

"No way that'll happen," Stuart said. There was no answer on the radio, and Hank slowed to ninety-five knots and lowered the landing gear. He entered downwind. "Look at that," Stuart said. The small airport was jammed with aircraft and vehicles. Hank called turning base leg on the radio and slowed to seventy-five knots. The Legend may have been a demon at speed, but it was a docile and forgiving aircraft in the landing pattern. They rolled out on short final.

"Jesus H. Christ," Hank breathed, "they got aircraft parked everywhere." It was true. Every available spot was taken, and aircraft were lined up against the narrow runway. Hank touched down on the centerline and ripped the throttle aft.

An all-terrain vehicle met them at the end of the runway and led the way down a narrow, aircraft-lined corridor to the fuel pumps. An FBI agent was waiting for them. "What the hell are you doing here?" he barked.

"I don't recall reading any NOTAMs that the field was closed," Hank replied. NOTAMs were "Notices to Airmen" that provided time-critical and recent flight-planning information.

"It was posted two hours ago."

"Sorry," Hank said. "We were airborne, and I never saw it. We'll refuel and get going."

His reply seemed to pacify the special agent. "Nice airplane," the agent said. "You build it?" Hank nodded. "I've been thinking of building one," the agent continued. "But my wife gives me fits every time I mention it."

"I had the same problem," Hank conceded. "You just gotta do it."

Stuart climbed out of the cockpit to help Hank refuel. He stood on the wing and looked around. A large group of police and FBI agents were milling around four blue Cessna Skymasters, a twin-engine, pusher-puller type of aircraft, at the far end of the parking ramp. "Isn't that Brothers to the Rescue?" he asked, pointing at the Cessnas.

"It *was* Brothers to the Rescue," the agent said. "Now it's Brothers to the Slammer."

"You've arrested them?" Stuart asked.

"Let's just say we permanently grounded them," the agent replied.

"Why?" Hank asked, exploiting their common interest in homebuilt aircraft.

"You'd think they were running a regularly scheduled airline into Cuba," the agent said. We had to stop it before someone got hurt." He jumped on his ATV and sped away.

"Lovely," Stuart moaned. "I guess this was all for nothing."

"What were you trying to do?" Hank asked.

Stuart doubted he could he explain it in a few words. He unfolded his map of Cuba and circled Cienfuegos. "When I was sailing in the Caribbean and got caught by Hurricane Andrea, we followed a ship into Cienfuegos. Well, it seems we shouldn't have seen that ship, and somehow it's tied to my problems. So I called the port captain to get the ship's name and registry, but the phone lines are down. Then I read a news report that Brothers to the Rescue was flying people and supplies into Cuba, and I was hoping they could get me to Cienfuegos."

"Cuba is coming apart. It must be pretty important if you were going now."

"I don't really have much of a choice."

Hank studied the map and measured off distances, first to Cienfuegos, and then on to the Cayman Islands. A wicked look captured his face.

·※·

"How current is your chart?" Hank asked.

"I have no idea," Stuart said.

"We're betting the homestead on it," Hank replied. He scrutinized the chart, looking for high terrain and obstacles. "The highest point is three hundred ninety feet until we reach Cienfuegos, where there's a couple of high smokestacks on the west side of town."

"Hank, you don't have to do this."

"Yeah, I do. What did Sam Peckinpah say?"

"The movie director?"

Hank grunted. "He said something like 'Life's about fuckin' and fightin'. Everything else is a surrogate.' Well, I haven't done enough of either." He gave Stuart a long look. "The most alive I've ever been was when I was up there with Maggot trying to bring Chalky and your kid down." He folded the map when the FBI agent came over.

"When you taking off?" the agent asked.

"We're about ready," Hank said. "Sorry about the delay, but I had to get my radar transponder fixed." There was nothing wrong with the Legend's IFF, but Hank had used it as an excuse to delay his departure.

"No problem," the agent said. He cranked his ATV and sped away.

Hank glanced at his watch and mentally ran the numbers again. It was 160 nautical miles to Cienfuegos, and at a speed of three hundred knots, they should make it in 32 minutes. But he wanted to arrive when it was dark, and that was driving his takeoff time. After depositing Stuart at Cienfuegos, he planned to head straight south for the Cayman Islands, another 150 nautical miles. "Okay, let's do it." He took a deep breath and climbed into the cockpit. Stuart followed him, and they strapped in without saying a word. Then Hank quickly unstrapped and jumped out. He stood behind the tail, unzipped his pants, and relieved himself on the tarmac.

"That's the last thing Maggot says he does before he flies a mission," Stuart said. Hank climbed back in and started the engine. He taxied slowly past the parked aircraft and waved at the FBI agent. The agent waved back. Hank made a radio call announcing he was taking off and then took the runway. He started his takeoff roll and at twenty knots, firewalled the throttle. The Legend sprang forward like a Thoroughbred out of the starting gate. They came unstuck at six hundred feet and were airborne.

Hank snapped the landing gear up and climbed to five hundred feet before he slowed to 120 knots indicated airspeed. They headed to the northeast and Miami—just two more tourists out sightseeing. When he judged they were out of eyesight of the airport, he slammed the Legend down to fifty feet above the water and firewalled the throttle as he turned south to Cuba.

Stuart glanced at the superaccurate GPS mounted on the instrument panel. Cuba was on the nose at eighty-six nautical miles.

When they were well over international waters, Hank climbed to five hundred feet. He engaged the autopilot and wiped the sweat from his face. He had never flown so low, so fast, for so long before, and he needed a breather. He dialed in Guard, the emergency radio channel, on his VHF radio. He had every intention of maintaining radio silence, but one never knew what might happen. The radio crackled with a woman's voice. "Southbound aircraft at five hundred feet, fifty miles south of Marathon, be advised you will penetrate the Cuban ADIZ in five minutes." The ADIZ was the Air Defense Identification Zone, the airspace extending approximately twenty miles offshore, where they could be intercepted and shot down in the name of air defense.

"I guess she's talking about us," Hank said. "Too bad I can't hear her, whoever she is."

"Most likely," Stuart said, "she's on board an AWACS patrolling the area." The AWACS was an Airborne Warning and Command System aircraft equipped with a highly sophisticated radar.

"Southbound aircraft at five hundred feet," the woman repeated, "identify yourself and reverse course immediately. You're subject to interception and hostile fire."

"Well, duh," Hank said. "At least they don't know who we are."

"They'll figure it out," Stuart said.

"Yeah, but I'll come back in through Mexico and deny I was ever here with my dying breath. Let them prove it."

Stuart shook his head. "You've got a screw loose somewhere."

"Hey! I'm not the guy who wants to run around Cuba playing James Bond." He thought for a moment and handed Stuart the aircraft's first-aid kit and a handheld VHF radio. "Take these. I'll hang around the Caymans for a few days and fly an orbit as close as I can get to Cienfuegos thirty minutes before sunrise and thirty minutes after sunset. Listen up on channel 123.4. If I get high enough, we should be in range and able to talk. I'll come and get you."

"Thanks, Hank. I really appreciate it."

"What are friends for?" Hank glanced at the GPS. Cuba was twenty miles ahead of them, and they were inside the ADIZ. He squeaked it down to fifty feet. "We'll climb to four hundred feet when we coast in." He inched the airspeed up to 320 knots indicated.

"I thought the Legend was redlined at three-ten," Stuart said.

"It is," Hank replied, sweat streaming down his face.

"Brave soul," Stuart muttered, seriously questioning why he had ever asked for Hank's help.

Somewhere over Cuba

They coasted in over coral reefs as Hank lifted the Legend to four hundred feet above the ground and nudged the throttle up. The airspeed needle bounced off 325 knots. A low hill loomed in the moonlight, and for a split second Stuart was certain they were dead. But they cleared the hill by ten feet. "Damn," Stuart gasped.

But Hank was into it. "No guts, no glory. Check the GPS," he ordered, not about to look inside at the instrument panel and lose the horizon. "I need an ETA to Cienfuegos."

Stuart looked over Hank's shoulder at the GPS. "Seven minutes, forty miles on the nose."

Hank looked up and scanned the sky above them. "Oh, shit." They were flying directly below two dark silhouettes. "Fighters."

Stuart looked and could make out the distinct planform of two old Soviet jet fighters framed in the bright moonlight. His mouth went dry. "Frescos," he said. "MiG-17s. I'm surprised the Cubans have any flying."

"You sure?"

"Yeah. I started life as an intelligence officer in the Air Force and taught aircraft recognition to fighter pilots." The two men watched as the two fighters slowed and started to descend.

"I'll be damned," Hank breathed. "I think they're landing at Cienfuegos."

"Then it's for damn sure we're not landing there," Stuart told him. The two fighters started to weave back and forth. "They might be looking for someone. Probably us. Let's get the hell out of here."

Hank was breathing hard. "They haven't seen us. Let's stay right where we are." They followed the jet fighters as they carved a lazy circle around the city. "Not a single light on down there," Hank said. The two fighters turned to the north and slowed even more. Ahead of them runway lights blinked on. "There's the air patch," Hank announced, "and our boys are on final." He peeled off to the left and turned out over the city. "Let's get the hell outa Dodge." Below them a wide boulevard cut through the city like long runway. It was completely deserted. "I can land there if you still want."

Something inside Stuart snapped. "Why not? We came this far."

"Gotcha," Hank said. He dumped his airspeed and circled to land. "Downtown Charlie Brown," he said to himself. He lowered the gear.

"What about power lines?" Stuart asked.

"What about them?" Hank replied, breathing hard. He turned on his landing lights. The broad boulevard scanned clean. He touched down just as a MiG roared over them. "Ah, shit! They didn't land." He stomped on the brakes and dragged the Legend to a stop. At the same time he raised the canopy.

Stuart grabbed his shoulder bag and jumped out. He slid off the wing and stumbled as the Legend started to move. "Which way is the harbor?" he yelled.

But Hank didn't hear him. The canopy was down, and the Legend was rapidly accelerating. The second MiG rolled in behind the Legend, its twin twenty-three-millimeter cannons flashing in the night. Shells walked down the pavement reaching for the Legend. Stuart dived for cover in the entrance of a three-story building as the pavement exploded behind him. A coppery taste flooded his mouth. Hank was dead.

Stuart rolled on the ground and raised his head, not believing what he saw. The Legend was airborne and turning out over the rooftops as the MiG's cannon fire walked into a building. Stuart gasped. He had no idea of the havoc high-explosive shells could create. The old building seemed to fall apart and collapse in on itself, sending a cloud of dust and debris down the street. In the distance he heard the high-pitched whine of the Legend's turboprop as Hank raced for the ocean. The second MiG flew down the street on a strafing pass, its cannon firing.

Stuart wrapped his arms over his head.

In the aftermath the silence was overpowering. Stuart blinked and started to stand up. A sharp kick in his side drove him back to the ground. A man holding a machete was standing over him. He shouted in Spanish, waving the big knife.

※

Hank was flying by the seat of his pants as he looked over his right shoulder. He was total concentration as he watched the MiG-17 turn into him. He had done acrobatics before, but never so low to the ground and never at night. "Shit!" he roared, wondering how the MiG could find him so easily. Two big smokestacks loomed in front of him, reaching well over three hundred feet into the sky. He hardened up his turn as the MiG closed, hoping to get the smokestacks between him and his attacker. Then it came to him. He still had his wing-mounted landing lights on, and he was a beacon in the night for anyone to see. His left hand flicked out and hit the toggle switch, shutting the lights off. At the same time he set the Legend on its wing and flew a knife-edge between the towers. A bright flash lit the sky behind him, and he was certain he was dead. He pulled up and looked back. The smokestacks were engulfed in a pillar of fire and the MiG was gone.

"Oh, my God," he whispered. The MiG had lost sight of him when he doused his lights and ran into the smokestacks. His head came up. He had a kill! He dropped the Legend onto the deck and ran for the open sea. The Caymans were 150 nautical miles on his nose. When he was outside the ADIZ, he climbed into the bright night sky. He kept shaking his head and repeating, "I got a MiG." But who would believe him? Hank laughed aloud. *He* would always know, and that was what counted. He reached out and patted the top of the instrument panel. "Thank you."

Hank Langston had fought the good fight and won.

⁕

Rough hands dragged Stuart into the room and dropped him to the floor. A man shouted at him in Spanish. *"No habla español,"* Stuart said.

"I speak English," a woman said. The man with the machete waved it at him and yelled in Spanish. "He says the planes were chasing you. Why?"

"They wanted to kill me," Stuart said.

She translated, and there was more yelling and swearing in Spanish. "The planes killed many of our neighbors instead," she told him. "Now he wants to kill you." Someone produced his shoulder bag and dumped the contents on the floor. The woman picked up the first-aid kit. "We need this," she said. "Now tell me why you are here before we cut you to pieces."

Stuart gulped hard. The only thing that would save him was the truth. "Because I need to see the port captain." Again she translated and another round of Spanish. But this time he heard something different.

Two men pulled him to his feet and tied his hands behind his back. The woman tied a blindfold over his eyes. "You are fortunate," she told him. "The port captain is a good man. He is one of us."

Who is "us"? he wondered.

34

Cienfuegos, Cuba

Stuart was in misery when he felt the sun on his face and the dark of his blindfold fade to a lighter shade. He wiggled his fingers, but his hands were numb and his arms cramped with pain. He had been tied up too long. He forced his mind to work, anything to quit thinking about his pain. *It must be Monday morning*, he decided. *That means I've been tied up for thirty-six hours.* He heard thunder in the distance. *Rain should cool things off.* He came alert at the sound of someone opening the door. He recognized the footsteps. It was the woman. He felt her untie his blindfold. The light blinded him. "Thank you," he murmured. She worked at his bindings, and his hands hurt as the flow of blood replaced numbness. Slowly his eyes adjusted to the light as he massaged his hands. The man with the machete was standing in the doorway.

"Thank you," he said again. In the distance the thunder grew louder. "Is it going to rain?"

"Those are cannons," the woman told him, "not thunder. They are fighting over the airport. We think the army is winning."

"Is that good or bad?"

An expressive shrug. "Who knows? It's happened before. The army comes, then it goes, while we survive." She helped him stand up. "Come."

"Where are we going?" he asked.

"You said you wanted to see the port captain. I will take you there. But once you are finished, you must leave Cienfuegos immediately. If the army finds you, they will kill many of us." She handed him his shoulder bag. "There is food, a water bottle, and your radio."

"Why are you doing this?"

"Your medical kit saved a child's life."

"My God. Are things that bad?" There was no answer.

✳

The port captain sat behind his desk in full uniform as if he were expecting important visitors, which he was. "*Si, señor.* I remember *Temptress* and Señorita Ryan. She was most kind and gave me food and gifts for my family."

"She never mentioned that," Stuart said.

"How may I help you?" he asked.

"There was a ship that arrived with us. I need its name and any information you may have about it."

"A simple thing," he replied. He heaved his bulk out of his chair and opened a file. "Do you remember the date you arrived?"

"Early Wednesday morning, August twenty-one of last year."

"That was during the hurricane. Most unusual."

"Unusual? The hurricane?" Stuart could hear the sound of sporadic gunfire in the distance.

"No. The ship. Ah, here it is." He handed Stuart a bundle of forms.

So easy, Stuart thought. His hands trembled as he thumbed through the papers: a customs declaration he couldn't read, a crew list with no names he recognized, more papers. Then he saw the ship's name—*Laser Explorer.* "Who owned the ship?" he asked.

The port captain took the form and read it. "A company in the United States, Laser Explorations, New Orleans, Louisiana." He sighed. "Have you ever been to Mardi Gras? I want to go before I die." The sound of the gunfire grew louder.

Stuart couldn't believe what was happening. He was trapped in a scene straight out of a film noir. "Aren't you worried?" he asked, gesturing outside.

"Of course," the port captain replied. "Regardless of who wins this time, I must perform the duties of my office. In other matters I am neutral. The army and the Guardians know this. In fact, I have relatives on both sides."

"Do you know who chartered the *Laser Explorer*?"

Again the port captain thumbed through the pages until he found the form he wanted. "A company from Dallas, Texas. Ah, the name is, ah, I think you pronounce it RayTex."

Stuart took a deep breath. He had what he needed. "Can you make a photocopy of these pages?" he asked.

The man gave him a condescending look. "Please. This is Cuba. But I can make a handwritten copy for you." Stuart nodded, and the port captain pulled out blank forms. He uncapped his fountain pen and filled in the blanks, carefully copying the two other forms. Outside, the gunfire moved closer. But the man refused to be hurried. Finally he signed both forms with a flourish. He was done. "That will be ten pesos, *señor*. Five pesos for each form." Stuart fished out his wallet, but he didn't have any Cuban pesos. He handed the man a hundred-dollar bill. The port captain looked at it. "I don't have change," he said.

"It's okay. You may have saved my life." Stuart shoved the two forms into his shoulder bag and ran from the office, the woman's warning fresh in his mind. Outside, he pulled up short and stepped back into the doorway. At the far end of the block a group of soldiers was dragging a man and woman into the street. Stuart watched in horror as the soldiers forced them to their knees. A big man pulled a pistol from his holster and shot each one in the back of the head. The port captain came out of his office at the sound of the gunfire and took in the scene. "The army is winning. I suggest you leave, *señor*."

"Where to?"

The man shrugged and pointed to the east. "That way is Guantánamo Bay. Perhaps six hundred kilometers." He pulled Stuart into his office and shoved him out the back door. "Tell the CIA that Fernando Batista was neutral and performed his office." He shoved the hundred-dollar bill back into Stuart's hand. "*Vaya con dios*, my friend." He shrugged in resignation when Stuart disappeared. Had he done the right thing? He didn't know. But survival in Cuba was always a chancy thing, and he had merely opened another door.

Dallas

L.J.'s house in Highland Park was alive with activity as RayTex's corporate office returned to work Monday morning. Workers in the backyard were busy installing a fence around her swimming pool so no child from the day care center would take an unexpected dip in the cold water. Inside, L.J. assigned space for the various offices, while Shugy retrieved RayTex's files from their offshore computer. After that it was business as usual.

Shortly before noon, one of the RayTex geologists brought L.J. the daily report from the drilling ships. He spread out the charts on her desk that compared the core samples from each of the three ships with a normal seismic scan. "We're finding exactly what we expected," the rock-tapper told her. "I don't think there's oil there. You might want to cut back to one ship."

"Which of the three looks the most promising?" she asked.

"Take your pick."

L.J. thought for a moment before she punched a number into her satellite phone to call the captain of the ship that had drilled the deepest. She put his voice on the monitor for the geologist to hear. The captain confirmed what the geologist had told her. "Are you having any trouble with the Cuban navy?" she asked.

"Not a bit. But we are being flooded with refugees. Mostly former government workers and army officers. We've got over a hundred on board right now. We're hearing some real horror stories of executions and that sort of thing."

"See if the Coast Guard will take the refugees," L.J. told him. "And keep drilling."

"How deep do you want us to go?"

"Try for twelve thousand feet."

"That's gonna be expensive," the captain said, telling her the obvious.

L.J. broke the connection as Shugy came in and handed her a sealed package. "This was just delivered by special courier from Felix Campbell at British Petroleum," she said. "For your eyes only. The courier says he's to wait and take it back today."

L.J. knew what it was and thanked her employees for their help. She waited until she was alone before opening the big envelope. As expected, it was the paperwork transferring 60 percent of her stock in RayTex to

British Petroleum in the event they failed to discover oil. It was a clever transaction, using offshore corporations as cutouts and the electronic transfer of funds into secret bank accounts in Switzerland and the Cayman Islands. A brief note from Campbell said that it had to be signed and delivered by midnight, London time, or the deal was off. She glanced at the carriage clock on the mantel. Midnight in London was 6:00 P.M. her time. She paced the floor.

I can still cut and run, she thought. It would cost her dearly in the informal world of contacts and deals that was at the heart of the oil business. Of course, she would still have control of RayTex. But the thought of how Felix Campbell would crucify her in the locker room at Wentworth Country Club, the golf mecca of international oil, was frightening. *What if Seismic Double Reflection doesn't work?* Her dream was back, vivid and real. With the same sickening realization, she knew that Seismic Double Reflection was a con, and she had fallen for it. All she had to do was look at the evidence the drilling ships were supplying on a daily basis. She paced some more, her arms folded tightly. "Damn!" she swore to herself. She desperately needed to talk to Marsten.

She wandered outside and climbed the steps to the maid's quarters above the garage, where she had placed the day care center. As always, the sight of happy, healthy children was a tonic, and her spirits soared. She was still there when the FBI arrived.

The lead FBI agent was waiting at the front entrance with his team as a light rain started to fall. "Miss Ellis," the agent said, "we seem to have a misunderstanding." He handed her a search warrant.

She unfolded it. "Really? What about?"

"Among the items we were searching for were your backup files."

"You got them."

"Then how are you conducting business?"

"I don't hire fools," she answered. "Or is that also illegal?" She handed him the search warrant and pointed to the garage. "The address on the search warrant is for that half of the property, not this side."

The agent made the mistake of trying to bluff her. "Then you do not wish to cooperate?"

"I wish for you to act within the law," she replied.

"Don't go away," the agent said. He punched at his cell phone and explained the problem. He listened for a moment, then said, "We'll have a new search warrant here shortly."

The rain was falling harder. "You can wait outside or in your cars," she told him, closing the door in his face.

A U.S. Attorney from the local DOJ office delivered the new search warrant two hours later. "Please come in," L.J. said, holding the door open. Fifteen wet FBI agents slogged inside.

"May we speak in private?" the attorney said, presenting his card.

"Certainly, Tom." She led the way to her office. She sat down and fixed him with a steady gaze. "How may I help you?"

Tom Fine waited for her to call for her lawyer. He smiled to himself when she didn't reach for the phone. How many times had he seen a person under investigation commit legal suicide by not calling in a lawyer? "I think it's obvious that Lloyd Marsten is under investigation in the attempted assassination of the president of the United States, and we're concerned there may be a connection to your company."

"Are you here to arrest me?"

"No, ma'am. We're here to gather evidence," he said. "By not turning over your backup files during our first search, you withheld evidence."

"I believe that search warrant applied only to our corporate offices in the Fountain Plaza building, as this search warrant applies only to my residence. Or am I confused?"

"You're splitting hairs," Tom replied, "and concealing evidence."

"Oh. Then your search warrants also apply to our offices in other countries?"

"I didn't say that. But what you're doing is an obvious attempt to subvert the intention of a search warrant."

"Which, in this case, is punitive in nature. Is that the intention of a search warrant?"

"I didn't say that." Suddenly Tom wished his immediate superior were there to advise him. At the outside there were maybe two lawyers in the United States able to argue the points she was hammering him with. And they probably worked for a major corporation. He decided to pull off the gloves and regain control of the interview. "What I'm saying, Miss Ellis, is, don't play games with us by downloading backup files from an offshore computer site while this investigation is in progress."

She smiled. "And you have a court order allowing our communications to be tapped?" From the stunned look on his face, she assumed they didn't. She was deliberately patronizing. "Tom, you can have full access to our files anytime you produce a valid search warrant. But you do not have the authority to stop us from doing business through the mechanism of a search warrant and a vacuum-cleaner confiscation of evidence."

"Don't play legal games with me, Miss Ellis."

"The legal games we will play, Tom, will be in a federal court, and my lawyers are more than capable of dealing with any prosecutor DOJ can bring forward. Count on it."

"Miss Ellis, you don't seem to understand the seriousness of what's happening here. We have an outstanding arrest warrant for Lloyd Marsten."

"And the charges?"

Tom gave her a smug look. "The charge sheet runs over fifteen pages long and includes conspiracy, attempted murder, possession of illegal explosives, smuggling, terrorism, wire fraud—do you want me to go on?"

"Oh, Tom, we at RayTex are as shocked as you and will do anything we can to help you in your investigation. But like so many others in matters like this, we are innocent victims."

"It would be in his best interests if he surrendered voluntarily and, of course, any cooperation you give us would be to your benefit."

"Can you explain how that works?" she asked. "Or are you making a proffer that we can't refuse?"

That was when Tom lost it and his ego took over. "If I find one thing that implicates you or RayTex—"

She interrupted him. "Then I sincerely hope you'll be as diligent in protecting our rights as you are the rights of other innocent people whose only mistake was standing too close to a crime."

"Have you ever heard of RICO? We'll start by impounding your bank accounts."

"Interesting. I wonder what the Commonwealth of the Bahamas will have to say about that?" She punched at her intercom and called her comptroller. "Marcia, please give Tom—he's the handsome young man from DOJ—access to all our bank records in the Bahamas. Of course, don't reveal the account numbers." She listened for a moment. "Yes, that's right, the same records we provide to the IRS." She broke the connection and smiled at him. "As you are aware, there is no requirement for us to bank in the United States. Is there anything else I can do for you?" She handed him a box of miniature microphones and video cameras her security crews had found in her corporate offices. "I believe your people left these behind last time. See, we are trying to cooperate with your investigation."

Tom's eyes narrowed. "I'm going to shut you down."

"Thank you for sharing that with me," she replied. He stormed out of her office. L.J. sighed and buzzed for her chief legal counsel to come in. He was there in less than thirty seconds.

"Did you record all that?" she asked. The lawyer nodded. "What do you think?"

"Cut your losses and give them Lloyd."

Her eyes flared with anger. "I can't—I won't do that. Besides, they can't touch him where he is."

"Your call," the lawyer said. "But this guy was a lightweight. The next time won't be so easy. They can close us down anytime they want. Unless you give them a reason not to."

"If they close us down, can we protect our stockholders?" she asked.

"Only to the extent our assets are held offshore." They talked for a few more moments before he left.

L.J. began to pace again, wearing a path in the Persian rug the shah of Iran had given her father years before. "Oh, Lloyd," she breathed. "I screwed this one up." She collapsed on the couch and closed her eyes.

✳

A voice reached out from a hidden niche deep in her memory. "Save yourself." It was Marsten, and they were in Eritrea. It was all back—the horror of their captivity—and he was lying on the dirt floor of the small tent, near death after being tortured and emasculated by the local warlord who had taken them all hostage.

"We're not leaving you," she promised.

A shallow breath. "I'm dying. Go."

She stood up, and the seven men looked at her. "I'm going to kill the son of a bitch," she announced.

"What good will that do?" one of the men moaned.

"I intend to find out."

She marched out of the hut and into the team's big tent, which the warlord had taken over as his headquarters. The tall, bearded man laughed when she demanded their freedom. "Why should I do this?" he asked. His second in command translated into Tigre for the other men in the tent.

"Because the Koran ordains mercy, justice, and tolerance. We have done nothing contrary to your law."

"I am an educated man, so tell me why I should listen to a woman who is unclean?"

"And if I am clean, will you listen to me?"

He decided to play with her. "Perhaps."

"Then how do I prove I'm clean?"

The man laughed and said something in Tigre. Then they all laughed uproariously as the warlord searched through the small library of books L.J. had brought with her. He found a copy of the Bible and threw it on the floor. "What does this tell you to do? Read where Allah wills it to open."

She picked it up and read from the Book of Judges. " 'Then Jael Heber's wife—' " She stopped, unable to go on.

The man laughed. "Do you know what Jael means? It means 'the wild she-goat.' How can a wild she-goat ever be clean?"

"Try me," she challenged.

"Now I will do as my book commands me!" He uttered one word and she blanched, her knees weak. He sneered, "Clitoridectomy is the right word, yes?" She nodded. "Do you still wish to be cleansed?" Again the low drone of the translator's voice filled the background. The tent echoed with shouts and laughter.

She raised her head. "There must be one man among you," she said, taunting them. "Show me how a true man pleasures a woman." She slowly undressed. The tent was silent as she shed the last of her clothes. The rumors of Western women and their wanton ways were part of their folklore, and, to a man, their faces filled with lust.

The warlord grabbed her hair. "Stay inside," he ordered the others as he dragged her outside.

When it was over, L. J lay on the rough ground. She had used every trick she knew and done things she didn't think she could to wear the warlord down. It had worked, and he was snoring peacefully. She slowly came to her knees and searched around her, finding a rock that fit her hand. Then she crawled to the next tent and worked one of the tent pegs free. She came to her feet and padded back to the sleeping man. She bent over him, her long hair dangling down, and drove the tent peg into his temple. The snoring stopped.

She smeared a little of his blood between her legs and walked into the big tent, still naked and holding the rock. The men were silent as she stood there. "You speak English," she said, pointing to the man who had translated earlier. "As Allah wills, be my interpreter." The man nodded, bewitched by the apparition in front of him. She picked up the Bible that was still lying on the ground and found the passage from the book of Judges. She read, " 'Then, Jael Heber's wife took a nail of the tent, and took a hammer in her hand, and went softly unto him, and smote the nail into his temples, and fastened it into the ground; for he was fast asleep and weary. So he died.' " The man translated as they stared at the blood between her legs, the mark of a virgin. She held up her blood-covered hand, still holding the rock. "This is my hammer! Come!" She led them outside and pointed to the body. An eerie light played on the corpse. "He commanded me to do as my book said, and you saw how the choice was made. It was the will of Allah. Now I command you to be compassionate and merciful or fear the wrath of Allah, for I am clean!"

※

She blinked her eyes as Marsten's voice echoed in her memory, this time much louder and surer. "It's business and not personal. Optimize your options and do what you must."

"But it *is* personal," she said aloud.

"Never mix the two," Marsten's voice answered.

But she knew how the Department of Justice worked, and it was only a question of who got RayTex—the government or British Petroleum. It wasn't really a choice. She grabbed a pen and signed the agreement Felix Campbell had sent by special messenger. She stared out the window, tears in her eyes. "Oh, Lloyd. Please forgive me." Then she picked up the phone and buzzed her lawyer. "Cut a deal," she said. "I'll deliver Lloyd in exchange for immunity." She broke the connection and called Shugy.

"Please call ARA. I need to speak to our case manager." She waited while Shugy made the connection. A man's voice came on the line. "I need to get a message to Lloyd Marsten in Cuba," she said.

"We can do that," the man assured her.

"Can you arrange transportation out?"

"I'll look into it," he said. "There have been some flights evacuating diplomats and stranded tourists."

"Please see what you can do." She hung up and leaned back in her chair. *I hope the FBI was listening*, she thought.

They were.

35

Cienfuegos

Stuart sat under a tree at Playa Rancho Luna outside town and eyed the small sailboat pulled up on the deserted beach. *It's a possibility*, he thought. He discarded the idea. *No passport. So how did I get here?* The answer was so simple, he smiled. He was a tourist stranded by the chaos sweeping Cuba, and his passport had been taken at a roadblock. The more he thought about it, the better it worked. But he would have to be a very cautious tourist. He took a long swig of water from the bottle the woman had given him. When he put it down, he saw the two little girls watching him. They were obviously hungry but too shy to approach him. He reached into his bag and held out the small package of food the woman had given him earlier.

The oldest of the two darted up and grabbed the food. "You're welcome," Stuart said as they ran away. He lay back on the ground and waited for the sun to set. What had Hank said? Monitor channel 123.4 thirty minutes after sunset. He slept.

"*Señor*," a voice said, waking him. He opened his eyes. The sun had set. A young woman was standing on the sand holding the hands of the two girls. "*Muchas gracias*. My daughters forgot their manners."

He smiled. "Look at me. Can you blame them?"

"It was very kind of you."

"It was nothing," he said. The woman nodded gravely and walked away with the two little girls. "She could use a good meal herself," Stuart said under his breath. He reached into his bag and pulled out the radio.

He dialed in 123.4 and adjusted the squelch. "Please be there." He lay back and waited. Again he dozed.

"Hey, good buddy, are you up?" It was Hank transmitting as promised.

Stuart grabbed the radio and hit the transmit button. "I got the info. Ready to copy?"

"I was getting worried about you. Go ahead."

"The ship was the *Laser Explorer*, owned by Laser Exploration out of New Orleans. It was chartered by RayTex of Dallas. Call General Butler in Washington and tell him. He'll know what to do." He rattled off the phone number.

"Copy all," Hank said. "So where do I pick you up?"

"Don't even try. It's chaos here, and we were unbelievably lucky the first time. I'm playing stranded tourist and headed for Guantánamo Bay."

"Good luck," Hank said.

"Thanks, Hank. I owe you."

"Roger that."

Stuart turned off the radio and took stock. If he was an innocent tourist, he definitely did not want to be caught with the radio. He dug a hole in the sand and buried it, along with his military ID card. Then he stood up and walked back to the main road. The young woman was waiting for him, this time without her daughters. She had on a pretty dress and her hair was combed out and fell over her shoulders. "*Señor,* perhaps . . ."

Was she offering herself to him? He didn't know. He pulled a hundred-dollar bill out of his pocket. It was the same one the port captain had refused. "For your daughters," he said in a low voice.

She looked at him, tears in her eyes. "How can I thank you?"

"Just remember there are still a few good Yanks around."

"Where are you going?"

"I'm not sure. Guantánamo Bay. But it's a long way away."

"Take the bus," she told him.

He couldn't believe it. Even in the midst of the killing, starvation, and chaos, people were getting on with their lives and jobs—like the port captain. She walked with him to the bus stop, over two miles away. As they talked, he realized that small kindnesses still made the difference with the Cubans. It was a lesson he would always remember.

Confinement Facility, Andrews Air Force Base

The two prosecutors from DOJ were in the interview room when the security policewoman brought in Sophia James. She clutched the light gray shapeless dress around her as she sat down and hunched over. "You wanted to see us?" the lead prosecutor said.

"I want a deal."

Neither man was surprised. She had been held for twenty-three days, since February 17, and the reality of prison life had finally kicked in. "What have you got?"

"What do you need?"

The two men stood up to leave. "What we need, Miss James, is the truth."

She took a deep breath. "It's not that much."

They sat down. "Let's hear it. Then we can talk deals."

"I was hired by Lloyd Marsten to penetrate the Group."

"We know that."

Sophia panicked. Any chance she had of getting a reduced sentence was rapidly evaporating. "It was a separate deal that had nothing to do with ARA."

The two men looked at her, their faces blank. "Why?" the younger man asked.

"Marsten wanted to use them, and there was no way ARA would go along with it."

"Use them for what?"

"He wanted them to blow up a drilling rig. Insurance, I suppose."

"Then neither you nor Marsten knew about the plot to assassinate the president?"

She shook her head. "I figured it out when they were holding me hostage, but there wasn't anything I could do about it. They had taken my clothes and I was watched, constantly."

That checked with what they already knew. "What can you tell us about the waiter from Café Martí in Little Havana?"

She was ready with an answer in case they made that connection. "Luis killed him. They had an affair, and after they broke up, he was afraid the waiter would sell him out."

The lead prosecutor checked his notes. "As a matter of fact, he did. But he didn't tell us about the homosexual activity."

"I don't think he would," Sophia said. "That's everything. Have we got a deal?"

The men stood up. "If this all checks out, who knows? Maybe five years with time off for good behavior."

Relief flooded over her face. She would be thirty-two years old when she got out and still have a life in front of her. "I'm always on my good behavior." She smiled at them as they left.

Outside, the two men climbed into a staff car and headed for the main gate. "Do you believe her?" the younger man asked. The senior prosecutor shrugged in answer. "So are you gonna cut her a deal?"

"Hell no," the older man answered. "Too much money was changing hands. I figure she probably killed the waiter to make her bones with the Group."

"We'll never prove it."

"We're not even going to try. We'll go with what we got, and she'll be an old lady when she gets out."

The junior prosecutor shook his head. "Too bad. She's a beautiful woman." They drove in silence as he considered what they knew. "Will we ever figure it all out?"

"Oh, yeah," the older man replied. "Proving it is another matter."

Varadero

Most of the men guarding the roads leading into town recognized the burly truck driver and waved him past. But the teenager at the checkpoint leading into Avenida Primera demanded to see his identification and thoroughly searched his truck. Besides the normal tools all he found was a compact satellite-communications radio. He held the radio in one hand as he played with the controls, but all he could get was a loud hissing sound. He glanced at the driver, who was holding two hundred-dollar bills in his right hand. "For your family," he murmured, taking the radio and pressing the money into the teenager's hands. The boy hesitated. "I am one of you," the driver said in a low voice.

"Where do you get this kind of money?"

"Don't ask," the driver said, climbing back into the driver's seat. He drove away.

The teenager immediately found his sergeant and showed him the money. "That was Rogelio," the sergeant said, taking the money. "You want to be his friend." The boy nodded in understanding.

Rogelio drove down Avenida Primera. A surprising number of tourists were in the bars and cafés, and pretty *jineteras*, some younger than usual, walked the streets marketing their wares. Nothing had really changed. He drove up to the luxury hotel Sol Palmeras and ran into a barricade and heavily armed men. The acting captain recognized him and escorted him to a parking place. Again a large amount of money changed hands. Rogelio gestured at the hotel. "The trial?"

"*Sí,*" the captain said. "He's been talking for two days."

"What are they going to do with him?"

An expressive shrug. "Who knows? I'm betting they'll execute him."

"Firing squad?"

"That would give him dignity," the captain replied. He wrote out a pass. "Who do you want to see?"

"The Englishman," Rogelio answered.

"Which one? Many reporters are here for the trial."

"The one called Marsten."

Rogelio pushed his way through the swarm of people pressing into the main ballroom where the trial was being held. He had to present his pass four times and was searched twice before he saw Marsten. The Englishman was sitting in a back row with the woman who had become his constant companion. Again money exchanged hands as Rogelio bought the seat next to him. "Señor Marsten," Rogelio muttered. "I have a message." A guard walking the aisle motioned him to silence as the seven judges took the stand. Then the defendant was brought out. He was wearing a fresh set of his trademark fatigues, and his beard was freshly trimmed. He held his head up and stared at the judges, challenging them. The chief judge called the court to order and said a few words. The defendant came to attention and started to talk, presenting his defense. His words echoed over the ballroom.

The truck driver listened attentively. It was the same rhetoric he had heard all his adult life. "Has he said anything new?" The woman with Marsten shook her head, and a guard again gestured for him to be quiet. He waited patiently for two hours as the defendant spoke. It was a long, rambling discourse on the morality and goals of the *revolución*. Finally the chief judge called a recess, and the defendant was led back to his makeshift cell in the basement of the hotel.

"What's your message?" Marsten asked.

"L.J. says she needs you. Transportation has been arranged. A diplomatic flight to Montreal."

"I'm not leaving without Amelia."

"That can be arranged," Rogelio answered.

"And I want to stay until the trial is over."

"Why?" Rogelio asked. "The judges will find him guilty but cancel his sentence."

Marsten stared at him in disbelief. "I don't believe that."

Rogelio snorted. "Your Spanish is not good enough to hear it. He has—what do the Americans call it?" He searched for the right word.

"It is called Alzheimer's," Amelia said.

A look of relief spread across Rogelio's face. "That's the word."

❄

Rogelio left Varadero and drove west along the coast road for sixteen miles before turning inland toward Juan Gualberto Gómez Airport. For Marsten it was sixteen miles of hell, as Rogelio drove around the burned-out hulks of cars and trucks. It grew worse as they neared the turnoff to the airport, and Marsten counted four dead bodies lying beside the road. "The fighting is over here," Rogelio assured them. "But there is still fighting in many cities. Santa Clara, Camagüey, and Holguín are the worst."

"What about Havana?" Marsten asked.

"The Guardians hold Havana for now. But there is much hunger, and the people are waiting for someone to feed them."

Marsten felt sick to his stomach. No matter how he rationalized, he was partly responsible for the killing and destruction surrounding them. He kept asking himself if it was worth it. He looked at Amelia sitting beside him and felt tears well up in his eyes. Because of him she had lost her husband and only son. Amelia saw his tears and held his hand. "It's not your fault," she told him.

For those simple four words, he would always love her.

Rogelio turned into the airport, where a single plane was parked on the ramp. The distinctive red maple leaf of Canada was painted on its tail.

36

The sound of the engines changed slightly as the Canadian airliner started to descend. Marsten was instantly awake, and every instinct told him they were descending too soon. He wished he had a watch to check the time. He glanced at Amelia sitting beside him. She was asleep, but her blanket had fallen away and she was huddled up. He gently pulled up the blanket, and she cuddled into her seat. He loved the way she slept, so serene and innocent. It amazed him that at sixty-four years of age he had finally fallen in love, and he wanted nothing more than to protect her.

The captain's voice came over the public-address system. "Sorry to disturb you, folks. But Air-Traffic Control has diverted us into Newark, New Jersey. I don't expect to be on the ground for very long, and we should be airborne in thirty minutes or so. We'll arrive in Montreal only a few minutes late." A few lights came on as passengers started to stir.

What's going on? Marsten thought. *It's not a mechanical problem, because we're only going to be on the ground for a few minutes.* Instinctively he worked the problem. The plane was full of diplomats and consular officials, and maybe someone important needed to get off. Another thought came to him. *Or be taken off.* He removed his belt and separated the seal, splitting it apart. He still had half the gold Krugerrands left. He emptied them into a handkerchief. Then he pulled off his left shoe and twisted the heel back. It was hard to do, and he broke a fingernail in the process. He dumped those coins with the others and quickly tied the handkerchief into a neat bundle. He dropped it into Amelia's handbag, redid his belt, and donned the shoe. Then he lay back and waited.

＊

The engines were still running when the steward made the announcement. "Will Mr. Lloyd Marsten please come forward?"

Marsten held Amelia's hand. "I put something in your purse that you'll have to declare when you go through customs." He smiled to reassure her. "I'll be all right. You can contact me through my company, Ray-Tex, in Dallas. Speak to L.J. Ellis and tell her that I asked for her to help you. She'll understand." She lifted her head to kiss him, but he drew back and touched her lips with his fingertips. He stood and walked forward.

Two federal marshals were waiting for him. "Mr. Lloyd Marsten," one said. "You're under arrest for murder, conspiracy to assassinate the president of the United States, and colluding with a foreign power to incite a revolution. Anything you say—"

Marsten tuned him out and looked back into the cabin, hoping to catch a last glance of Amelia. But all he could see was the top of her head.

The Old Executive Office Building, Washington, D.C.

Ann Silton found her way to an open seat in the conference room on the third floor and sat down. It was the first time she had attended a meeting with the nation's power elite, and she smiled nervously. The last person to enter was a shaggy bear of a man wearing a rumpled brown plaid suit. "Good afternoon, Patrick," Mazie Kamigami Hazelton, the national security adviser, said. Every eye turned and looked at the latecomer. They all knew that Patrick Flannery Shaw was the president's special assistant, although no one knew exactly for what. He was a legend and, by documented fact, had direct access to the president at any time and any place. By default, that made him the third or fourth most powerful person in the constellation that ruled the Imperial City.

The director of Central Intelligence shot a hard look at the director of the FBI and for a moment seriously considered walking out in protest. A quick head shake from the FBI chief convinced him not to do it. Shaw looked around the room and took the only open seat, next to Ann Silton.

"G'afternoon, ma'am," he drawled. Shaw was infamous for his attraction to members of the opposite sex, and for an instant Ann panicked, certain he was going to ask her to dinner.

Lieutenant General Butler shifted mental gears. If Shaw was at the meeting, he was speaking for the president.

"Well," Mazie began, "exactly where are we?"

The director of the FBI stood up. "We're now certain the Puerto Ricans who tried to assassinate the president were acting alone and not linked to Cuba in any way."

"But what about the James woman?" Mazie asked.

"She was employed by RayTex Oil," the director replied, "to penetrate the cell after they blew up RTX Farming Supplies, a subsidiary of RayTex. We're still working the contours of that relationship, but we think that to gain access to the Puerto Ricans, James killed an informant."

A voice asked, "So she's going to jail?"

"Yes," the director said, "but not for that. Lloyd Marsten, the CEO of RayTex, used the hysteria surrounding the assassination attempt to start a revolution in Cuba."

"Why would he do that?" another voice asked.

"Because RayTex thought they had discovered a huge offshore oil deposit in Cuba's territorial waters and wanted the concession. To get it, they had to get rid of Castro."

It was Butler's time to speak. "There's a huge irony here, sir. That so-called oil discovery is based on a process called Seismic Double Reflection, which, it turns out, is totally bogus."

Ann Silton couldn't contain herself. "So the three ships RayTex chartered are out there drilling for nothing?" It was the first time her voice had been heard at the executive level, and it felt good. She wanted more.

"That's correct," Butler replied.

The director of Central Intelligence spoke in a low voice. "How did you discover that this Seismic Double Reflection was a con and tie RayTex into all this?"

"An Air Force lieutenant colonel named Mike Stuart," Butler explained, "was working on a committee for me and got caught up in it. He put it all together." He decided to save the details for later. That was all they needed to know for now.

"What are you going to do about RayTex Oil?" This from Ann Silton.

"We've cut a deal with RayTex so we can indict Marsten," the attorney general said.

"So that means," Ann said, "that big business can start revolutions in other countries and get away with it?"

"Renege on the deal," Shaw growled. Everyone looked at him.

"Why?" the attorney general asked. "Getting rid of Castro was a good thing—for us, for the Cubans."

Shaw heaved his bulk out of the chair and ambled to the door. He was surprisingly light on his feet and walked with a rolling gait. He stopped. "No oil, no deal."

Ann was incensed. "Does that mean oil is the final arbiter of what's right?"

Shaw shook his head in disbelief. "Yes, ma'am, in this case it certainly does." He disappeared out the door, leaving silence in his wake.

The meeting was over, and Mazie asked the DCI and Butler to join her in her office. When they walked in, Patrick Shaw was waiting for them. Mazie came right to the point. "Mike Stuart did good work for us. What happened to him?"

"The last I heard," Butler replied, "he's still in Cuba."

"Get him out," Shaw said.

"We'll look for him," the DCI said, "but we're resource-limited outside Havana."

Near Camagüey, Cuba

It was time for his Spanish lesson, and Stuart pretended to be asleep when the two boys climbed into the bus seat in front of him. He cracked an eyelid. Their two faces were grinning at him over the back of the seat. "Go away," he moaned in Spanish. "I'm sleeping." More grins.

"It is time for your lesson," the oldest boy replied in English.

"Let me wake up first," Stuart said in Spanish. He had been on the bus eight days as it made its haphazard way down the island. At first it had been easy going when they were on the Ocho Vías Autopista, the eight-lane highway to the eastern end of the island. But the pavement had ended at Sancti Spíritus and the construction at Ciego de Avila. From then on it had been stop and go as they bumped along dirt roads, breaking down, spending nights in rural villages, the passengers taking up collections when the bus needed gas. The passengers had come to accept Stuart as a stranded tourist, and the two boys had befriended him, as much to practice their English as to talk about baseball. The bus ground to a stop, and Stuart looked up, now fully awake. It was another road-block. "Army or Guardians?" he asked.

One of the boys darted up to the driver and was back in a moment. "Guardians this time. Go back to sleep." It was a well-rehearsed drill, and Stuart slumped in his seat and pulled his straw hat down over his face. One of the boys uncorked a bottle and spilled a little rum on his shirt. Two rough-looking men climbed on board the bus, both carrying AK-47s. They spoke to the driver and, not liking his answer, dragged him off the bus. The two boys watched, their eyes wide. "Something is wrong," one said. "I don't know who they are."

Stuart chanced a glance. "*Bandoleros,*" he said. Bandits. More shouting from outside. "What are they saying?" Stuart asked, this time in English.

"They want money."

"Take up a collection," he said, handing them a U.S. twenty-dollar bill. It had happened before at the army roadblocks, but never at the ones manned by the Guardians. The older boy grabbed it and ran forward, collecting money, mostly pesos, from the passengers. Stuart folded together a few pesos and four U.S. dollar bills, two hundreds and two twenties and stuffed them in his shirt pocket along with his bus ticket before handing the boy his wallet. "Hide this, *por favor.*" He uncorked the bottle of rum, took a long pull, and fell back into his seat, still holding the bottle and pretending to be drunk.

The two men stormed back onto the bus, waving the twenty-dollar bill, demanding to know where it came from. "Tell them," Stuart muttered under his breath. The younger boy was frightened but did as he was told. He jumped out of the seat and pointed to Stuart. Then he ran past the armed men, crying in fear. The two men marched down the aisle, and one jammed the muzzle of his submachine gun against Stuart's neck. He snorted in disgust at the smell and slapped him. Hard. The man swung his AK-47 onto his back and used both hands to pull Stuart to his feet. The thug searched him with rough hands and quickly found the few bills and bus ticket in his shirt pocket.

"He's a drunk American," an old woman said, confirming what they saw. The man threw Stuart back into his seat and swung his AK-47 around. He thumbed the selector lever to single and shot Stuart in the right thigh. The sound echoed through the bus, leaving a strained, tension-filled silence in its wake.

"So much for drunk Yankees," the thug growled. He walked back down the aisle, glaring at each passenger.

"For the love of God," the old woman said, "leave him his ticket." The man shot her in the stomach. He laughed as he got off the bus. The bus driver climbed into his seat and started the engine. He mashed the gears and pulled away.

"We're close to Camagüey," the driver shouted.

A woman bent over Stuart and pressed a rag against his wound, trying to stop the flow of blood. Sweat bathed his face, and he gave her a grateful look. Then he passed out.

The smell of rum assaulted his nostrils, bringing him around. "The woman they shot?" he asked. No answer. The bus slowed as they came to another roadblock on the outskirts of town. Stuart turned his head to see, sweat pouring off him. He felt dizzy from the effort.

"They're Guardians!" the driver shouted as Stuart again passed out.

❄

Stuart came awake at the pain. For a moment he lay there, panting. Slowly the spasm yielded, and he was able to focus. He was in a comfortable bed in a well-lighted room. Another spasm racked his leg. It was the worst pain he had ever experienced, and a bolt of fear shot through him. Amputation! Had they cut it off? He struggled upright to see if it was true. He fell back into the bed, relieved to see he still had two legs. He breathed deeply, drenched in perspiration. A woman came by the open door and saw him. "Doctor," she called, "the American is awake."

A young man, his face prematurely aged by all the injury, disease, and pain he could not treat for lack of supplies, walked in. "Good morning."

"Where am I?"

"My home in Camagüey. It serves as my clinic. I am Dr. Roberto Silva. May I have your name?"

"Michael Stuart. The old lady, the one they shot, did she—"

Silva shook his head, despair in his eyes. "No. I couldn't stop the bleeding."

"Are we safe here?"

Dr. Silva gave him a very Cuban look. "It is chaos in the countryside. Many of the farmers support Castro, while the towns support the Guardians. The situation is confused because there are many bandits and thugs who are murdering and stealing. But for now you are safe." He stood up. "You have two visitors." He called out, and the two boys from the bus bounced into the room. For a moment they stood there, not sure what to say. Then one handed him his wallet. "I hid it in my baseball glove," he said.

Stuart took out half the money he had left and handed it to the boys. "Give this to your parents," he said.

Silva nodded. "You're a good man, Michael Stuart."

The Pentagon

The secure phone buzzed as Butler walked out the door of his basement office late Wednesday evening. He picked it up as he fumbled for the encryption key. "Yeah," he grunted, not bothering to identify himself. It was the director of Central Intelligence. He listened for a moment and inserted the key in the phone. When the DCI was ready, they turned their respective keys to scramble the conversation.

"We found Stuart," the DCI said. "NSA monitored a phone call from a doctor's office in Camagüey." NSA, the national security agency, had Cuba wired for sound. It was an easy task because of the proximity to the U.S. mainland and because there were so few phones. "He's been shot in the leg and is in the doctor's clinic. It was an AK-47, not good."

"Can you get him out?" Butler asked.

"No resources in that area."

"Why am I not surprised?" Butler allowed.

"Speak to Congress," the DCI replied. "They're the ones who cut us off. The Boys got anything available?" "The Boys" were the Boys in the Basement.

"We've got the same problem."

Now it was the DCI's turn. "Why am *I* not surprised?"

"I need a current Sit Brief on the area," Butler said.

"It'll be waiting for you," the DCI promised. They broke the connection, and Butler extracted his key from the phone. He locked it in his safe and headed for the Ops Center on the mezzanine level of the basement, where he held his hand against the palm reader on the steel door leading into the big vault area. The door clicked open, and he went inside, where the duty officer was waiting for him.

"The Situation Brief is on the screen," the duty officer said, pointing to a computer in a side office. He joined Butler as they scrolled through the latest intelligence from the Camagüey sector of Cuba. "Hum," the duty officer grumped. "How do they tell who the players are without a program?"

"They don't," Butler allowed. "And that's part of the problem." He focused on the Ignacio Agramonte Airport on the northeast side of town. "I didn't know the Cuban air force had a fighter base there."

The duty officer checked his order of battle, the detailed listing of Cuba's military. "Two squadrons. One of MiG-21s, the other MiG-23s. Five or six all told may be operational, if they're lucky."

"Are they still loyal?" Butler asked. "Or have they gone over to the Guardians?"

"Which way is the wind blowing today?" the duty officer replied.

Butler scanned the satellite imagery of the area. "What's this?" he asked, pointing to what looked like a long straight stretch of paved highway ten miles southeast of town.

"A highway airstrip for deployment of aircraft in wartime," the duty officer explained. "The Soviets built it for operations against Guantánamo Bay." He pointed to what looked like a tourist pavilion on the far end. "This is a parking shelter so our satellites can't see what's parked there." He traced the taxi path that led from the highway strip into the shelter and circled back to the highway. "It's a drive-through shelter, open on both ends so aircraft can use it as a turnaround."

"Clever devils, the Russians," Butler said. "So what's in the shelter?"

"Nothing."

Butler thought for a moment. "Call Andrews and lay on an aircraft to Navy Key West."

37

Chalky Seagrave was working in the Gray Eagles' office early Thursday morning when the nondescript man wearing three stars on his epaulets and carrying a briefcase walked in. The Englishman came to his feet in one easy motion, always the proper RAF officer. "Morning, sir."

"I'm looking for Colonel William Stuart," Butler said.

"He's in the hangar," Seagrave replied. "This way, please." He led the way as Butler followed.

"How's it going?" Butler asked.

"A bit frustrating. Been here over three weeks and haven't flown a single mission with the Air Force. Cuban thing got in the way, and it appears that your chaps forgot we were here. We may have to go home early. Pity. The Eagles are rather enjoying it." It was true. All around them the Gray Eagles were working, re-creating a time from the past when they were young. "There he is. Shanker! You have a guest."

Shanker crawled out from under the Lightning and stood up. He recognized Butler from the arraignment hearing when the general had vouched for his son. The two men shook hands. "What brings you down here?" Shanker asked.

"Is there someplace we can talk?" Butler asked. "With Commander Seagrave?"

Shanker led the way back into the building, and they found a deserted office. Seagrave closed the door, and Butler came right to the point. "We found your son."

"I didn't know he was lost," Shanker replied.

"Then you haven't talked to Hank Langston lately?" The two men shook their heads. "Langston," Butler continued, "flew Mike into Cuba and dropped him off."

"What the hell for?" Shanker demanded.

"Let's just say he was there on business."

Shanker snorted. "Mike doing something like that? Bullshit."

Butler fixed Shanker with a hard look. He had seen it before. "Sometimes," he said, his voice even but stern, "parents can't see their children for what they really are."

Seagrave understood immediately. "Always a pity."

"The trouble is," Butler continued, "he's wounded, and he can't get out."

Shanker froze. Like most fathers, he would rather be hurt himself than see one of his loved ones injured. "How bad?"

"We're not sure. Apparently he was shot in the leg with an AK-47."

"Do you have any idea the damage an AK-47 can do?" Shanker asked, his voice low and contained.

"Unfortunately, I do. He needs to be in a hospital."

"Can you get him out?" Seagrave asked. Butler paused. Then he shook his head. "Bloody hell," the Englishman muttered.

"What about Brothers to the Rescue?" Shanker asked. "I heard they were flying in and out like they owned the place."

"The FBI shut them down."

"Jesus H. Christ!" Shanker roared. "Whose side are we on?"

"Sometimes I wonder," Butler replied.

"I can't believe I'm so thick," Seagrave muttered under his breath. "You want us to go get him."

"The thought had crossed my mind." Butler snapped open his briefcase and pulled out a chart. He spread it out on the table. "We know he's under the care of a doctor in Camagüey. The city is quiet at the moment and appears to be held by the Guardians."

"The Guardians are the good guys, yes?" This from Seagrave.

"We hope so," Butler said. "But the DAAFAR has a main fighter base just outside Camagüey."

"DAAFAR?" Shanker asked.

"*Defensa Antiaérea y Fuerza Aérea,*" Butler explained. "That's the

Cuban Air Force. At last report they were still loyal to Castro. But that seems to be negotiable on a daily basis."

"Are they any good?" Seagrave asked.

"Apparently not. We have an unconfirmed report that Langston downed a MiG on the way out."

The two men stared at the general in disbelief. Shanker choked when he tried to speak. Finally he managed "Hank got a MiG? How?"

"You'll have to ask him," Butler said.

"That's gonna cost us a few beers," Shanker declared.

"So where do we land?" Seagrave asked.

Butler pointed to a stretch of paved highway ten miles southeast of town. "This is a highway airstrip the Soviets built for wartime operations against Guantánamo Bay."

Seagrave was interested. "So what's there?"

"Over two miles of concrete with a taxi-through shelter at the eastern end for parking and turnaround." He pulled out three high-resolution photographs of the highway. "Satellite imagery from two days ago." He handed them a magnifier. The two men bent over the photos and passed the magnifier back and forth as they went over every square inch of the photos.

"There's nothing there," Shanker said.

"And the concrete looks clean and is in good shape," Seagrave added. "A bit narrow, though. Good thing for that turnaround. What's the DAAFAR got?"

Butler pointed to the airfield four miles northeast of the city. "A squadron of MiG-21s and a squadron of MiG-23s plus the usual antiaircraft defenses. Our latest reports indicate they may have five or six aircraft operational. Most have been cannibalized for parts."

"Fuel," Seagrave said, now into it. "How far?" Fuel, or the lack of it, was a fact of life for the Lightning. Butler produced another chart used for flight planning, and Seagrave quickly spanned off the distances from Key West to Camagüey. "A bridge too far," he said. "We'll need a tanker for air-to-air refueling."

"Boom or drogue?" Butler asked.

"Drogue," Seagrave replied.

"No problem," Butler replied.

"You can arrange that?" Shanker asked.

"If I can't, it's time I retired."

The two pilots bent over the chart and worked the problem for the next hour while Butler called the station commander and arranged for an airborne tanker. Finally Seagrave straightened up. "We can do it with a tanker on the way in and a little deception. High-low profile in, low-high profile out." As far as he was concerned, the decision was made. "We land on the highway, taxi through the shelter to turn around, and pick Mike up. Piece of cake. All your chaps have to do is get him there."

Butler shook his head. "We don't have anyone in the area. But we can get a message to him."

"How?" Shanker asked.

"I believe the telephones are working in that area," Butler replied. The two men stared at him in disbelief. Butler couldn't help himself and laughed. "So it's stupid. But it works."

"If it's stupid but works," Shanker intoned, "it ain't stupid."

Camagüey

The stream of patients into the clinic finally tapered off in the late afternoon, and Dr. Silva was able to look in on Stuart. He took his temperature while changing the bandage on his leg. The row of neat stitches was mute testimony to the doctor's skills, but the telltale marks of infection were beyond his ability to treat. Even if he had the money, there were no antibiotics available. He checked the thermometer: thirty-nine degrees.

"How bad, Doc?" Stuart asked.

Silva converted the number to Fahrenheit. "A hundred and two degrees," he said. He methodically bathed the wound. He had seen this before, and it was only a matter of time. "We will do what we can," he said. When he was finished, he retreated to his office and buried his head in his arms, his frustration and anger consuming him. He took a deep breath and resolved to go on. The telephone rang, and he picked it up. He listened for a few moments. "We need antibiotics," he said, hanging up. He walked briskly back to Stuart's room.

"There was a telephone call from Brothers to the Rescue," he said. "They're sending a plane to pick you up tomorrow morning, soon after sunrise."

"Where?" Stuart mumbled.

"There's a highway eighteen kilometers to the southeast where an airplane can land. I'll take you there."

"It's too dangerous for you to go," Stuart said.

"They promised to bring antibiotics," Silva replied.

Stuart started to say that Brothers to the Rescue was out of business, thanks to the FBI. But the look of hope on Silva's face kept him silent.

Navy Key West

The Lightning's dark gray paint glistened under the floodlights as the Gray Eagles pumped a hundred pounds of fuel into each of the two external fuel tanks mounted on top of the wings. Normally each tank held 2,160 pounds of fuel but they were only putting in enough fuel to check for transfer prior to takeoff. Shanker took one last walk around. He made a swipe with his rag at imaginary dust speckles on the seeker heads of the training AIM-9 air-to-air missiles, one under each wing. For a moment he considered telling the Eagles to download the missiles and pylons. But Seagrave had said to leave them. Besides, with the missiles there was no doubt what the Lightning was. He wasn't so sure about the external fuel tanks. Mounting one on top of each wing was contrary to logic, and they should have been slung underneath where they belonged, next to the missiles. But that was the British. He wiped at the British roundel on the side of the fuselage underneath the cockpit. Lightning One was as ready as he could make it.

Shanker climbed the ladder and strapped his flight helmet on the right seat for his son to wear on the flight back. Butler's words about parents not understanding their children were seared in his mind. All he had ever wanted was for Mike to be a fighter pilot like Maggot. But now he knew the truth. Mike had become his own man, on his own terms, and he, Shanker had missed it. He touched the helmet, hoping it was enough. He was still on the ladder when a blue staff car drove up and stopped. Seagrave and Butler were back from the briefing with the Navy. Seagrave walked over to the Lightning while Butler opened the back door and pulled out a box. "What's that?" Shanker asked, still standing on the ladder.

"Antibiotics," Butler replied, passing the box up to him. Shanker placed it on the right seat and buckled it down with the helmet. He climbed down, and Seagrave scampered up the ladder to strap on the jet. Shanker stood back as Seagrave brought the number-one engine on-line. Then number two cranked. He gave them a thumbs-up and snapped his oxygen mask in place. Then he looked back inside the cockpit to finish running his checklist. He lingered a moment when he checked the external fuel tanks. Both were feeding, and the fuel gauges were functioning. His head came up and looked around as he radioed for clearance. Then he fast-taxied for the runway.

Shanker stood back and saluted the departing fighter. He glanced at the general, who was also saluting.

Seagrave snapped the gear up the moment the Lightning came unstuck. At five hundred feet he turned to a heading of 120 degrees and climbed into the early morning dark. Ahead of him the first glow of sunrise cracked the eastern horizon. He checked the master chronometer on the instrument panel: twenty minutes to sunrise. Timing was critical, for he wanted full light when he coasted in and flew low-level over Cuba. Low levels were difficult under the best of conditions, and he would never find the highway strip in the dark, much less land. Air-Traffic Control came over the radio. "Panda One, confirm destination is San Juan Airport."

"That's affirmative," Seagrave transmitted.

"Are you HF-equipped?"

"Negative high-frequency radio," Seagrave said. "VHF and UHF only." The Lightning's radios were line-of-sight with a maximum range of 180 nautical miles at altitude.

"Roger, Panda One. You are cleared to destination airport, flight level three-five-oh. Remain this frequency until entering Havana FIR." Havana FIR was the Flight Information Region that extended over international waters and was monitored by the Cubans. "Contact Havana on 133.7 for flight following. Avoid Cuban airspace and monitor Guard."

"Copy all," Seagrave replied. "Monitor Guard," he mumbled to himself. "Are they expecting trouble?" He hoped not. Four minutes after liftoff he was flying straight and level at thirty-five thousand feet and .9 Mach, or 530 nautical miles per hour. He took a deep breath and tried to relax. So far the deception part of the plan was working, and he was simply routine traffic flying to Puerto Rico. "Fuel check," he told himself, talking to remain calm. Internal and wing fuel were feeding nicely, and of course the overwing tanks were dry before he took off. One of the idiosyncrasies of the Lightning was that during a long climb all the additional fuel carried in the overwing tanks was virtually canceled out by the extra weight and the power needed to climb. But once at altitude he could make good use of the tanks. Now he had to find the tanker the Navy had promised, or it was no go. On cue he saw a flashing rotating beacon ahead and below him. He checked his position on his handheld GPS and gave silent thanks to the geniuses who had created the system. The Lockheed Viking S-3A was on station waiting for him.

Near Camagüey

The old car jerked and rattled as Silva followed the dirt track out of town. Only one headlight still worked, and he could barely follow the ruts that passed for a road. Still, he didn't have a choice if he was to avoid the roadblocks his patients had told him about. And ultimately they were the reason he was taking the American to his rescuers. With a supply of antibiotics he could save lives. He kept looking at Stuart, deeply worried that his fever might start to spike, a very bad sign. But if everything went right, the American would be in a hospital in Florida in a few hours and the infection under control. He stopped and checked on Stuart. The bandage was clean, and his temperature was warm but stable.

Silva slipped the car into gear and edged forward. Two kilometers later he joined the main road and turned to the east. Again he checked on Stuart, who was asleep. Ahead of him he could see the glow of sunrise. *Just a few more kilometers*, he thought. Suddenly the car hit a large pothole, and Stuart groaned as the car jerked to a stop. Silva gunned the engine, and the car clunked forward with a horrendous screeching sound before it ground to a complete halt. They got out to survey the damage, and the doctor slumped to the ground when he saw the broken rear axle. "A pothole," he said, totally defeated.

"Hey, Doc," Stuart said, looking into the hole, "I've got a dead moose we can bury there."

Silva snorted. "We have our own sacred cows for that."

"Let's start walking," Stuart said. The doctor shoved a water bottle into his medical bag and handed Stuart a walking stick.

Over the Straits of Florida

"Panda Two," Seagrave radioed, "I have you in sight."

"Cleared for contact," the Viking pilot replied. A hose with a drogue basket fed out from the buddy refueling pack under the S-3A's left wing as Seagrave moved into position. He barely had enough light to see and was thankful for the refueling light on the drogue. He retarded the throttles a hair and flew into the drogue, making contact on the first try. The old skills were still with him. The fuel transfer went smoothly, and he monitored the seven flight-refuel lights on the upper left console. One by one the lights went out. When the last one blinked off, he had a full load of fuel, including 4,260 pounds in his overwing external fuel tanks. He moved the refuel switch to normal and broke contact.

"Many thanks," Seagrave radioed, climbing to thirty-five-thousand feet.

"Our pleasure," the pilot answered. "Sorry we couldn't clean your windscreen. By the way, our gear was active."

Seagrave frowned. The "gear" was the Viking's radar warning receiver, and "active" meant that the Cubans were painting them on a search radar. He took a deep breath. Time for the next, oh-so-critical step. He punched 133.7 into the radio and hit the transmit button. "Havana Control, Panda One with you at flight level three-five-oh, destination San Juan Airport, Puerto Rico."

A woman with a heavy Spanish accent acknowledged the call.

Dallas

The clock's blanking luminescent numbers read 5:00. L.J. gave up trying to sleep and crawled out of bed. She hadn't slept a wink all night and was exhausted. But the conversation was still fresh and clear in her mind. RayTex's chief legal counsel had called her after dinner with the news that the Department of Justice had reneged on all deals. They were back to square one. "Expect a search warrant first thing tomorrow morning," the lawyer had warned.

L.J. pulled on a robe and sat on the edge of the bed. *First Lloyd, now this,* she thought. *Damn the bastards to hell!* She stood and walked to the French windows overlooking her garden. All the toys from the day care center were gone, and only the fence around the swimming pool was left as a reminder of the children who had played there. She was going to miss them. She hugged her arms to herself. *I should have seen this coming when the county enforced that ordinance forbidding businesses in private residences.* She wanted nothing more than to crawl back into bed and sleep. But her relentless mind drove her on, forcing her to face the inevitability of the coming day.

"Expect a search warrant first thing tomorrow morning" echoed in her mind. Their strategy was obvious. Every time RayTex opened for business, the FBI would be there with a search warrant.

"Well, do it right," she said to herself. She walked into her big closet and carefully selected the clothes she would wear.

Near Camagüey

Silva had his arm around Stuart as they hobbled down the road. "I think I'm bleeding," Stuart said. The doctor helped him to a low tree, and they collapsed on the ground. For a moment neither said a word, breathing deeply. The light was rapidly improving, and Silva examined the bandage. His lips drew into a grim line, and he reached for his medical bag. He removed the bandage and cleaned the wound.

"The exercise makes it bleed," he said. "It's okay for now. But I don't think you should move."

"We may not have to," Stuart said. He pointed behind the doctor. Stretching away from them into the early-morning light was a long strip of concrete.

Over Great Bahama Bank, the Caribbean

Seagrave punched at the GPS and highlighted the TRIP field. He pressed the enter button, and the number 250 flashed at him. He had flown 250 nautical miles since taking off. "Time, gentlemen," he muttered. He checked the fuel gauges. He still had a thousand pounds remaining in each overwing tank, and all the others were full. "Very nice," he said to himself. He punched up Guard, the emergency frequency, on his radio and made the announcement. "Pan, Pan, Pan. This is Panda One on Guard." He worked to put the right amount of panic in his words. "I have an emergency and am descending at this time, heading for Exuma International." Exuma International was on Great Exuma Island in the Bahamas. "Repeat, I have an emergency and am diverting to Exuma International."

He turned to the northeast, away from Cuba, racked the throttles to flight idle, and nosed over. He was going in the wrong direction but would be on the deck and below radar coverage after traveling less than fifteen miles. Not a long diversion, he reasoned, if the Cubans bought it and he disappeared from their radar screens. He scanned the instruments as he plummeted earthward. His radio squawked with a heavy Spanish accent asking him to state the nature of his emergency. He ignored it. With nothing else to do, he reached out and wound the clock.

Passing through two thousand feet, he broke his rate of descent and leveled off a hundred feet above the ocean. He turned due south, toward Cuba, and set his airspeed at 340 knots. "Might as well save some fuel," he told himself. "No need to hurry. At least not yet." He scanned the sky, looking for aircraft. Cuba was seventy nautical miles on the nose, twelve minutes' flying time. The ocean was gray below him as the sun cracked the horizon. Soon it would be a bright blue, and the Lightning's dark gray paint would stand out like a harsh shadow. But for now it was the perfect camouflage. The minutes passed. He glanced inside the cockpit at his GPS—thirteen miles to the coast. Then it was only another five minutes to the highway strip.

Again he searched the sky. He coasted in over some mangrove swamps and across the western end of Cayo Sabinal Island. He turned to the southwest. That was also part of the plan. If anyone saw him, they would assume he was heading for the fighter base at Camagüey. The land was flatter than he expected, and he squeaked it down another twenty-five feet. His eyes swept the sky in a constant search, looking for the bandits he assumed were out there. He wasn't happy when two dots appeared at ten o'clock high. Just maybe they were heading for the base and not out looking for him. But it was an assumption he wasn't willing to make. He nudged the throttles up, touching 420 knots, and altered course, all part of the plan. A quick glance at the fuel gauges for the external tanks—almost empty. Get rid of them before he was jumped and had to maneuver. A glimpse at the GPS to confirm he was on course and well clear of the base. His left hand automatically lifted the cover guarding the external-fuel-tank jettison switches. "Damn!" The two dots had become a pair of MiG-21s, and they were turning onto him, ready to slice down. Shanker had told him how difficult the small MiG-21 was to see, but he never imagined an engagement could develop so quickly. He started to reef into the lead MiG but hesitated. The MiG pilot wasn't turning as aggressively as he should, and that was puzzling.

Seagrave hardened up his turn a little as his eyes padlocked on the MiG. Although he was less than a hundred feet above the ground and traveling at over seven hundred feet a second, he had no trouble maintaining a level turn. The MiG's nose seemed to wobble as the pilot made constant corrections. "Okay," Seagrave muttered. "So you're afraid of the ground." He almost smiled as the MiG slowly closed to a firing solution. His left hand flicked out and hit the dump switch, opening the rear end of the overwing tanks. Fuel streamed into his slipstream. "Reheats," Seagrave said as he shoved the throttles full forward. The afterburners cracked and lit the raw fuel in the slipstream, sending a torch eighty feet behind the Lightning. At the same time Seagrave hardened up the turn, increasing his G load, and hit the overwing jettison buttons. The two tanks separated cleanly, tumbling up and backward, barely clearing the vertical stabilizer. They came together like two hands clapping and fireballed right in the face of the MiG pilot. Seagrave was never sure what happened next. Either the tanks hit the MiG, causing it to explode, or the pilot maneuvered to avoid the fireball and crashed into the ground.

But it didn't matter. "Sorry for the bad day," Seagrave grunted. He rolled out and looked for the other MiG. But it was gone. "Stalwart fellow," he muttered. He glanced at the GPS and turned toward the highway airstrip. Less than two miles on the nose. He racked the throttles aft and climbed to a thousand feet as he hit the speed brakes to slow down.

He overflew the field as he decelerated to approach speed. As soon as his airspeed touched 250 knots, he dumped the flaps and gear. He turned on a short downwind to scan the highway. The concrete was clean, and he could see the parking shelter at the far end. He circled to land and touched down. He popped the drag chute and got on the brakes, dragging the fighter to a slow roll. He shut down the number-two engine as he taxied into the shelter, the drag chute bumping along on the ground behind him. Once inside the shelter, he jettisoned the drag chute and let the cable drop to the ground underneath the tail.

He raised the canopy and looked around for Stuart. But Seagrave was totally alone. He scanned the highway and sky. Both were clear. *Are they still looking for me?* he thought. "Come on, Mike," he urged under his breath. "Where are you?" He glanced at his watch: 6:42 local time, twenty-two minutes after sunrise. Again he looked around and scanned the sky. Nothing. "Time to go," he told himself. "But who in their right mind is out and about this early when fools are shooting up the countryside?" He glanced at the box of antibiotics still strapped onto the seat next to him. "Besides, someone needs this, and you're quite safe for the moment." His instincts told him to take off. "Don't be stupid. Make a decision."

He did.

38

"I think we should leave," Silva said, still not sure what to make of it all. He was standing in the open, staring down the long highway. The sight of a jet fighter flashing overhead and then circling to land was so far beyond anything in his experience that it had created sensory overload.

Stuart staggered to his feet, feeling dizzy. He still couldn't believe it. At first he had thought it was a MiG. But the moment the aircraft had circled and he saw the aircraft's planform, he had recognized the Lightning. And when it flew past them as it landed, there was absolutely no doubt that Chalky Seagrave was at the controls. "It's okay," he assured Silva. They stood there and waited for the Lightning to taxi back.

"Where is it?" Silva asked.

"I don't know." Stuart squinted, trying to make out the jet in the distance. "I think he's turning around." But the jet never reemerged on the highway. "Can you see anything?" he asked.

The doctor shook his head. He stared at the tree for a moment. Then he quickly pulled himself up into the branches and climbed as high as he could. "I can see him. He's stopped in that shelter or whatever it is next to the highway."

"Oh, shit," Stuart moaned, finally figuring it all out. "The concrete is too narrow to turn around. We have to go to him."

"It's a long way, maybe four kilometers."

"Two and a half miles," Stuart said, putting it in terms he understood.

He picked up his walking stick and hobbled out onto the concrete. "You coming?" he asked.

※

Seagrave was starting to sweat. He pulled off his helmet and unstrapped. He reached for the canopy bow and pulled himself up, standing in the seat to gain every bit of height he could. He squinted, looking down the highway, and could barely make out two figures walking toward him. His instincts told him one of them was Stuart. Then the sound of a low-flying jet caught his attention, and he automatically looked up. But all he could see were rays of light streaming through the cracks in the shelter's roof. The sound grew louder as a shadow passed over the ground. The jet pulled up and turned away, disappearing in the sky. But even at that distance Seagrave had recognized the distinctive shape of a swing-wing MiG-23, the fighter known to NATO as the Flogger. It was a formidable opponent, and he wanted nothing to do with it. He looked at the two figures in the far distance. "Get the thumb out," he urged.

"*Señor*," a voice said behind him. Seagrave almost fell out of the cockpit as he whirled around.

※

The sight of the second jet fighter was too much for the doctor. He turned around and ran. Stuart watched him for a moment. "Can't say I blame you," Stuart muttered to his back. He headed for the waiting plane, his steps dragging and unsure. He felt something warm, and he looked down. His pant leg was soaked in blood. "Hey, Doc!" he called. "I sprung a leak." But he doubted if Silva heard him. He took a few more steps and collapsed to the ground. "This ain't gonna work," he announced. He was on the verge of passing out.

"Do not give up yet, my friend." It was Silva. "I lost my nerve for a few moments." He bent over Stuart and examined the wound. But lacking an operating room, there wasn't much he could do. He applied a fresh bandage and then wrapped his belt over it. He formed a loop in the belt and stuck a small stick through it. He twisted it down, making a tourniquet. The bleeding stopped. He helped Stuart to his feet.

⁎

The four boys stared up at the pilot, who was still standing in the cockpit. "Well, gentlemen," Seagrave said to them, "what do we have here?" He estimated the oldest was maybe ten or eleven years of age, the youngest seven or eight. The boys just looked at him. "I see we have a failure to communicate."

"*¿Americano?*" one of the boys asked, finally finding his voice.

Seagrave shook his head as an idea formed in the back of his mind. He pointed at the unfamiliar roundel on the fuselage beneath the cockpit. "Russian," he said. They weren't convinced. What name had the general used? "*Defensa Antiaérea y Fuerza Aérea,*" he said, looking hopefully down at them. They babbled in Spanish, at last falling for the story. They had heard too many confusing stories about how the Russian Bear had been their friend and was now poor like them. Besides, the plane was definitely not like those flown by the Americans. One of them pointed at the drag chute lying on the ground underneath the tail. "That would be too much to hope for," Seagrave muttered. He made a rolling motion with his hands and arms. The boys pounced on the chute and quickly rolled it up. It took two of them to hold it up for his inspection. "*A presento,*" he said, pointing to them.

The boys were beside themselves as they talked. Seagrave checked his watch. He had been on the ground over an hour. He looked at the two figures struggling down the highway and estimated they were still a half mile away, but he could see that one was definitely limping and supported by the other. How much longer did he have? Maybe he could speed things along. "Gentlemen," he called, gaining the boys' undivided attention. He pointed down the highway at the two figures and made an underhand waving motion. "Go help them." No response. "Help?" he looked hopeful. One of the boys got it and shouted. They bolted out of the shelter and ran to the men.

The youngest skidded to a stop and ran back. He pointed to his chest. "Me fighter pilot."

Dallas

It was business as usual, more or less, when L.J. arrived at RayTex's offices shortly after seven o'clock that morning. The computers were all up and running, and Shugy had made coffee, waiting for the staff to arrive. "My, you look nice today," Shugy said. "I've never seen that dress before."

Normally L.J. wore a business suit with a skirt or pants to work. But this morning she was wearing a very pretty, exquisitely feminine dress. "I was saving it for a special occasion," she said, thinking of how Marie Antoinette or Mary, Queen of Scots must have felt on the last day of her life. She walked into her office to wait for her executioners.

Near Camagüey

The sun was well above the horizon as the heat started to build. Seagrave checked his watch. He had been waiting in the cockpit for over two hours. "Come on," he muttered. Outside, the doctor and four boys were half carrying Stuart as they covered the last few feet to the shelter. "Good show," Seagrave called when they finally made it. The two men collapsed to the ground. "What kept you?" the pilot asked, almost conversationally.

Stuart's face was bathed in sweat, obviously not from the heat. "We hit a moose hole," he said.

"I see," Seagrave replied, not understanding at all. "Well, perhaps it's time you came aboard."

"How?" Stuart asked. The cockpit was almost ten feet above the ground and there were no recessed handholds in the fuselage, even if he had been strong enough.

"A bit dodgy," Seagrave allowed. "If the doctor can get you up high enough, you can step on the refueling probe and I can pull you in." Silva translated for the boys, explaining what they had to do. They surrounded Stuart and helped him to his feet while Silva got on his knees. Stuart was so weak from loss of blood that the boys had to hold him while he stepped on the doctor's shoulders. The doctor slowly stood while the boys propped Stuart up, holding him against the fuselage. Finally, Stuart was able to step onto the refueling probe as Seagrave grabbed his shirt and pulled, dragging him into the cockpit. A trail of blood dripped down the side of the fuselage.

"Very good," Seagrave panted. He passed the box of antibiotics down. The sound of a jet passing overhead deafened them. "Bloody hell. The bastard's back."

Dallas

Tom Fine, the U.S. Attorney, arrived at exactly eight with a large team of FBI agents. He presented a search warrant to Shugy with a curt "I think you'll find everything is in order."

"Please," Shugy replied, "may I see your identification cards?" He ignored her and set the team to work. Shugy buzzed L.J. with the news that the FBI was in the building. But L.J. was on the phone talking to her lawyer. Shugy hung up and asked Tom if he would like some coffee. Again he ignored her.

The FBI was very thorough that morning and stripped the offices bare, taking all the computers and every shred of paper, file, record, and address book they could find. When they were finished, L.J. walked through the offices and sent everyone home. She knew when she was defeated.

Near Camagüey

Stuart was strapped in, his helmet on and plugged in to the oxygen and intercom. Silva was still standing beneath the cockpit, clutching the box. "You must release the tourniquet about every twenty minutes to let the blood flow. Then tighten it back down."

"Now?" Seagrave asked.

"Yes, now."

Seagrave did as the doctor ordered, and blood gushed down Stuart's leg, pooling on the floorboards. Then he retightened the tourniquet, and the blood slowed to a trickle. "I don't know about that," he said to himself.

"I'll be okay," Stuart mumbled.

"Time to go," Seagrave said. "Doctor," he called, "please look outside, and if you see that jet fighter, give me a thumbs-down sign." Silva nodded and told the boys what he wanted. They all ran outside to search the sky as Seagrave began the start-engine sequence. He quickly brought the engines on-line and did a cockpit check. He glanced at the doctor and the boys, who were standing outside the shelter, their eyes scanning the sky. He lowered the canopy and taxied forward into the full sun, then turned onto the concrete to line up. He paused to salute the doctor and boys. They all had their hands out, thumbs down.

Dallas

The top two floors of the Fountain Plaza Building were eerily quiet when Ann Silton's office called.

But Shugy refused to put the call through until Ann was on the line and not her assistant. It was all gamesmanship, but Shugy was a fierce gatekeeper when it came to defending her employer. Like most bureaucrats, Ann was very brave on the phone. "L.J.," she said, "so good to speak to you again. I just wanted to let you know that the injunctions against offshore drilling until all ships and rigs are certified environmentally safe are back in place. I'm afraid your three ships are grandfathered only through today. They must stop all operations after midnight and return to port for certification or be subject to heavy fines."

"Thank you for your concern," L.J. replied.

"There is one more thing," Ann said, triumph in her voice.

Near Camagüey

Seagrave shoved the throttles full forward. The afterburners cracked, and the Lightning rapidly accelerated down the narrow highway. The nose gear lifted at 90 knots, and at 150 Seagrave moved the stick smoothly rearward. The Lightning came unglued from the ground at 180 knots. Seagrave snapped the gear up and hugged the ground as they accelerated. "Where are you?" he shouted. He set the Lightning on its tail and climbed straight up at .9 Mach. He looked back, desperate to get a visual on the MiG he knew was in the area. "Goddamn!" he roared. Behind him a MiG-23 Flogger was strafing the highway as the doctor and four boys ran for cover. The shelter where he had been parked only moments before exploded in flames. Since he was in front of the Flogger, there was no doubt the pilot had seen him and had chosen to go after the people on the ground. "*I'm* the fucking target!" He ruddered the Lightning over to turn into the Flogger.

Dallas

L.J. dangled the phone by its cord from her fingertips. But she could still hear Ann's voice. "We know who made the videotape. I believe that the FBI wants to have a few words with you about that. And a check is in the mail reimbursing you for my wardrobe. Thank you for the loan. It was most kind."

"You're most welcome," L.J. said. "And I do believe that was *two* more things." She hung up without waiting for a reply and walked to the big window overlooking Dallas. She loved the way the buildings rose majestically out of the flat prairie, challenging the sky. She sighed, recalling what her lawyer had told her. Without a deal with the Department of Justice, RayTex was history.

"So close." She looked at the big whiteboard where she had originally conceived the Trojan Sea. The irony of it all struck her. She had only managed to deceive herself. Marsten had warned her off, and even her subconscious had seen through Steiner's Seismic Double Reflection. But she wanted to believe and had convinced herself otherwise. Now the board was wiped clean, like RayTex. "But I had to try," she said aloud. At least the government wouldn't get the company, and BP would take care of her employees.

She stood at the window for the last time.

Near Camagüey

A fighter pilot lives and dies by a few very basic truths and high on that list is "Know the opposition." Unfortunately, Seagrave knew what he was facing. The MiG-23 Flogger could outaccelerate and, thanks to its swing wing, outturn the Lightning. It didn't help that the Flogger was armed with a twenty-three-millimeter, five-barreled Gatling gun in a belly pack and probably two air-to-air missiles. All Seagrave had were two AIM-9 training missiles. The seeker heads could track a target, but the missiles could not guide or detonate. All he could do was jettison them by launching them off the rails. Equally high on the list of truisms was "Honor the threat." And that was exactly what Seagrave had in mind, provided he wasn't flying against a Cuban version of Baron von Richthofen. He armed up his missiles for jettison as he arced down onto the Flogger.

The Flogger pilot saw the Lightning and pulled off straight ahead as he swept his aircraft's wings back. He started to climb as Seagrave hardened up his diving turn to cross behind the Flogger. For a brief moment the Lightning's nose was in front of the Flogger's, and Seagrave mashed his pickle button. The left missile leaped off the rail and, as programmed, went ballistic. It streaked across the Flogger's nose. The Flogger pilot saw the missile, honored the threat, and did the right thing. He turned into the Lightning and pulled up even harder. The two aircraft came together head-on, the Lightning going down, the Flogger up. Just as they merged, Seagrave rolled left and brought the Flogger aboard, canopy to canopy, with less than fifty feet separation. He was fully aware that the Flogger's Gatling gun was firing at him. "He's good," Seagrave growled.

Seagrave slammed the Lightning down onto the deck and headed due east, hoping the Flogger pilot had opted to disengage and kept going in the opposite direction. He took a quick look at Stuart. Because of the violent maneuvering and G forces, his leg was bleeding under the tourniquet. Seagrave jerked the Lightning left, then right, to check his six-o'clock position as his head twisted with the check turns. The Flogger was high above and sweeping down on them in full afterburner. "How did you do that?" Seagrave muttered. The ability of the Flogger to turn and accelerate was awesome, and the Cuban pilot was not going to let him disengage. Seagrave's eyes were padlocked on the Flogger as he stroked the afterburners and pulled on the stick. He climbed into the sun.

When he judged that the angles were right, Seagrave pitched back into the Flogger, again coming at him head-on. But this time the sun was at his back, and he had the sun advantage. The Flogger pilot momentarily lost him in the glare and hesitated for a split second. Seagrave heard a loud growl in his headset, telling him his one remaining AIM-9 was tracking, not that it made any difference. This was strictly seat-of-the-pants flying. His right thumb mashed down on the pickle button. The missile came off the rail and went ballistic as it flew directly at the Flogger.

The AIM-9 flew up the Flogger's right intake. The MiG's big turbo-fan engine simply came apart and exploded. The aft section of the Flogger mushroomed as the Lightning flew past.

"Holy shit!" Stuart shouted. "What was that?"

"The golden BB," Seagrave replied. He pulled the throttles out of afterburner and climbed as he turned to the north. They were still over Cuba, but it had been an incredibly long engagement and now fuel was critical. They had to get to altitude.

Dallas

L.J. had slipped out of her shoes and was still standing at the window. Her arms were outstretched, her palms against the glass as she leaned forward, her head down, between her arms. The intercom buzzed, but she ignored it and didn't move. It buzzed again. Still she didn't move.

Shugy burst into the office. "It's the captain from one of the drilling ships."

L.J. shrugged it off. What did it matter? "Which one?"

"I don't know," Shugy answered. L.J. waved her hand, dismissing her. But the secretary picked up the phone and handed it to her. When L.J. wouldn't take it, she punched on the monitor. "Miss Ellis's office," she said.

"We hit it!" the man shouted. His words echoed across the office. "We hit the biggest god-awful strike—" He sputtered, searching for the right words. "It's humongous! Big!"

"Which ship?" L.J. asked, suddenly alive.

"All of 'em! Every goddamn one!"

L.J. closed her eyes for a moment. She wanted to ask how, why the oil was there. But that could wait for the rock-tappers. She looked at her watch. It was midnight in London. But it didn't matter. "Shugy, please call Felix Campbell. I know he won't mind being disturbed." Another thought came to her.

"And please leave a message for Ann in Washington. Tell her we'll be glad to pay the fines."

"Yes, ma'am," Shugy sang. She ran to her desk to make the calls.

L.J. closed her eyes and tilted her head back, her palms pressed against her temples. Then she shook her hair free and twirled around, her spirits soaring.

Over Santaren Channel, the Caribbean

"How you doing?" Seagrave asked.

"Makin' it," Stuart replied. His voice was weak, and he was drifting in and out of consciousness. Seagrave checked the blood-soaked bandage and took another twist on the tourniquet. But no matter what he did, the blood was still flowing and pooling on the floorboards.

How much blood can a man lose? he asked himself. He didn't know, but he knew he had to do something. He grabbed the GPS and checked the distance to go: 138 nautical miles to Navy Key West. He did the math in his head. Sixteen minutes plus another two or three for approach and landing. He hit the go-to button on the GPS and called up the nearest emergency airfield. The window flashed and Nassau International appeared, 135 nautical miles to the northeast. *Not worth it*, he reasoned. Then his brain kicked in, and he cursed himself. He should have thought of a diversion sooner, when they were much closer to Nassau. But he was dog-tired from the engagement, and Stuart hadn't been bleeding as badly then. Besides, fuel wasn't a problem. Or was it? He rechecked the fuel gauges. Twenty-three hundred pounds remaining with 135 miles to go. They'd be landing on fumes, but they should make it. If the gauges were accurate.

Time to talk to someone friendly and have help waiting for us. He dialed in a new frequency. "Miami Control, Panda One with you at flight level three-six-oh. Destination Navy Key West."

A bored-sounding controller answered. "Panda One calling Miami, say again. You're coming through broken."

Seagrave's head came up. He wasn't a Panda. That had been the call sign they had used as part of the deception plan. He was a Lightning returning from combat. But there was more. It was the only time a Lightning had seen action, and he had downed two aircraft. He mashed the transmit button. "Correction, Miami. This is Lightning One."

"Aircraft calling Miami, you're unreadable."

"Lightning One transmitting in the blind. Inbound to Navy Key West with wounded on board and will require medical assistance on landing. Declaring minimum fuel at this time. Request a tanker and priority handling." Again the response was the same, and he wondered if he had taken battle damage. He scanned the instrument panel. Everything was as it should be, except for the low state of fuel. He'd try again when he was a little closer.

Out of the corner of his eye he saw a jet flash by at his eight-o'clock position going straight up. His head twisted as he watched it climb high above him. Instinctively he paddled off the autopilot and check-turned to the left to better follow it. It was an F-16 with the letters HO on the tail. Stuart was conscious and had also seen it. "An interceptor out of Homestead," he said. Seagrave kept the turn coming another twenty degrees and found the second aircraft. It was rolling in at his deep six.

"Shit! They think we're hostile!"

"They won't fire unless they have a positive ID," Stuart assured him.

"Right," Seagrave muttered, not believing him. If the first aircraft had shot through his altitude to identify them, then why was the other F-16 rolling in for a firing pass? But he didn't have time to discuss it. He racked the throttles to flight idle and hit the speed brakes, slowing down as quickly as possible. He had to get his landing gear down, the traditional sign for a surrendering aircraft. Much to his surprise, the second F-16 overshot him and spit out in front. But the first jet was slicing back down on them.

Seagrave lowered the gear. He knew what it would do to his fuel consumption, but he didn't have a choice. He inched the throttles up and wallowed along at a leisurely two hundred knots. A voice came over the Guard channel. "Westbound MiG, identify yourself and say intentions."

"This is Lightning One." He put on his thickest English accent. "I'm a British aircraft with RAF markings. What do they teach you bloody fools in the name of aircraft recognition?" He didn't wait for an answer and sucked the landing gear up. He nosed over for a long-range descent. "I'm minimum fuel with wounded on board and recovering at Navy Key West. Request a radio relay." He couldn't help himself. "Or is that asking too bloody much?" He looked over at Stuart, who was smiling feebly at him. "It's not funny, lad," Seagrave said.

"Yes it is."

"That little diversion played havoc with our fuel."

Navy Key West

The two men stood on the ramp as the Lightning came down final. All around them the Gray Eagles paced nervously. They had monitored the radio transmissions and knew what Shanker was going through. The last crash truck raced by to take its place on a taxiway. "They got to be flying on fumes," Shanker said to no one.

"Will they have to eject?" Butler asked.

Shanker shook his head. "I doubt if Mike could survive if they did." They held their breath as the Lightning touched down. Shanker saw it immediately. "Fuck me in the heart! No drag chute!" His face was grim as Seagrave got on the brakes, dragging the fighter to a halt. Smoke poured off the brakes as he ran out of runway. Finally he came to a halt on the overrun. Shanker and Butler jumped into their pickup and raced for the runway. They slowed just long enough for two Gray Eagles to pile into the back.

When they reached the Lightning, the canopy was up and Seagrave was motioning for a boarding ladder. "Come on!" he yelled. "I've got a wounded man here. He's bleeding to death." A fireman banged a ladder against the cockpit, and Seagrave scampered down to let them extract Stuart. On the ground he ripped off his helmet. His face was lined with fatigue, and his eyes were bloodshot. "Flamed out on landing," he muttered.

"Thanks," Shanker said. "I owe you big time."

"I mucked it up," Seagrave said. "Should have recovered at Nassau, or called for a tanker sooner."

"It wouldn't've done any good," Shanker said. "None were available." Shanker watched as the crash crew lifted his son out of the cockpit. He knew better than to get in the way. "Don't go beating yourself up." He tried to act nonchalant, the unruffled fighter pilot who could take anything in stride. But it was all a façade to hide his worry. "How'd it go?"

"Not bad," Seagrave replied, playing the same game. "Got jumped going in and coming out. Had to splash two of the poor buggers."

Shanker looked at him in amazement. "You got two?" A nod in reply. "I never did that."

"My dear chap, you were simply flying the wrong fighter."

Shanker gave the Englishman his moment. He had earned it. By every standard Shanker valued, Seagrave was a superb fighter pilot and the Lightning an outstanding warbird.

The crash crew lowered Stuart gently to a stretcher, and two medics bent over him. One held a plastic bag above his head as the other found a vein to insert the needle. "I need another unit of blood!" the medic yelled.

"Sweet Jesus," Shanker said, shedding the last bit of restraint. He hurried over, the worried parent. "I'm his father," he said, pushing through. Tears were in his eyes. He looked down at his son, certain he had lost him.

"I'm okay, Pop."

Shanker took a deep breath. There was so much he had to say. But for now it could wait. He brushed away his tears. "What the hell am I supposed to tell your mother?"

Stuart thought for a moment. "Cheated death again?"

Epilogue

The White House

Butler had to walk. He stepped out of the entrance to the West Wing and savored the lovely March day. It was good to be alive. Mazie Hazelton joined him. As usual, she was wearing a stylish suit, but she had traded her high-heel pumps for white walking shoes and socks. "May I join you?" He nodded, and they stepped onto the road and walked briskly for the west appointment gate. They were totally mismatched, the gray and hunch-shouldered spook and the petite and beautiful politician.

"Maddy's going to recognize Cuba's new government this afternoon," Mazie told him.

"Does she really have a choice?" Butler asked.

"Not if she wants the oil," Mazie replied.

"Who would have ever thought?" Butler said. "Cuba about to become the wealthiest oil-producing nation in the world?"

"And all thanks to L.J. Ellis," Mazie added.

"What are you going to do about her?"

"Nothing," Mazie said. "Lloyd Marsten will have to serve some time but, like Shaw said, it's a whole new ball game now."

"Indeed it is," Butler allowed.

"By the way," Mazie said, "the president asked if you'd be interested in serving as her first ambassador to Cuba."

The San Blas Islands, Panama

Eric steered the battered *Zodiac* inflatable as they rounded the point and headed for anchorage inside the reef. The noisy outboard motor coughed and sputtered before it caught again. "Dad," he called, "isn't that *Temptress*?" He headed for the only boat in sight.

Stuart squinted his eyes against the spray. "I think so." The outboard sputtered again and died. The silence was a relief. Eric pulled at the starter rope a few times before giving up. He grinned and crawled forward to row.

"What a great spring break!" he said. "Becky and Andy are really going to be jealous when I tell them." The two neighbor girls had become his inseparable companions. He pulled at the oars and found the rhythm as he rowed across the lagoon.

"Hello, *Temptress*," Stuart called as they approached. They coasted to a stop about twenty feet away. A head popped out of the companionway and darted back inside. But not before Eric got a good look.

"Dad, I don't think she had any clothes on."

Stuart made the best of it. "Don't be silly." How could he tell a twelve-year-old boy that when you were alone in the tropics with not another person within ten miles and a limited water supply, running around starkers was more efficient than washing clothes?

Jane came on deck wearing a tank suit. She cocked her head and studied him for a few moments. "How did you find me?"

"I have my sources," Stuart replied.

"We asked on the Net," Eric said. The Net was the informal single-sideband radio channel that cruisers monitored to exchange information.

"We?" she asked. Eric bobbed his head enthusiastically. "What do you want?" she asked, giving them only four words.

"You, just you," Stuart replied. Eric's head was on a spring bouncing up and down.

She relented a little. "You two are crazy." A little smile flickered across her lips.

Stuart caught it. "About you." He upped the ante. "You get two for the price of one."

"Is someone still out to get you?" she asked.

"Not anymore. I got them."

Eric had to chime in. "But he had to go to Cuba and he got shot and almost bled to death. He's still kinda weak, so I'm rowing."

Her head came up. "Are you serious?"

Stuart stood in the *Zodiac* as it rocked back and forth. "Very serious." He pleaded his case: "I love you, and Eric can't stop talking about you. In fact, Jenny screams every time he mentions your name."

"Which I do every day," Eric called.

Stuart feigned dizziness and fell into the water. He pretended to sink. Jane didn't hesitate and dove in, cleaving the water cleanly. Five strong strokes and she was with him, holding him up. "Were you really shot?"

"Sure was," he burbled. She threw her arms around him, and he could feel her heart beating against his chest. "Eric!" Stuart yelled. "We could use a little help here."

Eric rowed away. "Grown-ups," he muttered under his breath. "Sink or swim," he called.

Club Fed, Eglin Air Force Base, Florida

The phone call from the director of the Federal Bureau of Prisons had been short and simple: Roll out the red carpet. When the warden heard the name of the visitor, there was no doubt that he was facing a command performance, and he was waiting under the canvas marquee at the entrance long before the scheduled arrival time. His practiced eye swept his domain, Federal Prison Camp Eglin. Everything was ready.

To the uninitiated it looked like a military compound on a military installation. The lawns were neatly mowed, the barracks painted, the sidewalks swept. There was only a standard eight-foot chain-link fence surrounding the compound. There was no barbed wire, no armed guards. In fact, the fence was more to establish the installation's boundaries and keep stray animals out than to keep the prisoners in. The real boundaries were painted lines on the ground that no inmate crossed without a pass. Not for any reason whatsoever. If any did, it was a very quick one-way trip to a regular prison.

The media referred to FPC Eglin as "Club Fed" or "the country club." But every inmate would tell a different story. It was a tough place *because* there were no walls or barred windows, and the rules were self-enforced.

The warden saw the helicopter the moment it came into sight. He turned to the unarmed guard next to him. "Get Marsten."

Lloyd Marsten walked out a few moments later. He was trim and tanned and glowed with health. His dungarees were freshly washed and pressed. "Lloyd," the warden said, acknowledging his presence.

"Good afternoon, sir," Marsten replied. The noise of the helicopter settling to the ground drowned out any further conversation. The door flopped open, and a steward helped L.J. Ellis step down.

The warden sucked in his stomach. He had seen photographs in the newspapers and, of course, the coverage on TV. But he was not prepared for the reality of her physical presence. "A beautiful woman," he murmured.

"Indeed," Marsten said.

She walked with long strides across the grass, and Marsten made the introductions. L.J. exchanged the customary courtesies with the warden before coming to the point. "Can Lloyd and I talk in private?"

"Of course," the warden replied. Whatever this woman wanted, short of Marsten's release, she would get. He motioned to the wooden picnic tables dotted around the lawn.

L.J. and Marsten walked into the shade and sat down at a table opposite each other. She reached into her bag and handed him a first edition of Ernest Hemingway's *A Farewell to Arms*. He touched the book lovingly. The dust jacket was unblemished, and the book was in perfect condition. He turned to the title page and saw the author's autograph. "Thank you. You must have paid a small fortune for it." She shrugged. Money was truly meaningless now. A soft silence came down. Then, "Thank you for taking care of Amelia."

"She's a lovely woman. Do you see her often?"

"Every Saturday."

"How're you doing?"

"Much better than expected," he allowed. They were silent for a moment. "How's Duke?"

"Surviving," L.J. admitted. "He's with Billy."

Marsten shook his head. "A dog in a nursing home?"

"The administration thought it was a good idea when I suggested it." She didn't say which administration.

"I imagine they did."

Her hand reached out and covered his. "Oh, Lloyd, I'm so sorry, so sorry. I didn't know what else to do."

A gentle shake of his head. "It was one of those times when you didn't have a choice." His words echoed in her mind, a gentle reminder of the lesson her father had taught her so many years ago when she had to bury her teddy bear.

He gazed at her, his face at peace. "I'm so proud of you."

Shanker's Rules

Colonel William "Shanker" Stuart, USAF (Ret.), was, above all else, a fighter pilot. As a young man he flew F-4C Phantoms in Southeast Asia and logged two-hundred combat missions over North Vietnam. When he volunteered for a third tour, the Air Force assumed he had a death wish, which he did not, and refused to send him. As a fighter pilot he had three qualities that few men, and only a small percentage of pilots, possess. He was the master of his aircraft, he was a hunter, and, most important, he had situational awareness. Situational awareness can best be defined as the state when perception matches reality. In the air and in combat Shanker had it in abundance. But not necessarily on the ground or in his personal life. He lived his life by the principles he learned as a fighter pilot, and he had distilled them to a set of simple rules. With the exception of Rule Number One, there is no priority.

1. Check six.
2. Honor the threat.
3. When things go wrong, get aggressive.
4. The guy who shot you down is the guy you never saw.
5. Always know when to get out of Dodge.
6. Always know *how* to get out of Dodge.
7. Speed is life.
8. The ground has a kill probability of 1.0.
9. Lose sight, lose the fight.
10. In a knife fight (one versus one), one of you isn't coming home.

11. Train like you plan to fight.
12. It ain't over until you've filled out the paperwork.
13. A plan never survives the first thirty seconds of combat.
14. Use the sun.
15. Never fly in the same cockpit with someone braver than you.
16. If it's stupid and works, it ain't stupid.
17. When all else fails, select guns.
18. Know the opposition.
19. Tell me the threat and I'll tell you my tactics.
20. Never forget Rule Number One.

Acknowledgments

While this novel is a work of fiction, I tried to base it in reality. In it I went far beyond my own area of expertise and am indebted to those who shared their experiences and knowledge. Mike Curtis spent hours introducing me to the complex and fascinating world of oil, while Perry Fisher, *World Oil* magazine, was willing to take the time to answer a host of questions from a complete stranger and provide invaluable leads.

Brian Carroll, who logged nearly three thousand hours flying Lightnings—first for the RAF, where he served as the Chief Flight Examiner Strike Command (Fighters), and later as Chief Flying Instructor Royal Saudi Air Force—spent a weekend captivating me with the saga of the Lightning. He then had to spend countless hours tutoring me in the details. And while I was a poor student, I enjoyed every minute.

A word about the Lightning. A total of 337 Lightnings were built by English Electric, now known as British Aerospace, and served in the RAF from 1960 to 1987. They were also flown by the Kuwaiti and Royal Saudi Air Force. The Lightning was unique and a classic fighter, and the only supersonic jet built by Britain on its own. Designed as a point defense fighter, it exceeded all expectations in its superb performance, and its initial rate of climb of fifty-thousand feet per minute was breathtaking. It is a pilot's airplane in every respect, and it was a sad day when they were finally phased out of service.

Jeff Ackland of Performance Aircraft was kind enough to allow me to write about the Legend, and his aircraft does perform as described. Dr. Richard Hawkins made the Sabreliner come alive and, in the process, made me deeply envious. At the Pentagon, Mr. Robert Boyd intrigued me with the plans-intelligence interface, which is worth a story in itself, and Colonel John Gunselman of Installation Logistics and POL gave me a quick education in what logistics is all about and, in the process, impressed me beyond measure.

Karen Frost of Frost Media Relations went far beyond the call of duty in showing me the Dallas–Fort Worth area, while Jack and Mary Holstein gave meaning to the term "Texas hospitality." Finally, Paul Woodford shared his insights and humor into the nature of fighter pilots, and William P. Wood was always there with his sage advice and cool insights, keeping me on track.

To all, many thanks.